No Safe Harbor

Center Point
Large Print

**This Large Print Book carries the
Seal of Approval of N.A.V.H.**

EDGE OF FREEDOM
Book One

NO SAFE HARBOR

ELIZABETH LUDWIG

CENTER POINT LARGE PRINT
THORNDIKE, MAINE

This Center Point Large Print edition is published
in the year 2012 by arrangement with
Bethany House Publishers,
a division of Baker Publishing Group.

Scripture quotations are from the
King James Version of the Bible.

The text of this Large Print edition is unabridged.
In other aspects, this book may
vary from the original edition.
Printed in the United States of America
on permanent paper.
Set in 16-point Times New Roman type.

ISBN: 978-1-61173-556-7

Library of Congress Cataloging-in-Publication Data

Ludwig, Elizabeth.
No safe harbor / Elizabeth Ludwig.
pages ; cm.
ISBN 978-1-61173-556-7 (library binding)
1. Young women—Fiction. 2. Irish Americans—Fiction.
    3. New York (N.Y.)—History—19th century—Fiction.
    4. Large type books. I. Title.
PS3612.U33N6 2012b
813'.6—dc23

2012018856

To Peg and Seth

On this side, there was no safe harbor,
and so God took you home.
We miss you every day.
Looking forward to . . . someday.

No Safe Harbor

1

Ellis Island, 1897

A mischievous wind lifted the tips of Cara's hair and tossed them into her eyes. She brushed the strands away, then blew on her shaking fingers to warm them. The day was overcast, like every day before it for the past two weeks, but thankfully the snow had stopped and the sea had settled into something less than raging. She stood against the rail with no fear of being tossed over.

Few passengers crowded the rails of the ship *Servia*. Most were kept belowdecks by the frigid February temperature and the choppy Atlantic Ocean, but not Cara. Bad weather had lengthened the crossing, made her longing for her first glimpse of America sharper.

America. And Eoghan.

Just thinking of her twin brother brought a wash of hot tears to her cheeks. Eoghan was alive. After two years of bowing under the villagers' whispered condemnation, of bearing in silence the brand given her family name . . . finally . . . the chance to uncover the truth behind his disappearance. His letter in hand, she'd scrambled aboard the first ship to America she could find.

Her fingers crept inside her coat to press the precious scrap of paper against her chest.

Soon, my sweet lad. I'll be at your side! And then we'll prove you were no traitor to your church or your country.

Gently she caressed the twisted leather bracelet encircling her wrist. Eoghan wore one identical to it—a gift from their father on their sixteenth birthday.

"Ah, Miss Hamilton. You made it on deck, I see."

Cara tucked the bracelet into her sleeve, then turned toward the boisterous voice. Douglas Healy was a kind man. A bit loud for her liking. Nonetheless, his generosity had rescued her from steerage—a fact for which she would be forever grateful, and his good-humored jokes had made the trip across the Atlantic bearable. His presence had also kept some of the more amorous lads at bay, since they'd assumed mistakenly that he was her father.

She greeted him with a smile. "And you, as well, Mr. Healy. Here to catch your first glimpse of America?"

He snorted, his full mustache stirred by the force. "I've seen it before. This is my fourth crossing. Business, you know."

His gray eyebrows bunched as he claimed the spot next to her at the rail. Teased by the wind, the fedora on his head lifted slightly. He caught it with a gloved hand and jammed it firmly back in place. "You, however, have yet to reveal your reasons for making the journey. Still no hope of finagling the information?"

Her heart thrumming, she smiled and turned her face to the waves. Always the same question. Every night, at dinner, she was forced to hide the answer, even when he tempted her with treats he'd bribed from the steward.

"Ah, my coy Irish lass, that winsome grin will get you far in the New World." He leaned forward to rest his thick forearms on the rail. "I only hope you do not undertake those challenges alone?"

Cara shook her head, though in truth she did not know what awaited her in New York. Her plan, like Eoghan's letter, was vague: find her brother, force him to tell her what he'd done, and then convince him to return home. "I . . . have kin in America. I hope to reunite with them when I arrive."

He clucked his tongue and dipped his head to peer at her over his spectacles. "The city is quite a large place for a mere hope."

"But 'tis more than I had a few weeks ago," she whispered, pressing her hand against the letter at her chest. A stiff breeze tore at her words and carried them away.

"I'm sorry?" Mr. Healy bent his ear toward her, out of the wind.

She cupped her hand around her mouth. "I said

I'll be fine. Do not worry yourself, Mr. Healy."

He gave a satisfied nod and straightened. "All right, then. Still, you might be able to use this." He removed a piece of paper from a pocket of his woolen overcoat. "An old friend of mine runs a boardinghouse near Battery Park on Ashberry Street. Amelia Matheson is her name. I've listed the address there in case you need a place to stay." When she lifted her brows, he added, "Until your relatives arrive, or until I can check on you—see how you be faring."

Cara accepted the piece of paper and studied the unfamiliar handwriting. When she looked up, Mr. Healy watched her, his kind gaze dark with concern. She patted his hand, warmed by the compassion on the elderly gentleman's face.

A bright sheen filmed his pale blue eyes. "I had a daughter once, not quite your age. Did I tell you?"

She shook her head, surprised by the waver in his voice. Not since stepping foot on board the *Servia* in Liverpool had she seen Mr. Healy without a smile creasing his wrinkled face. "What happened to her?"

A deep sigh seemed to rumble from the depths of his soul. He cast his gaze upon the sea, a vacant look in his eyes that said his thoughts, too, had gone adrift.

"She was only seventeen, and oh, so beautiful. She had red hair like her mother . . . and you."

The wind snatched Cara's hair again, sending coiled strands spiraling into the air. She caught them with one hand and jammed the tangled curls into the collar of her coat.

Mr. Healy watched, a sad smile curving his lips. "Olivia used to do that same thing, just so."

A flock of sea gulls circled overhead, their mournful cries providing a fitting backdrop to the sorrow with which he spoke.

She slid her hands into the pockets of her coat. "Olivia. That was her name?"

He nodded. "After her mother."

A lump formed in Cara's throat. She, too, had been named after her mother, and she felt a strange affinity for this lass whose story mirrored hers. "How did she die?"

Surprise flitted across Mr. Healy's face and as quickly disappeared. "Ah, 'tis a tragic tale, that. One I'll not trouble you with today." He mimicked her brogue in a gentle way that inspired no ire and turned toward the rail, his finger jutting out over the edge of the ship. "Look, there. Do you see?"

Her hand shading her eyes, Cara squinted toward the horizon, where a strange gray haze dipped in and out of the waves. "What is it?"

"Wait," Mr. Healy said, patting her back.

Salt spray washed high on the side of the ship, but Cara remained welded to the deck, excitement building inside her chest as the haze thickened and took shape. "Is that . . . ?"

"It's what you've been watching for, me dear girl, the reason you made this voyage."

Cara tipped her head back and searched his face. He smiled in the way her father used to when bestowing a gift. Faster and faster her heart raced, until the pulse pounding in her ears drowned out the roar of the ship's steam engines.

His broad mustache twitched, then parted to reveal even teeth and his hand swept over the rail. "Miss Hamilton, welcome to America."

"Welcome to America, Miss Hamilton."

For a second, Rourke Turner thought he'd heard wrong. After months of watching and listening, his senses had gone dull, though with the clamor of crying infants and shouted questions in myriad languages echoing from the ceiling, he was surprised he'd caught the name at all. He jerked his head up and scanned the crowded Great Hall. It was his cousin's turn to stake out the island. Rourke had swapped places with him reluctantly, and only after much haggling as to who would assume the duties the rest of the week. Could it be that today . . . ?

There.

His gaze locked on a tall redhead accepting her registration papers from a dour-faced inspector. Rourke eased through the press of people, stepping around baggage and parcels, until he could hear clearly.

"I am finished?"

The inspector shuffled a stack of papers. "Everything appears to be in order. You have money and a place to stay."

In the girl's hand was a scrap of paper. She gripped it until her knuckles turned white.

"You passed your medical exam proving your ability to work," the inspector continued, "and you have family who will be meeting you once you leave the island." He bobbed his head once, twice, and then handed her a small card. "You're free to go."

"My thanks to you," the redhead murmured, a distinct quiver in her voice. She looked to the right and then the left. In her other hand she clutched a leather valise whose worn edges testified to its age. The voyage had soiled and dampened the hem of her blue traveling skirt, and her curls lacked luster, but no one could dispute her beauty, even with worry lines marring her face.

Beautiful, yes . . . but was she the girl he sought? He rather hoped not. A pretty lass such as she could prove a welcome distraction. He forged closer, straining for a glimpse of her eyes.

The inspector did not react with impatience as expected. Rourke had spent enough time on Ellis Island and witnessed enough immigrants passing through the Great Hall to be surprised by the sudden change that came over the man's face.

His scowl disappeared, and with one finger he nudged the rim of his spectacles higher onto his bulbous nose.

"The Kissing Post," he said gently.

The woman swung back to look at him, her fine brows lifted in surprise. "Your pardon, sir?"

Setting down his pen, he pointed toward a flight of stairs. "Go down those steps and to your right. You'll see a row of benches near the exit for the steamer to Battery Park. The pillar by the door is where people usually wait for their loved ones to arrive. If you're expecting someone, that's likely where they'll be."

Her face cleared of anxiety as she reached out to clasp the inspector's hand.

"Bless you!" she breathed, then ducked out of the line and hurried in the direction the man pointed.

Rourke followed at a distance. The crowd on either side of the aisle had become a living thing, swelling and undulating like a wave upon the sea. At any moment he expected them to part and release one of their number to greet the woman. Instead, she reached the place nicknamed the Kissing Post and whirled, her face hopeful as she searched the people bustling past.

So, she *was* looking for someone. Anticipation flared in Rourke's chest. Settling against another of the square pillars stretching toward the ceiling, he assumed the casual posture of the other men gathered to await the arrival of a loved one. One by one they were joined by wives, brothers, sisters, or fathers whose faces had been freshly bathed by tears. Excitement high, they showered one another in kisses and then made their way out of the Great Hall.

At first, the woman straightened every time a happy shout indicated another joyful reunion, but gradually the hopeful gleam faded from her eyes. A full hour passed before she reached for the valise at her feet and turned hesitantly for the exit.

She was leaving!

Rourke's heart raced. Likely he'd never find her again in a city the size of New York, if indeed that was where she was headed.

He shoved away from the pillar and cut a path toward her through a family shouting in loud Italian. Somehow he'd learn the truth. Somehow he'd find out if she was tied to the man he'd spent years looking for . . . the man he intended to kill.

2

With a roar of the engines, the last ferry of the day lurched away from Ellis Island. The ship rode low on the waves, her deck packed from bow to stern with sweaty, tired passengers. Cara hugged the small valise in her lap, glad for the comfort of something to hold after the trauma of health screenings and inspectors back on the island. Many around her clung to nothing but the hand of a person they loved. Still, she'd have traded everything she owned for one glimpse of Eoghan. Of their own will her fingers crept to the bracelet on her wrist.

A man hunched on the seat next to her elbow, his jaw clenched and face pale. With every roll and pitch of the boat, he groaned and bent lower, clutching the edges of the bench they sat on. Stirred with compassion, Cara wondered how he'd managed a voyage across the ocean. As though in answer, the man stumbled to his feet and staggered across the deck toward the lavatory. No doubt he'd remain there until they docked. Lucky for him it wouldn't be long. She'd heard an hour at most.

Once the steamer gathered speed, a stiff breeze lifted the cloying scent of unwashed bodies and swept it out to sea. Cara turned her nose into the wind and breathed deep. The hint of fish on the salty air was not unlike Ireland. Different yet familiar.

As if conjured by the longing in her spirit, a man's voice thick with an Irish brogue pulled her attention from the waves.

"This seat be taken?"

Cara looked up into the bluest eyes she'd ever

seen. Thick, dark lashes framed those eyes, and a friendly smile lit the man's face. He gestured to the seat next to her. "Would anyone be sitting there?" he repeated.

Cara glanced toward the lavatory. Green as the man had looked, it was unlikely he'd be returning soon. "No. Please, help yourself."

He lifted a dark eyebrow as he sat. "Irish?"

She nodded, her heart thumping. Eoghan's letter had warned against speaking to anyone until he'd had a chance to fill her in on who they could trust. But this man was only making conversation, she chided herself.

"Me too." He pointed to the tweed cap on his head and scarf around his neck and laughed. "In case you couldn't tell."

She returned his smile with a careful one of her own.

The boat pitched and the man reached out to steady her, then just as quickly pulled his hand away. "What part of Ireland are you from?"

"Derry." It was out before she could consider whether she should reply.

His head bobbed. "Ah, a northerner. I have kinfolk up that way."

Her fingers closed around the handle of her valise, but she forced her voice to remain light. "Really, now? So, what brings you to America?"

Despite his friendly demeanor, his eyes narrowed and Cara felt he was studying her. "I'm looking for someone. I thought perhaps I'd find them coming on a boat from England."

"You're not . . ." She swallowed, hoping he'd missed the hitch in her voice. "You are not just arriving, then?"

"No. What about you?" He flashed a quick smile, and then his gaze fell to her clenched fists. "Your pardon, miss. I did not mean to unnerve you. It's just, you looked a bit forlorn, and when I saw you sitting here alone, well, you reminded me of my sister, is all. I've not laid eyes on her in almost a year."

An embarrassed blush colored his cheeks. He braced his hands upon his knees and moved as if to rise. "If you'd rather I left . . ."

He had a sister. Was that the person he'd been looking for? Cara winged a prayer for direction heavenward.

The shock of finding out her brother lived, combined with his mysterious letter, kept her on edge. But despite Eoghan's dire warning, the prospect of facing America alone birthed terror in her heart. She wouldn't tell this man about the purpose behind her trip, but maybe she could ask a few questions. He had a kind face, after all, and he was bound to know more than she about the city looming in the distance.

She stayed the stranger with a light touch on his arm. "Forgive me. The voyage has robbed me of my manners. Please, stay." She motioned around the crowded ship. "It's unlikely you'll find another seat."

He hesitated, but then settled back on the bench. "True enough."

"Cara Hamilton," she said with a dip of her head.

"Rourke . . . Walsh," he responded.

"Pleased to meet you, Mr. Walsh."

"The pleasure's mine, Miss Hamilton. Or is it Mrs.?"

Heat fanned her cold cheeks at the flirtatious gleam in his eyes. "I am not married." Cara pulled the note Mr. Healy gave her from her pocket. "You said you have lived in New York a while?"

He nodded and looked at the paper curiously. "Almost a year. My family was hit hard by the famine a few years back. We had to sell much of our land. I came here looking for work."

Cara took care opening the note and pressing it flat. "I . . . thought you were looking for someone?"

"I am. I have a cousin who is supposed to be joining me, but I'm not sure when. I went to the island hoping for word."

He crossed his arms, his wool coat pulling at the shoulder seams. He was a big man, obviously fit and heavily muscled. Undoubtedly, he'd had no trouble finding work. Her heart fluttered. Maybe he knew Eoghan. Only how to ask without giving herself away? She couldn't. Her gaze fell to the name on the note.

"What have you there?"

Cara held out the paper. "I wonder, would you be knowing this person?"

He took the note, glanced at the writing, then handed it back. "I'm afraid not." His voice lowered, but he leaned forward so she still heard him clearly over the noise of the ferry's engines. "Is she family? Was she supposed to meet you today?"

Her throat tightened. Too quickly his questions had turned to a topic rife with risk. Her fingers clutched the collar of her coat. "No . . . I . . . I do not have any family. My parents died years ago."

That much, at least, was true. The rest? Up until a few weeks ago she'd believed that true, as well. She breathed a prayer for forgiveness at the half-truth and dropped her chin.

"But . . ." Hesitancy filled his voice. "The island?" His dark brows bunched as he peered at her.

"What?"

"Single women dinna often make it through registration alone."

Shame flooded her. "I told them Amelia Matheson was my grandmother."

"Forgive me. I should not have pried."

Was that relief mixed with the compassion in

his voice? Cara's head, and her heart, lifted. "Thank you, Mr. Walsh."

"You're welcome, and please, call me Rourke." His shoulder bumped hers. "We're two Irishmen in a land of foreigners, after all."

The gleam in Rourke Walsh's eyes as he studied her left no doubt that he liked what he saw.

So did she. Her gaze drifted down the length of his strong jaw and settled on his mouth. Fortunately a stiff breeze blew up, and Cara used the motion of brushing the hair from her face to hide her embarrassment. "You have that wrong. Here, we be the foreigners."

Rourke laughed and settled against the seat. "True. So? What will you do when you reach the city?" He caught the fluttering end of his scarf, then jammed his hands into his pockets and hunched deeper into his coat.

Cara shrugged. "Search for Mrs. Matheson, I suppose. See if she can offer me a place to stay. After that, I'll need to find—" she glanced at him and away—"work."

He extended his hand. "May I see the note again?"

She dropped the slip of paper into his palm and then blew on her stiff fingers. What she wouldn't give to curl up someplace warm tonight, with the quilt her dear mother had sewn for her snuggled under her chin and a peat fire crackling in the hearth.

"Ashberry Street?" Rourke frowned and returned the paper to her. "I know the area. You say she runs a boardinghouse?"

She nodded. "That is my understanding. Mr. Healy said she's an old friend. Though I only just met him, he seemed quite pleasant during the crossing."

"I don't know." He shook his head slightly. "There be many unsavory people in the city. Are you certain this Mr. Healy can be trusted?"

Cara laughed, surprised to admit his concern ignited an excited tickle in her belly. "I've only just met you, too. How do I know you can be trusted?"

A roguish smile curled his lips. "A fair question." Instead of answering, he shrugged. "I'll help you find the place. Check it out, perhaps, just to make sure it's safe."

Suddenly Eoghan's warning rang clear in her mind.

"Trust no one. Speak to no one until I come for you."

Rourke dashed the cap from his head and laid it across his chest, then followed with a wide smile. "Upon my honor, miss, no harm will befall you so long as you be under my care."

Cara laughed outright. Good or bad, the exaggerated concern on his face put her apprehension to rest. Eoghan used to tease her in a similar manner, before his new friends pulled him farther and farther away from the family and home. Aware of Rourke's steady gaze, she resisted the urge to touch her bracelet.

"Very well, sir. Ashberry Street it is. Are you certain you know the way?"

"If I didn't, I wouldn't admit it now and risk losing my chance to escort a pretty woman."

She hid a smile and narrowed her eyes. "Fie. I'm sensing a bit of the blarney in ya."

"More than a bit."

They laughed, and for the first time Cara allowed herself to relax against the back of the bench. It felt good to let go her guard, if only for a moment. She hadn't done so since receiving Eoghan's message.

She gave a quick lift of her chin. "So, what about you?"

"Me?" Rourke slapped the cap back on his head. "I'm as boring as a milk bucket. Not much to tell."

"But you work in the city?"

"I do. Odd jobs mostly, and whatever I can wrangle at the wharf. They always be looking for a bit of muscle unloading the ships that come into the harbor."

Cara cast a longing glance at the shore growing larger in the distance. That had to be how Eoghan intended to find her. Perhaps he'd be waiting when she arrived, his bonnie eyes welcoming, his arms spread wide to wrap her in a hug as he'd done when they were children. She clasped her hands in her lap, afraid Rourke would see their trembling and know there was more she wasn't telling.

A quiet murmur rose from the other passengers, and almost as one they shuffled toward the rail, rocking and bobbing in rhythm with the boat, pointing at something Cara couldn't see.

"What is it?" She craned her neck to look over Rourke's shoulder.

He smiled, his eyes sparkling. "You haven't seen it, then?"

"Seen what?"

"The statue."

She nodded. "From afar. We caught a glimpse as the ship was docking, another as the barge carried us back to the island."

"It's different up close." He rose and held out his hand, then guided her to a spot near the stern. "The ferry always passes by so that those coming to America for the first time can get a glimpse of her."

Looking up into the Lady's earnest face, Cara gasped. She'd seen a tintype of her features cast in stark relief, but this close . . . Never had she imagined the way the sight would make her feel. No wonder people who intended to make their home in America were filled with such hope. Like the passengers gathered around her, Cara fixed her eyes on the glowing torch splitting the overcast sky.

"Beautiful, isn't she?"

Tears filmed Cara's eyes. Clutching the edges of her coat shut, she managed a weak "She is indeed."

In fact, the image impacted her so, it burned onto her memory. Long after they passed, she pictured the spires of Lady Liberty's crown piercing the air, like the points of a star reaching toward the sky. Among the folds of her robe, Cara imagined the souls of foreign lands taking shelter—orphaned children yearning for a mother. Was that why Eoghan had chosen to hide in America?

Rustling stirred among the passengers as the ferry docked, the excitement in the air almost tangible. Cara rose, but before she could reach for her valise, Rourke hefted it for her.

"Ready?" He smiled as he motioned toward the gangplank.

A tremor weakened Cara's knees. Departing here was different from the landing on Ellis Island. Here, the land was vast, the city stretching farther than her eyes could see. She had not the means to return to Ireland alone. If Eoghan wasn't waiting on the dock, if she couldn't find him . . .

Drawing a deep breath, she shook the melancholy from her limbs and walked forward, down the wooden gangplank that rumbled with the footsteps of many passengers, onto the dock.

From this moment forward, her feet would seek a new path. Which way it wound, she couldn't guess, but for better or worse it led through American soil.

3

"Marta! Wring out those damp clothes and bring them to me. Don't let them drag. It took me hours to get them clean."

The strident voice curled on fingers of wood-smoke rising from the alley. Soon a young woman carrying a basket laden with laundry ducked out of a shop door. Marta, Cara assumed. The girl spared Cara a brief glance before she plodded around the corner of the building and disappeared. Down the street and along the side-walks, children in patched coats darted and ran.

Cara's feet faltered on the path. Before her rose a large gray building, the bricked sides mottled with dirt and soot. Shutters framed each window, but with the shades half drawn and no light peeping through they merely gave the house a sleepy-eyed look she found daunting.

"It'll be all right, lass. God's help is nearer than the door."

Her mother's words ringing in her head, Cara let her gaze drift upward. At the boardinghouse's peak, twin dormers stood guard beside a massive chimney from which plumes of gray smoke spiraled. At least the place promised to be warm, she thought as she drew near to a flight of stairs that angled up to a large door, topped with a leaded fan light and framed by wooden pillars, none of which looked inviting in the early evening gloom.

Her stomach sank. Compared to Derry, what she'd seen of New York was cramped and dirty, nothing like the rolling hills back home. Worse yet, she was alone, for Eoghan had not waited on the dock to meet her as she'd hoped.

Blinking to ward off tears, she unfolded the note with Amelia Matheson's address scribbled inside and then searched the forbidding structure for numbers.

"Are you certain this is the right place?" she asked, a tremor in her voice.

"Quite." Rourke eased past her and forged his way up the steps to the door, his fist half raised. "Shall I knock?"

What choice did she have? With no place to stay and only a few meager coins in her pocket, Mr. Healy's note had proven a godsend. Her feet leaden, she followed Rourke to the door. He made room for her, then lifted his hand and knocked.

Standing so close, Cara felt very small, and wished suddenly that she knew Rourke Walsh better. Maybe then she could ignore the echo of Eoghan's warning.

"Are you cold, lass?"

Captivated by the intense hue of his eyes, rational thought fled her brain. "Pardon?"

"You shivered just then, so I thought you might be cold."

Cara shook her head. "No. It's just . . . all so new."

Empathy spilled over his face. "You'll adjust. New York can be overwhelming at first, but it's not a bad city. You'll see."

Just then the door swung open and a portly woman stood framed in the entrance. A dingy white apron wrapped her girth, and upon her head she wore a mobcap that drooped into her eyes.

With chubby fingers she jabbed the cap further back onto her head. "Yes?"

Cara swallowed, hard. "My name is Cara Hamilton. I was told you have a room for let?"

The woman eyed her from head to grimy toe. Cara hardened her jaw and tried not to squirm. There was nothing for it. She hadn't had time to wash up before leaving the ferry.

"Just arriving, are ya?"

The gruffness of her voice matched her rough exterior. Surely this wasn't Amelia Matheson? Cara had expected someone with a humor like Mr. Healy's. She bobbed her head, once.

"Who sent ya?"

"Douglas Healy. He and I sailed from Liver-pool."

"You're not English."

Did it matter? Irritation stiffened her spine. "No."

"Eh . . . Irish. Well, come in then." The woman swung out of the doorway and motioned for them to enter. "Can I take your coats?"

Stepping into the front hallway, both she and Rourke slipped out of their outer garments and gave them to the woman. She took them and then, cupping her hand to her mouth, bellowed up a flight of stairs. "Amelia! Boarders."

She called her employer by her Christian name? Cara glanced at Rourke to see if he was as taken aback as she. He merely shrugged.

Jabbing her thumb toward a brown and gold settee with a deeply carved crown, the house-keeper said, "Wait there. Mrs. Matheson will attend you shortly."

With that, she turned and lumbered down the hall, disappearing at the end through a narrow doorway.

" 'Tis a wonder she didn't get stuck."

Cara started at the low voice so near her ear. So that's what was meant by a devilish grin, she thought, cheeks burning as he motioned for her to precede him to the settee.

"Shall we?"

Once again his light banter loosed the tension

31

snaring her limbs. What was it about this man that reminded her so of Eoghan? They looked nothing alike, for Eoghan's hair was red like hers, and his eyes a sultry hazel, not deep and blue like Rourke's.

She sank onto the settee still pondering, but only briefly. Light footsteps echoed in the hall and Cara looked up to see a small woman approaching, a welcoming smile stretched across a very pleasant sort of face.

"Mrs. Hamilton?" She extended both hands to take Cara's.

Cara rose and slipped her cold fingers into the woman's warm grasp. "Aye, I am Cara Hamilton. You must be Mrs. Matheson?"

"That's correct, dear. It's a pleasure to meet you. Laverne tells me you are a friend of Douglas's."

Assuming Laverne to be the woman who met them at the door, Cara nodded. "Although, in truth, I only just met Mr. Healy some days ago, when we departed Liverpool for America."

Amelia Matheson smiled, her gray eyes sparkling with humor. "Ah, but it doesn't take him long to make friends, does it? That man has more charm than a debutante at her first ball." She turned to Rourke. "And you must be Mr. Hamilton."

Judging by the raised eyebrows and parted lips, Rourke was as befuddled as Cara, but he recovered quickly. A rakish smile replacing his confusion, he looked Cara over and then shook his head. "I fear not. I've known Miss Hamilton less time than Mr. Healy. My name is Walsh. Rourke Walsh."

Nonplussed, Mrs. Matheson waved a slender hand. "Well, it's a pleasure to meet you both. Please, join me in the parlor. We'll sit and enjoy some tea while you tell me all about yourselves."

"There's not much to tell, I'm afraid," Cara said, following Mrs. Matheson into a simply furnished room.

Darkly paneled, the place still managed to look cheery with a fire crackling in the overlarge fireplace. Boughs of evergreen covered the tables and mantel. With her cap of snowy hair, Mrs. Matheson looked right at home among the leftover Yuletide decorations. She motioned toward a cameo-back sofa, then took her place in a wing chair drawn close to the fire and arranged her skirt over her legs.

"So, Miss Hamilton, Mr. Walsh, what brings the two of you to New York?"

Despite the fact that she ran a boardinghouse, she was obviously a lady of breeding with her genteel manner and careful speech. Cara grew even more conscious of her soiled traveling clothes and unwashed hair. On top of it all, she probably smelled like fish!

Rourke shook his head. "You misunderstand, Mrs. Matheson. Miss Hamilton was aboard the ship, not I."

33

Mrs. Matheson's gaze shifted to Cara. "I see. Forgive me. I assumed you were family traveling together."

Rourke gestured to the valise he'd carried in and set by his feet. "Simply doing a favor for a friend."

"Then . . ." Her eyes clouded and she brought her finger to her lips. "You're not looking for a room . . . together, I mean."

"No!" Cara gasped. What on earth had given the woman such an idea? Apart from the fact they'd arrived at her door together, he carrying Cara's valise, and she otherwise unchaperoned . . .

She colored at the implication and shifted further from Rourke. "No," she repeated softly. "Just me. Alone."

The worry lines lifted and Mrs. Matheson smiled. "Wonderful. I wasn't so sure, what with the larking about of the younger folk nowadays, but I must tell you, I don't allow that sort of thing here."

"That be well and good. Da would roll over in his grave if I even pondered such a thing."

Compassion softened Mrs. Matheson's face. "Your father is dead?"

She nodded. "My ma, too, over six years ago."

"And you have no other family."

Though not a question, she answered with a shake of her head.

"Ah, so that explains your presence, then."

Cara swallowed the lump of guilt rising in her

throat. They'd only just met, but she liked Mrs. Matheson and wasn't keen on deceiving her. "Among other things, yes."

"And where are you from, Miss Hamilton, if you don't mind my asking?"

"Northern Ireland. A town called Derry."

"What about you, Mr. Walsh?"

Cara's gaze traveled with hers to Rourke. He'd grown so quiet and listened so intently, she'd almost forgotten he was present.

"Excuse me?"

"What do you do?"

Rourke crossed one long leg over the other. His manner said he was at ease, but the set of his jaw hinted otherwise. "This and that. I do enough to get by, but only when absolutely necessary."

Behind a delicate cough, Cara saw Mrs. Matheson hide a frown. She turned to Cara. "My boarders are all hardworking Christian women. I do employ one man to help me run the boarding-house. He's older, however, and he occupies a couple of rooms on the third level of the house, the women the second."

She studied Cara a moment before nodding her head as though she'd arrived at a decision. "I have a room, if you're interested. The rent is reasonable and includes the cost of your meals. Most of my boarders work during the day, but they all return in time for supper. I lock the doors at eight."

No longer homeless, Cara felt herself relax.

Indeed, Mr. Healy's note was a godsend. "It sounds perfect. Thank you." She hesitated. "I cannot pay much . . . at least . . . not at first. I hope to secure employment, but until then . . ."

Mrs. Matheson waved her hand in dismissal. "It doesn't take long for my boarders to get on their feet, dear. What can you do?"

The trip across the Atlantic had afforded ample time to ponder her answer. She lifted her chin. "I am skilled with a needle. Also, I can read and write, and I'm good with figures. My *daed* taught me." A twinge of sorrow fluttered in her stomach. She plunged onward before it took root. "I speak a bit of French, though I cannot claim to be fluent. And I can operate a household well enough. I managed my father's house after my mother passed away."

Mrs. Matheson nodded, her expression guarded. "All good skills."

Cara clutched her hands in her lap and leaned forward. "I am also good with children. I thought perhaps I might find a family in need of a governess."

Mrs. Matheson's bunched eyebrows revealed the answer. "There's not much call for Irish governesses in the Battery, I'm afraid."

Cara bit her lip. Indeed, that was what she'd feared. Of all domestic servants, Irish girls were paid the lowest and prized the least.

Rising, Mrs. Matheson crossed the room to a

36

desk. She pulled out the center drawer, ran her hand inside, and retrieved a small book. The pages rustled softly as she flipped through it to the middle. Finding what she sought, she stopped and returned with the book.

"Here we are. This man might be able to help. He owns a small candle shop. From what I understand, he's looking for someone to manage the finances." Her lips spread in an indulgent smile and she waved toward some long tapers burning in sconces on the walls. "He's a wonderful candlemaker, but he has no sense when it comes to money."

A candle shop? It wasn't what Cara had envisioned, but then nothing about America had been what she'd imagined. She nodded and took the book. "James O'Bannon?"

"That's him. He's a good sort. He's from Ireland, like you, though I couldn't tell you which part. I think you'll like him." Mrs. Matheson collected the book from Cara and replaced it in the drawer. Meanwhile, Cara spared a quick glance at Rourke. He shrugged, and she knew he thought the idea as plausible as she, though why his opinion should matter, she couldn't fathom.

She waited until Mrs. Matheson returned before she spoke. "Beggars in my position are thankful for whatever scraps they can get, I suppose. If you deem the opportunity worthwhile, I'll look into it."

"Good." Mrs. Matheson laid hold of a bell resting on the table next to her chair, gave it a ring, and then sat down and folded her hands in her lap to wait. The housekeeper appeared a moment later. "We'll take some tea, Laverne, and set two more places at the supper table." She lifted a brow toward Rourke, who shook his head.

"I appreciate the invitation, ma'am, but I'm afraid I won't be joining you for supper. I am long overdue. My friends will be wondering where I've gotten to."

Mrs. Matheson *tsk*ed softly. "Perhaps another time?"

Rourke nodded and moved to rise while Laverne fetched his coat. Cara joined him in the hall.

"I . . . cannot thank you enough for accompanying me today. For sure I would've been lost without your help."

He bowed slightly. "It was my pleasure."

Cara flushed with embarrassment. She'd only known the man a short while. She shouldn't feel so taken by a few kind words or a ready smile, and yet . . .

Rourke cleared his throat. "I have some business that is going to take me out of town for about a month, but when I return . . . that is . . . I'd like to call on you again, just to see how you're faring," he finished quickly. "Would that be all right?"

Cara's heart thumped with excitement. In a day or so she would have reunited with Eoghan, and then she could speak freely with Rourke, tell him all about her reasons for coming to New York. She smiled her agreement. "I would like that."

"Good. I'll be in touch," he said softly.

Laverne appeared with his coat. He took it, shrugged inside, and with one last glance over his shoulder, he slipped out the door.

Aside from the inspector, Rourke was the first person Cara had met in America, and she felt a bit forlorn at his going.

"Come away from the door, dear," Mrs. Matheson called. "The others will be arriving soon, and I want you to meet them all. But before that happens, we still have much to discuss."

Unfortunately, until Eoghan appeared, there was not much Cara could tell.

Where was he? Why hadn't he met her at the dock? Her fingers closed around her bracelet, as though with that touch she could somehow forge a connection to her twin.

A sigh building in her chest, she turned and went back into the parlor, the story she'd concocted on the journey from Liverpool ready on her lips. For now she would stick to the ruse, but for how long she didn't know. Still, something inside warned it would be much longer than she thought, and the story much more difficult to maintain.

Eoghan ducked deeper into his coat as the door to the boardinghouse swung open. His heart pounded against his ribs, but not with excitement as it had earlier when he watched the *Servia* steam into the harbor. This time it was dread that made his brow bead with sweat and his limbs tremble.

He'd warned Cara. The instructions in his letter had been as explicit as he could make them. Speak to no one. Trust no one. Why then had she disembarked the ferry with a stranger? Without a doubt they had been together. The man carried her bag, walked with her to the boardinghouse, leaned almost protectively toward her when she shuddered. Surely, she would not have been so careless as to tell the man why she'd come, unless . . .

His stomach sank. Could it be?

His place in the shadow of an awning did not provide nearly the cover he would have liked. Fortunately for him, the man swinging down the boardinghouse steps appeared distracted. He cursed the cap pulled low on the man's head. It hid half his face. If only he could see his eyes!

Though it meant risking exposure, Eoghan wheeled and left the hollow between the seam-stress's doorway and the alley. He had to know. If they had found him, if they'd tracked him to his sister, he wouldn't risk endangering her further. He'd wait, bide his time until the attention had turned from her before seeking her out.

He timed his entrance to the street, waiting for

an approaching carriage before drawing even with the man.

Four steps. No more.

The moment the carriage passed, he paused for one searching glance and then veered left, back into the crowd and maze of vendor stands.

Cold air bit his lungs as he drew in a sharp, angry breath. He didn't know how, or when, but somehow the Turners had traced him to New York, and to his sister.

His bunched fists shook with rage as he stalked the cobbled street. Cara was the only family he had left. Waiting two years to contact her, living like a fugitive, alone and hunted, had nearly killed him. Worse, every day he'd borne the anguish of knowing Cara lived in torment—believed him dead. And now, when he'd finally dared hope for a new start, they'd found him. Again.

With each angry step he cursed the infernal Turner persistence. Maybe it was time he stopped running. It wasn't like he hadn't tried to stop what had happened. Maybe if he faced them instead of hiding . . .

A snarl ripped from his throat. He drove his knuckles into the side of a tall brick tenement, welcoming the blood and pain that followed.

There was no mistaking those piercing cobalt eyes. It had to be Rourke Turner himself who'd accompanied Cara from the ferry.

Running his palm over his face, Eoghan forced

his breathing to slow, his heart to calm its wild racing.

They'd found him. So be it.

Cara knew nothing of his activities, had no idea of his whereabouts or how to contact him. For her own safety, he'd made sure of it. He would simply wait the Turners out, and when their guard was low, he'd send her a message, secret her out of the city.

His long strides carried him swiftly from the street and down a dark alley. America was wild and vast. He and Cara would find a place free from the intrigue of his past. If not, if the battle between him and the Turners somehow snared his sister, he'd stop running. He'd fight to protect her with every ounce of strength in his body. One way or another this hellish war would end, and either he would be dead or he'd have scoured every last Turner from the face of the earth.

4

Dipping his head against the biting wind, Rourke hunched his shoulders and wound through the dimly lit streets of New York. At this hour of the night, most of the city's residents lazed in front of their home fires, their bellies full from supper and their eyelids heavy with sleep. With Rourke's dark coat and his cap pulled low, he doubted anyone noticed as he slipped past. Still, he hugged the shadows, avoiding the glow of the street-lamps, ears perked for the sound of footsteps.

A little used alley beckoned just past a clockmaker's shop, where timepieces of every kind stared out from the windows. Next to the clockmaker sat a Polish bakery, whose warm rolls on chilly morns made Rourke's mouth water. Carefully arranged boxes blocked the entrance to the alley, but a quick sidestep and a quarter turn of his shoulders pushed him into the gaping hole of a darkened doorway.

"Turner?"

Rourke tipped back his cap and let the dim glow of the moon, peeking between buildings, spill across his face. "Aye."

Body rigid, he waited. To move too soon or too suddenly would bring swift and certain retribution. After a moment, a rap sounded and the door scraped open. Rourke slipped into the circle of feeble light cast by one sputtering candle.

As expected, two of his kinsmen stood guard on the other side. The one who had spoken to him in the alley remained, and would remain, hidden in the shadows outside.

Malcolm, his uncle, welcomed him with a clap to the shoulder. "Rourke, me boy, you've returned."

"Did you doubt?"

Malcolm snorted and motioned for Rourke's cousin to assume his place at the door. As the man passed, he offered a quick embrace and a quiet word of greeting before Rourke joined his uncle in the hall.

Malcolm's snowy eyebrows rose in anticipation. "I take it you have news?"

Reluctance thickened Rourke's tongue. "Of a sort."

Emptying his mind of Cara's green eyes and honest face, he concentrated on the narrow paneled hall and the large room that waited at the end. When they reached it, Malcolm pushed open the door and let Rourke precede him inside.

A fire glowing in the belly of an iron stove chased away the worst of the night's chill, but the breaths of the ten or eleven men gathered around a squat table still rose in wispy columns.

The place had once been a shoe store. Rourke dodged the wooden boxes that littered the corners of the room as he greeted his kinsmen and then grabbed a chair from alongside the wall and swung it to the table. As one, the men shifted to make room.

Malcolm remained standing, his stern glower and graying hair so reminiscent of Rourke's father it made him wince.

Chest swelling, Malcolm braced both hands on his hips and tipped his head toward Rourke. "Well, lads, I think I speak for all of us when I

44

say it be good to lay eyes on me nephew again."

A hearty round of *ayes* followed Malcolm's statement. Indeed, it had been several weeks since Rourke had anything to report. Gazes bright with anticipation fixed on him, but once again a pair of green eyes flashed across his memory.

"Rourke, lad?"

Rourke's head jerked toward his uncle. Malcolm and his father, Daniel, had always favored each other, but never more than when Malcolm's furrowed brows dipped so low they nearly covered his eyes, an intimidating skill unique to Turner men. Though his father was older, he was still only fifty-six when he died—too young and too good a man to have been felled by a coward's bullet. Rourke's resolve hardened, crowding out guilt and a small voice inside that said his father would not have been pleased.

"A woman arrived on the *Servia* earlier today. A redhead named Hamilton."

Across from Rourke, a gruff voice cut in. "There be many Hamiltons. How do you know she is the one?"

Rourke turned to the oldest—and often most cynical—member of his family present.

"I have a feeling, Angus O'Hurly, that is all. I need to keep me eye on her."

Angus was his mother's brother, with no blood ties to Rourke's father in the truest sense, but when she and Daniel married, the two men had become fast friends. "Closer than brothers," Daniel always said, even though he was Angus's junior by several years.

A smirk carved through Angus's lined face. "Well, nephew . . . so long as you have 'a feeling.' "

Rourke stiffened at the baleful gleam in his eyes. Angus blamed him for his father's death. No more than he himself did, but he still bristled at being called out in front of his kinsmen.

"Tell us what you know, lad," Malcolm interrupted, probably sensing the rage boiling in Rourke's belly.

Rourke tore his focus from Angus and clapped it on Malcolm. Swallowing his anger, he forced himself to recall everything Cara had told him.

"She is a young lass, maybe twenty-one or -two. Traveled alone, which I thought odd, though she did make a couple of friends while on board the ship. She said her parents are dead. Claimed to have left Ireland in search of a fresh start."

"Eoghan Hamilton's parents are both dead." Clive Turner, Malcolm's youngest son, leaned forward and placed both elbows on the table. "They died years ago, and I did hear it rumored that Hamilton has a sister."

Several heads bobbed in agreement. Malcolm's gaze, sharp as blue ice, fixed on Rourke. "What else?"

"She's a northerner . . . from Derry. And she appeared to be looking for someone."

At this, the men gathered around the table drew a collective breath. Malcolm leaned forward on his knuckles. Even old Angus's brows rose with interest.

"She told you this?"

Rourke nodded and looked over at Malcolm. "She warrants watching, at least until I can figure out who she's searching for."

Malcolm's eyes roved the faces of the assembled men. With each nod he moved on until he returned to Rourke. "We be in agreement, then. What do you intend?"

"She asked to be taken to a boardinghouse on Ashberry Street. I think I can find work nearby without drawing too much attention."

Malcolm rubbed his hands together eagerly, an action Rourke well understood. Two years had passed since his father died. Two years ago that he and his kinsmen vowed revenge, and this was the first lead that offered more than a little promise.

"Take Hugh with you."

Caught off guard, Rourke jerked around to stare at old Angus.

Angus's grizzled head bobbed toward the eldest of his seven sons. "He's a knack for this sort of thing. You'd do well to have him close."

Rourke had seen firsthand the sort of "knack" Hugh O'Hurly was known for. He wanted him nowhere near Cara or the other boardinghouse residents. But to deny Angus . . .

Malcolm came to his rescue. "If it be true she was searching for someone on the island, there's a good possibility she might return there. But the city is a large place. Best if we keep our men spread out and our ears open." He chuckled. "This could be the chance we've been waiting for, lads. Fate has shined her bonnie face on us at last."

Murmured approval drifted upward toward the ceiling, and with it Rourke's sigh of relief.

No one wanted to see his father's murder avenged more than he, but for the first time it wasn't at the expense of everyone . . . or everything . . . else.

Conviction seared him—an old, tired argument he'd grown weary of having. Taking one last glance around the table, his gaze collided with Hugh's. A tiny sneer curled his cousin's lips, as though he alone were privy to Rourke's thoughts. In Hugh's eyes shone a glimmer of the cruelty he kept hidden beneath a silken veil of charm and good looks. Hugh possessed the kinds of qualities Rourke knew they needed in their quest for a killer. He'd just never imagined that quest would involve a woman.

5

Stirred by a gust from the open door, Cara's red curls gently tickled her neck. It wasn't a pleasant feeling. More like troublesome gnats. She rubbed the spot. Perhaps her disquiet was caused by her nerves, riled by the commotion shaking the boardinghouse. She turned her head to watch the cluster of women filling the hall.

"Come, dear. Meet the other residents."

Mrs. Matheson's voice lilted like the River Foyle on a soft summer day, a direct contrast to the icy breeze blowing in from the street. Summoning her courage, Cara rose from the seat where she and Mrs. Matheson had been sharing a pot of tea. Their scarves half unwound from around their necks, two of the women paused to eye her curiously. The rest shrugged out of their coats and hung them on a row of hooks flanking the door.

Mrs. Matheson motioned her forward. Faced with a half-dozen measuring gazes, Cara couldn't help but press close to her side. While the boardinghouse residents continued shedding their outer garments, Mrs. Matheson slid her arm around Cara's waist. "We have a new boarder, ladies." She gave Cara an encouraging nod and gently pushed her forward. "I'd like you all to say hello to Cara. I know you'll help me make her feel welcome."

Cara waited, her breath captive in her chest. How she hated these moments, when the attention of a crowd felt like a woolen cloak pulled tight around her face. She startled as she felt her hand grasped between chilly fingers.

"Pleased to meet ya, lass. I'm Breda."

Breda's eyes were kind and inviting, and her wrinkled cheeks, kissed rosy by the wind, lifted in a friendly smile. "Where you be from?"

Again with the questions. But since she'd already spilled the answer to Rourke and Mrs. Matheson, she saw no reason to hide it now. Cara swallowed the lump in her throat and forced a smile. "Derry, ma'am."

Pleasure flared in Breda's gray gaze. "A northerner!" Her head dipped closer, and with it came the scent of yeast and warm bread. "Be ya Protestant?"

"Breda," Mrs. Matheson scolded, wagging her finger, "you know we do not hold to distinctions here. Everyone is welcome, regardless of their beliefs."

Breda chuckled, revealing gaps in her uneven teeth, and patted Cara's shoulder. "That's the British for ya. Always pretendin' like there's no fly in the buttermilk." Drawing back, she winked and passed a rounded sack to Mrs. Matheson.

"Rolls to go with the gravy. You know I dinna ken to those stones old Laverne bakes."

Mrs. Matheson took the bag with a smile. "I'll tell her you said so."

"Huh!" Breda snorted, her plain cotton skirt swishing as she ambled to the parlor.

"Don't mind her," a gentle voice soothed. "The food here is quite good, and there's plenty of it, so none of us have cause to complain." Soft brown eyes peered from a sweetly rounded face. "I am Ana."

Cara's fingers shook as she accepted Ana's outstretched hand. "Pleased to meet you—"

Her voice broke as she looked down to the twisted hand she clasped. In places, the skin was smooth and supple, but in others, red and purple scars puckered the young woman's flesh. They looked like burns, healed over with age but crippling nonetheless. She dragged her eyes upward and swallowed. "Ana."

A pink flush crept up from Ana's slender neck as she averted her gaze. "Pleasure's mine."

"Them's northern manners for ya."

The bitter-tinged voice silenced the chatter. All eyes swung to the slender figure of a woman who stepped from the shadows like a wraith.

"Deidre." Mrs. Matheson frowned her displeasure. "This is not the time."

"It's the truth, Amelia." Deidre went on as though Mrs. Matheson hadn't spoken. "Never

51

met a northerner what knew how to hold their tongue."

Deidre was a tall redhead—taller even than Cara herself by an inch or more. Her face was thin and pinched, her green eyes narrowed and glittering. Crossing her arms over her angular frame, she glowered first at Cara, then at Mrs. Matheson. "Well? Will we be standing here in the hall until our dinner gets cold, or can we make our way to the dining room? Stones or no, I've a hankering for some warm bread and bit of pork to go with it." Whirling, she stalked from the hall.

"Yes, of course," Mrs. Matheson clucked, shooing the rest of the women toward the dining room with a flustered wave. "Plenty of time for introductions later. Come, ladies. Supper will be ready soon. There's just enough time for you to wash and dress."

In fact, Cara barely had time for the embarrassed flush to cool from her cheeks before Ana took the seat next to her at the dinner table and Mrs. Matheson signaled they should join hands for grace. As heads bowed, Cara stole a quick glance around the table. Settings for seven lined the narrow pine plank. Six women and one man to whom she had yet to be introduced occupied the chairs.

"Father, we thank you for this bounty," Mrs. Matheson began, prompting Cara to lower her head. "We thank you for the friends gathered here, and for the warm beds that await us at the end of this day. Bless us with your peace, we pray, in your Son's holy name. Amen."

"Amen," they chimed as one.

Curious, Cara watched as a couple of them followed with a touch to their forehead, chest, and both shoulders.

"Like Amelia said," Breda whispered, leaning across the table to hand Cara a roll, "we make no distinction here."

A cold knot formed in Cara's stomach.

"God makes no distinction, Da. Protestant or Catholic, it matters not so long as one holds to the Savior."

Her words had felt so right spoken in the vehemence of youth, even in the wake of her daed's icy fury. She swallowed hard and took her time arranging her napkin in her lap.

"You call Mrs. Matheson by her Christian name?" It was conversation only, something to divert Cara's chaotic thoughts, but Breda nodded brightly.

"Aye. She insists on it. You'll see soon enough."

"Potatoes, Cara?" Ana held up a bowl brimming with the hot, buttery vegetable. "They're from Breda's garden, and their flavor is grand. We squeezed enough into the cellar to last us clear through the winter."

"The woman could grow turnips in a trash pot," the man said.

Ana leaned to whisper in Cara's ear. "That's Giles, Amelia's gardener and handyman."

Cara nodded her thanks.

Giles's chin jutted toward Breda and then he jammed his thumb against his own chest. "Me? I kinna keep daisies alive."

" 'Twould help if you watered 'em once in a while. Some gardener," Breda said with a huff. She chuckled as she jabbed a fork into a plate piled high with hearty slices of pork. Plopping one onto her plate, she replaced the fork and then passed the dish to the next girl, a shy lass Cara had only heard referred to as "the bairn."

The talk continued around the table, several of the women engaging one another with the details of their day and the savory flavor of Breda's potatoes—except for Deidre, who watched Cara in silence from her place at the end of the table.

"You say you hail from Derry."

Focused on picking out names from among the women's chatter, it took Cara a moment to realize that Deidre had addressed her. She passed the gravy bowl to Ana, then turned toward Deidre.

"I'm sorry, what did you say?"

"Derry. You said you hail from that place."

Cara nodded hesitantly, her fingers fumbling for the fork that lay alongside her plate. She hefted it, calmed to hold something . . . anything . . . of substance.

"What brings you to America? Haven't you family in Ireland?"

Accompanied by Deidre's disconcerting stare, the questions left Cara with gnarled anxiety in the pit of her stomach.

"Trust no one. Speak to no one."

She could almost feel the brush of Eoghan's soft whisper against her ear. Clearing her throat, Cara adjusted her fork so it rested lightly against her index finger. "No family. Both my parents are gone." She left out any mention of Eoghan.

Ignoring her full plate, Deidre leaned forward. "No brothers or sisters? No uncles? Aunts?"

Cara's grip on the fork tightened. She didn't like being forced into a lie by Deidre's pointed questions, but neither would she risk Eoghan's safety. She squeezed one word from her stiff lips. "None."

"How sad," Ana whispered from Cara's side.

Unaware she'd been listening, Cara spun toward her with raised brows.

"You be an orphan then, like—" Ana swallowed hard and continued—"myself and our Tillie." She motioned to the one they called the bairn.

Lifting her eyes, Tillie stared at Cara and then tucked back into her meal without a word.

Cara swallowed a swell of sympathy, mingled with the bitterness of her deceit.

Oh, Eoghan . . . come quickly, lad, so I do not have to lie to these good people long.

She forced her gaze not to waver. "Aye, Ana, but I do not feel an orphan. I have my faith in God."

Mrs. Matheson cleared her throat and smiled at Cara from the head of the table. "That's good, child. Faith can see you through many a trial. Many a trial, indeed."

"I dinna believe Amelia gave us your last name," Deidre interrupted, her untouched plate of food shouting at Cara like a banshee.

Suddenly, Cara wanted to lie, to keep the truth of her ancestry from Deidre without knowing why. "It be—" her mouth watered and she swallowed, twice—"H-Hamilton."

Already hard, Deidre's features turned to stone. Except for her eyes, Cara realized. They flashed emerald fire.

"Ham-il-ton?" Each syllable dropped from Deidre's lips like ice. "I be knowing quite a few Hamiltons up Derry way."

A gruff voice cut in from the foot of the table. Giles gestured at Cara with his fork. "She don't look much like them, however. Most of them be a dark-haired lot, with eyes to match. Not fair and red, like her."

Resisting the urge to touch the hair curling at her neck, Cara nodded. "I am told I favor my mother's side."

"Then she must have been beautiful," Mrs. Matheson said gently.

By now, everyone had turned in Cara's direction, a situation she'd hoped to avoid after the first time. She sank a little deeper into her chair.

"Is the pork not to your liking?" Breda asked, cutting the silence but intensifying the stares. "You haven't touched your food."

"Oh, leave her be, Breda," Mrs. Matheson said. "It's her first day in a new home and new country. No doubt this is all a bit overwhelming."

Cara glanced at her plate, shocked to realize that Deidre wasn't the only one who'd let her food get cold. She jabbed her fork into the potatoes and took a hearty bite, aware as she chewed that all still watched. Swallowing with difficulty, she forced a smile. "Delicious."

The lines on Breda's face softened with relief, and Mrs. Matheson's good nature returned full force. Loosed by her approval, the women's chatter resumed.

Like a flock of birds, Cara thought, careful to keep her gaze from wandering to Deidre as she sliced a bite from the pork on her plate and put it in her mouth. No longer concerned with learning the names of the other residents, she ate quietly, the food sliding untasted down her throat. She'd nearly finished eating when curiosity raised her head.

From across the table, Deidre continued to watch her, her eyes sparkling green slits and her plate of food still untouched.

6

Rourke eyed the boardinghouse door and the shadows slinking backward over the dormered peaks. It was early—the sun had yet to crest the tallest city buildings. Up and down both sides of Ashberry Street, many a vendor cart sat empty. In little more than an hour, they would all be full and shoppers would cram the street, leaving sparse room for horses or carriages. Maybe then he wouldn't look so conspicuous lugging the same basket of poultry back and forth in front of the boardinghouse.

"You there! Are you lost?"

Irritation swept up from Rourke's belly and burned the back of his neck. It was impossible to conceal his presence forever, but he had hoped to linger long enough to catch Cara leaving for the chandler Mrs. Matheson had told them about. Hunching his shoulders, he grunted before facing the glowering man perched in the entrance of an apartment building across the street.

"Aye. I'm supposed to deliver these here birds to the boardinghouse of one Amelia Matheson. Are you knowing it?"

The potbellied man shook his bald head as though he thought Rourke daft. Hitching his thumb, he pointed and said, "That's it. You've only been wandering around in front of it for thirty minutes."

Fie. So he'd been watching. Rourke hoisted the basket higher and saluted the man with a tip of his cap. "My thanks to ya. Wouldn't want to keep Mrs. Matheson's cook waiting any longer."

Instead of moving back inside, the man hooked his thumbs on his suspenders and braced one large booted foot on the railing that flanked the apartment steps. Rourke tamped his rising anger and lumbered toward the boardinghouse door.

"Not there, man."

Casting a glance over his shoulder, Rourke paused and lifted an eyebrow. The man shook his head, one great paw rubbing at the cotton shirt stretched over his potbelly.

"That's the main entrance. You want to go to the servants' entrance." He jabbed a finger toward the alley separating the boardinghouse from the dressmaker's shop next door. "Around the back."

The look that followed said clearly that Rourke should have known this fact. Angered by his own ineptitude, Rourke growled an apology and ambled off the stairs into the alley. His carelessness was going to give him away. He shot one last glance at the man and gave a nod of thanks before slipping to a narrow wooden door with a heavy iron knocker.

Now what? The birds were intended for a

restaurant several streets over. He'd only brought them as cover. Before he could decide, the door swung open and he stood face-to-face with the woman he and Cara had met the day before.

Surprise widened Laverne's eyes. "Wha—" She spotted the basket in Rourke's hands. "Oh. The poulterer sent you?"

No recognition shone in the woman's eyes. Rourke breathed his relief.

Sighing heavily, Laverne propped her meaty hands on her hips. "Well?"

Rourke held the basket out for inspection. "Aye. Told me I was to come by bright and early."

She murmured her approval. Drawing back the cloth covering the birds, she poked one, then another, and finally bent down and took a deep whiff. Settling back on her heels, she gave a satisfied nod and stepped aside so Rourke could enter.

"They're fresh, all right. Better be, for the price I paid." She motioned toward a solid wooden table at the center of the large kitchen. "Put 'em there."

Bustling to an iron stove, she grabbed a towel, wrapped it around a thick metal handle, and swung open the door. Coals glowed in the bowels of the massive beast. Carefully stirring them to life, Laverne added several logs to the fire and closed the door.

Rourke slid the basket of poultry onto the table and stood aside to wait.

Laverne returned, a hitch in her step, wiping her hands on a white cotton apron wrapped around her midsection. "Don't just stand there," she scolded. "Get 'em out and be on your way."

"My apologies," he mumbled, quickly removing the birds from the basket and hustling to the door.

Laverne said nothing. Rourke reached for the knob.

"Hold it there."

He stiffened and turned.

She stood with her arms folded over her chest. After a moment, she gave a nod and fumbled in her apron pocket, retrieved a coin, and held it toward him. "I figure you've earned this."

When he didn't take it, she waved it in his face, her hand slowing as recognition flared in her eyes. "Hold up a minute. Ain't you the man what brought Miss Hamilton to the boardinghouse yesterday eve?"

Impatient to resume his vigil, Rourke jabbed at the brim of his cap with his thumb and nodded. "I am."

Her jowls shook as she bobbed her head. Resting her ample hip against the table, she slapped the coin down and motioned toward the basket. "Got a job with the poulterer, I see."

"A man's got to work," Rourke said, smiling as his hand inched toward the doorknob. Heat flamed his cheeks. His daed would have argued it be honest work.

Laverne scratched absently at the hair poking out from her mobcap. "I suppose that's right."

"I'd best be about it, then. Good day, madam." With one last bow, Rourke reached for the door, but once again it opened just as he touched it.

"Sorry I'm late, Mrs. Bennett—" The man at the door broke off as he came face-to-face with Rourke. "Beggin' your pardon. I thought you was Mrs. Bennett."

Who? Rourke quirked a brow. The man was older, though stoutly built. In his arms he carried a load of wood almost as large as himself. How he'd managed to wrest open the door, Rourke could only guess. He shoved aside and bade the man enter.

Moving with surprising quickness, Laverne maneuvered to Rourke's side and flashed a beaming smile. "There you are, Giles. I wondered what was taking you so long. Your coffee's gone a mite cold. I can warm it for you, if you like."

"Dinna bother," Giles said, squatting next to a woodbox as big as Rourke's bed. He deposited his armload of firewood and then swept his hands together to brush away the dust. "You know I'm not picky." His wiry eyebrows wiggling, he flashed a look at Rourke. "And who is this?"

Rourke extended his hand. "Rourke Walsh, sir."

"The poulterer sent him," Laverne added.

Giles chuckled as he grasped Rourke's hand. "Well, I don't know how I could have mistaken

62

him for you, Mrs. Bennett. He's nowhere near as pleasant on these old eyes."

"Posh. You're more of a flatterer than my poor dead husband." Swatting at him with her apron, Laverne shuffled to the table, retrieved the coin she'd abandoned earlier, and dropped it into Rourke's palm. "Anyway, he was just leavin', weren't you, Mr. Walsh?"

"Aye, ma'am. That I was."

"Good day, then," Giles said, tipping his hat.

Rourke returned the gesture and left the two to their coffee—and whatever else was afoot. Strange, he hadn't pictured Laverne as the flirtatious type after their meeting the day before, but women were women no matter where they lived. It didn't take a lot of blarney to win them over—a fact Rourke found not altogether pleasing. True, it made for easy and amusing company from time to time, but deep down he craved a more challenging conquest. Not that he had time for such nonsense these days.

Shrugging away his futile thoughts, he rounded the corner of the boardinghouse, casting a look in both directions before stepping from the alley.

The street had begun to fill, though he saw only merchants and a couple of paper boys with stacks of newspapers at their feet. Good. Perhaps he hadn't missed Cara's departure. For the next few days he'd keep an eye on her dealings, making note of whom she met and with whom she spoke. With any luck he'd find out quickly if she was tied to the person he sought.

Tossing the basket into the alley, he sidled close to the wall and settled down to wait. He didn't like being seen, but there was naught he could do about it now. He'd act as though he had come to escort Cara to her new place of business. If anyone asked, he'd say he hadn't been able to help himself. He'd been compelled to see her again.

Ana hadn't seemed the talkative type when Cara first met her, but since they'd left the boarding-house bound for James O'Bannon's candle shop, her words had flowed nonstop.

"It be a beautiful morn, eh, Cara? The kind you want to drink in and save for a rainy day." She took a deep breath and spread her arms wide.

Cara shivered inside her coat. It was a nice day . . . or promised to be. Breakfast had been hearty and warm, and filled with friendly conversation since, just as Breda had promised, Amelia had insisted that she call her by her first name. Why then could Cara not shake the chill from her limbs?

The sun peeked playfully over the roofline of a row of apartment buildings across the street. No doubt by midday it would have chased away the nip that accompanied the crisp February morning. That meant good business for the vendors who were readying their wares with happy shouts and bright whistles.

She dodged a vegetable cart half loaded with beets, turnips, and potatoes. Lifting an eyebrow, the vendor measured her from her neatly pinned curls to her buttoned boots before returning to his careful stocking.

Giving a sniff, Cara continued down the sidewalk alongside Ana. She had to admit, it wasn't the weather that had her feeling so cold. She'd barely slept the night before, her mind wracked with worry and thoughts of Eoghan.

"Now, Mr. O'Bannon knows to be expecting you. Amelia sent him word by Giles yesterday eve." Ana patted Cara's arm with a mittened hand. "You'll like Mr. O'Bannon. He's a good sort. Never has a harsh word to say."

Ana shivered and drew in her arms to slide her hands into the pockets of her wool coat. Reminded of the scars she'd witnessed at supper, Cara couldn't help but wonder if the terrible burns still pained her.

"What do you do for Mr. O'Bannon, Ana? Do you work in his shop?"

Ana nodded, the gray scarf she wore wrapped around her head tipping gaily. "Can't be too near the fire, what with these fingers of mine"— she rolled her shoulders but left her hands in her pockets—"but I can do other things Mr. O'Bannon can't, like pour the wax and trim the wicks. Mr. O'Bannon says I be skilled at keeping the candles nice and straight like the people on the Upper East Side prefer. They're picky about their candles, you know," she said, lifting her nose. Her lips curved in a quirky smile Cara found irresistible. She smiled back.

"Anyway, Amelia's right when she says he's in need of someone to help with his books. Never known a finer man, but he kinna add a row of figures to save his life."

Just in time, Cara spotted a large icy puddle and managed to skip over it without wetting her boots. "How does Mrs . . . Amelia know him? Are they friends?"

"Friends, yes, and members of the same church." Ana nodded down the street toward a large stone building framed by a gabled roof and capped with a pristine white cross.

"Mr. O'Bannon's a northerner, and Amelia, British."

Heaviness pressed on Cara's chest. She knew exactly what Ana meant. Like Mr. O'Bannon and many others from northern Ireland, her father had held to the belief that the Irish should remain loyal to British rule and to the Church of England. None of that mattered to Cara. She would trade religious tradition and loyalty to the Crown for the knowledge that her father died loving Christ, not just the church.

"Here we are." Ana motioned to a squat shop

nestled between two narrow buildings, one a milliner, the other an apothecary. The door to the candle shop had been painted a cheery yellow—an indication of the owner's temperament? Cara hoped so.

She glanced down the street in the direction they'd come. On a bright day it wouldn't be a bad walk, especially with Ana's chatter eating up the distance, but she shivered to think what it would be like on a dreary day.

"Don't worry," Ana said with a laugh. "Amelia lets us take the carriage when the weather be frowning." She shoved the door open, a bell fastened above the transom tinkling a welcome. The moment they stepped inside, the scent of beeswax and a touch of cinnamon met their noses.

Adding to the merriment, a jovial voice called, "Is that you, Miss Kavanagh?"

"Aye, sir. And I have Cara with me, the lass Mrs. Matheson told you about."

"Ah, good. Good." From the rear of the store, a portly man ambled. Black tufts of hair peppered with white stuck out over his ears. Bushy eyebrows gave him a comical look. The strings on his leather apron barely touched, but somehow he'd managed to get them tied. Rather than unfasten them, he lifted the apron over his head, ruffling his tangled hair even more, and dropped it onto the counter.

"So you are Miss Hamilton. Bless me, but

you're a vision. Hair the color of fire, just like me sainted mother."

Cara felt a blush heat her cheeks as the chandler's gaze swept her up and down. Finally, he took her hands and peered at her over his spectacles. "You're an answer to prayer, me dear. Truly. The calluses on these old knees bear witness to the hours I've spent pleading with the good Lord for help with these books." He patted a ledger dotted with dried wax and picked absently at it with his thumbnail while he watched her with lifted brow. "Mrs. Matheson tells me you're good with numbers?"

Cara nodded. "Aye, sir. My da taught me."

After depositing her coat and scarf on a carved hat tree next to the door, Ana moved toward a stack of crates. "The paraffin has arrived, I see. I'll work on getting it stocked."

Gentle as a whisper, she disappeared into the back room. Probably to give Cara and Mr. O'Bannon time to get to know each other.

Cara risked a glance around the crowded little candle shop. Pillars and tapers of every sort lined shelf after shelf. More hung drying from uncut wicks over racks. Across the floor were wooden molds of varied description. If the condition of the store said anything about its owner, James O'Bannon was an honest man, straightforward and simple, with nothing to hide and no secrets to keep.

Mr. O'Bannon gestured to a small table where coffee and a basket of scones waited. "Are you hungry, lass?"

Cara patted her full stomach as she sat across from him. "We broke the fast with Mrs. Matheson at the boardinghouse."

Head wagging, Mr. O'Bannon poured a cup of coffee for her and one for himself, then helped himself to a buttery pastry. "Of course. Amelia Matheson always takes good care of her boarders. And that Laverne is a gifted cook. Her meat pies . . ." He trailed off, his tongue licking at his lips. "Just wait. Won't take long before you see what I mean."

A giggle rose from Cara's belly at the urgency in his twinkling eyes. Though supper had slipped down her throat untasted last night, she knew it wouldn't be so once she reunited with Eoghan. "I'm sure you're right."

He smiled, his eyes gleaming like copper. Lifting his cup, he brought it to his mouth and sipped. Cara did the same, the hot liquid instantly warming her chilled limbs.

Pinching off a piece of scone, Mr. O'Bannon popped it into his mouth and took his time savoring the treat. After a moment, he nodded in satisfaction. "Good, as always. That baker, Josef Kaczynski, he knows his bread."

Cara felt herself relaxing. Amelia was right. The candle shop would prove the perfect place for her to work and wait for word from Eoghan. She wouldn't need to be on her guard here, with this gentle chandler and Ana as company.

As though reading her thoughts, Mr. O'Bannon smiled and reached out to pat Cara's hand. "So, lass . . . tell me about your brother."

7

Though it hadn't been long since he last checked, Rourke pulled a watch from the pocket of his coat and glanced at the time. Half past the hour. What could be keeping Cara?

No longer empty, Ashberry Street bustled with vendors and patrons taking advantage of the amiable weather. Rourke found himself jostled again and again by hurrying women and men loaded with crates of goods. Everyone but Cara. Was it possible he'd missed her? He'd only been with Laverne a moment, but could Cara have slipped past unseen?

Pushing off the wall where he leaned, Rourke took one step into the street. Fingers bit into his shoulder from behind. He whirled, fists ready.

Hugh's crooked grin mocked Rourke's tense stance. "A touch late for fisticuffs, eh, cousin? If I wanted you dead, 'twould have been easily done when I came up behind you in the alley."

Rourke forced himself to relax, but only a bit. Apparently he'd been less observant than he hoped if both Cara and Hugh had escaped him. He grunted, tugging his coat back into place as he straightened.

"What are you doing here? I thought Malcolm gave you orders to keep watch on the island."

Hugh's smirk disappeared and he poked his cap over his brow with his thumb. "He did, and I will, but first I thought I'd best look after you. Good thing I did—"

Just then the boardinghouse door swung open. As one, Rourke and Hugh melted into the alley, their backs pressed against the walls. Neither said a word as they watched a slim redhead emerge. She perched on the top stair a moment, working her fingers into a pair of knitted mittens. Then, with her scarf tucked safely inside her coat, she left the steps and turned north.

"That her?" Hugh stiffened and moved as if to follow.

Rourke stayed him with a hand to his arm. "Easy, cousin. That's not the woman I met yesterday." Indeed, though she favored Cara in form, she did not have her bonnie green eyes or ready smile.

Hugh grunted and relaxed against the wall, his muscled arms crossed over his thick chest. "Where is she, then? Dinna tell me she shook free of you already?"

The hair on the back of Rourke's neck rose, and his skin prickled. His fight wasn't with Hugh, but the man sure enough could make him itch for it to be so. Biting his lip, he resumed his vigil of the boardinghouse door.

"So tell me about this Hamilton woman, cousin," Hugh said, snatching a crate and flipping it over to sit. Obviously he meant to keep Rourke company. He tipped back against the wall, crossed his legs, and then pulled a knife from the waistband of his trousers and proceeded to clean his nails with the blade. "Is she a bonnie lass?"

The muscles in Rourke's stomach clenched. Hugh's appetite for pretty women was widely known. There could be little doubt why he asked.

Eyes narrowed, Rourke swept him critically from head to toe. "Too bonnie for the likes of you."

Hugh barked a laugh. "Or you, I wager."

Finished with his nails, he gave a quick flick of his wrist and gripped the knife by its blade. Satisfied by its weight, he slid it back into his waistband, then studied Rourke through hooded lids.

"It be your daed we've come to avenge, you know."

As if he could forget. Rourke tensed and went back to watching the street. "So?"

Hugh shrugged. "Just thought you were needin' a reminder, cousin—something to keep you from being blinded by a comely woman. Wouldn't want you to lose sight of the prey."

Anger stirred Rourke's blood to fire. He leaned toward Hugh, an outraged retort on his lips, but before he could speak, the man's fist butted against Rourke's chest. Not hard enough to drive the wind from him, but solid. Silently, Hugh turned his palm up and uncurled his fingers. Confused by the gleam in his eyes, Rourke looked down to see what he held.

Nestled in Hugh's meaty palm lay a scarred piece of lead.

The angry words melted in Rourke's throat. "Where . . . where did you get that?"

"I think you know."

Indeed, he did know from whence Hugh had plucked it. Rourke lifted the shot, its weight burning and heavy in his hand. It was a bullet.

And it had come from his father's wounded back.

For a moment, Cara doubted she'd heard correctly. Mr. O'Bannon hadn't asked about her brother. She'd misunderstood his question, surely . . .

Mouth dry, she thought back over her words. What could she have possibly said to trigger his suspicions? Panic shook her limbs, and the cup rattled as she replaced it on the saucer.

"My . . . brother?"

"Aye." His jovial expression slipped as she deposited the cup on the table with a thump. "I say, are you all right?"

Cara tensed. *Careful, lass. For sure and for certain, you will give yourself and Eoghan away.*

Forcing the smile to return to her lips, she clasped her hands in her lap to hide their shaking and said, "What makes you believe I have a brother?"

Confusion wrinkled his brow. "You're from Derry, is that not so? At least, that's what Mrs. Matheson told me." He pointed at her bracelet. "And that trinket there be fashioned by one Shamus McDougle? His work is well known throughout the region. Since you traveled alone, I assumed you were not married. Therefore, those twisted strands could only mean—"

"A brother. My twin."

He nodded. "Or a sister, though by your reaction I assume I guessed correctly."

Of course. Hadn't Amelia told her Mr. O'Bannon hailed from northern Ireland? Self-consciously, Cara tugged the sleeves of her cotton dress over her wrists.

"Ah. I see." Compassion dimmed Mr. O'Bannon's cheery eyes. "He's passed, has he? Forgive me, lass. I did not mean to vex you. Blast my ignorant tongue." He pounded the table with his gnarled fist. "When will I learn to keep the bridle where it belongs?"

Such anguish filled his face, Cara felt compelled to offer comfort. She patted his shaking hand. "Please, sir, don't fret. You could not have known, and I do not hold you to blame for asking questions."

"You dinna understand." Swallowing, he drew a deep breath and then clasped her fingers. "I had a brother once . . . a twin, like you."

Sudden tears welled in Cara's eyes. "What happened to him?"

He shook his head sadly. "The famine took him. It was years ago now, but sometimes"—he pressed his wrinkled hand to his heart—"it feels like only yesterday we laid him to rest. My mother, too, not long after, bless her sainted heart. She couldn't live with the suffering caused by William's passing, so she followed him to the grave."

That was one thing, at least, Cara had been spared. Her parents preceded Eoghan in death—at least she'd thought so, before his letter arrived. She lowered her eyes to keep Mr. O'Bannon from reading the truth.

"I'm sorry, sir. It must have been difficult losing your family so."

"Indeed, though it was much harder on Da. He was never quite the same."

Unable to form a single word, Cara simply nodded and prayed he would press no further.

Sighing heavily, Mr. O'Bannon retrieved his

cup and took a careful sip. "Ah, well. No sense dwelling on the past, eh, lass? Or filling our minds with regrets we are helpless to do anything about?"

"I suppose so."

Like him, she sipped from her cup, content to allow a comfortable silence to settle between them. When they finished, they joined Ana in the storage room.

Within minutes, Cara was seated behind Mr. O'Bannon's desk, a quill in her hand and an open ledger before her. It took some time for her to collect her thoughts enough to concentrate on the figures, however. Her mind kept slipping to Eoghan, and how near she'd come to giving away their secret despite her attempt at caution. Obviously her only hope was that he would come to her quickly so they could both return home to Derry. Only then would things feel normal. They would be together. Safe. And then, finally, this pretense would all be over.

8

For several hours, a slow, steady rain had streaked the windows outside Mr. O'Bannon's candle shop, but as the temperature dwindled, so did the rain, changing finally to wet snow. The wooden chair where Cara sat creaked as she leaned back to rub her eyes. Four solid hours she'd spent poring over the candle shop's figures. That on top of the three weeks she'd already been at it, and still the books weren't completely sorted out. The hard work felt good, though, the jumble of numbers enough to keep her mind occupied and off of Eoghan.

March still meant shorter days, and though it was only five o'clock, Cara had been forced to light a candle in order to see clearly. She smiled as she pulled the slim taper close and blew out the flame. Mr. O'Bannon was indeed a fine chandler. His candles did not flicker and sputter out like the ones made of tallow she used back home. His burned evenly and left very little soot to darken the walls next to the desk.

"Ready, Cara?" Ana poked her head inside the dim office, her scarf already twisted around her neck and tucked inside the collar of her coat. "We'd best be gettin' on home before it gets too late. Mrs. Matheson will already be holding supper for us."

Wearily, Cara rose and stretched the stiffness from her back. Except for the half hour she'd spent with Ana and Mr. O'Bannon over the sandwiches Laverne packed for their lunch, she hadn't left the desk. "Is it time to go already?"

"Past time. Mr. O'Bannon bade me fetch you. I think he was afraid you'd sit there all night otherwise." Ana's pleasant smile lit the darkened door. She glided the short distance to the desk and held out Cara's coat. "Here you are."

"Thank you," Cara said, sliding her arms into the sleeves and then fastening the buttons.

In the other room, Mr. O'Bannon was hunched beside a large metal safe, his keys in hand. More wax had been added to the flecks already dotting his clothes. Ana's, too, Cara noted. In spite of that, they both looked cheerful after a hard day's work.

Mr. O'Bannon patted the locked safe and then straightened with a smile. "There you are, Cara. I'd begun to think you might not come out." He crossed to them, his brow puckered in a frown. "You didn't work too hard, I hope. No sense trying to untangle a year's worth of mess in a few short weeks."

Cara stifled a grin. More like *several* years, but she wouldn't tell him that. "Not at all, sir. It feels good to stay so busy."

"Indeed. Ana and I have been quite busy ourselves, haven't we, Ana? One benefit of this foul weather hanging over our heads the past few weeks—people need candles." He craned his neck to peer out the window at the overcast sky.

Ana gave a dimpled grin. "I do not mind it. Like Cara said—feels good to stay busy."

Mr. O'Bannon nodded, then turned from the window. "Bless me, it's gotten quite dark, and those clouds don't look welcoming." His fingers worried the bottom of his chin. "Perhaps I should see you ladies home—"

As he spoke, the door to the shop swung open, accompanied by the tinkle of the little bell Cara had heard rung over and over throughout the day.

"No need, sir. I will be glad to see the ladies safely to the boardinghouse." Rourke wiped the moisture from his coat and stepped inside.

Cara's heart thrilled at the deep voice. Self-consciously she smoothed her skirt and patted her hair before moving further into the shop. "Why, Mr. Walsh. What a pleasure to see you again."

Eyes gleaming in the dim light of the candles, he stepped forward to take her hand. "You, as well." His voice lowered. "And my name's Rourke."

Heat suffused her cheeks. Unwilling that he should notice, she turned and motioned first to Mr. O'Bannon and then Ana while she made the introductions.

It had been some time since she'd seen him, but Rourke made as dashing a figure as Cara remembered. She admired the way he shook hands firmly with Mr. O'Bannon, then just as deftly took great pains to hold Ana's hand gently after just the slightest glance at her scars.

When they'd finished their greetings, Cara turned to Rourke. "I don't understand. Last time we spoke, you said it would be a month or more before you came by."

"That was me intent," he said, a devilish twinkle in his eye. "I found I couldn't wait."

Mr. O'Bannon's chortle set his belly to bouncing. "Oh, ho! Perhaps these two maidens would be safer with me."

He clapped Rourke on the shoulder, his merry smile saying he meant no offense. Rourke's answering grin said none was taken. Obviously, the old chandler charmed him as quickly as he had Cara.

Still smiling, Mr. O'Bannon turned to her, his pudgy fingers ruffling his tousled hair. "Well, me dear, if I see you tomorrow, it will mean nothing I can do will scare you away." Leaning close, he offered a wink that made Cara giggle. "I hope not. Ana and I enjoy your company."

"For certain, we do," Ana agreed.

Rourke swept open the door. "Then I'd best be getting these ladies home before either of them changes her mind."

They laughed, and after bidding Mr. O'Bannon good-night, they started down the lighted street toward the boardinghouse.

No longer packed with vendors, Ashberry Street felt strangely empty, even with a couple of urchins darting in and out of the emptied carts, their pockets bulging with the leftover scraps they scrounged from the wet, icy ground. Lifting a mangled turnip high, one of the boys gave a victorious whoop, but then ran off before his counterpart could snatch it from his hand.

Teasing . . . just like Eoghan used to do.

"So, lass?"

She cast a startled glance at Rourke. He quirked an eyebrow.

"How do you like working at the candle shop?"

Shoving aside all thoughts of her brother, Cara tried to sound lighthearted. "The work is plentiful and I couldn't ask for better company than Ana and Mr. O'Bannon." Ana was walking to Cara's left. She squeezed her arm. "You were right about him, Ana. He is a kind sort. I feel as though I've made a fast friend, even though I've known him such a short while."

A chill mingled with the night air. Pulling her scarf over her ears, Ana nodded. "Never a cross word to say, that Mr. O'Bannon. He bears a saint's heart, for sure."

And perhaps a saint's discernment. Cara's face still burned when she recalled how he'd reasoned out the truth about her brother. Longing for Eoghan pricked her heart. He said he would find her, but how? And when? How would he know where she lived, or even that she'd arrived in America?

Never one to suffer exceedingly with patience, Cara felt the itch to ask questions tickle her tongue. She bit down hard to keep them from escaping her lips.

"Sounds like luck has smiled upon you," Rourke said, keeping pace on Cara's right.

"Luck . . . or the Lord?" Awash with gratitude, Cara breathed a silent thank-you for having come so far in safety.

"You've a strong faith, then?" Ana said, the cold muffling the words on her tongue.

Startled, Cara realized both she and Rourke had gone silent after her remark. Could it be neither of them knew the Savior?

Eyeing Ana's mittened hands, Cara could only guess what tragedy had tested her faith. But what about Rourke? His face had gone rigid, but not with anger. It looked more like guilt.

She nodded, carefully. "Aye, I've a faith. Strong or no I figure will be for the Lord to decide."

She waited, and then opted against saying more, certain if she did, she'd be tempted to talk about her childhood. And Eoghan.

Dislodging her thoughts with a slight toss of her head, she looked at Rourke. "And what about you, Mr. Walsh? I take it you have found plenty of 'this and that' to earn your bread?"

He gave a smile that chased the somberness from his expression. "I have. Fortunately for me, people still enjoy a plump bird for their suppers. It's kept me busy enough."

"The poulterer?" Disappointment charged through Cara's midsection. "I thought you said you had business out of town."

"I did. I meant I started working for the poulterer when I got back," Rourke said, his face coloring.

"I figured you'd go to work on the wharf. A bit of muscle unloading the ships," she added, hoping he wouldn't sense her frustration. Surely, that would be the place where Eoghan would search for her. She'd rather hoped to glean a bit of information from Rourke about the men he saw day to day. Not that she could ask questions. Once again, resentment filled her at the bridle Eoghan had placed on her tongue.

Rourke's broad shoulders rolled in a shrug. "The wharf, the poulterer . . . it makes no difference so long as I've earned a coin at the end of the day."

Something about his rakish smile made Cara hesitate. She'd seen that look before, but usually it was on the faces of wealthy British dandies who had no cause to worry about earning a living.

Her gaze dropped to his worn coat and scuffed shoes. Both had seen better days and offered scant protection against the biting wind and slushy snow. Rourke wasn't wealthy, and he certainly wasn't British. She must be wrong.

"So, Mr. Walsh, how long have you been in America?" Interest lit Ana's eyes, and as she walked, her wool skirt swished pleasantly from side to side.

With a start, Cara realized how pretty Ana was, especially with the dimple on her cheek accentuating her smile. Apparently Rourke thought so, too. His grin broadened.

"A couple of months shy of two years, though the harsh winters here in the city make it seem longer." Hope warmed his voice as he laughed and pulled his collar higher around his ears. "What I wouldn't give to see the rolling hills of me home back in Ireland."

"Why not go, then?" Ana's cheeks flamed as her lashes swept down to cover her brown eyes. "I mean, if you want to go back . . ."

Judging by the longing in her voice, Cara and Rourke weren't the only ones with aspirations of returning to Ireland. Cara felt a swell of pity and suddenly wished she'd bothered to learn more about her companion.

Rourke cleared his throat, shooting a glance at the glowing streetlamps, the carriages rumbling by . . . anywhere but at Ana.

Unease trickled through Cara's veins like the icy water running in rivulets down the snow-packed streets. He acted as though Ana's questions made him uncomfortable, like one who might have something to hide.

Clutching her arms to her chest, she quickened her steps, anxious of a sudden to return to the boardinghouse. There, at least, she could find a place to think—to sort out her thoughts and clear her head. Before another word passed her lips, she would sit down and figure out exactly what she knew about Rourke Walsh.

• • •

A light snow had begun to fall as the day waned, settling in the folds of Hugh O'Hurly's coat like a fine feathery web. He didn't mind it. In fact, he remained motionless so long, lodged between the worn sides of the boardinghouse and a naked old oak, that the layer of snow grew quite thick. Finally, his kinsman's muscled figure ambled into view, two women by his side.

Scowling, Hugh burrowed deeper behind the tree. "Rourke, me boy, what have you been about?" he said under his breath.

Still muttering to himself, he watched as Rourke bid first one of the women, and then the other a good-night, then disappeared into the dusk.

Hugh dug into the tree's rough bark. One of these was Cara Hamilton, but which one? It was impossible to tell with the waning light and the scarves over their heads. He dipped further into the shadows as a third person appeared. Framed in the door was the woman he'd once mistaken for Hamilton, a surly frown upon her face.

"You're late. Amelia is holding supper."

" 'Twas my fault, Deidre. I lost track of the time." The woman, shorter than her companions by nearly a head, removed her scarf, revealing a mass of brown hair.

So, the other was Cara.

Hugh strained for one last look as the door closed. He caught only a glimpse, but it was enough. He was tired of waiting, wondering. Tomorrow he'd know just who to watch for when the women left the boardinghouse. 'Twould be unfortunate if the shorter girl was with her, but that was all . . . unfortunate. For her.

A swing in his step, Hugh ambled in the opposite direction Rourke had taken, past tightly bundled shops with their darkened, staring windows. His kinsman wanted to make certain they had the right Hamilton woman before taking action. Hugh wasn't so picky. He'd ask questions, all right, but whether she answered or no, he'd see to it there was one less threat to his position—one less risk to his secret.

Tomorrow he'd make sure there was one less Hamilton.

He'd gone but a few feet when a trail winding through the fresh snow from the rear of the boardinghouse made him pause. Footprints? He squinted into the gloom, straining for sounds on the snow-muffled street. He'd not witnessed anyone come this way, but no falling snow blurred these tracks. They were fresh.

He jerked his head as a figure darted across the street into an alley. Whoever it was had obviously been waiting and watching, just as Hugh had been.

Hamilton?

Elation coursed through Hugh's veins. Maybe his cursed luck had finally changed.

Shifting directions, he matched the man's

strides through the city's winding alleys for almost a mile until the street opened, exposing a row of decaying lean-tos and shanties. Rotting sewage and smoke from a dozen cook fires spewed from a dozen run-down town houses and thickened the air, making breathing distasteful. Farther down, one meager streetlamp spat a feeble glow onto the vexed street.

Hugh pressed himself to the side of one of the town houses and waited until the man passed under the streetlight. Drawing a pistol from the pocket of his coat, he cocked the hammer and stepped into the street.

"Hamilton!"

The man froze, craning his neck in confusion. It wasn't until their eyes met that Hugh knew for certain. He raised the pistol. Hamilton whirled to run. A second later, the crack of gunfire split the air.

9

Warmth flowed through the open boardinghouse door, mingled with the inviting scents of frying bacon and yeast bread. Rourke didn't linger on the tempting fragrances. Instead, he dragged his cap from his head and gave both Cara and Ana a slight bow.

"Good morning, ladies."

Muffled by her scarf, Ana's soft voice sounded even more waiflike. "Why, Mr. Walsh . . . this is an unexpected pleasure."

Judging by her tight lips and downcast eyes, Cara wasn't nearly as pleased. She mumbled curt agreement, however, before pulling her coat from a hook on the wall and shrugging into it.

Ana tugged the scarf from her face and tucked it into her coat. "On your way to the harbor?"

Rourke nodded. Sometime during the night he'd decided his efforts at finding out all he could about Cara would be better served in the open. Rather than prying the information from her in bits, or learning what he could by spying from darkened alleys, he'd play the interested suitor. Women were funny that way. If they found a man attractive, they became pliable, easily seduced into revealing everything about themselves. Cara would be no different. He'd just have to take care to make no mention of his real intentions.

"I hope you don't mind . . . I thought I might see the two of you to the candle shop since it's on my way."

Ana's eyes flashed with pleasure, but Cara's remained hidden behind her thick lashes.

Working the buttons on her coat closed, she chewed her bottom lip as though she were pondering. "You say you be headed to the wharf?"

"Indeed. Several ships came into the harbor last

night. I'll find work there today, sure enough."

Finally, Cara did look at him, interest evident in her emerald gaze. For just a moment, Rourke's breath caught, but then she turned and secured the door tightly behind her before moving down the steps to the street. He and Ana followed.

"I wonder . . . what can you tell me about these ships?" Cara said, wrapping the strings of a plain brown bonnet around her fingers and then fashioning a bow that she snugged under her chin. The bonnet, added to a merry red and green scarf around her neck, made her look cozy and warm.

An odd question, but at least she was talking. Rourke stepped aside for Ana to precede him, then swung alongside Cara, between her and the crowded street to protect her from injury.

"Most of them come from Europe. They're loaded with merchandise for the stores—things like cloth, food, medicine, and spices." He laughed at the look of concentration on her face. "Those that are not packed with people, I mean."

Cara ignored his attempt at jest and bunched her slender brows. "And these boats hire you to help with the off-load?"

"The boats, no. The shipping companies."

"I do not understand. How do they find you?"

He shrugged one shoulder. "That's easy enough. Men looking for hire stand at the wharf when the ships dock. The company foreman rounds up the help he needs and puts them to work."

Excitement filled her eyes. "How interesting."

"Interesting?" Ana snorted. "Sounds dull to me. And smelly. Have you been to the wharf?"

Cara ignored her and shook her head. "I'd like to learn more, Rourke." Mindless of the puddles swirling about her feet, she stopped in the middle of the sidewalk and clutched his arm. "Do you suppose it would be possible to see them . . . the workers, I mean?" Her voice lowered a bit, and though her eyes still gleamed, it seemed embarrassment replaced her excitement, for her cheeks turned red and she stuttered, "I've always b-been fascinated by ships."

Earlier, Rourke had accused women of being pliable, but it was he who found himself melting beneath the fiery warmth of her touch. "I . . . suppose . . ."

"Oh, please, Rourke? It would mean a great deal to me." She paused, looking from him to Ana. "I could go during my lunch hour, if you don't think Mr. O'Bannon would mind, Ana."

Confusion troubled her brow, but Ana gave a shrug. "He will not mind, but are you certain you want to bother, Cara? Ships come into port all the time."

"I'm sure," Cara replied, too quickly. Her gaze returned to Rourke, sharper than before and more earnest. "Well?"

The feeling of disquiet grew in Rourke's belly. "I'll fetch you around midday."

"Thank you."

Dropping her hand, Cara continued down the street. Her steps were lighter than before, her shoulders erect. There could only be one reason for the change, one thing that could chase the worry from her eyes and change it to a hopeful glimmer.

She expected to see someone at the wharf, and Rourke had a dreadful feeling that someone was Eoghan Hamilton.

A shudder took him, followed by the tiny pinpricks along his neck that one felt when another was watching. Searching up the street one way and down the other, he scanned the sea of faces for one that showed unusual interest. Finding none, he followed after the women, smiling at Ana as she sent a worried glance at him over her shoulder. No need alarming the women.

He was plenty alarmed for them all.

Deidre's fingers tightened around the handle of the blade she carried in the pocket of her plain brown dress. Though she despised the knife, it was never far from her, its hard steel a vivid reminder of all she'd lost.

Pain flowed like a river through her heart, the path of it carved by the knife in her hand. Close on its heels came rage, as familiar as her own reflection. It bubbled up inside her, heating her neck and face. Helpless to do anything but watch

Cara and Ana walking away with the tall stranger, she ducked under the covering created by a canvas tarp stretched over the street.

A burly shopkeeper poked his head out from behind a stand of leather goods. "Shine your shoes, mum?" He held out a corner of the soiled apron fastened around his expansive waist. Above his head, a wooden sign painted with a woman's boot swung from iron hinges, creating a rusty song that mingled with the usual clatter of the busy street.

Deidre shook her head, irritated to have to take her eyes off of Cara for even a moment.

Who this Hamilton was she could not yet be sure, but before long she vowed to know if the woman was tied to the man whose knife she clutched so tightly it cut her palm.

"Are you certain, mum? Won't cost much, just a nickel for me trouble—"

Cara passed out of sight, swept into the crowd by the stream of people making purchases up and down the street. Ignoring the shopkeeper, Deidre stepped from the shadows. His voice followed her, but she cared not. She'd waited this long—two long, empty years. Another day mattered little. She had plenty of time.

Uncurling her fingers, she withdrew her hand from her pocket, surprised by the warm, sticky flow that trickled over her wrist. Instead of grimacing in pain, she smiled.

How ironic . . . and fitting.

She plucked a handkerchief from her sleeve and wrapped it around her wounded hand before continuing toward the milliner where she worked. Her needlework would be hindered now, but she'd work slowly to ensure her stitches remained even.

She had time.

Dodging grimy drifts and the icy puddles that pooled between the cobbles in the street, she repeated the words in her head, even hummed along when the rhythm became a mantra.

She had time. Eoghan Hamilton, on the other hand, did not. She would see to it, even if it cost her the very last breath in her body.

10

Pain lingered in the dim light of morning.

Instead of dispelling its white-hot fingers, the sun peeking through the tattered curtains only intensified the agony and stoked the burning fever.

Two faces hovered close, one a wizened old man, the other a thin hawkish figure whose only feminine quality lay in the gentleness of her touch.

The woman blew a sigh of relief from her thin lips. "There now, he's awake. See, Charlie? I told you he'd make it through the night. Ain't much my poultice kinna cure."

The old man grunted, withdrawing his head and letting more blazing light filter through the grime-crusted window. "Who is he, Maggie, and how do ya reckon he come to this condition?"

Water wrung from a cloth trickled into a bowl. A moment later, the cool rag provided blessed relief from the scalding fever.

"Said his name is Ow-en, or some such thing. Couldn't rightly make it out, what with him so sick."

Sucking in a breath, Eoghan struggled to raise his head, failed, and flopped back against the sweat-soaked sheets.

The woman—Maggie—leaned forward and patted his shoulder.

"There now, no need to fidget. You're safe here."

"No . . ."

His tongue thick, Eoghan fought to form the words pounding inside his head, but the fog returned, swirling around him, threatening to drag him back to the murky depths from which he'd clawed.

Concern widened Maggie's eyes, and then Eoghan felt it—the bone-chilling cold that swept over him a second before he tasted bitter, metallic brine upon his tongue.

Blood. His blood.

Panic soured in his belly. He couldn't give in to

it, the relentless tug that promised freedom from the pain. Spasms claimed his limbs. Though he tried, he couldn't control their trembling.

"Charlie!"

Maggie should have been louder, the desperation in her voice sharper, but the buzzing in Eoghan's ears drowned her out. Even her face grew fuzzy, as though he saw her from a distance. Instead of a mottled gray, her hair became soft and red, her features young and refined. On her wrist lay a twisted leather bracelet—an exact replica of his own.

Longing for his sister filled him, drawing him away from the dingy room and lifting him from the confines of his torturous bed.

The raging fever Eoghan had fought to overcome fanned to life, licking over his flesh like fire. Regret stabbed through his brain, adding to the pain wracking his body.

Cara would be alone now. He couldn't protect her . . . warn her.

"It'll be all right, son. God's help is nearer than the door."

Though his mother's words rang in his head, the agony of his failure was too much to bear. Instead of battling the pain, Eoghan ran toward it. Giving a strangled cry, he dove headlong into the welcoming bliss that opened up and swallowed him whole.

No more could he fight.

No more . . .

• • •

The row of figures danced before Cara's eyes, mocking her attempts to sort them into some semblance of order when all she could think about was Eoghan.

Soon she would see him again.

Her heart thrilled with the possibility. He would be watching for her at the wharf, she just knew it. Certainly he'd warned her not to look for him, to wait until he sent her word, but it had been several weeks. Surely, once he caught sight of her, he'd forget all about that, wrap her in his arms, and take her home to Derry.

Tears leapt to her eyes, joined by the smile that sprang to her lips. It had taken a conscious effort to keep from staring at the hands on the clock above Mr. O'Bannon's desk. Each moment ticked by more achingly slow than the one before. She tapped the tip of her quill against the open ledger, leaving tiny blotches of ink against the paper as she strained for the sound of the bell.

At last, it rang.

Leaping to her feet, Cara snatched her scarf and mittens from the desk and carried them to the entrance, where Rourke waited, his cap in hand.

"Good day, Mr. O'Bannon. Ana. Cara." Rourke tipped his head to each one as he said their names.

"Ah, here's your young man," Mr. O'Bannon said, giving a hearty chuckle as he poured the last bit of wax from a kettle into a mold. When he finished, he replaced the kettle on the hook over the fire, dusted off his hands, and thrust his chin toward Cara. "Lunchtime couldn't come soon enough for that little miss, I tell ya. Isn't that right, Ana?"

Taking the wooden mold from Mr. O'Bannon, Ana replaced it alongside a row of others of varying heights and then nodded. " 'Tis a kindness to be sure that you've agreed to escort her, Mr. Walsh. Cara could hardly sit still long enough to work on the books."

Too anxious to be embarrassed, Cara hurried to him. "Thank you for coming."

His blue gaze unguarded for a moment, Rourke appeared almost reluctant as he removed her coat from the hall tree and held it aloft for her to wiggle into. "No trouble, me dear." Arm held out to her, he motioned toward the door. "Shall we?"

Sliding her fingers over his bent elbow, Cara let him lead her to the candle shop door. "I'll be back soon, Mr. O'Bannon," she said over her shoulder.

"No hurry, lass. Business is a mite slow today. Enjoy learning about your new country."

The tinkle of the bell accompanied his cheerful voice. Sick at her stomach over the lies she'd told, Cara turned into the crisp March breeze and took a deep breath. The fresh air couldn't wash away her guilt; only telling the truth could do that. But until she found Eoghan, she'd find a way to live with the troublesome stains.

"Are you all right, lass?"

Startled, Cara slowed her steps and looked at her companion. Already her feet carried her toward the harbor. She hadn't even bothered to hide her anticipation. What must he and Mr. O'Bannon think of her?

A deep ache scoured her heart. Her heavenly Father, too, was certain to be disappointed by her actions, but what else was she to do? If her silence insured Eoghan's safety, surely He understood?

Realizing she'd taken too long to answer, Cara moistened her lips and cast her gaze to the frozen ground. "I will be . . . soon. Thank you for your concern."

A frown pulled at Rourke's dark brows, but thankfully he asked no questions.

"Do you see those buildings?" He pointed at a row of brick and glass structures stretching taller than the rowan trees that grew back home in Ireland. "Those are some of the oldest houses in New York. And that way"—he pointed east, away from the harbor—"is Federal Hall, where this country's first president, George Washington, was inaugurated. The actual building is long gone, of course, but the one that stands there now is similar." His sigh created wispy clouds around his head. "Ach, but I would have loved to have been alive then, to see the birth of a free nation."

He means to distract me from my troublesome thoughts.

Cara's gaze wandered the planes of his handsome face. He didn't seem the sort to concern himself with the worries of an anxious female, and yet here he stood, idling away the distance with chatter regarding local lore . . . for her.

The realization settled over her slowly, like molasses—sweet and warm.

Blushing despite the cold, she slid her hands deeper into the pockets of her coat and then measured her steps to equal his. "Tell me about yourself, Rourke. 'Tis plain you have a love of history."

"Very true."

Before he continued, he grasped her elbow and led her around a stack of newspapers that tipped at a crazy angle and threatened to fall. Safely on the other side, his hand dropped, leaving a cool spot where the warmth of his touch had been. Hard-pressed not to rub her elbow, Cara found the heat traveled up her arm and settled around her neck.

"I've always had a fondness for the past," Rourke continued, "especially America's past. She is a beautiful country with a bright future, assuming her leaders take care to guide her properly."

Cara gave a nervous laugh. "Politics, too? You're well versed."

He cast a hurried glance at her and then away. "Aye."

Rather than dwelling overlong on how his nearness affected her, she focused on extending the conversation and cleared her throat. "So tell me, what is it about government that appeals to you?"

He hesitated and his jaw worked to form an answer. And why not? It was most unusual for even the most educated women to discuss government and politics with a man. It ranked next to religion—a fact she knew well thanks to her father's stern admonition.

She tugged at a string on her mittens. "Forgive me—"

"My da was very active back in Ireland," he said in the same moment.

Glancing at each other, they shared a smile and then Cara motioned for him to continue. As they walked they passed a line of evergreen shrubs lightly crusted with snow. Rourke brushed absently at them, his expression as clouded as the gray sky overhead.

"Da was a great believer in giving voice to the common man. He loved his country. Wanted the best for Ireland and her people."

Here, a hard edge replaced the melancholy in his tone. Cara found herself searching his face for clues as to the cause. Though the wind bit at her nose, she sniffed and pressed on. " 'Tis obvious you loved him a great deal."

Rourke gave a stiff nod but refused to say

more. Well did she understand why. It was not so long ago she could scarce but speak Eoghan's name without drawing tears to her eyes.

Other couples strolled past them, along with men in coats and top hats who hurried faster and kept their focus on the path ahead. Cara lowered her voice so as not to be overheard. "May I ask how long it has been?"

"Since he passed?"

Cara nodded.

Rourke's features became as pale and lifeless as the landscape—his eyes, twin chips of azure ice. "Just under two years."

How similar their grief! Though Cara wanted to offer comfort, she dared not reveal more than she already had about herself or her family.

Rourke's hand lifted and he pointed to a couple of sea gulls circling above their heads. "We're getting close."

Indeed, the scent of salt water tickled Cara's nose. Ships' bells replaced the rumble of carriage wheels. Rigging creaked and groaned as great crates were lifted from the vessels and settled onto the shore. With a start, Cara realized they had come a long distance without her once thinking to look for her brother.

Rourke pulled her to a halt, his arm sweeping to encompass the length of the harbor. "Where would you like to start?"

"The workers," Cara said without hesitation.

His crooked grin said he thought her selection odd, but he nodded. "Very well, but I warn you—they're as salty as the sea. This is not the most fitting place for a lady."

She gave a casual shrug of her shoulders. "According to most gentlemen, not many places are."

He gave a snort of laughter, then moved with her toward one of the piers that jutted out over the water. Before they quite reached it, Cara heard Rourke's name above the din of the ships being off-loaded.

"Rourke! That you, me boy?"

Rourke craned his neck in the direction of the voice and grunted. "Madigan. He's one of the foremen with Larson and Greene."

He pointed to a large warehouse farther down the wharf, then lifted his hand higher and waved a greeting. In return, Madigan gestured for him to come closer.

"Business?" Cara asked.

"I'm thinking so, since he appears quite adamant about speaking with me." Rourke moved to stand in front of Cara. "Would you excuse me a moment while I inquire as to what he be wanting?"

She nodded. It was only after he left with a promise to return quickly that she was struck by the preciseness of his manners. Earlier, she'd teased him about being a gentleman, but the longer she knew him, the more curious she became as to his true breeding.

Sighing, she turned from Rourke and Mr. Madigan to scan the shoreline. Ships large and small dotted the pier. Many out on the open water spread their sails wide to catch the crisp breeze, but several steamers chugged along as well, their stacks belching clouds of puffy white smoke. Still others, driven by wood or coal, left less appealing traces of their passage.

"Give me that, ya mongrel!"

"Ho, ho! Not likely. You come and take it."

The raised voices echoed from a place just out of sight behind several boxes almost twice Cara's height. Curious, she inched toward them.

"I mean it, Luke. That's my hat. I won't tell you again to hand it over."

"And I said come and get it!"

The closer she came, the louder the voices grew, and more full of jest. One even sounded familiar. Through the gaps in the boxes, Cara glimpsed a flash of red locks beneath a shaggy wool cap.

Eoghan?

Heart racing, she sped around the first crate and stopped. Two men were circling each other. One, large and heavyset, leapt for his hat. The smaller man kept it clasped tightly in his fist. Though his back was turned, it was easy enough to see he outmatched the larger man in speed and agility.

Her breath caught. He was the right build and

had the right color hair—judging from the waves curling around the edge of his cap. He even had the same teasing manner.

She stepped forward, away from the shadow of the crate. It was Eoghan. It had to be! His name rose to her lips.

Before she could call out, a firm hand grasped her shoulder. She whirled, expecting to see Rourke. Instead, she stared up into a pair of hostile gray eyes.

11

Hugh could hardly believe his good fortune. Since the night Hamilton slipped through his fingers, he'd been determined to kill both him and his sister, but instead of scouring the streets for her, Rourke had plopped the woman into his lap. And a pretty little filly she was, what with her long red hair and curved figure that even her heavy coat couldn't hide.

Seizing the opportunity, Hugh stepped into her path. Her full lips parted in surprise as they collided. His gaze was immediately drawn there.

"F-forgive me," she stammered. "I did not see you."

In the same instant she jerked back, her hip slamming against a stack of cargo crates. Hugh reached to steady her, reveling in the way her eyes widened when his fingers closed around her upper arm. Even through her coat he felt her tremble. A fire lit in his belly.

"Be ya looking for someone, lass?"

"I . . ." She swallowed and shook her head, tousling that glorious hair. "No. I mean . . . yes. My friend."

"On the wharf?" Hugh quirked an eyebrow. "He must be a scoundrel if he left you to fend for yourself."

Confusion furrowed her brow. "You misunderstand, sir. It's not like that at all. It's just . . ."

She strained to see around the crates, exposing the long pale line of her neck. Though Hugh's fingers itched to roam there, he resisted. No sense alarming her . . . yet.

Whatever she sought, she did not find. She turned back to him, dismay etched deep on her face. "Please, sir, if you wouldn't mind letting go of my arm? I'm all right now, really."

All right? Hugh bit back a chuckle. She was far from all right. In fact, with just a tug he could pull her into the corner created by the shipping crates. A firm swipe of his blade and that pretty neck would be covered in blood.

'Twould be a shame, that.

Finishing the woman here would have to be quick. He'd have no time to savor the delights of her silky flesh. And if she somehow managed to scream, to draw the attention of the sailors scrambling across the decks of the ships anchored in the harbor . . .

And yet, he dared not risk her spilling a bit of unfortunate information, especially now that she'd seen his face. His grip on her arm tightened as he reached for the waistband of his trousers.

"Hugh."

The low, deadly voice penetrated even the throaty calls of the ships' horns. Turning, Hugh released the woman and watched her scurry away, then pasted a smile on his face for his kinsman.

"Rourke. What a surprise."

"What are you doing here, Hugh?"

Hugh tipped his head toward the water. "On me way to the island. You?"

A scowl slashed across Rourke's face, dispelling the ridiculous civility of their conversation. "My doings are not your concern."

"I think they are, especially if they involve her." He thrust his chin toward Cara's retreating back. She darted in the direction of the pier, her head twisting from side to side. Hugh's lips curled in a smirk. "Who do you suppose she be searching for among all these crusty sailors?"

"I don't know," Rourke said, jamming his curled fists into the pockets of his coat.

"I think ya do." Hugh shoved closer, until mere inches separated his face from Rourke's. He lowered his voice. "She's the one."

"You don't know that," Rourke shot back.

"We don't have time to waste wondering if I'm wrong."

"We do if it means sparing an innocent life."

Frustration spread like fire through Hugh's veins. There was none better than Rourke in a fight. His head for strategy had saved their hides more than once, but today Hugh had no patience for his cautious ways. Not when one small slip could cost him everything.

Breathing deep, Hugh uncurled his fingers and forced a nonchalant shrug. "Fine, cousin. Do what you will. It's none of my business how you handle the woman." At this, Rourke's eyes narrowed. Hugh clapped him on the shoulder and feigned a laugh. "I'll ask around, see if I can't figure out who she's searching for."

Before Rourke could protest, Hugh whirled and strode for the dock, rage making his nerves tingle.

Rourke couldn't protect the woman forever. Sooner or later, Hugh would get to her. Sooner, he amended, gritting his teeth until his jaw hurt. Soon.

For several long moments, Rourke stood listening to the cry of the gulls circling above his head and watching his kinsman stride the length of the dock. Finally, Hugh ducked beneath a gangplank and disappeared from view.

He was hiding something, of that Rourke was

certain, and somehow it involved Cara. He'd read it in the eagerness on Hugh's face when he first mentioned the woman at the shoe store. He saw it again now in his clenched fists.

Shaking off a feeling of foreboding, he turned to look in the direction Cara had gone. Instead of her gray wool coat, he saw only her scarf, a twisted slash of red and green against the muddy slush piled along the wharf's wood planks.

Striding forward, he retrieved the scarf and then continued toward the pier. It wasn't until he rounded the last stack of waiting cargo that he caught sight of her. She was standing with her face toward the sea . . . no . . . a ship, he realized as he came closer. A handful of men rousted and joked as they made their way on board. She watched them, unmoving.

"Cara?"

Rourke's gut clenched as she turned to look at him. Pain shadowed her green eyes, and her skin, already pale, equaled the snowbanks for pallor.

He went to her and took her elbow. "What is it? What's wrong?"

"I thought . . . I mean . . . for a moment . . ."

She got no further. Dipping her head, she covered her face with her hands and cried. The sound she made seemed rent from her—like one lost . . . or who had lost. Deep inside, it resonated with the grief Rourke had felt as he clutched his father's lifeless body, a grief not even

God himself could cure. Though he told himself not to, he reached out and patted her thin shoulder.

"There, there, lass," he began awkwardly. "It's all right. Whatever you thought, it cannot have been so bad."

She shook her head, her sniffs coming between gasps for air and jerking hiccups. "You don't understand. It's . . . it's . . ."

Rourke stiffened. She wanted to say more. With just a little prompting he could pry the truth from her. He bit the inside of his lip, the dull pain reminding him of why he'd come to America.

"You . . . were looking for someone?" He phrased the question carefully, despising himself for asking, then held his breath while he waited for her answer, which was several seconds in coming.

Finally she lifted her head and wiped her tears on the tips of her mittens. "No, I was not. Please, forgive my folly. I thought I saw someone I knew, is all, and it . . . made me homesick."

Oddly relieved, Rourke blew out a breath. Well he knew that longing for the rocky cliffs and rolling moors of Ireland. He felt it himself, late at night, when he could almost imagine the wind howling through the bustling streets of New York was really an Irish breeze whistling up from the sea.

"Ah . . . I see." He loosed the ends of her scarf until it dangled free and then gently draped it around her neck. "I believe this belongs to you, eh, lass?"

This close, he could see the golden flecks in her eyes as they widened in surprise.

"My thanks," she murmured and then pressed her lips tightly closed.

Something about the way she stared—a desperate mix of fear and pleading—made Rourke want to linger, to brush his fingers against her cheek. She looked so soft. Vulnerable. Like one meant to be protected from sinners and scoundrels such as he.

A sinner once redeemed, he reminded himself, casting into his memory for an evening alongside Da, Rourke's adolescent cracking as he pleaded with God for salvation.

And then his father's pale countenance flashed before his eyes.

Gulping a deep breath, Rourke straightened and gestured toward the street. "We'd best be getting back. Mr. O'Bannon will be wondering where we've gotten to."

"Aye. I suppose you're right."

She looked in no hurry to leave, however. She took one last slow look around the harbor, ending where she'd started, with him. A sigh escaped her, cut short by a hopeful gasp and a brightening of her eyes. Rourke's heart thumped as she clasped his arm.

"Rourke, Ana said ships come into port every day."

"Aye, that's true. Or almost every day."

Tugged free by a sharp wind, a lock of Cara's hair whipped across her face. She brushed it impatiently aside. "Well then, I do not suppose you would consider bringing me again tomorrow? I mean, if it wouldn't be too bothersome?"

Suspicion coiled in Rourke's belly. This was no ordinary interest Cara displayed. Despite what she said, he sensed she *was* searching for someone. But why did she deny it?

He fixed a charming smile to his face. "Accompany a beautiful woman? Nay, I would not say 'tis a bother."

"Oh, thank you, Rourke. This . . ." Her face flushed, she dropped her hand and stepped away. "Well, this means so much."

For just a moment, joy sparked in her gaze. Rourke knew better than to think he was the cause. It had more to do with the wharf . . . and the mysterious person she sought. He held out his arm, but this time no warmth flooded him at her touch. Instead, anger at her deception folded him in its grasp.

Though she was working hard to hide it, somehow he'd glean the truth. He'd find a way to get closer to her, learn her secrets. By one means or another he'd know if the person she searched for—the one she thought she'd seen today—was the man who'd murdered his father.

Eoghan Hamilton.

12

Cara stared out her window at the furious wind and snow lashing the boardinghouse. For two days she'd been locked inside, only venturing out when Giles came in the carriage to collect her and Ana in the morning, and again in the evening when he came to bring them home from the candle shop.

Even the frigid temperatures seemed determined to see she remained indoors. With each passing hour the fire sputtering in the fireplace warmed a little less, the drafts squeezing through the floorboards and around the windowpanes chilled a little more. In fact, it had been so cold that morning at breakfast they hadn't attempted the trip to the candle shop at all.

Sighing, Cara pulled her shawl tighter around her shoulders. There was naught to be done about it. She hadn't seen Rourke since the first time he'd accompanied her to the wharf, when the storm began.

A soft knock sounded on her door. Pushing away from the window, she let the heavy curtains fall back into place and went to answer.

"There you are, dearie. We've all been looking for you. We missed you at lunch."

Despite her cheery smile, Breda's appearance failed to dispel the melancholy Cara felt. Clucking like a hen, Breda bustled into the room and wrapped a wiry arm around Cara's shoulders.

"*Tsk, tsk.* No sense going to the goat's house to look for wool. Come, warm yourself by the fire and enjoy a cup of Laverne's mulled cider." She closed one eye in a wink. "I'll even sneak a drop of brandy in it for ya, if ya like. It'll warm your bones," she said, wheedling.

Cara wagged a finger at her. "Breda, it's barely past three!"

Cackling, Breda shoved off through the door. "C'mon then, just cider for you." She paused when they reached the stairs. Eyeing Cara from beneath lowered brows, she added, "Though I dinna think a slice of Laverne's apple pie would hurt ya none. Put some meat on them bones. It's a wonder ya haven't caught a chill. Come along," she said, still muttering as she led the way down the stairs. "Everyone's in the back. The rooms are warmer there, and the fire a mite more cheery."

Though Cara had little appetite, the inviting scents of cinnamon and nutmeg stirred a rumbling in her belly as she entered the library. Seated around the roaring fire were all the women of the boardinghouse—except for Deidre, Cara noted, which didn't bother her in the least. The woman barely spoke to her, and when she did, it was with icy matter-of-factness. Perhaps it *was* her way, as Ana insisted, but still, Cara was grateful for her absence.

"Ah, there you are, dear." Amelia rose from her spot on a leather settee. Snapping a book closed, she crossed to Cara and clasped her in a brief hug. "You didn't come down for lunch. I hope you've not taken ill?"

Cara smiled and shook her head. "Not at all. Just a bit of melancholy, I'm afraid."

"And why not, what with this wretched weather." Amelia motioned toward a set of tall windows framed by heavy drapes. Blowing snow blasted the frosted panes.

Ana poured another cup of cider and held it toward Amelia, who collected it and then pressed it into Cara's cold hands. "This will chase away the chill. Come here and sit by the fire."

Scooting aside, Tillie patted the cushion next to her. "Here you go."

Her voice was scarcely above a whisper, but her face reflected a friendliness that had grown since the first time they'd met. Cara gave her a warm smile and sank onto the seat next to her. "Thank you, Tillie."

Blushing, the girl ducked her head. She couldn't be more than seventeen or eighteen. What circumstances had driven her to the boarding-house and Amelia's sheltering wings? Her eyes remained hidden as she lifted her own cup and took a small sip.

Amelia crossed to a large oak cabinet nestled between shelves bulging with books. "Well, ladies, it's not often we get to enjoy one another's company for an entire day like this. While the foul weather forces us to remain indoors, I can't say I'm sorry." She laughed lightly and withdrew a slim ledger from the cabinet. "It gives us an excuse to get to know one another better." Returning to her seat, she folded both hands over the ledger and glanced around the room. "All right now, who wants to play The Minister's Cat?"

Tillie's head lifted. "The Minister's . . . ?"

"Cat," Amelia finished for her. "We'll go around the room, and each of us will give an adjective beginning with the letter *A* that describes the minister's cat. You cannot repeat a word given by another player, however. Once everyone has described the minister's cat, we'll move on to the letter *B,* and so on."

As she spoke, Cara felt her spirits lift. If the weather forced her to remain inside, perhaps Eoghan, too, was kept behind doors. Relief made her limp. Of course. That was why she'd seen no sign of him. Once the weather cleared, he'd come, she would convince him to return to Ireland, and everything would be put to right. For now, it wouldn't hurt to enjoy the company of these fine women.

Smiling, she leaned forward and gave a nod to Amelia. "I'll play."

"Me too." Tillie matched Cara's posture eagerly. She set down her cup and motioned to Ana. "Come, Ana. Play with us."

Looking pleased to have been invited, Ana placed the cider pot on a tray and went to sit next to Tillie. Her lips curling in an impish smile, she said, "Well, I heard it be told that the minister's cat is an *amiable* cat."

"Ho-ho!" Amelia said, laughing. She clapped her hands together, then flipped open the ledger to keep track of the words as the game went on. Indeed, it was several rounds before any of them were put out. Even Breda took part, her forehead wrinkling in concentration every time it came to her turn. Finally she stood up, stretched her arms out to her sides, and then plopped her hands on her hips.

"That's it for me, then. I'm not nearly as quick-witted as the rest of you. Think I'll check on Giles, see how he's doing on the sidewalk."

"He's shoveling away some of the snow," Tillie said, leaning forward to speak in Cara's ear.

Breda gave a hearty chuckle. "Most likely he's finished with that and gone on to warm himself at the stove in Laverne's kitchen."

"Hush now. Leave them be," Amelia scolded, but with a teasing twinkle in her eye.

Ignoring her, Breda swished from the library and closed the door firmly behind her.

"Do you really think he's taken a shine to

Laverne?" Tillie asked, scooting closer to the fire and holding her hands toward the blaze.

Amelia shrugged. "One can never tell for sure, though I daresay, neither of them would be averse. I've seen the way he watches her, and she, him. Like cats eyeing a bowl of sweet cream."

"I've seen it, too," Tillie said, a touch sadly. She heaved a sigh that shook her whole body.

Ana and Amelia exchanged a quick glance, and then Ana reached out to pat Tillie's shoulder. "Be ya remembering your braw lad?"

Tillie's head dipped once, twice, and then she pulled her hands back to wrap around her waist. "Beggin' your pardon, ladies . . . I should go see if Laverne needs any help getting supper around."

Cara glanced at the clock on the mantel. The hands showed quarter of five, but Amelia gave a silent nod anyway, and Tillie slipped from the room. It appeared to Cara, however, that before she disappeared from view, Tillie swiped at her eyes, and then the door closed with a soft click.

"Is she all right?" Cara's gaze shifted between her two remaining companions.

Amelia closed the book in her lap and laid it aside. "She will be in time, and with the Lord's help."

Though she felt uncomfortable asking, curiosity won out. "What happened to her?"

Ana fell silent, her hands stilling in her lap.

After a long pause, Amelia said, "Tillie wasn't

married when she ran away from her parents' house to follow her beau to America. They were young and so desperately in love. Both thought it would nigh kill them that her parents refused to allow her to be with him."

"They objected? Why?"

Ana lifted her head. "He was Catholic. Got himself mixed up with the Fenians."

"Her parents, too, were Catholic, but they didn't approve of his involvement. Thought the group too radical," Amelia added, "and feared their desire to achieve Irish independence from England by force would lead to persecution, even excommunication from the Roman Catholic Church."

Pity washed over Cara. "They ran away . . . so they could be together?"

Amelia's face colored as she nodded. "I have no doubt Tillie and her young man intended to marry once they reached America, but alas, he never made it that far. He took ill aboard ship and died during the crossing."

"Leaving Tillie all alone." Cara shuddered. She knew exactly how the girl felt.

Ana shook her head. "Not quite." She glanced at the door, and her voice fell to a whisper. "She was in the family way."

Cara stared at her, dread growing in her chest. "Pregnant? But . . . what happened to her baby?"

Both women's eyes filled with tears. Finally,

Amelia spoke. "The day the ship's captain brought Tillie to us, she was feverish and swollen with child. We did what we could, but we were fortunate just to save her life. There was naught we could do for the child."

Stillborn.

Grief for all Tillie had endured squeezed Cara's heart. "And on top of everything else, she couldn't go back home."

"No," Amelia said softly. Sniffing, she ran the tip of her finger under her lashes. "Ruined as she was, she feared her parents wouldn't accept her, and so she stayed on here, with us. Not long after, we got word that her parents had died in a carriage accident."

No wonder she kept to herself so. Her sorrow and guilt kept her locked inside. Cara closed her eyes for a moment. "Oh, if only she knew what forgiveness could be found in the Savior."

When she opened her eyes, both Amelia and Ana were watching her.

"I mean . . . real forgiveness. Then she would see herself as God sees her—not ruined—precious. And redeemed."

Clutching her hands beneath her chin, Amelia nodded. Ana, however, looked uncertain. Her troubled gaze fell to her scarred hands, and once again Cara wondered what tragedy she hid. Before she could ask, a snort of disgust sounded near the door.

"Forgiveness?" Deidre's hard stare was even more icy than normal, and her cheeks were blotched and red.

She stalked into the room. Resisting the urge to rise, Cara nodded. "Aye, Deidre. God's grace extends to all men, no matter their past."

"Then perhaps God doesn't know what it is to have your husband snatched from your arms," she spat, her lips white.

"Deidre—" Amelia began, stretching out her hand hesitantly.

Deidre cut her short with an upraised palm. "Stabbed, and left to die in the street. That be how I found my Sean. You dare speak of forgiveness? I'll tell you—"

Swift as the wind howling outside, Ana rose and stood between them. "That's enough, Deidre."

"No! What does she know?" Her finger shook as she jabbed it toward Cara. "Nothing. She's never had to watch as dirt covered her beloved's face. She's never wanted to crawl into the grave beside her lover . . . to die . . . ."

Slowly she trailed off, and though tears glittered in her emerald eyes, she refused to let them fall. Ana met her gaze, unmoving, resolute.

Seconds ticked by on the mantel clock. Finally, Deidre closed her mouth and lifted her chin. "Fine." She stared down at Cara, her face devoid of expression. " 'Tis no use talking when the harm is done."

"Exactly," Amelia said, too eagerly. She wrapped her arm around Deidre's shoulders and pulled her toward the door. "Come, dear. Supper should be ready soon. Laverne's cream gravy will soon make us forget all about this unpleasantness."

As she bustled away, Ana close on her heels, Breda's remark about a fly in the buttermilk echoed in Cara's head. Indeed, Amelia seemed content to pretend that Deidre bore no animosity, but Cara had seen for herself the hatred in the woman's eyes. And hatred it was, whatever anyone else might say.

A shudder took her as slowly she rose to follow. What she had done to incur Deidre's ire, she knew not, but somehow she'd made an enemy of the woman. Until she knew why, she'd have to watch her words . . . and her back.

13

Cara lay in the stillness of her darkened room, straining for a clue to the strange noises trickling in from the hall. Muffled sobs? A creak in the floor?

She threw aside the covers, immediately assailed by the frosty night air. Would spring never come? Shivering, she grabbed a shawl from the back of a chair and tossed it around her shoulders. At least the large oval rug kept her toes from turning to ice. She skittered to the highboy that sat directly across from her bed, pulled a pair of wool socks from a top drawer, and slid her feet inside them before hurrying to the door.

The pale glow of a single candle rounded the corner just as she poked her head into the hall. Though the light disappeared, the sound she'd assumed to be muffled sobs remained.

Tillie?

Cara scanned the row of doors. Except for the one closest to hers—Tillie's—they remained tightly shut. She slipped into the hall and closed the door behind her. Though she wanted to catch Tillie, she wouldn't risk waking the others. She hurried down the hall on her tiptoes, pausing when she reached the top of the stairs. Below her, the candle floated from the stairway, across the foyer, and through the door toward the library.

Bereft of even that feeble light, Cara stuck out her hand and felt for the banister. Why hadn't she thought to bring her own candle? Puffing out a breath, she inched down the stairs, guided only by the moonlight glinting off the snow that shone through the windows.

At the library, Cara paused. One of the pocket doors had been pushed back. Through the entrance she saw a cheery fire crackling in the fireplace, the only sound in the otherwise silent room. Still, Cara was certain she'd seen Tillie come this way. She moved closer.

"Tillie?" Something about the situation called for a whisper. She cleared her throat. Hand on the jamb, she leaned further into the room. "Are you in here, lass?"

"Cara?"

Cara swung her head toward a tall shelf filled with books. Like a wraith, a shadow separated itself from the darker shroud surrounding it. She held her breath, waiting, until Tillie stepped into the light cast by the fire.

Made even more pale by the shimmering moonlight through the tall library windows, Tillie's face had a surreal quality as she stood, brow bunched, her slender hand at her throat. "What are you doing up?" She lowered her eyes. "Did I wake you?"

Cara released the air from her lungs in a rush. In the same moment a shiver took her and she rubbed her hands over her arms. "No. I couldn't sleep, and then . . . I came looking for you."

Tillie crossed to her. "Me?" Grasping her elbow, she pulled Cara toward the fire. "Why?"

"I thought I heard . . ." Cara trailed into silence, studying Tillie's swollen red eyes. "Are you all right?"

Sighing, Tillie moved toward the fireplace and dropped into a high-backed chair. "I will be. It's just . . . tonight . . ." She lifted tear-soaked eyes. " 'Tis the eve of Braedon's birthday."

Braedon? Cara slid into the chair opposite Tillie's. "Your young man."

Tillie lifted a brow. "You know?" When Cara nodded, she shrugged. "I shouldn't be surprised, I suppose. 'Tis a hard thing keeping anything secret in the boardinghouse."

Cara leaned forward to grasp Tillie's hand. "Don't be angry. Ana and Amelia told me. I think they were concerned that you seemed so sad this afternoon."

"Ach, 'tis true, I was sad. Though he's never far from my thoughts, today of all days . . ." She paused and drew a shuddering breath, then lifted the sleeve of her nightgown to rub her nose.

Cara wished she'd thought to tuck a handkerchief into her sleeve the way Ma always did when she was little. She reached out to pat Tillie's knee. "I'm dreadful sorry, I am. Is there anything I can do for you, Tillie?"

The girl looked up, her gaze measuring. Whether the lateness of the hour, the eve of the event, or Cara herself that prompted Tillie to speak was unclear. Regardless, she leaned toward Cara, her face pinched and earnest.

"Would . . ." Her mouth twisted, as though the words pained her. "I'd like to tell you about him, if you wouldn't mind. Tonight . . . his memory . . . I feel like he be slipping away."

So faint was her voice, Cara strained to hear. She nodded, her throat thick.

Tillie's head lowered and she bit her lip. She took her time, and by the tense set of her shoulders, Cara could almost see her mustering the courage to speak.

Finally a handful of words rasped from her lips. "We met at the market in the village where I lived."

Cara waited, silent. Down deep, she sensed what Tillie needed was simply to talk, to share the grief she'd carried alone for so long.

The fire popped, startling Tillie and drawing a nervous giggle. She turned her gaze to meet Cara's head-on. "You must think me foolish."

Cara's thoughts winged to her own family and how she'd felt when she thought she'd lost them. She shook her head. "Succumbing to grief never made anyone a fool."

The reassurance seemed to soothe Tillie. She sank against the back of her chair. Overcome by memories, her eyes clouded. Cara waited, listening to the wind howling outside, the hiss of the fire, and Tillie's steady, even breathing.

Then a smile flitted across her lips and disappeared. "I was fifteen. Braedon was older, but not much. Still, I always admired him more than the other lads in the village. He seemed such a strong man to me, so full of life and vigor."

Cara smiled. "He was a braw lad, too, I wager."

Tillie blushed and dropped her chin. "Ach, that he was. He had the finest head of hair—so dark and full."

As if she were running her palm over silky tresses, Tillie's fingers flexed, and then she recoiled and pulled both hands into the sleeves of her nightdress.

"How did you meet?" Cara prompted gently, hoping to draw her away from whatever painful memory pinched her face.

A ghost of a smile appeared, followed quickly by an impish gleam in Tillie's eye. "I arranged to deliver the eggs from my mother's hens to the market on the same day that I knew Braedon and his family would be selling wood."

Women and their wiles. Cara gave a low laugh. "And it worked, did it?"

"Aye, but not exactly how I'd planned. A stray dog ran into me. Knocked me off my feet, the mongrel, and sent me basket of eggs flying into the air. Ach, but Momma was cross when I came home empty-handed."

"Well, not quite empty," Cara teased.

Tillie's smile widened. "No, not quite. Braedon saw what happened. Rather than laugh like the other people at the market, he helped me up, dusted me off, and took me to sit with his family until I'd calmed me crying. Such a gentleman, he was. Always looking out for me. Even on the boat as we were crossing over, when he thought . . .

when he was weak and confined to his sickbed . . ."

She drew a heavy breath. Fingers trembling, she pressed them to her mouth and whispered the next words. "Got lung fever, he did." Anguish swept over her pale features. "If only they had let me tend him, but women weren't allowed in the men's quarters, and with so many taken ill, well, they figured it wasn't safe."

"They feared an epidemic aboard the ship."

"I reckon that was the way of it." Tillie's chin dropped to her chest.

In the dim glow of the firelight, Cara could see the tears that washed from her eyes to soak the front of her nightdress.

"Only on that last day," Tillie whispered, "when my poor, braw lad was so weak he could barely lift his head, did the ship's captain take pity on me and allow me go to Braedon's side." She clutched both hands to her chest. "I held him while he drew his last ragged breaths, watched as his life ebbed away like the tide."

She quieted then, the silence filled only by the crackling of the fire and the low wail of the wind.

"You arrived in America alone, like me," Cara whispered.

Tillie nodded.

"And you've never thought of going back? You have other family besides your parents, aye?"

Her jaw hardened. "Even if it were possible, I wouldn't go back there. 'Twas their rejection of

Braedon, theirs and my parents, that forced us out of Ireland in the first place."

An idea formed in Cara's mind—whispered remembrances that until now she'd not put together before. Bits of speech Eoghan had made, ideas that Da said sprang from nowhere.

She leaned forward, her hands clasped in her lap. "Tillie, tell me about the Fenians."

Tillie's head jerked up. Her gaze bright, she stared at Cara. "Who told you about them?"

Cara shrugged. "No one, I guess. Just what Ana and Amelia said about your parents' fear of them."

"Not them, people's view of them."

Cara held her breath, waiting.

"My parents believed the same things Braedon did, wanted the same things; they simply weren't brave enough to do anything about it. Braedon didn't want violence," she continued, her voice turning strident, her fingers clenched around the arms of her chair. "He just wanted freedom from Britain. Freedom for us and for our *bairns*."

Her hand went instinctively to her midsection. Then, as though remembering, she slumped and dropped her hand to her lap.

"It's true then? He was part of the Fenians?"

She nodded. Cara bit her lip, drawing courage from her desperate desire to know of her brother's whereabouts.

"Tillie, did you ever meet the others in the organization?"

As quickly as it had opened up, Tillie's expression closed. Her gaze became wary, narrowed. "Never. Why?"

She was lying. Cara knew it instinctively, yet to draw the truth from her would require telling her about Eoghan, and his warning for her to remain silent still rang too vividly in her head. Disappointment settled heavily on her shoulders, though she tried to appear unperturbed.

"Just curious, is all."

Her gaze still wary, Tillie looked away and back. "Perhaps . . . you be breaking your shin on a stool that isn't in your way, Cara."

Cara blinked. "What?"

Some of the harshness melted from Tillie's expression. She rose, her hand light on Cara's shoulder as she turned for the door. "Dinna look for trouble. Sure, and it'll find you all on its own."

With that, she left the library, taking the one sputtering candle and leaving Cara to sit alone to ponder her words by the light of the fire.

Deidre pressed tighter into the shadows, her nails pinching half-moons into her palm. She hadn't heard everything that passed between Cara and Tillie, but she'd heard enough to confirm her suspicions. Cara was in New York under false pretenses.

"I'll find out who you are, Cara Hamilton," she vowed under her breath. Her words, like venom, tasted bitter on her tongue, yet she relished them.

She peeked through the library door at the object of her hatred. Cara remained seated in front of the hearth, the firelight casting an orange sheen on her bent head.

"And if you had anything to do with my husband's death, I'll make you pay, if it be the last thing I ever do."

Longing for her knife made her fingers ache. How simple it would be to take Cara's life tonight, with her back unguarded. But when the creaking of the floor roused her from slumber, she hadn't thought to grab it from her nightstand. Easing toward the hall, she took grim satisfaction in the knowledge that soon her thirst for revenge would be quenched. Cara would be dead, as would her traitor of a brother . . . or was it husband?

Even shrouded by darkness, Deidre paused and quirked a brow. The possibility had not occurred to her before. A slow smile curved her lips. Even better. Justice would truly be served if Eoghan Hamilton were her lover and not her flesh and blood. Maybe she would let her live, then. Let her savor the bitter loneliness of a too-empty bed.

But seeing the horror on Eoghan's face as he watched her slit Cara's throat was too tempting a draw. Deidre rounded the hall and skipped lightly up the steps. No, she wouldn't be able to resist killing Cara when the time came. Indeed, she would take great pleasure in it, exceeded only by that which she would feel once she'd closed Eoghan's eyes forever.

Yawning, she moved from the stairs to the landing and down the corridor to her room. All this sneaking about was exhausting. No doubt she'd be bleary-eyed in the morning.

She closed the door with a soft click and then crossed to her bed. Drawing back the covers, she slid her cold feet between the crisp sheets and fell asleep before her head fully settled on the feather pillows.

14

"I dinna understand, lad. Is this woman kin to Hamilton or isn't she?" Of all the faces on all the men gathered around the table, the one most perplexed was Malcolm's. He cocked his head to one side and scratched his temple. "You'd best be making your meaning clear."

Rourke thumped his knuckles on the table and stood, toppling his chair in his wrath. "That's just it, uncle, I cannot be certain. That is why—"

"Fie!" Hugh also stood and kicked aside his chair. "It's because she's a woman that you've let sentiment cloud your judgment." His head swung to Malcolm. "Let me question her. I'll get to the truth." He cast an accusing glance at

Rourke. "And it wilna take me a month, either."

"No!" Rourke's fingers tore his hair. "What I mean is, there is no point. I do not believe she is Hamilton's sister, and even if she was, she could not give us his whereabouts."

"Why is that, nephew?" Angus asked, his gnarled fingers pulling at his beard.

"Because she doesn't know." Rourke paced the floor. At least he didn't think she knew. If he were honest, his judgment did tend toward cloudiness where Cara was concerned.

"But ya just said she isn't his sister. Which is it, Rourke? Surely ya have a feeling one way or the other?" Hugh demanded.

Rourke's guard rose. Hugh was pushing, showing unreasoning persistence. Why? "If I waver," he said carefully, "it is because I know Da would want us to be assured of our course before we act."

"That be certain," Malcolm said, holding up his hand when Hugh moved to interrupt. "My brother esteemed a man's reputation highly. He never made accusations based on assumptions."

Angus sat up and propped both elbows on the table. "What do ya recommend we do, Malcolm? Sit around and wait for the lass to escape? What if she can lead us to the Hamilton lad?"

Malcolm pressed the fingertips of both hands together. For several seconds he said nothing. At long last, he looked at Rourke. "Two weeks. That should give you plenty of time to get close to the girl, win her trust."

Though unease simmered in his belly, Rourke nodded.

Malcolm's head swung to Hugh. "The chandler who hired her—find out what you can about him, see if they have connections outside of the shop."

Hugh's eyes rolled, but when Malcolm's brows dropped into a glower, he sighed. "Fine. I'll ask around."

"Good." Malcolm turned to his son Clive. "Any word from Derry? You said you would write the others back home, find out if anyone knew anything about Hamilton's sister."

"None," Clive said.

Angus, too, shook his head. "This weather has slowed the ships some. It could be word is on its way."

"Keep on it," Malcolm said, rising. To the others in the room he gave brief instructions before dismissing the group entirely.

Weariness seeped from Rourke's bones, made his feet heavy. Despite Malcolm's support, his kinsmen weren't happy. Hugh especially eyed him critically as they left the shoe store and parted ways.

Turning up his collar, Rourke stepped out into the dark street. Rain mixed with bits of ice razed his face. He squinted to protect his eyes and hunched deeper into his coat. Though he quickened his pace, he couldn't escape the questions pounding his brain.

Why hadn't he told the others about his suspicions regarding Cara? How could his loyalties be so divided?

A twinge of guilt bit at his conscience. He'd been fighting divided loyalties ever since he ignored God's admonition and set out seeking revenge, but he loved his father. Didn't he deserve to be avenged?

Anger at himself flared to life, making him oblivious to the houses he passed and the streets he crossed, so that he was surprised to look up and see the tenement where he roomed looming ahead. He took the stairs two at a time, slid a key from his pocket, and jammed it into the lock. It turned easily, but he still had to wrestle for several minutes, kicking the slushy snow piled in front of the door out of the way before he could shove it open and slip inside.

Stark walls. A single gas lamp. Dismal gray paint. Never had he felt the solitude of the place so keenly, and all because of a peculiar need to protect someone he barely knew from his own flesh and blood. What was the Hamilton woman doing to him?

A row of doors stretched down the hall to his left, another to his right. His was the second from the end.

Brushing the snow from his shoulders and

stomping it from his shoes, he moved down the hall until he reached his apartment.

A gray sliver of light splayed across the dusty floor, a reflection through the window of the snow outside. One more step and the faint light spilled across his legs. He stared a moment, his fingers reaching for the knob that should have been pulled closed but wasn't. He flattened against the wall, listening.

No sound escaped from inside, but if the intruder heard him coming . . .

Silently he cursed his lack of caution. At home in Ireland he would never have been so careless, so preoccupied by foolish thoughts.

He yanked a short-handled knife from the waistband of his trousers. Jabbing at the door with his toe, he pushed it open far enough to see inside. He had few belongings, only a bed and a writing desk to cast shadows on the walls. Not that any more would fit in the tiny space. Opposite his bed, the chair to the desk had been pushed close to the window.

A large figure was slumped against the ladder-back chair, long legs stretched out and crossed at the ankles. Rourke stared, wrestling with the dark to make out the man's face.

A low voice rumbled out, splitting the night. "Welcome home, cousin."

Hugh. He'd followed him?

Rourke let go a relieved breath and fully entered

the room. The knife, he returned to hiding beneath his shirt. Then he closed and locked the door—though the irony of the action did not elude him. Hugh had gotten in without much trouble.

Behind him, a match struck. The glow from a single candle illuminated his kinsman's face.

Beneath Hugh's hooded gaze, Rourke crossed to the bed and sat. "I left before you. You must have been in a hurry. I assume by your presence you want to speak with me?"

Hugh tossed the spent match on the floor. "Wasn't difficult beating you here, cousin. You be getting careless in your old age."

Rourke let that pass. Bracing his elbows on his knees, he sat forward and waited.

Hugh snorted. "We need to talk."

"About?"

"I think you know."

Rourke stood. "Get on with it, then," he snarled, pacing the length of the cramped apartment.

To his surprise, Hugh let out a low chuckle. "Just like your father. Did I ever tell ya about the time Uncle Daniel caught me pinching coins from the offering plate at St. Peter's?"

What was this about? Rourke paused and scratched his temple. He was furthest from the candle and shrouded by shadows, so he doubted Hugh saw, little though it mattered. Hugh's face was turned toward the window—the candle and his eyes forming ghostly reflections on the glass.

"I was thirteen. Still a lad, but as thieving as a fox's snout. Our whole family used to file into church Sunday after Sunday, come sun or hail. Did you ever wonder why I refused to sit anywhere but the end of the pew?"

Drawn by memories, Rourke returned to his seat on the bed. He and Hugh had been close once, as boys. He shook his head.

"Ah, well, you wouldn't. You were much younger than I."

"Three years."

"Is that all?" Hugh's brow furrowed. "I thought it was more." He shook himself and smiled. "Anyway, it was just easier slipping the money out sitting there. I'd make sure I had a coin between my thumb and the plate, and when I passed it on, the money fell into my hand. Easy." He barked a laugh. "Until your daed saw me. I knew the moment I'd been caught." He looked at Rourke, not with anger or grief. His eyes were steady. Calm. "He stared at me exactly the way you be looking now."

Rourke dropped his gaze. "Make your point, Hugh."

Despite his prodding, Hugh refused to be hurried. His head shook from side to side. "I thought for sure and for certain he would tell my father what I had done. Da was never as forgiving as Uncle Daniel. Maybe your daed knew, and that's why he didn't tell."

"Uncle Angus never found out?"

"Not so far as I am knowing."

"So what happened?"

Hugh lifted a brow and crossed his arms. "Uncle Daniel made me go to the priest and admit what I had done. Sure, and Father Duncan was a saint for not turning me in, though I think your da had some to do with it. Father Duncan assigned me a penance—three days a week coming by the church to help serve meals and clean."

The memory of begging Hugh to play and his refusing flashed into Rourke's mind. "It happened right after Candlemas."

Hugh gave a slow nod.

"I wondered why you were always so busy." Rourke tilted his head, thinking. "It was nigh unto a month, wasn't it?"

"Two. And I remember complaining to Uncle Daniel that my punishment was too long."

A smirk curled Rourke's lips. "Sure, and that went well."

Hugh laughed—an easy laugh, like when they were boys.

"What did he say?"

Sobering, Hugh sat up in his chair. Even by the dim light of the candle, Rourke read the sorrow in his face. "He told me to get on with it. Only that. Like you just did."

Da's voice echoed in Rourke's ears. What wouldn't he give to hear him speak one more time? Chiding or encouraging . . . it mattered not so long as it was his deep, rumbling voice. Aching grief stabbed Rourke's heart.

Too ashamed to let Hugh see the emotions flooding over him, Rourke propped his elbows on his knees and rested his chin on his clasped hands. He struggled until finally he was able to speak.

"You came a long way, on a cold night, to tell me about something that happened a long time ago, Hugh. Why?" He lifted his head. "I ask you again, what's your point?"

Rourke had the uncomfortable suspicion it was his jumbled emotions that caused the strange satisfaction gleaming in Hugh's eyes. His kinsman rose and clapped him on the shoulder.

"I just thought you needed to hear it, cousin. Hear, and be reminded why we came. What we lost." He leaned down to whisper in Rourke's ear. "You turned soft on me once, remember? You quit hanging with me and the lads because you said *God* wouldn't approve of our activities. Well, God might not like what we're doing now, but it's your father who died. You'd do well to remember that."

As though he needed reminding. Rourke wanted to reply, to inject his words with pain and sarcasm, but though his throat worked, he made no sound. Instead, he watched as Hugh turned and walked slowly to the door.

No one knew better than Rourke what had been lost. How dare Hugh make such an accusation? He wouldn't let him leave—not thinking he'd forgotten his da or that he'd let go his vow to see justice administered. He tried bolting to his feet, but even his legs felt weak.

"Wait—"

He was too late. The door closed with a firm click behind Hugh, and Rourke . . .

Rourke was left alone, with only the keening wind outside to cover the ragged sobbing of his heart.

15

Cara woke slowly, pulled from slumber by the bright rays streaming through a gap in the brocade curtains covering the window.

Sun.

She vaulted from her bed and scurried to the window to look outside. Indeed, the winter storm had finally subsided and a gay sun scattered its rays on the glittering drifts. Though it was Saturday, a few brave souls had already ventured out. Footprints broke the pristine beauty of the fallen snow. One pair led from the street straight to the boardinghouse door.

She was right. He had been waiting for the

storm to relent. It was the blizzard that had kept him away. Her breathing quickened, frosting the windowpane until she could no longer look out.

But why stand here, when even now Eoghan could be downstairs?

Joy flooded her heart. He'd been so anxious to find her, he hadn't waited for a decent hour. He'd come before breakfast, probably demanding to be let in and was even now explaining his presence and his identity to Amelia.

How did he know where to look?

She ignored the niggling doubt prodding her brain as she let the curtains fall back into place and hurried to wash and dress. He was here. He had to be. And he was waiting.

Her fingers trembled with excitement as she crossed to the largest piece of cottage furniture adorning her room—a massive armoire painted white and decorated with flowers. Inside, her meager belongings hardly filled the space.

Pulling her best dress from the back, she laid it across the bed, then threw her nightdress over her head. In moments she smoothed the blue muslin skirt over her hips. Crossing to the vanity, she jerked a brush through her curls and twisted her hair into a knot at the nape at her neck. The simple bun would have to do. She didn't have time for anything more complicated. Besides, Eoghan wouldn't care how she looked. He would just be glad to see her.

She danced from the room, her slippered feet so light she barely touched the stairs. Voices drifted from the parlor, one of them masculine, confirming her belief that Eoghan had indeed found his way to her. Her heart pounded harder.

Two years! For two years she'd suffered and thought him dead, and now he was here. She would see him at last, and he would explain why he'd allowed the lie that broke her heart. Rounding the door, she burst into the parlor without knocking and skidded to a stop on the lacquered wood floor.

Shock bit her tongue, for it wasn't Eoghan seated alongside Amelia on the settee, sharing a cup of steaming coffee. It was Rourke.

Both gave her a startled glance, and then Amelia put down her cup, the newspaper on her lap rustling as she laid it aside and stood. "Cara, dear, you look positively white. What is it? Is something wrong?"

When she didn't answer, Rourke stood, too. "Cara?"

"Oh," she improvised feebly, hiding her wringing hands behind her back. "Forgive me for intruding. I . . ." It was too much. Disappointment pierced her like a knife. Her knees shook, leaving her weak.

"You'd best sit down." Taking her by the elbow, Amelia led her to the settee and poured her a steaming cup from the coffeepot. "Drink this, dear. It'll warm you right up."

Cara lifted the cup and took a sip, too numb to wonder how she would explain her curious behavior. She'd been so certain Eoghan had come today, so hopeful that once the storm passed, they'd be reunited. So, if it was not the frigid temperatures and blowing snow that kept him away . . .

Her heart dropped like a stone into her stomach. Only one thing would keep him now. There was only one thing whose victory Eoghan had somehow stolen but which had now returned to claim its prize.

Death.

Eoghan was dead.

The cup clattered from her fingers and crashed to the floor. A second later, Cara followed.

Cara crumpled before Rourke's eyes. Leaping forward, he caught her in his arms moments before she hit the floor.

"Cara!" The pot slid from Amelia's grasp, scattering the cups and dribbling coffee over the table and onto the rug. "Good heavens, Mr. Walsh. Is she all right?" Without waiting for an answer, she grabbed her skirts and ran to shout into the hall. "Laverne! Laverne, come quickly!"

Whirling, she hurried back and stood with her hands clasped at her waist, an anxious frown turning her lips down. "What's wrong with her? Should I send for the doctor?"

Rourke eased his arm under Cara's legs and gently lifted her to the settee. Though she rested quietly, he found it impossible to release his hold. Instead, he adjusted his arm until he encircled her shoulders and knelt beside her on the floor.

Her lashes spread like fans against her pale cheeks. Smoothing a stray lock of auburn hair from her forehead, he let his hand linger. Her skin felt clammy to the touch but not feverish. Ignoring Amelia's worried babbling, he leaned forward to whisper in Cara's ear.

"Cara, darling?"

She stirred, like an angel rousing from slumber.

Throat tight, he caressed her cheek with the back of his fingers. "Lass, wake up."

"Is she . . . will she . . . ?"

Laverne's stout form rumbling through the doorway cut Amelia short. "What in heaven's name is all the fuss—bless me!" Catching sight of Cara, she halted near the door, her hand pressed tight over her heart. "I'll fetch some water."

She spun and disappeared.

Cara sighed—the sweetest sound to reach Rourke's ears in the last hour—and her eyes fluttered open.

Rourke held his breath.

"What . . . happened?"

Clucking like a hen, Amelia bent over the back of the settee to clutch Cara's hand. "You fainted, dear."

"Fainted?" She blinked and her eyes lost their dazed look, replaced by something deep and mournful. "Oh."

The color had returned to her cheeks, but the tears brimming in her eyes removed any hope of easing the tension crushing Rourke's chest. Whatever was wrong wasn't physical, but to her it was no less distressing. Whipping a handkerchief from his pocket, he pressed it to her palm. "Here."

"Thank you," she said in a low whisper. She looked up at Amelia. "Forgive me. I'm fine now. Truly."

Amelia patted Cara's hand, then released her hold, forcing Rourke to do the same. Reluctantly he removed his arm from about her shoulders and stood. Taking a step back, he relinquished his place at Cara's side to Amelia, who huddled close and felt for her temperature.

"I don't understand it," she said, her hands fluttering from Cara's forehead, to her cheeks, to her wrist. "No fever. No high color. No signs of illness at all."

Laverne entered bearing a tray laden with a bowl, a towel, a pitcher of water, and a glass. At her heels trailed Ana and Tillie, more than likely roused by the commotion. "There, there now," Laverne muttered. "Let me in. I'll see to the lass."

Ana leaned close, peering over the settee at Cara, her eyes wide with worry. "What's the trouble?"

"What happened?" Tillie echoed. "Is she hurt?"

Splashing water from the pitcher into the bowl, Laverne dunked the towel, wrung it out, and pressed it to Cara's forehead all in a matter of seconds.

Cara struggled to sit. "Please . . . don't trouble yourselves. I'm fine. It was just . . ."

Her chin dropped and she went still. Too still. Rourke looked to see what had captured her attention.

Cara was staring at the newspaper Amelia had discarded. In the excitement, it had slipped from the settee to the floor. Bending, Rourke picked it up. Only Cara watched. The others were too busy fussing over her to notice. Her gaze turned pleading, and somehow he knew she begged him to keep silent regarding her interest. Folding the paper carefully, he slid it into his shirt.

Suddenly her chin lifted and she appeared to regain her strength. "Honestly, none of this is necessary. I am fine now." She caught Laverne's hands and gently pushed them away. Leaning forward, she lowered her voice to a whisper. "I have not been drinking enough fluids for . . . the time which it be. Please, Laverne, pour me a glass of water from that pitcher and I'll be right soon enough."

Understanding dawned on the faces of the women. As one, they heaved a collective sigh. Rourke, however, remained skeptical.

Amelia crossed to him, her palm held high and her stern face saying she'd brook no argument. "I'm afraid you'll have to excuse us, Mr. Walsh. In the excitement we forgot we had a gentleman present. You are welcome to stop by later this afternoon if you'd like to see how Cara is faring."

Chagrin made his face hot. Just like that, his visit was cut short. But he wouldn't risk offending his host. "Of course. Ladies, if you will excuse me . . ."

He dipped his head, but Cara put up her hand before he could turn to leave.

"Wait, Rourke. Don't go." Sliding her feet to the floor, she freed herself from Laverne's worried hands and stood. "Amelia, I have something I need to discuss with Mr. Walsh. I'm afraid it simply cannot wait."

Ana looked to Laverne, who looked to Amelia. Tillie's head swiveled between all three. Eventually all of their gazes fluttered to perch on Rourke. He shrugged. Whatever Cara had to discuss more than likely had to do with the paper pressed to his side, but obviously she wasn't ready to share that fact. For now, he'd keep her secret.

Amelia returned to Cara's side and gently stroked her arm. "Are you certain it cannot wait, dear? You gave us a terrible fright, you did. I'm sure Mr. Walsh would understand—"

"It can't wait," Cara said, cutting her short. She turned her stare to Rourke, and for the life of him, he couldn't . . . wouldn't refuse. He nodded.

"Very well, then," Amelia said, spreading her arms wide and ushering the women from the room as though she were herding chicks. "I'll be in to check on you shortly, Cara."

The last to leave, she exited slowly, her concerned face disappearing between the closing oak doors.

"Let me see it." Cara wasted no time shooting out her hand. "The paper. Please. I must see it."

Resisting the urge to scan the contents, he reached inside his coat and pulled the paper free. Barely had he done so than she snatched it from his hand and carried it to the settee. Never had he witnessed a more earnest face. Her brow puckered, her fingers worried her bottom lip, but in her eyes . . . what on earth could she be reading to produce such a hopeful gleam?

She flipped the paper around and jabbed her finger at one of the pages. "What do you know of them?"

"Who?" He leaned forward to read the headline.

VIOLENCE FORCES FENIANS INTO HIDING

The article spoke of a group of Irish immigrants whose presence had begun to be felt in New York. He quirked an eyebrow. "The Fenians?"

She nodded too eagerly.

Rourke took care to measure his response. "Not

but what I've heard rumored. It's a political group, known variously as the Fenian Brotherhood or the Irish Republican Brotherhood. John O'Mahony helped organize it. It's said he gave them their name. Why?"

She frowned and yanked the paper back. As she read, her lips moved—faster and faster. Even the pages quivered, rustling like dry leaves on an autumn day.

Dismay swept over Rourke like the tide. Her fascination could only mean one thing.

No, Cara. Dinna tell me yours is more than casual interest in the group.

But his plea went unspoken and unheard. She kept reading, an almost crazed look of glee upon her face. Whoever Cara was, one thing was certain. She was somehow involved with the Fenians . . . and that meant she was his enemy.

16

There was only one place Cara could go to risk learning all she could about the Fenians.

Tipping her head back, she stared at the tall stone structure looming over her head. St. Paul's was an imposing place, with its arched entrance and rising pillars. Catholic worshipers, beckoned by the ringing of a massive bell, streamed from the city streets, passing her with nary a glance.

She drew a deep breath. No more waiting and hoping. No more jumping at every knock on the door and imagining she saw her brother around every corner. From now on, she intended to take the search for her twin into her own hands.

Merging with the tide, she mounted the wide stone steps, her reticule a shield behind which to hide her shaking fingers. The article in the newspaper said increasing violence had forced the Fenians underground. She could only assume . . . no, pray . . . that meant Eoghan, too. But here, in a house of God, maybe this was where she would reunite with her brother.

Thankfully, Amelia had not questioned her overmuch when she insisted she wanted to attend mass this Lord's Day rather than ride to church with the others in the carriage. Even more surprising, it was Deidre who had volunteered the location of this large cathedral upon learning of Cara's interest.

Her feet hesitant, she entered the church's marbled foyer. Inside, candles blown by the breeze of the open door flickered and danced. There were so many, even had some gone out, Cara doubted anyone would notice. She briefly wondered if any of them had been made by Mr. O'Bannon's skilled hands. Behind her, someone cleared his throat.

She jerked her head around to look. A portly

gentleman in a tweed coat tipped his hat toward a marble bowl carved from the wall.

Of course. Cara mumbled an apology and then ducked aside so the man could dip his fingers into the holy water. She was so preoccupied by her thoughts she'd forgotten the rituals.

Once the man moved on, Cara, too, touched her fingers to the water before dabbing her forehead, chest, and each shoulder. Finished, she eased into a wooden pew whose carved arms rivaled the most intricate work of art. This row was empty but many others were not. Still, she failed to spy a familiar redhead among those gathered.

As more people filed in, Cara's gaze drifted to the crucifix suspended at the front of the sanctuary.

"Forgive me," she pled, her spirit trembling. God knew her reason for coming, for surely nothing was hid from His sight. She only prayed He'd see fit to show mercy at her deception.

Sliding to her knees, she bowed her head in earnest prayer. The pew creaked as someone joined her, but she didn't lift her eyes to look. Instead, she breathed a heartfelt amen and then pushed her mittens into the pockets of her coat just as a pipe organ, more grand than any she'd ever seen, wheezed its first trembling notes.

"I've not seen you here before."

Cara turned to see who had spoken. The man looking back at her had a friendly enough face.

He was older than she, rugged but clean-shaven, his eyes so blue they almost rivaled Rourke's. About his neck he wore a bonnie scarf, twisted and tucked into the front of his wool coat.

She bowed her head. "No, 'tis my first time to worship at St. Paul's."

"Welcome, then," he said, pinning her with a jovial smile.

Cara relaxed and returned his smile. "Thank you."

"Are you new to the city?"

"Somewhat. I arrived on the *Servia*."

His dark head bobbed like a bird on the waves. "You came from Liverpool, then."

She nodded.

"Am I correct in assuming you're from Ireland?"

Cara held her breath. How much should she say? But wasn't this why she had come? To glean what information she could? She opened her mouth and spoke carefully. "You be correct."

"Whereabouts?" he asked, removing his coat and scarf and draping them over the back of the pew.

The man softened his abrupt question with another smile, yet something inside Cara warned against candor. She waved her hand dismissively, grateful when he did not press.

A hymn started, and the congregation rose as one, their voices echoing from the vaulted ceiling and multiplying into a crescendo. Cara fidgeted, hardly able to stand the impatience that built inside her as one song stretched to two, and then three. Finally a priest garbed in crimson robes stepped to the front and invited the people to sit. Casting caution aside, Cara situated herself closer to the man in the pew with her.

He shot her a curious glance.

Her lips suddenly dry, Cara licked them before tilting her head to whisper, "So, by your accent, I assume you, too, hail from Ireland."

He smiled and tipped his head.

Cara swallowed. "And you are Catholic?"

He lifted one eyebrow and gave a merry wink.

Silly question, considering their surroundings, Cara chastised herself. How to ask the real question simmering on her tongue?

"Are you—?"

"Let us pray."

Aargh! Like the rest of the congregation, Cara slid to her knees and closed her eyes while the priest intoned a blessing. When she opened her eyes, the man alongside her watched.

"Am I . . . ?" he prompted, to which several heads turned in their direction.

Cara felt her cheeks grow hot. She mouthed an apology at the people behind the irritated glares and waited until attention had returned to the priest before responding.

Her voice lowered to just above a whisper. "I am new to this city," she continued. "I was wondering where a lass could go if she wanted to . . . connect . . . with people from home."

He gave a knowing nod. "Homesick, eh?"

"Yes." She fumbled to a halt. "Not exactly. I mean, it would be easier were I surrounded by others from back home." Drawing a deep breath, she leaned toward him and lowered her voice. "People with similar interests."

He appeared puzzled a moment, and then a deep red flush crept up from his neck to cover his cheeks. "Lass, I'm not sure I understand what you be searching for, but one thing's certain, unless it's forgiveness, you'll not be finding it here."

"What?"

"This is a house of God. Sure, it was made for sinners such as you and I, but if you think to be bringing some kind of worldly—" His voice had begun to rise. He stopped himself, put his hand to his chin, and resumed more quietly. "Listen to me, lass. If it's help you're needing, maybe wisdom on how to escape an unsavory way of life, you've come to the right place."

Unsavory—

Shame descended on Cara like fog. "You misunderstand me, sir."

His brows lowered in a frown. "I hope so. I hope it's repentance you're seeking and not something else." He frowned. "We dinna ken to people dragging havoc in here with them."

Cara lifted a hand to stop him. "Please, allow me to explain."

Singing had resumed—the perfect cover. She scooted closer, praying she'd find the words to convince him to help her.

"I need information, sir. Nothing more."

He eyed her skeptically. "What kind of information?"

She dared not mention Eoghan. Better to stick to gleaning what she could about the Fenians. She drew a breath. "Where I'm from, there were those willing to risk everything to see Ireland free from British rule. A brotherhood of sorts, from what I heard rumored."

He glanced right and left, then back to her. "The Fenians?"

She clasped her fingers tightly in her lap. "They're the ones."

He gave a slow shake of his head. "They're a militant group, emigrants mostly, bitter about the way things are between Ireland and Britain. Some were forced here to escape execution, and a few would do anything—" he paused and dipped his head closer—"anything, including terrorism, to get what they want." He withdrew, freeing Cara to breathe. "Now, what would a young lass like you be wanting with the likes of them?"

Cara forced the words from her dry mouth. "Certain things have happened, certain events, that make me want to learn all I can about them."

"Good things?"

She grimaced, her fingers twisting in her lap. "I cannot say, sir. Forgive me."

He took his time measuring her from tip to toe. Finally, his jaw working, he shook his head. "I kinna help you, lass."

"Oh, but—"

Cautioning her with a raised finger, he cut short her protest. "I kinna help you, save to give you a name."

Her breath caught. She waited, afraid to move, to utter a sound. Finally he gave a nod and bent toward her.

"He be known as The Celt."

She bobbed her head once to show she understood.

"He took over leadership of the group after John O'Mahony died. He's been known to frequent Canal Street, but be careful who you ask. An untimely question could mean an unfortunate accident, if you be following my meaning."

"Of course."

The final benediction given, people began to rise. The man to whom Cara had been speaking also rose, his face marred by a worried frown.

"I must be going now. 'Twouldn't be seemly for me to be seen speaking with you this way." He paused and looked down at her, his lips thinned and white. "Be careful, lass. The Fenians are not to be trifled with. Be sure and be certain of your actions before you go seeking them out."

With that, he spun and made his way down the aisle.

It wasn't much, but at least she had something —The Celt. Cara twisted the name over and over in her mind. She'd start with that, and tomorrow she'd learn all she could about the mysterious Fenians.

"Well?" Deidre motioned Jacob Kilarny closer, impatience making her throat tight. Father Pat often went late on his sermons, but today he'd been especially long-winded. "What did she say?"

Jacob ducked into the small alcove with her. It was off the main entrance, away from prying eyes and hidden by a flight of stairs. Normally it was reserved for the altar boys who waited there for the service to begin. One of them had left his surplice on the floor and would probably be chided later.

Deidre grabbed Jacob's arm and dragged him close. "Well?"

Jacob's head bobbed. "She asked after the Fenians, just like you said."

Deidre relaxed her grip. As she did, the scarf he'd draped over his arm slipped to the floor. He bent to retrieve it and wrapped it around his neck while Deidre paced the stone floor.

She pounded her fist into the palm of her other hand, then regretted the move when pain sliced clear to her wrist from the cut caused by Eoghan Hamilton's knife. "I knew it. I knew there was something she wasn't telling."

"Doesn't mean she's a spy, Dee. Maybe she's just—"

Deidre whirled. "I never said she was a spy. And don't call me 'Dee.' "

"A traitor then."

"She's not Catholic. Why else would she be here asking about the Fenians?"

"How should I know?" At her frown, Jacob's voice turned placating. "You and I asked about the Fenians once upon a time. Who's to say she's not a patriot looking for a way to fight for her beloved country?"

Deidre snorted and laid her hand on the room's one piece of furniture—a carved wooden chair with a straight back. "You're as dumb as this here seat if you think that, Jacob."

Immediately she regretted the remark. Jacob wasn't the most cunning man she knew, but he didn't take kindly to insults. She relaxed her posture and batted her lashes at him. "And since we both know that's not true . . ."

Though he faced the opposite direction, Jacob moved to stand alongside her, their shoulders barely touching. He turned his head slightly to glance sidelong at her. "I knew your husband, lass. I fought alongside him at Belfast and other places. He was a good lad, and I grieved when he fell. But dinna think for one moment"—he did look at her then, a steely glare that sent shivers up Deidre's spine—"dinna think I'll allow your private quest for revenge to endanger everything we've fought for." He leaned closer, his breath a fiery lash against her neck. "You hear me, lass? Dinna be using our cause to pursue justice for your lover's death."

She dared not move a muscle for the deadliness of his tone. Deidre simply nodded once and blew out a sigh when at last he moved away.

"Jacob?" Deidre called, catching him as he prepared to slip through the door.

He looked back at her, one eyebrow raised.

"It's not just revenge I'm after."

"No?"

She shook her head. "Believe it or not, I care as much about the cause as my Sean did."

He looked her up and down before twisting his lips into a grimace. "If you say so."

She strode forward until she stood toe-to-toe with him. "I do. And like it or not, Jacob Kilarny, you'd best be warning your cohorts about that young lass out there." She jerked her chin toward the sanctuary. "Maybe you're right. Maybe she's not a spy, or a traitor, or anything else I said. But let me ask you this. Can you afford to be wrong?"

His jaw clenched and he said nothing.

Satisfaction simmered in Deidre's gut. She

smiled and backed away. "I didn't think so. Now, when you and whoever you answer to are ready for the truth, you come see me. I think you know where to find me."

Taking the end of Jacob's scarf, she threw it over his shoulder and gave his cheek a pat before slipping through the alcove door and out of the church.

The sun's brilliant rays sparkled off the dripping icicles and melting snow. Deidre inhaled a lungful of crisp, fresh air and blew it out with a smile. The meeting hadn't gone as she'd planned, but she was happy with the result.

Very happy, indeed.

17

Rourke slid out of his coat and deposited it into Tillie's waiting arms.

"Thank you," he said, brushing away the moisture lingering on his sleeves and in his hair.

"Not at all," Tillie said, smiling. "I'm sure Cara will be glad to see you. This way." She indicated the parlor and then ducked into the hall. "I'll fetch her for you."

She dissolved like a mist under a hot sun. Rather than sit, Rourke crossed to the window and looked out. Nature promised a return to spring with budding trees and glimpses of green peeking through the melting snow, but now, just after noon, Sunday carriages had turned the roads and sidewalks into gray mush.

"Rourke?"

He turned from the window. Cara was watching him from the door, a mixture of surprise and pleasure on her face. Better if she'd only looked surprised. He dared not allow himself to be befuddled by her pleasure.

He gave a stiff nod. "Cara."

Pressing her hands to her midriff, she entered, a wary smile on her lips. "Tillie said you were looking for me."

He nodded and met her near the settee. "Aye, that is . . ." Why hadn't he bothered to think of an excuse for stopping by? He couldn't exactly say she'd made him suspicious with her interest in the Fenians. Inspiration struck him like a blow to the head. "How are you feeling? Better, I hope?"

She blinked. "Excuse me?"

"You fainted the other day. I thought I'd come by to check on your recovery."

A blush rose to her cheeks, and he knew he'd succeeded in flattering her. Good. Let her think she'd deceived him with her shy glances and pretty looks.

"I'm much better, thank you." She motioned toward the settee. "Shall we sit?"

Rather than answer, he sank onto the seat

without waiting for her. Puzzlement furrowed her brow as she sat next to him.

Easy, me lad. You'll never coax the truth out of her by being churlish.

Rourke immediately feigned a contrite grimace. "I'm sorry for not coming sooner. I thought it wise to give you time to recuperate before I imposed on you with my company."

"No imposition." She clasped his hand, a timid smile on her face. "Besides, your coming gives me a chance to pass along me thanks. I couldn't earlier, what with all the other women about."

He waited, hardly daring to breathe. "Oh?"

Her head bobbed so hard a curl worked loose and dangled against her cheek. He longed to stroke it back into place.

"Rourke, I've felt so alone here. So . . ." She released his hand and dropped her gaze. "I realize we haven't known each other long. Thank you for being a friend to me. I cannot tell you how grateful I am for your silence the other day."

Heaven help me! Why did it have to be her? Why couldn't the one I seek, the one who would lead me to my father's murderer, be someone else? Anyone else?

Only she could make you want *to forgive.*

The thought brought a wince. Had his quest already made him so callous? He curled his fingers into his palms. And what was it about this woman that made her so different?

"My family was always so close," she continued, her fingers working at something hidden beneath the folds of her sleeve. "Da was strong-minded and very opinionated, but he taught us to love one another, and to love the Lord. Momma was just the opposite—about being strong-minded, I mean," she clarified softly.

She smiled as though remembering. "I always thought the Lord had my ma in mind when He said a quiet spirit was something to be desired."

Like his own mother. Rourke couldn't help but recall her gentle voice and winsome smile. Both had disappeared the day they'd come home with the news that his father was dead. It was like she'd faded into herself, lost, it seemed, without her stronger half.

He cleared his throat and motioned for her to continue. "What happened to her, your mother?"

Cara dipped her head. "She died when I was very young."

"I'm sorry about that."

"Thank you."

"And . . ." He paused, framing his next question carefully. "What about your father? Or brothers and sisters?"

"I have no other family." She looked at him then, her wide eyes saying she wished she could say more.

He clenched his teeth. This was the woman who would help him to forgive?

Why do you lie, Cara? What are you hiding?

The questions danced on Rourke's tongue, itching to be spoken. He leaned toward her, close enough to smell the delicate lemon perfume that clung to her skin, to see the flecks of gold mingled with the green in her eyes. He could shake the truth from her, but kissing her until she bent to his will would be so much more pleasurable.

As though she read his thoughts, her lips parted. Just an inch closer and he'd savor their sweetness. One more breath—

"Home from church, I see."

Cara jerked back, breaking the spell that had held them both captive. Irritated, Rourke turned his head.

Deidre walked—no, *sauntered* was more the term—into the parlor, her fingers trailing over the mantel and the tops of the chairs. When she looked at them, her eyes glittered with spite. Rourke straightened, instantly on his guard.

He stood. "Good morning, Deidre."

"Mr. Walsh." She drew to a halt next to the chair opposite the settee. "Cara."

If she sensed the hostility emanating from Deidre, she made no sign. Cara simply nodded at Deidre and indicated the wing chair. "Will you join us?"

Deidre narrowed her eyes. "I will."

Amelia swept into the parlor, Ana, Breda, and Tillie on her heels. "Mr. Walsh, what a pleasure to see you. We weren't expecting a visit this morning. We were about to sit down to lunch. Will you join us?"

Frustration wound Rourke's nerves into knots. Just when he'd been about to glean the truth from Cara! Still, he managed a smile. Perhaps all wasn't lost. He'd find a moment to be alone with her, and then he'd make her tell him all. "Thank you, Amelia. I'd like that very much."

She clapped her hands, her eyes twinkling. "Wonderful. Tillie, will you ask Laverne to set another place at the table?"

"Of course." Tillie bobbed and scooted into the hallway, once again disappearing before Rourke could blink.

"Now, Rourke, how was your morning? I take it you came by to see how our Cara is feeling?" Seating herself in the floral-covered chair next to Deidre, Amelia fixed him with an interested stare.

Rourke stood until Ana and Breda had taken their seats, then resumed his place on the settee. "Yes. I was rather anxious wondering about her, though Cara insists she be fine now."

"She attended services this morning," Breda volunteered, with a smile in Cara's direction.

"Deidre was kind enough to point me in the direction of St. Paul's," Cara said.

"And what did you think of the place?" Deidre asked, her voice low. "Was it all you expected?"

Cara appeared as confused by her question as Rourke felt. She gave a small nod, though the lines that furrowed the skin between her brows remained. "It was indeed pleasant. Thank you again for recommending it."

"Pleasant. Is that all—pleasant?" Deidre leaned forward. Her fingers were surprisingly white, as though she were clenching the arms of her chair instead of resting her hands there lightly. "I would have thought you found it much more interesting than that."

"Hogwash. Why—" Breda began.

Tillie popped her head back into the room. "Lunch is ready. Laverne said we'd best eat before her stew gets cold."

"Of course." Amelia rose and beckoned the others. "Come along, then, shall we? We all know how Laverne fusses when we keep her waiting."

Rising, they followed her light laughter down the hall to the dining room, where Laverne had a hearty spread waiting. Giles, the handyman Rourke had met the day he claimed to be working for the poulterer, carried in a large soup urn and set it on the table.

Rourke took a deep whiff, savoring the whisper of sage and pepper that mingled with the beef and vegetables. His mother's kitchen had smelled like this once. Years ago.

Amelia patted a chair at the table, next to the

one occupied by Cara. "Here you are, Mr. Walsh. Please, sit."

"Thank you, Amelia." He allowed his elbow to brush Cara's arm as he sat. As desired, a flush rose to her neck, but instead of the satisfaction he expected, Rourke felt a bit ashamed of himself. Da, certainly, would not approve of his methods. And his mother?

"Your pardon," he whispered, for Cara's ears alone.

She inclined her head. The move revealed the slender line of her neck and jaw, the slight, almost perfect tilt of her chin. Rourke tore his gaze away as Amelia invited everyone to participate in blessing the food, Giles included. The handyman took the seat opposite Rourke and bowed to pray with the others.

At the last amen, Rourke lifted his head, looking everywhere but at the woman at his side. No matter how beautiful he found her, he had to keep himself focused on his reason for coming. Across the table, Deidre appeared to have taken the opposite approach. She was watching Cara like a hawk eyeing its prey. Rourke found himself leaning protectively closer.

"Rourke?"

He startled at Cara's soft voice. "Aye?"

She held the soup urn toward him. "Stew?"

He took it, flushing when his fingers brushed hers—accidentally, this time. "Thank you."

"So, Cara, how was the service at St. Paul's?" Amelia asked cheerfully, plucking a biscuit from a platter and passing it to Tillie.

"Wonderful," Cara said, though by her voice it was anything but. "I have missed our family church back home in Derry. It felt good to be in the company of other Christians."

At the last, a strange flush covered her cheeks.

Tillie had passed the platter across the table to Ana and was generously buttering a biscuit. "I've never been to St. Paul's. Deidre has, haven't you, Deidre?"

The woman nodded, accepted the platter Ana held toward her without taking anything from it, and passed it on to Giles.

"I've heard it be beautiful inside," Ana said. She dipped her spoon into her stew, took a bite, and gave a satisfied nod. "This is delicious. I'll have to tell Laverne."

Were it not for Deidre's stare, Rourke would have found the conversation entertaining. As it was, he couldn't help but feel she was biding her time, waiting to strike. He pretended to participate in the banter hopping around him, all the while keeping watch. Oddly, though he had his own reasons for mistrusting Cara, he didn't like that Deidre might, as well.

Tillie regaled them with the antics of a couple of children who'd spent the morning tickling each other in church, and with their flustered parents, who'd struggled to keep them quiet. It was the most he'd heard her speak.

Breda, too, seemed comfortable and shared how the preacher's message about redemption had touched her. Tears soaked Amelia's eyes as she listened. Obviously there was something she knew that the others didn't. Even Giles and Ana chatted happily once Laverne joined them at the table.

As the meal went on, Rourke allowed himself to relax. Perhaps his suspicions regarding Deidre were false. He didn't know her all that well, after all. It could be she was somewhat like his uncle Angus—mistrustful of everyone.

He glanced at her. Though she was following the conversation, her eyes flitting from person to person, her fingers lingered on her knife, stroking the blade in a way he found disconcerting.

At last, her hand flashed out and she gripped Tillie's arm, stopping the girl midsentence. "This has all been quite entertaining, but I really be interested in how Cara's morning went."

Cara's head lifted, her beautiful eyes wide and confused. "Your pardon, Deidre?"

"Come, Cara. You've said very little, really. What did you think of St. Paul's?" She stressed her words, pausing between each syllable and punctuating them with an iron stare.

Heavy silence settled over the table until Amelia cleared her throat. "What is this, Deidre?"

"Why, it be simple curiosity, of course," Deidre said, her smile hard. "Cara?"

"Cara already said she liked the service," Ana said, a bit defensively.

Deidre gave a regal tilt of her head. "But that is all she's said. I want to know what she thought of the sermon."

Rourke's gaze passed from Deidre to Cara. It was obvious she had a point, but she was clearly taking her time making it.

"It was . . . very good," Cara whispered.

"And did you meet anyone of interest?" Deidre pressed.

"She hardly had a chance." Though Tillie tried to sound light, her voice came out too high. It didn't help that she followed it with a nervous giggle. "It was her first visit." When Breda shook her head at her, she trailed into silence.

For some odd reason, Tillie's defense of Cara seemed to infuriate Deidre. Her face flamed to match the color of her hair. Slowly she slapped both palms on the table and leaned forward. At that moment, Rourke noticed the slender strip of cloth encircling her right hand. When had she hurt it?

"For heaven's sake," Deidre said, "it is a simple question, one I am quite sure the lass be capable of answering for herself. Well?" She directed her glare at Cara. "Did you?"

"I . . ."

She waved her hand. "Come now, don't be shy. I saw you speaking to someone."

"What do you mean, you saw me?"

"Were you spying on her, Deidre?" Ana asked, squaring her shoulders. With a just lift of her chin, she showed her outrage.

Deidre was unperturbed. "St. Paul's is the church I attend. I told Cara that this morning."

"Aye, but—"

"Besides, *spying* be more a word I'd apply to her."

"What!" Ana braced both hands on the table and matched her stance.

"I do not understand your meaning, Deidre," Cara said. "I am a Christian. Of course I went to church on the Lord's Day. Aside from that, I merely made conversation with a man who showed kindness, and asked a few questions."

"A Christian." Deidre's brow arched to form a blazing peak against her ivory skin. "What a very *Protestant* thing to say. And what, pray tell, was a Protestant doing asking questions in a Catholic church?"

"Enough!" Lifting her hand, Amelia brought the tumult to a halt. All heads turned to her, Rourke's included. Though her face had gone white, Amelia's eyes had taken on the stormy appearance of the Atlantic on a winter day. She blew out a breath, then turned to look at Ana. "Be seated, Ana."

The girl complied, her hands shaking as she retrieved her napkin and placed it in her lap.

"Thank you." Amelia turned her head and directed a firm glance at Deidre. "Cara is new, Deidre, so besides the apology you owe her for those unwarranted accusations—"

Deidre tossed her napkin on the table, scoffing. "Apology? I think not."

Rather than argue, Amelia simply stared at Deidre until the woman dropped her gaze. "Everyone is welcome here. You know that, Deidre. We make no distinctions. I hold you responsible for raising a topic you know to be forbidden at my table."

Deidre answered not, though her chin remained hard.

Amelia looked to her left and captured Breda's attention. "Will you help Laverne with the coffee? I think it best we move on to dessert."

Both Breda and Laverne nodded hastily, as though neither of them could wait to get out of the dining room.

Pushing back her chair, Deidre rose stiffly, her nose in the air. "I'm finished."

"Good," Ana said beneath her breath.

Except for the sharp look Amelia directed at her, Rourke doubted anyone else heard.

"If you do not mind, I think I'll retire to my room," Deidre said.

Amelia nodded, too graciously in Rourke's

opinion. "Of course, dear. Get some rest. I'll call you when it's time for dinner."

"No need." Deidre cut her eyes to Cara. "I've lost my appetite."

Flouncing from the table, she left the room, sliding the dining room doors behind her with a snap.

For the first time, Rourke glanced at Cara, gauging her reaction to the scene Deidre had created. Her skin had gone quite pale, and her hands, he noticed, trembled as she took the napkin from her lap and placed it on the table.

"I'm afraid I'm not very hungry anymore, either." She followed this with a weak laugh. "If you would excuse me?"

"Oh, but Laverne has made a peach cobbler from the preserves she put up last summer," Ana protested.

Tillie nodded. "It's one of her best desserts. My favorite."

"Save me a piece." Cara looked to Amelia. "Do you mind?"

Amelia leaned back in her chair, a sad smile on her face. "Of course not, dear. I truly am sorry about all of this." She glanced toward the doors where Deidre had gone. "I don't know what has gotten into her."

Unfortunately, Rourke feared he did. Deidre's words pounded through his brain, adding to the dread that had been building ever since he met

Cara. If Deidre's accusations were true, what *was* a Protestant woman doing in a Catholic church, and asking about the Fenians no less?

There could only be one answer.

Cara was a spy—but for which side?

18

Eoghan somehow managed to pry his eyelids open, even though the light filtering through his crusted lashes burned his eyes.

"Well, hello there! Glory be. I thought to never see you open your eyes again."

Confusion muddied Eoghan's thinking. Who was the woman hovering over his bed, clucking like a chicken about to meet with the angry end of an ax? He pushed up with his elbow, shook like a leaf cast about by the wind, and collapsed back onto the pillow.

"Where . . . ?" He licked his dry lips.

"Are you?" the woman finished. She pressed her wrinkled hand to her chest. "Lancaster Square. This be my home—mine and my husband, Charlie, that is."

Eoghan scanned the frayed curtains hanging from hooks at the windows and the soot covering the walls. He'd hardly call it a home. Exhausted, he let his eyes drift closed.

"That's right. Rest now."

A thin hand patted his shoulder lightly.

"I'll be back to check on you in a couple of hours."

Hours?

"No." Eoghan peeled his eyelids open again. "No, wait. Please, I must speak with ya."

The woman's wrinkled face clouded with concern. Jamming her fingers under the kerchief on her head, she scratched vigorously and then frowned. "Not sure about that, lad. You be weak as a kitten."

Lifting his head, Eoghan fixed the woman with a stare. "I beg you. I must know what happened. Where you found me. How long I've been"—he gestured around the dingy room—"here."

He managed a swallow, though with his dry throat it was more like an involuntary convulsion.

Sensing his thirst, the woman lifted a pitcher, poured a glass of water, and brought it to Eoghan's cracked lips. "Here now, take a sip of this."

Liquid relief slipped down his throat. Too soon she pulled the cup away and dried the dribble from his chin with the back of her hand.

"That's enough for now. Wouldn't want ya overdoing it." She laughed—a thin, rasping sound —then took a cloth from the washbasin and laid it over his forehead. "How's that?"

"Heaven."

Indeed, it was. Were it not for the fact that he felt the seconds ticking away, he'd have languished beneath the comfort of the cool rag. Instead, he patted the bed beside him, inviting the woman to sit.

She did, though her slight weight was barely enough to rustle the ticking.

"Now," said Eoghan, gathering his strength, "tell me everything."

"Not much to tell," she replied with a shrug. "Charlie and I had gone to fetch wood for the fire"—she motioned toward the stone hearth—"and we saws ya lying in the road, your life's blood seeping onto the cobbles."

She shuddered, an act Eoghan would have copied had he the strength. He closed his eyes, fighting to remember.

A blast that split the night. Fiery heat that ripped from his shoulder down his back. "I was shot."

The woman—Maggie, his memory supplied—nodded. "Whoever did it thought to kill ya. Snuck up on ya from behind, they did. Guess that's why my Charlie and I was so keen on helping ya. Neither of us care for that particular brand of cowardice." Her saggy lips puckered in a frown.

Eoghan had seen . . . and done . . . worse. He cleared his throat. "Maggie, did you see anyone? The shooter, did he leave any clues?"

More scratching. "Charlie thought he caught a

glimpse, but just a small one. Before he could call out, they were gone." She sniffed. "Good thing we came by. They might have finished the job otherwise."

Her sneer revealed yellowed, uneven teeth. Were it not for the kindness shining from her face, he'd have felt repulsed. She patted his hand and stood.

"Maggie, wait—"

Turning, she shook her head at him. "I'll be back. Just going to fetch Charlie. He's gonna want to hear what ya have to say as well as I."

Her cotton skirt swished as she moved to the door and stuck her head out. Eoghan used the respite to catch his breath, gather his strength. In a moment, Maggie returned, her husband in tow.

Hitching his thumbs into the waistband of his ragged trousers, Charlie rocked back on his heels and gave a nod. "Well, lad. Glad to see you be feeling better."

Better? Eoghan rolled his shoulder, gasped at the searing pain that struck straight to his lungs, and collapsed against the pillow. He was alive, not necessarily better.

"How long have I been here?"

Charlie spat on the floor, adding to the grime caking the place. It was a wonder Eoghan hadn't died of infection.

"Eight days, near 'bouts." He cocked an eyebrow at Maggie, who nodded in agreement.

Eight days. Eoghan bit back a groan.

"Any idea who done this to ya?" Charlie asked, sinking onto a rickety stool next to the bed.

The possibilities were too many to count. The shooter could have been anyone. Eoghan shook his head.

"What could they have been after?" Maggie chimed. " 'Cept for your clothes and a couple of coins in your pocket, you had no other belongings. We didn't even know your name, where ya come from, for the longest time, 'cept what ya was able to tell us when ya were half-conscious."

Thinking so hard raised beads of sweat on Eoghan's brow. Maggie took the cloth, rinsed it in the basin, and replaced it on his head.

"No, I . . ."

He had very little money to carry, no watch or jewelry of any kind. Except for . . .

He lifted his arm and stared in horror at his wrist.

"O-wen?" Maggie struggled with his name, pronouncing it in syllables, slowly, like she was daft. "What is it? What's wrong?"

For a moment he couldn't speak. Could only stare. Finally he licked his lips and managed a raspy "My bracelet."

Maggie glanced at Charlie and back. "What bracelet?"

"It was on my wrist when . . . have you seen it?" He threw his gaze about the room, searching.

Helplessness twisted her features. "There, lad, I'm sure it'll turn up." She patted his hand. "Charlie can look for ya, back on the street where we found ya, ain't that right, Charlie?"

His grizzled head bobbed. "Sure, lad. Dinna trouble yourself."

Eoghan refused to be comforted. Whoever shot him and left him for dead hadn't bothered to check his pockets for gold. In fact, the only thing they'd taken had no value whatsoever but what it meant to its owner.

And that could only mean one thing.

The shooter knew who he was—and what the bracelet meant. No doubt he owed his life to Charlie and Maggie's timely interruption. Otherwise, they'd have taken more than his bracelet. On top of that, they had an eight-day head start on finding Cara. But why? Why did they care if he had a sister, or whether or not she was in the city?

Helplessness and fear settled in his gut, adding to the queasiness he'd been fighting since he woke. Cara was in danger. Why and from whom was a question he couldn't begin to answer, at least not until he'd regained his strength. In the meantime, he had to try and get in touch with her, somehow send her a warning.

He rolled his head on the pillow and clasped Maggie's hand. He didn't know her or Charlie, but they'd saved his life.

He had to trust them.

Her eyes widened, revealing the milky edges of her pupils.

"Maggie," he said, urgency making his throat tight. "There's something I be needing ya to do."

19

Though the weather had cleared and a bright sun held the promise of spring, it was still cold. Every evening, frost painted the windows with icy fingers that crept through the sash, challenging the warmth radiating from the fireplace. Running her thumb over the binding of the book she held, Cara sighed and replaced it on the shelf. Her thoughts were in far too much of a jumble to concentrate.

The boardinghouse was quiet, with everyone wrapped in individual pursuits. Left to her own devices, Cara had sought the privacy of the library after supper. A soft knock sounded on the door, and then Rourke poked his head through.

"Cara?"

She turned, her hands clasped behind her back. "Aye?"

"May I come in?"

She only hesitated a moment. Having someone —anyone—to talk to might lessen the tension building in her chest. Which wasn't entirely true, she realized with a start. She was glad Rourke had come. She nodded and bid him enter, then joined him in front of the fire.

"Are you all right, lass?" Rourke said as each of them claimed a seat before the dancing flames. "Not still bothered by the things Deidre said the other day, I hope?"

More like the things she did not know—why Deidre hated her, who The Celt was and where she could find him, and why her brother had still not come.

Rourke's eyes were gentle as he peered at her. From the moment she'd arrived in this country, he'd been nothing but kind. Longing to confide in him tugged at Cara's heart. Her mouth went dry sorting through the things she could and could not say. She concentrated on his question. "I . . . confess, her words pricked me."

They more than pricked. Somehow she sensed Rourke knew that as he studied her, his gaze warm and steady. How good it felt to know someone cared! Tears threatened, but afraid of revealing too much she blinked them away.

Rourke smiled. "You did well not to allow her to goad you into responding."

In fact, it was the desire to protect Eoghan that had kept her silent. Suddenly the need for secrecy weighed heavily on her, making her weary to her bones. She sighed.

Rourke leaned forward, his head cocked to one side. "What is it?"

Nothing she could tell him. Her chest felt tight, squeezed until even the simple act of breathing was painful. Unable to bear sitting any longer, she rose and went to the window. The glass cooled her brow, if not the unease raging inside.

Rourke's voice was a soft whisper over her shoulder. "Cara? What's wrong?" When she didn't answer, he placed his hand on her arm and gently turned her to face him. "Tell me."

He was so close, his voice so sweet and tender. Even better, his hand lingered, igniting a fire that spread slowly through her veins. A few more seconds and she'd be unable to resist telling him everything. "I can't . . . that is . . ." Biting her lip, she trailed into silence.

How deep and intense his eyes appeared to be, how shadowed by urgency. She cast about in her mind for a way of escape.

Eoghan, where are you?

Rourke cleared his throat. "There was a time when claiming faith for myself was difficult."

Afraid to speak, she waited, silent.

Rourke moved away, but only slightly, and leaned his back against the windowsill. Arms folded, he still filled the entire frame. He looked so strong standing there, as though he could shoulder any burden a person cared to lay upon him. She licked her lips and rubbed the spot where his hand had been.

"My da . . ." He paused and started again.

"When my da passed away, many of the things in which I'd placed my faith disappeared. It was a difficult time for me."

"What happened to him?"

He flicked her a sharp glance. "He died. That is all."

She couldn't hide the hurt his words caused. About to look away, she saw his features soften.

"He was betrayed and it led to his murder."

He opened up to her! Why, she didn't know, but she wasn't so daft not to suspect what his vulnerability cost him. Tempted to reach out to him, she swallowed and shook her head. "Oh, Rourke, I'm so sorry."

He studied her a moment, the conflict warring inside him evident in the hard line of his jaw and white lips. He left the window and turned his back on her. His agitated stride carried him quickly to the fireplace.

"I have spent years searching for the man who betrayed him. It has consumed me, Cara, made me bitter. Unable to forgive." The seconds ticked by on the mantel clock. His voice lowered. "But then you came . . ."

Cara held her breath as he turned and moved toward her, not touching but caressing her with his gaze.

"Then you came, and I thought of something besides revenge."

"Rourke—"

"I tell you this because I want you to know there be nothing you need fear saying to me, even if it is difficult. Even if the truth of it makes you feel disloyal."

Which explained the battle she'd seen reflected in his eyes. She was a distraction, and that made him feel disloyal to his father.

But was she only a distraction?

She'd never know unless she first proved that she trusted him. She sensed it deep inside. A muscle in his jaw ticked as he watched her— wondering, no doubt, if she would return the faith he'd placed in her by opening up to him.

Do not trust him! You do not know enough about who he is, what he be doing here.

You know enough. Look into his eyes. See the goodness of his soul.

Two voices argued inside her head, both drowning out the even smaller voice that pleaded with her to seek out a higher wisdom. Ignoring them all, she gave in to the stirring in her gut that wanted to trust Rourke.

She twisted her laced fingers. "I have been lying to you . . . to everyone."

No surprise flickered in his gaze. It remained steady, prompting her to go on. "About?"

"My reasons for coming to America."

His silence urged harder than his questions.

"Please don't ask me more." She covered her face with her hands.

A moment later, Rourke pulled them away. With the tip of his finger he rubbed aside the tears clinging to her lashes. "Tell me about your childhood."

"What?"

"Were you happy growing up in Ireland?"

Relief flooded her. He wouldn't press, and that released the tension from her shoulders. Taking her hand, he drew her back to the fire. This time she allowed the cheery blaze to warm her bones.

"I grew up in a happy home. We didn't have much, but we had enough. Da always saw to that. And Ma, she saw to the rest."

"The rest?"

"She made sure our spirits were fed, after she nourished our bodies. It was always important to her that we knew the Lord, and that He knew us. 'God's help is nearer than the door,' she used to say." Cara smiled as she recollected how her mother's voice raised them from their beds on the Sabbath and urged them on to church.

"Your mother must have been a faithful woman."

"She was, but do not mistake me. Da was faithful, too, after a fashion. He was always just more—" she cast about for the word and finally found it—"legalistic."

Rourke quirked a brow.

A familiar weight settled on her heart. "Da

loved the church. Ma loved the Lord. I grew up knowing the difference."

He appeared startled by the matter-of-factness of her tone. It quickly dissolved into curiosity. "So what happened?"

Though Rourke's question was meant to be an innocent query about her parents, inside the words struck a different chord. She claimed to have grown up knowing the difference between religion and a relationship with God. What happened? When was the last time she'd experienced intimacy with her Savior? Or thought of anything but reclaiming her relationship with her brother?

Shame burned her cheeks.

"Cara?"

"I'm sorry. It's just, thinking about the past . . ." She ducked her head to hide her face.

Outside, the howling of the wind echoed the keening in her heart. To her surprise, Rourke placed a finger under her chin and lifted until she looked at him.

"It's not too late."

She swallowed, not trusting herself to speak.

"God will not hold your absence against you. He's waiting for you to come back." He gave a wry grin and dropped his hand. "I say this to myself as much as to you."

Something about the wistfulness of his words struck straight to her heart. Instead of closing him to her, his clasped hands and bowed head showed his vulnerability—and his pain. Gathering her courage, she reached out and touched his arm.

"Thank you," she whispered.

He nodded, but refused to look at her. When he finally did, there was a new understanding between them. She sensed it, and knew by the warmth in his expression that he did, too. It felt good. Too good. She needed to create some space.

Her skirt rustled softly as she stood. "Shall we find the others?"

He rose, too, but the movement only brought them closer. She smelled the clean, masculine scent of him, felt the energy that rolled from him in waves. Oh, but she could lose herself in his arms!

And in his eyes.

He winked, an almost roguish grin on his lips as he swept his hand toward the door. "After you."

Her breathing quickened. Sweat dampened her palms. Her heart beat an erratic rhythm. Who was she fooling, she thought as she walked on shaking legs toward the hall.

She was lost already.

20

Time was growing short. Each passing day tightened the urgency in Hugh's chest, increased the frantic need to act stirring in his muscles until the itch nearly drove him mad. Or perhaps he was mad already.

Growling, he punched his fist into the palm of his other hand. How long could he wait? How much longer? He'd lost one chance to rid himself of the threat to his secret. Two, he reminded himself with a low snarl. A second more and he'd have ended Eoghan Hamilton's worthless life a fortnight ago on the city's snow-covered streets. Thanks to a couple of meddlesome gnats, he was left to wonder if Eoghan still lived. Which made silencing Cara Hamilton all the more vital.

The back door to the boardinghouse swung open and a plump woman with the face of a hound stepped out. Hugh lunged into the shadows. A hairsbreadth later and he'd have moved too late. She'd have spotted him. Limbs quivering, he watched from the crook formed between the outhouse and a wall of split wood as she emptied a pail of dishwater on the ground. A moment later, a squatty fellow with an ax slung over his shoulder rounded the corner whistling.

His presence wrought an immediate change in the hound-faced woman's demeanor. She straightened and pasted a smile to her lips, her chubby fingers patting her hair into place.

"Good day to you, Giles," she said, bobbing like a debutante.

"Why, Mrs. Bennett. You're looking fair this morning."

More patting. "Thank you, sir."

Chuckling, Giles set the ax aside and took the pail from her limp fingers, his touch on her hand lingering a second too long. When she blushed, he ambled to the well. Five quick pumps and water streamed from the spout.

"So, Mrs. Bennett, heard you had a spot of trouble between the boarders," Giles said, filling the pail and lumbering with it to her side.

Mrs. Bennett clucked like a hen. "Terrible, that. Never had so much bickering in the boardinghouse before. It has me at me wits' end, I tell ya."

"There now, it can't be that bad. Nothing you kinna manage, eh?" He winked and handed her the freshly filled pail.

"I cannot say as I can, Giles," she replied, wagging her head until the mobcap she wore flopped over one eye. "It be frightful bad, the things I see happening. Every bit of it."

The door opened a second time and the target of Hugh's attention stepped out. He leaned forward. She was tall and graceful, slender in a simple cotton dress that hugged her hips.

"Good morning, Laverne. Giles."

Both heads bobbed in response to Cara's greeting.

She glanced up at the sky. "Nice to see the snow has finally let up. I'm more than ready for a few warm days."

"Aye. Still a mite cool in the evenings, though," Giles said, scratching his ragged beard with gnarled fingers. "I'll be taking you and Miss Ana in the carriage today, if that's all right."

Cara rubbed her hands over her arms. "That would be lovely. Thank you, Giles." She put a finger to her chin. "Oh, and Amelia asked me to tell you that the woodbox in the parlor is running low."

He touched the rim of his cap with his forefinger. "I'll take care of it this afternoon."

"Thank you, Giles." A smile and a wink and she disappeared through the door.

Giles patted his broad belly, then grabbed his ax and slung it over his shoulder. "Such a nice gal. Hate to think of the trouble she's seen."

"Trouble?"

"What brought her to America."

Mrs. Bennett's mobcap fluttered with her nod. "Same kind as what brings 'em all, I suppose."

"Even you?" He winked and chuckled low in his throat.

Her laughter matching his, Mrs. Bennett flapped her apron at him. "Go on with you now. The lasses will be waiting."

A couple more words, whispered so only Mrs. Bennett could hear, and Giles departed, the woman's laughter ringing on the chilly air.

Hugh's eyes narrowed. He'd watched the routine at the boardinghouse for several days now, and for several days it was always the same: breakfast, followed by Mrs. Bennett chatting in the backyard with Giles, then the occupants of the boardinghouse leaving for their prospective places of employment and returning before dark. But sometimes, on mornings like this one, Giles drove two of the women, Ana and Cara, to a chandler's shop located a couple of miles down Ashberry Street. They had the farthest distance to travel, he reasoned.

Regardless, it provided him with an opportunity.

A smile parted Hugh's lips as he eased away from the woodpile. Tomorrow, then, if the weather held. Tomorrow he'd rid himself once and for all of the troublesome Cara Hamilton.

21

Cara shivered, thankful that for the second time in two days, Giles would be delivering them to the candle shop in the carriage. Though the snow had ceased falling, the temperature continued to plummet, as indicated by the woodboxes that emptied faster than normal and the patch of ice in front of the boardinghouse that seemed to build while she watched. But what was troubling for her provided hours of enjoyment for the children from the tenement across the street.

Two boys slid by, laughing as they skated their way down the length of sidewalk, then turned and did the same coming back. Before long a line formed, and several children took turns on the icy walk.

Mindful of flailing arms, Cara stepped out of harm's way, smiling. Were it not for her thin boots, she might have joined them. As it was, her toes already felt numb. She clapped her mittened hands together to warm them. What could be keeping Ana and Giles?

"Miss?"

Cara startled at the unexpected voice. A few feet away stood a stooped woman, a soiled scrap of cloth that substituted for a scarf covering her head, and a ragged wool coat draped over her scarecrow-like shoulders.

Cara glanced about and then back at the woman. She pointed at herself. "Me?"

The woman bobbed her head and shuffled closer. "By any chance, be your name Cara?"

Mistrust made the hair on Cara's arms stand on end. She eased away until she reached the boardinghouse stairs. "Do I know you?"

"Not me, but perhaps we have a mutual friend. From Ireland." The woman's lips stretched into a smile that was probably meant to ease her fears, but the yellowed teeth . . .

Cara shuddered. "I'm sorry. You must have me mistaken—"

"I've checked every boardinghouse on Ashberry Street." She jabbed her finger at Amelia's front door. "This and one other place down the block a piece are the last I've left to try."

She waited, peering at Cara through slightly narrowed eyes. "No? Well, ain't no hair off my back. All I can do is tell 'im I tried."

She turned, still muttering, her ragged skirt making dirty swirls in the snow.

"Wait." Cara put out a hand to stop her. "Who will you tell? Who sent you?"

The children's merry voices faded, but the woman seemed not to notice as she ambled back, her bushy gray brows drawn in a frown. "All right then. Are ya the Cara girl, or ain't ya?"

Cara swallowed her apprehension and nodded. "I'm Cara. Who sent you?"

The woman shook her head and propped her fists on her hips. "Uh-uh-uh. First, your arm."

"My what?"

She thrust out her hand, her grime-caked nails curling like claws. "Let me see your arm."

A tremor weakened Cara's knees as the woman bent close and clasped her wrist in her bony fingers. Grunting, she shoved Cara's sleeve up her arm, twisted this way and that, and then did the same with the other. Finally she released her with a sigh. "You're not her. Sorry for your time."

Confusion kept Cara frozen in place like the icicles clinging to the boardinghouse roof. She didn't know the woman ambling away, had no idea if she could trust her, yet . . . something pushed her past the throng of children after her. When she reached her, she caught her by the elbow and yanked her to a stop.

"Wait!"

The woman eyed her angrily.

Dimly aware of Giles pulling around the boardinghouse in the carriage, Cara fumbled in the pocket of her coat until her fingers closed around her bracelet. Tearing it free, she held it aloft. "Is this what you were looking for?"

The hardness melted from the woman's face. Once again her lips split in a smile. "Cara. Cara Hamilton?"

Inside, Cara's heart beat like a hammer against her chest. She nodded.

The woman leaned closer. "I've been searching everywhere for ya, lass. I've a message from—"

"Look out!"

Terrified neighing mingled with the shouts of scattering children. Whirling, Cara watched in horror as a milk wagon thundered down the street straight toward Giles.

"Whoa!" the driver yelled, to no avail. The wagon's wheels skidded on the ice-packed street. The horse scrambled to recover its footing, but only succeeded in stumbling and scraping both knees in a frantic effort to right itself.

"Giles!"

Cara's warning came too late. The two vehicles collided and erupted in an explosion of splintered wood and screaming horses.

Springing forward, Cara grabbed a handful of children by the arms and shoved them out of the way of the horses' flashing hooves. The poor animals were so frightened, they kicked and struggled blindly against their harnesses. And where were the drivers?

Fortunately, the vendors who'd begun unpacking their wares along the street saw what had happened and hurried toward them. One of the men grabbed Giles's horse by the bridle and eased the trembling beast to its feet. A second man did the same to the milk-wagon horse. Still, the clamor of voices and questions escalated.

"Did anyone see what happened?"

"Is anyone hurt?"

"The drivers. Where are the drivers?"

"Here. There's one over here."

A thin man wobbled to his feet and rubbed a knobby palm over his head. "I'm fine. Fine." He blew out a breath. "Blimey, I don't know what happened. Never seen my animal spook like that."

A woman's voice rose above them all. "What about the children? Are they accounted for?"

"They're all here."

Nausea rolled in Cara's stomach. The force of the collision had driven both vehicles over the walk, straight onto the spot where she'd been standing. She, and a score of innocent children. But where was Giles?

Now that the horses had been freed from their rigging, she inched toward the overturned carriage closest to her, the one driven by Giles. It lay on its side, the wheels still spinning.

"Giles?" Her shaky whisper drifted on the frosty air, drowned out by the clamoring voices echoing off the boardinghouse walls. "Giles?"

The boardinghouse door flung open, and Ana, shocked and upset, tripped down the steps. "Cara! What happened? Are you all right—?" She broke off and clapped her hand over her mouth.

Following the direction of her stare, Cara eased around to her side of the carriage.

Giles's hand poked out from under the seat, limp and sprawled at an ugly angle. Worse, the pristine ice beneath him was steadily giving way to a sickening circle of red.

Unable to tear her eyes away, Cara fumbled blindly until she encountered Ana's arm. Grasping hold, she shoved her toward the boardinghouse. "Go. Find Amelia and . . . Laverne." Ana didn't move. Cara spun to face her. "Go, Ana! Get help."

Ana whirled, skirt flying, and sped up the steps.

Cara dropped onto the icy sidewalk near Giles's hand. "He's over here!" she shouted in answer to the continued query about the other driver's whereabouts. "Under the carriage. He's trapped."

She tried but couldn't quite block the gasps of horror that rose from the women gathering. Touching Giles's fingers, she breathed a sigh of relief that they were still warm.

"Giles, don't worry. We're going to get you out." His fingers twitched. She threw her head back to stare at the men gathering around the carriage. "Please hurry."

"We'll get 'im out, miss," a stout fellow said. He beckoned to the growing crowd. "Come on, lads. Let's see if we can't get this here buggy off 'im."

She heard the barked orders, sensed when the rest of the boardinghouse residents joined the watching crowd, even picked out Laverne's wail from the others. Ignoring them all, Cara clasped Giles's hand and concentrated on praying for his life.

"You might want to move, miss," the stout fellow said, laying his large hand upon her shoulder. "If this buggy should slip while we're trying to lift it . . ."

She shook her head and squeezed Giles's fingers tight. "Please, just get it off him." Her gaze flew upward. "Unless I'm in your way?"

His head wagged. "It's your own safety I'm worried about."

"I'll be fine. Please, hurry."

He lifted a brow, then shrugged and turned to the others. "All right, blokes. You heard her. Let's get this here thing moved."

Slowly, agonizingly so, the men circled the carriage. It moved only slightly at first, not even enough to slide Giles out from underneath, just enough for someone to peek.

"Easy, fellas," a man's voice said. Whose voice, Cara couldn't tell. It came from the other side of the carriage.

"Where's his head?" another asked.

"That way. Toward the rear."

"Get more men on that end, then."

"Careful on the ice."

"Someone fetch some salt so we can get a foothold."

Feet shuffled and then someone threw salt,

dirt, and ashes over the ice. Where it came from was a mystery. So, too, were the things the men said. Cara's prayers blocked them out.

But even with her eyes closed, she sensed when Rourke arrived.

The energy that rolled off of him forced her to look up. Their eyes met—his shockingly blue against the gray sky. Blue, like a promise from heaven, or at the very least an answer to prayer.

Instantly, tears burned the backs of her eyelids. "Rourke!"

His palm cupped her cheek. "Are you hurt?"

Her knees shook. Rourke was there. Everything would be all right. "It's Giles . . ." She looked at the hand clutched in hers.

Rourke nodded, then shifted to brace both feet.

"On three," the stout fellow shouted. "We all lift together. Move the buggy toward the street."

Rourke's hands went under the carriage next to her. Determination made his face look as though it had been carved from stone.

"One . . ."

Even with the cold air, sweat formed on Rourke's brow. Cara added him to her prayers.

"Two . . ."

Lord, give them all strength . . .

"Three!"

The carriage groaned. Or perhaps it was the men. Or Giles. Either way, the sound rasped in

Cara's ears and sent a shiver down her spine. Ages later, the carriage was moved and Giles was free.

Laverne hurtled down the steps. "How is he? Is he hurt bad? Giles!"

Rourke caught her and kept her from flinging herself over Giles's limp body. "It's all right, Mrs. Bennett. He'll be all right. Has the doctor been called?"

Amelia nodded. "I sent Breda and Deidre to fetch him."

"Good." Rourke motioned to a couple of the men still standing by. "Help me get him inside."

He turned to Laverne. "The doctor will be needing some fresh blankets. Maybe some bandages and hot water. Can you manage it?"

She could only give a numb nod at first, and then she flushed red and bobbed her head more decidedly. "Of course I can, if it'll help Giles."

She rushed up the stairs faster than Cara had ever seen her move. Grabbing Tillie's arm, Laverne shoved her through the open door. "Come on, girl. I'm going to need your help."

Gratitude shone on Amelia's face as she peered up at Rourke. "What can I do?"

"Find him a place to lie down."

"The parlor. It's closest. Ana and I will ready the settee." She clasped Ana's hand and the two women disappeared inside.

Apart from the dwindling crowd, that left just

200

Cara, Rourke, and the three men waiting to help carry Giles inside.

She squeezed Rourke's arm. "Is he . . . ? How bad is he?"

"No way of telling, lass. We'll have to wait on the doctor." He paused and laid his hand over Cara's. "You did good staying by him like you did. I'm sure 'twas a comfort to the old man."

His words were few, but they filled Cara with relief. So, too, the wink he gave her that she somehow sensed was meant to be reassuring.

She stepped back and let the men carry Giles inside. Only when she crossed the threshold to follow did she think to look for the woman who had spoken to her on the street. In fact, it was the woman who had spared Cara injury, for had she not followed after her, she'd have been standing in the very spot where the carriages collided.

The crowd had thinned, driven away most likely by the cold and lack of interest now that the carriages had been cleared and the drivers removed. Still, a few heartier souls remained, a couple of the men pointing and waving with enthusiasm as they reenacted the accident.

But the woman?

Cara searched up and down the street for a glimpse of her ragged coat.

She was nowhere to be found.

22

"He has a concussion. Some scrapes and bruises. But it's his arm I'm most worried about." Dr. Nelson straightened like a reed recovering from a brisk wind. "It's a bad break. Clear through the skin. I've set the bone, bandaged him up the best I can. You'll have to keep it clean and fresh, watch for signs of infection. When he wakes"—he pulled a brown-colored bottle from his medicine bag—"give him a spoonful of this mixed in water. It'll help with the pain. Call for me if he begins showing signs of nausea. Any questions?"

Rourke scanned the row of women listening with rapt attention to every word the doctor uttered. Except for Laverne. She huddled on a stool at Giles's side, crooning softly as she smoothed the graying hair from his forehead.

Amelia took the bottle and clasped it to her chest. "None. Thank you ever so much, Doctor."

He tipped his head. "No thanks necessary."

The doctor was a stern enough looking fellow, with raven hair and black eyebrows that slashed across his thin face. Still, there was a gentleness about him that shone from his gray eyes and manifested in his touch. Rourke had never seen anyone move with such care. Giles had barely let go a whimper while the doctor tended his wounds. Of course, it was probably a blessing that he'd remained unconscious throughout the setting of his broken arm.

And Cara . . .

Rourke marveled at the way she'd handled the situation—so confident and reassuring, she'd comforted the others in the room with nary a word, even assisting the doctor when he asked.

He added admiration to the growing list of things he liked about her, then carved it free with an inward snarl.

He didn't *like* her. Couldn't admire her. What he needed to do was find out all he could about her. Fast.

His tools packed, Dr. Nelson slipped into his coat and moved with his bag to the door. Laying a finger to the brim of his hat, he said, "Good day, ladies. Mrs. Matheson." He turned for a last glance at Rourke. "Mr. Walsh."

"Doctor."

When he'd gone, the women released a collective sigh.

"Thank the Lord he be all right," Breda said, clapping a hand on Amelia's arm. "Giles and me have had our disagreements, but this old place wouldn't be the same without 'im."

"No, it wouldn't," Amelia agreed. She cast a grateful glance at Rourke. "I can't thank you enough for your help."

He dismissed her thanks with a shrug. "It was nothing."

"Nothing or not, I'm glad you were there." Amelia motioned toward Ana and Cara. "Come now, girls. Let's give Giles a chance to rest. Laverne, will you be all right?"

The normally rotund cook looked like a half-baked loaf of bread, puffy and limp on one side, sunken in the middle. "We'll be fine. Thank you, Amelia."

Amelia wrapped her in a hug before leading the others from the parlor and closing the doors.

Cara paused in the hallway. "Where's Deidre?"

"She and Tillie went on to the milliner. There wasn't anything they could do here, so I told them they might as well," Amelia said, drawing her hand across her brow.

She looked tired, even slightly pale, as though the day's events had drained her of strength. Turning, she started for the kitchen. "Would anyone care for a cup of tea?"

Cara and Ana glanced at each other. Cara spoke. "Mr. O'Bannon will be expecting us."

Amelia cut her short with a wave. "There's no sense even going to the candle shop now. It's almost quarter of twelve. James will understand. Let's sit for a bit and grab something to eat. You, too, Mr. Walsh, unless you have somewhere you need to be?"

In fact, his business was here, but he could

hardly tell her that. Rourke agreed with a nod and trailed the others to the kitchen. Bustling to a monstrous cast-iron stove hunched against one wall, Breda muttered and clucked as she took a kettle from the back burner and filled it with water.

Amelia motioned the others to the table. "Sit, all of you. I'll fetch us something to eat. I think Laverne has bread around here somewhere."

She found it, along with a round of cheese and some freshly churned butter, and set everything on the table with a knife. "It's not much. Then again, I never claimed to have Laverne's skills." She gave a weak laugh that ended in a sigh.

"It's plenty," Ana said, reaching for the knife.

Cara slid her arm around Amelia's waist. "I doubt we could eat much, anyway."

Amelia's hand fluttered to cover her midsection in what looked like subconscious agreement. The room fell into dismal quiet, with only the hissing of the teakettle to break the silence.

Finally, Rourke clapped his hands and stood. "All right then. No sense sitting around here. Breda, how is the woodbox?"

She gave a shrug. "Low. Giles didn't have time to fill it."

Rolling up his sleeves, Rourke headed for the back door. "I'll see to it. Give a holler when that tea be ready."

He winked, and Breda blushed as he slipped outside. A short while later the woodbox was full, with a stack of split wood piled next to the door. A fine sheen covered Rourke's brow, but it felt good to do something with his hands. Something pure. Honest.

He swung the ax one last time, sending two halves of a log flying.

"You're good at that. You must have had some practice." Framed in the half-open door, Cara was a vision in her dark green dress. Her eyes sparkled as she smiled at him.

Pausing, Rourke leaned on the ax with one hand and wiped the sweat from his brow with the other. "I've had enough."

"Breda says the tea is ready. I would tell you to come in and warm yourself by the fire, but you look plenty warm already. This should cool you off." An impish grin on her face, she bent and scooped up a handful of snow, then chucked it at him before ducking into the kitchen.

He chuckled as he washed the dust from his palms with a handful of snow and then followed her inside. The time had allowed the women to collect themselves, and he was pleased to see them chatting as they carved slices from the cheese round and buttered several slices of bread. Amelia had produced a slab of ham and stood at the counter cutting it into portions. Breda filled several teacups and set them on the sideboard. One by one they helped themselves to a plate and sat at the table to eat.

"How is Giles? Has anyone checked?" Rourke asked when he'd finished and brushed the crumbs from his fingers onto his plate.

"Awake," Amelia said. "Laverne came in to let us know."

She put the finishing touches on a thick ham sandwich, added a steaming cup of broth, and laid them both out on a tray. Ana scooped up the lot and carried it to the door. "I'll take this to him, but I doubt Laverne will want to give up care of him for even a moment." She gave a wink and pushed the door open with her foot. "I'll be back shortly."

In the same moment, the kitchen erupted with activity. Cara stood and collected the dishes from the table, Amelia wrapped and stored the remaining food, and Breda emptied the water from the wash bucket into the sink to allow the dishes to soak.

Feeling rather useless, Rourke stepped outside and cleared the snow and ice from the walk to make it easier for them to navigate without fear of slipping, then strode toward the stable. The mare Giles used to pull the carriage had been rubbed down and fed, but her stall needed cleaning. The carriage itself needed considerable repair—work Rourke doubted Giles would be able to see to for some time, at least until his arm healed.

An idea formed in Rourke's head.

Setting to work, he tended the minor scratches on the mare's hindquarters and legs, then mucked out the stable and spread fresh straw. When he finished, he searched the feed bins for corn, found some, and filled a bucket that he carried to the hen house. He scattered a healthy portion on the ground, which the hens pecked up in a flurry of beating wings and loud squawks. If chickens could think, they were probably glad to see him and wondered why their meal was so late.

He replaced the feed bucket and then took care of the hogs and Amelia's milk cow in equal measure. Funny how he'd never stopped to consider it, but it made sense that the owner of a boardinghouse would own livestock.

Vegetables were another story, however. There were signs of a garden poking through the snow, but it wasn't large, and he assumed what produce she served in the winter months was purchased from the vendors that lined Ashberry Street. That, and coal, he quickly realized, taking note of a chute built into the back of the boardinghouse. Like most New Yorkers, Amelia probably depended heavily on the stuff, since it was more readily available than wood.

His steps light, he made his way to the stable to take stock of the damage to the carriage. He'd need to have a list of duties handy when he took his idea to Amelia.

Cara smiled as she watched Rourke carry yet another armload of kindling to the fireplace in the library. He'd been so industrious all morning, he had all of the woodboxes brimming again.

Amelia noticed it, too. She patted Rourke's shoulder as he stood and repeated her thanks. "You've been such a blessing to us, dear. I can't seem to thank you enough."

Rourke shook his head. "No thanks necessary. I do not mind the work."

He smiled, but something about the way he hesitated made Cara think there was a deeper meaning to his words.

"At the very least, you must let me pay you for your trouble," Amelia insisted, reaching for the small chain purse fastened at her waist. "You've lost an entire day's wages because of us. Certainly I don't know what we would have done if you hadn't been here."

She trailed off and bit her lip as if it suddenly occurred to her that with Giles's injury, she would be without a handyman. And why not? It had only just occurred to Cara. She looked over at Amelia, who appeared to be mulling over her dilemma.

"I'm only glad I could help." Rourke replaced the lid on the woodbox with a firm shove, then spread his hands wide. "Is there anything else I can do before I go? Anything at all? I won't mind helping if I can."

Still biting her lip, Amelia shook her head. "I don't think so. Giles keeps most things well tended."

"But he is going to be laid up a good while," Rourke said. "At least, according to the doctor."

He paused, and to Cara's thinking it was to let his meaning sink in.

Rourke cleared his throat and fiddled with the collar of his shirt. "Amelia, have you given thought to what you will do while Giles recovers?"

"What do you mean?" Cara said before Amelia could ask.

"There be much work to running a boarding-house," Rourke said. "Not to mention the repairs the carriage will be needing."

"Oh! I hadn't even considered the carriage," Amelia said, wringing her hands.

Rourke's head bobbed. "I took a look while I was cleaning out the stable." He paused, just a split second, but long enough that Cara suspected it was intentional. "I'm quite handy with a hammer. If you're interested, I'd be willing to take over as your handyman for a while. Just until Giles is back on his feet," he clarified quickly.

The uneasiness grew in Cara's stomach. Hadn't she been glad to see him when he appeared next to her on the street? What changed?

She licked her lips and addressed Amelia. "Are we sure that's necessary? Giles's injuries are not extensive."

Amelia shook her head. "No, Rourke is right. Giles will be very limited in what he will be able to do, even after he's back on his feet. Besides, I wouldn't want him overdoing it, as he'll be wont to do unless we get him some help." She smiled and stuck out her hand. "You have yourself a deal, Mr. Walsh, and thankful I am to you for suggesting it."

Rourke accepted her hand and gave it a slight shake. "I'll stop by tomorrow morning so we can work out the details."

"Nonsense," Amelia said, her smile broadening. "I have plenty of rooms here. If you're agreeable, I can include it, plus meals, in your pay."

"I'm agreeable," Rourke said, inclining his head. He stepped back and grabbed his coat from the arm of the couch. "In fact, I'll just collect a few of my things and return tonight."

Amelia clapped her hands in delight, relieved, no doubt, to have her problem so quickly and easily resolved. But it wasn't Amelia's actions that bothered Cara. It was the glimmer that shone in Rourke's eyes as he looked at her that made Cara think things had worked out exactly as he'd hoped.

Rourke shoved his arms into the sleeves of his coat and made his way to the door, said his good-byes, and left. It was then that Cara realized what troubled her so.

He was polite. He touched his cap and nodded to them both as he scooted through the door.

But he never once looked her in the eyes.

23

Scurrying through the back streets of New York, Hugh scowled. Blast the Hamilton woman's luck. Twice now, he'd had her in his grasp, and twice she'd escaped his clutches.

This last instance was especially frustrating. He'd waited for hours. Spooked the milk-wagon horse with his slingshot. Timed the angle. She moved seconds before his scheme reached culmination.

It was as though someone watched over her.

He spat into the snow, wishing he could as easily rid himself of the bitter taste in his mouth. He wasn't used to being thwarted. It didn't sit well.

Reaching a heavy wooden door tucked into the side of a tenement, he inserted a key in the lock and shoved it open, welcomed almost immediately by a blast of tobacco-scented air.

His father waited inside. Catching sight of Hugh, he stubbed out his cigarette on the floor.

Hugh stopped shy of the threshold. "You be out early."

Angus, for that was how Hugh thought of him, straightened and left his chair. "I was going to say the same about you. Where have ya been?"

Hugh slammed the door, tossed the key onto a small oak table, then shrugged out of his coat. "Taking care of business like Malcolm asked."

Angus crossed his arms. "You've been out to the island?"

Hugh took his time responding. Angus was baiting him, checking his activities. He didn't like it, but he knew better than to let it show. The old buzzard fed on that kind of rubbish. "The ferry doesn't run this early. I've been at the dock."

Angus watched him, his sharp gaze measuring. Ire roiled in Hugh's belly. Just how much did the old goat know? Or how much had he guessed? Hugh shoved his thumb at him. "What are you doing here?"

"You weren't at the meeting last night. Neither was Rourke. I saw fit to check on you lads, but Rourke's apartment was empty."

"So was mine, yet you deigned to come in anyway."

Angus lifted a shaggy brow. "I dinna think you'd have anything to hide."

"And Rourke might?" Turning his attention might be the only way to keep old Angus from asking uncomfortable questions. Hugh settled himself in the chair Angus vacated. "Why? What has he done?"

"Not what he's done. What he be doing." Pulling a tobacco pouch from his pocket, Angus rolled a fresh cigarette, clenched it between his teeth, then struck a match and lit it. "Is it true he asked you to keep your distance from the Hamilton woman?"

News traveled fast. Hugh nodded. "You know Rourke. He's afraid acting too quickly will draw attention, especially if she's not the person we be looking for."

"But you think she is."

"I think she might be."

Angus drew closer, the ever-present scent of woodsmoke and peat clinging to his clothing, even in New York. "So what do ya intend to do about it?"

He didn't like having to tilt his head back to look Angus in the eye, but rising would be perceived as defensive and Hugh needed to look relaxed. He shrugged. "I haven't decided yet. For now, I'll wait to see how Rourke handles the situation."

Angus gave a nod of his grizzled head. "For now, but perhaps it would be wise not to wait too long."

With a flick of his wrist he tossed the scarf dangling from his shoulders around his neck and wheeled toward the door. His hand resting on the knob, he turned back. "Some things are best laid to rest quickly, eh, son? Before too much is said . . . or exposed. I speak of your own well-being, of course."

"*My* well-being?"

"Ours," Angus corrected. "The family's." Slipping out of the apartment, he quirked an eyebrow and gave Hugh a knowing look before he closed the door.

Tension grew in Hugh's gut. Bolting to his feet, he strode the span of the small room and kicked one of the chairs next to the table, sending it clattering against the wall.

How Angus knew was of no interest to Hugh. The fact of the matter was the wily old badger knew, or at the very least suspected, and that made him dangerous. Old Angus never kept anything a secret unless it was to his benefit, and protecting a son wasn't benefit enough. But surely the shame that might befall them would make Angus bite his tongue, Hugh reasoned. The only thing the old man might gain by revealing his indiscretion would be a vacant seat in parliament.

Hugh bunched his fists. If he hoped to pluck the playing card from Angus's hand, he'd need to take care of Cara soon. To do that, he was going to need help.

He mulled the possibilities and finally settled on one.

Tomorrow, he'd seek an ally—an old friend who'd come to his aid before. If that didn't work, he'd kill Cara with his own hands, and soon, before Angus guessed too much.

And then he'd take care of his father.

24

Now that Giles was settled comfortably in his room, Cara felt free to retire to the peace and quiet of the library. A heartwarming blaze danced in the fireplace, ferreting the chill from even the deepest corners, but it was the more tantalizing scent of leather, soap, and wood tinged with a hint of heather that made her pause, her nose in the air.

"Rourke?"

He rose from behind Amelia's desk, looking as contrite as a schoolboy caught cheating on his papers. "Hello, Cara."

She left the doorway to press further into the room. "Are you looking for something?"

He swiped his hands the length of his trousers. "Giles's ledger. Amelia said he keeps it here, with her books."

She'd seen Amelia working on them on occasion. She pointed to the top drawer on the left side. "In there, I think."

He pulled the drawer out and lifted out a black ledger. "This must be it. She said it was black. Thank you."

She nodded and folded her hands in front of her. Dressed in a white high-necked sweater, pushed to his elbows, he was a banquet for the eyes. But the uneasy feeling from earlier lingered and chased any romantic notions she might have had from her mind. She shifted her weight to her other foot and gnawed her lip. "So, have you gotten settled?"

He circled the desk, watching her intently. "Amelia made sure I'd be comfortable."

She couldn't help herself—she backed up a step, adding to the distance between them. It helped her think. "It's good of you to fill in while Giles is abed."

He closed the gap as quickly as she'd opened it —more, since his broad shoulders blocked her view of the fire. "Cara, what happened this morning?"

"W-what do you mean?" A chair bumped the back of her legs.

"The wagon that hit Giles—what did you see?"

She wagged her head from side to side. "Nothing. I was talking . . ." She was about to say she'd been talking to the woman who asked about her bracelet, but caught herself in time. "Why?" she asked instead.

Rourke waved dismissively, but his expression remained troubled. Ignoring the voice in her head that warned against candor, she laid her hand over his arm and prompted again, "Why? Did not all seem as it should?"

He rolled his shoulder, then covered her hand before she could pull away. "Cara, have a care, aye? When you're out and about, stay watchful."

A shiver traveled her spine. His face was heavy with concern, as if he knew more than he was telling. She nodded, if only to be free from the power of his touch. When he dropped his hand, she sucked in a breath and rubbed the spot with her fingers.

He hitched the ledger high with a smile, but Cara took no comfort from his grin. It was too wide, and it failed to reach his eyes.

"I'd best be getting this to Amelia."

She swept aside to let him pass.

He paused, his hand on the jamb. "I'll see you at supper?"

"Of course."

He looked as though he wanted to say more but ended up passing through the door without another word.

Cara sighed. Just when she'd begun to enjoy the camaraderie between them, things were once again stilted and odd. Would the day never come when she could once more trust the people around her?

Not people, she corrected silently. Rourke. Her heart longed to reach out to him, to confide in him, to trust the man she saw reflected in his gaze at unguarded moments.

She moved closer to the blaze, but the fire no longer held the same warmth. She rubbed her hands over her arms to ward off the gooseflesh she felt rising. Rourke thought something amiss about this morning's accident, that much was clear. But what? And why would he not say more?

She thought back over the scene. If he were right, if it wasn't an accident but something more sinister, there could be only one explanation.

Someone wanted her dead.

Suddenly, every noise became a creeping step, every flicker of the fire, a shadow with evil intent. She glanced over her shoulder at the door, her shoulders sagging with relief when she saw it was securely latched. Never before had she felt unsafe at the boardinghouse, yet Rourke's words lingered in her ears, and with them, a name.

Deidre.

She alone bore animosity toward Cara—unreasoning hate she barely bothered to conceal. Could it be her words had given way to action?

Lifting her chin, Cara strode to the door. She'd never been one to stand idly by. Neither would she start now. She'd never been to the milliner where Deidre and Tillie worked, but she knew where to find it. With God's help, perhaps she'd find the answers she sought there.

She found Ana scrubbing potatoes in the kitchen and told her only that she'd be going out before dinner. Tying her cloak around her neck, she went out the back door to avoid raising further questions, then hurried north on Ashberry Street.

At this time of day, the street was far less

crowded than in the morning, making navigating the vendor stands much easier. Still, she stayed to the shadows just in case she failed to see Deidre returning home. A light snow had shaken loose from the clouds and drifted lazily over the shops. The flakes were fluffy and wide, just the kind Cara loved to catch on her tongue, but today she would take no time for such things. Shoulders hunched against the cold, she scurried down one street after another until she reached a painted brick building tucked between two others of similar build. A sign in the window bore the name Ferguson.

This was the place. Cara ducked into a narrow alley to wait. Thankfully the cold had barely pinched her fingers and toes before the door swung open and Tillie stepped out, alone.

"Good night," she called into the store, then shut the door firmly behind her. Afterward she blew on her hands and hurried in the direction of home.

Cara eased out of the shadows to stare in the milliner's window. Where was Deidre?

She waited another ten minutes, then twenty, until the door swung open again. This time, Deidre stepped onto the boardwalk, but instead of following the direction Tillie had taken, she turned north, her feet swift and sure.

Cara's breath caught as a figure swung from the opposite side of the street toward her. Deidre's pace never broke. Instead, the two joined paths and continued down the boardwalk side by side.

Obviously they knew each other, but Cara was quite certain she had never seen the man before. And where were they going?

Clutching her cloak tightly to her shoulders, Cara merged alongside a band of women headed in Deidre's direction. By keeping slightly behind and to the left, she managed to maintain sight of Deidre's proud head but lost herself in the press of women whenever it appeared she might look back. This went on for several blocks, until the thinning crowd no longer offered even scant protection and Cara feared she'd be caught. Still, she forced her feet on, determined to learn where Deidre was going and why.

Finally the man with Deidre veered left, into an alley. Deidre waited, shifting from foot to foot with impatience. The man appeared, motioned to her, and then they both disappeared into the alley.

Indecision tore at Cara's gut. How much could she risk? Surely, were Deidre to catch her spying, she'd only confirm what the woman thought. But how would she know what she was up to otherwise?

Though it was early, dusk crept along the street. Another hour and it would be dim enough for the streetlamps, which meant Cara would be hurrying home alone and in the dark. A shiver took her. She couldn't let this opportunity slip by. She slipped into the alley, surprised to discover it was not one but many narrow walkways, a series of twists and turns that wound in and around the tall city buildings.

Her heart beat faster as she pressed deeper into the maze. Here, the gloom was even denser than on the street. It weighed on her chest and at the same time drifted on the steamy plumes rising from the cobbles. The only snow here lay piled in dirty clumps along the walls. She quickly gave up trying to keep her hem from riding in the mud and concentrated on finding the path Deidre and her companion had taken. Several failed turns later and against yet another dead end, she gave up with a frustrated sigh.

It was hopeless. There was no way she'd find the pair now, or if she did, she'd certainly give herself away.

Dodging refuse that spilled from an overturned crate, Cara turned back the way she'd come. The hour had grown much later, the shadows longer. The only light lent to this cramped space came from a row of apartments high above. She'd be lucky to find her way home now.

Indeed, when she finally stumbled onto the main street, a slight panic had begun to squeeze her chest. But a moment to right her sense of direction and she was headed south toward the boarding-house as fast as her feet could carry her.

Even by the dim light of the streetlamps, the sight of the boardinghouse had never been so welcome. Cara scrambled up the steps and then nearly fell through the doorway in her haste to get inside. Immediately, warmth and laughter surrounded her, dashing the fear that had nipped at her heels down the street. Fingers trembling, she hung her cloak on the hook next to the door and made her way to the dining room.

Amelia rose from her chair, both hands flat on the table. "There you are, dear. We've been worried about you."

Cara managed an apologetic shrug and took her place at the table, all the while avoiding Rourke's inquiring gaze. "Forgive my tardiness. I lost track of the time."

Amelia resumed her place. "We all daydream now and again, but next time you go for a walk, take one of the girls with you. It isn't safe for a pretty young lady like yourself to be wandering about all alone, especially if she isn't familiar with the city. Heaven knows where you could end up. Isn't that right, Breda?"

Breda's head bobbed. "I wouldn't mind going with you. I fancy a bit of night air myself sometimes."

Even Laverne agreed, Cara noticed, though she looked a bit worn.

"How is Giles?" Cara asked once the others forgot her arrival and resumed their chatter.

"Much better," Laverne said, her plump cheeks lifting. "I took him something to eat, and now he's resting comfortably."

"That's good news."

"That it is."

Though she and Laverne talked, Cara felt Rourke's gaze heavy upon her. Finally she had no choice but to look at him.

"Where did you go?" he whispered.

Cara took a small bite of pickled beets, chewed them carefully, and swallowed before she answered. Even then, she pushed her food around her plate with her fork. "For a walk."

"I know that. Where to?"

"Just around the city. It started snowing and I thought it was pretty." She risked a peek at him. He looked quite angry with her, though why that should be, she couldn't guess. He leaned toward her with a scowl.

"I thought I told you to be careful."

"I was," Cara insisted.

"No you weren't. You were wandering alone after dark. Anything could have happened to you."

"It wasn't that dark yet."

"The sun set an hour ago. It was dark."

She set her chin stubbornly and opened her mouth to argue, but before she could utter a sound, the front door opened again and sent a chilly draft scurrying down the hall.

Deidre's voice echoed against the wood floors. "I'm home."

"Oh good. There's Deidre. We're in here having supper," Amelia called.

Deidre appeared in the entrance to the dining room, long tendrils of hair clinging to her flushed cheeks.

"Tillie said you and Mr. Ferguson would be working late. Come join us. Ana has your place all ready." Amelia motioned to a vacant chair, but Deidre shook her head.

"Thank you, but I'm not hungry. I think I'll get changed and turn in early, if you don't mind. Good night, everyone," she said, her tone unnaturally cheerful. She sent one last glance around the room and then left to a chorus of good-nights. One even fell from Cara's lips, though she barely squeezed it out.

Tillie wouldn't lie, which meant Deidre had deceived the girl into thinking she'd be working late. Turning to her right, Cara whispered into Tillie's ear, "Does Deidre work late often?"

Tillie nodded. "Two, sometimes three nights a week."

Thinking back, Cara did remember her returning home later than the others. "What about tomorrow?"

"Thursday?" She shook her head. "Nay. Probably not until next week. Why?"

"Just curious," Cara said, lifting her fork and pretending to eat.

So, it would be several days before she got another chance. She'd wait. Perhaps then she'd discover the truth behind what Deidre was really doing in the alleyways around Ashberry Street. And this time she'd have the benefit of knowing where to start.

25

Business remained light the rest of the week and early on Monday morning, so much so that by noon Mr. O'Bannon had complained profusely about the lack of customers, and by quarter of three he let Cara and Ana go home early.

Cara and Ana parted ways outside the candle shop, after Cara claimed to desire exploring a bit of the city. Though Ana had offered, she'd managed to convince her that she preferred going alone.

Now she scurried along the path she'd taken last week, retracing her steps to the milliner where Deidre and Tillie worked, and then winding her way back through the alleys until she reached the spot where she'd lost sight of Deidre. The view by daylight was not much better than it had been at night. Indeed, more than simple household refuse lined the alleys. She shuddered to think of her soiled dress and vowed to see it laundered by the end of the day.

Emerging from a particularly narrow alley, Cara stepped into a wide square. Ropes tied from window to window dangled overhead. Laundry hung to dry waved back and forth like painted wooden signs, stiff and frozen. Twice, Cara witnessed a window swinging open and barely managed to duck out of the way before a bucketful of dirty water cascaded down on her head.

She resisted the urge to pinch her nose. Derry was dirty, but nothing like this. Longing for home filled her heart. On top of that, curious glances had begun to drift her way, and she knew she wouldn't be able to loiter in these alleys long. She'd need to walk on or risk drawing attention.

Holding her head high, she moved around the square, pausing to peek into each alley as she passed. Several led nowhere, ending at high brick walls where one building abutted another. Others were lined with doors—row after row of them, and Cara knew Deidre could have been behind any one of them when she disappeared. A heated argument broke into her thoughts.

"She's trustworthy, I tell you. I'd stake me life on it."

The voice was unfamiliar, yet the accent caught Cara's attention. She turned and backed up, searching for the source.

"Yeah, and what do you know of her besides what she's told us?"

"Enough. I have me sources, too, ya know."

A sharp snort echoed from an alley to Cara's left. Running her palm along the wall, she drew closer to a slightly open door at the end from which the voices drifted.

"I've had the misfortune of dealing with your sources. A fine mess *he* made of things."

"The information was good. It's not his fault one of us didn't have the stomach for bloodshed and turned traitor."

"Tell that to Deidre. I'm willing to bet she'll say anything to get her hands on—"

"Quiet!" The man resumed, lower. "Regardless, Kilarny, her husband was one of us. As his widow, we owe her our trust."

Cara's heart quickened. She'd found the place! She pressed closer to the wall, thought better of it and looked around for someplace to listen without being seen.

"Trust. Loyalty. All just words. I want proof her motives extend beyond revenge."

"What more do you need than blood?" A pause followed, and then the man continued, urgently, "Besides, it's not up to you, Kil. She has ties to The Celt."

The other man snorted, stirring a memory in Cara's brain. What was it about the sound that seemed so familiar?

"More rumors. Besides, he'll be headed back to Ireland soon."

"True, but when the twig hardens, it's difficult to twist. Do you really want to risk raising The Celt's ire by pitting yourself against one of his kin?"

Though she could not see the men, Cara had crept close enough to hear one of them sigh.

"Fine. When is she coming?"

"Soon. Do you think you can put away your suspicions by then?"

"Do I have a choice?"

A bark of laughter followed. "I guess not."

The men were expecting Deidre soon. Cara *had* to find a better place to hide, but except for crates similar to the one she'd stumbled over last time, there was nothing. Worse, her breathing had become so shallow it seemed to echo against the very walls. Even her legs were a danger, for at any moment the knocking of her knees threatened to become audible.

Get out of here, Cara. The waters here be far too deep for you to swim.

The voice inside her head had never been louder, or she more inclined to listen. She retraced her steps, mindful of making any noise that would draw the attention of the men. Once on the street, she took a deep breath of frosty air, glad to be back among the bustling shoppers and cheery vendors. In minutes she'd be home, and any thoughts of rebels or mysterious strangers named The Celt would be gone.

The sound of the street soothed her ragged nerves. What could happen to her here, with so many people swirling by? Still, her feet itched to get moving. But before she could take a step, she felt herself grabbed by the shoulders and spun around.

A gasp caught in her throat. Fear clutched at her chest. Her lips parted, but words refused to come. She couldn't even call for help.

She jerked her head back. A pair of blazing blue eyes stared into hers—eyes at once familiar and frightening.

Not frightening, she realized at once. Comforting. The eyes staring into hers brimmed with passion and concern . . . and something deeper. Something that spoke directly to her heart.

She sagged in his grasp and expelled the breath caught in her lungs. "Rourke."

Slowly, the ragged pounding of Rourke's heart lessened. From the moment he'd left Mr. O'Bannon's shop in search of Cara to the moment he'd found her, an unexplained fear had driven him faster and faster through the streets of New York.

Angered at himself for his concern, he tightened his grasp on her shoulders. "Where have you been?"

"What?"

"I've been looking everywhere for you."

Her eyes widened. He wouldn't have thought it possible.

"You have? But how—?"

"Ana told me."

Confusion clouded her eyes, casting them an even darker, more beautiful forest green. She blinked, at the same time breaking the spell that held him bewitched.

"Oh. Of course. I was sightseeing."

She was lying. Rourke's heart plummeted.

Immediately she looked to the ground. Even so, a part of him begged her to be truthful. "What were you doing here, Cara?"

Her lashes swept up, but this time Rourke refused to be captivated by her beauty.

"What?"

"This isn't the best place to be sightseeing."

He felt a tremor shake her, and she shifted from foot to foot. "No. I . . . got lost."

She looked so small, so sweet and vulnerable, melting his resolve. "And are you found now?" The question slipped out unbidden.

She gave a slow nod, her gaze still fixed to his. "I think so."

He let go of her shoulders, but even still she held him. Though they didn't touch, he felt her.

The tip of her tongue slipped out to wet her lips. "You came just to look for me?"

231

"No. I . . . needed to purchase some things for the boardinghouse."

He knew he couldn't trust the pain he read on her face, yet a desire to recall the lie scorched his lips.

"I see."

Her withdrawal was tangible. Rourke was once again aware of where they stood—not on a quiet corner, with just the two of them, but a busy street with people and vendors.

Giving a mental shake, he drew a ragged breath. "Come, Cara. I'll walk you back to the boarding-house."

She reached for him. Real or imagined, heat from her touch burned his arm.

"No. Not yet. I'm not ready to go back."

"You're not?" He repeated her words like an imbecile, hope flooding him.

She shook her head. "Can we walk?"

Yes, he wanted to walk. At least here, away from the others, he could pretend only truth existed between them. He *was* Rourke Walsh and she was Cara Hamilton, and neither of them had anything to hide.

He held out his arm. Her fingers slid down until they linked elbows. Together, they moved along the street.

"So, you got lost. How much of the city did you see?"

"Not much." Her nose wrinkled. "What I did see was dirty."

He laughed, surprised by how easily he put the tension behind them. "That's because you weren't looking for the right things."

"Oh?"

He nodded. "New York can be beautiful, especially at night when the streetlights come on. In the meantime"—he motioned toward another, less busy street—"I want to show you something."

Now that the sun had sunk behind the buildings, night fell in earnest, but strangely the air had become less sharp. Perhaps it was the huddled buildings that protected them, or perhaps Cara's nearness. Regardless, warmth filled him as she threw back her head to stare up at the tallest structures, her face bright with wonder.

"It really is amazing how so many people can live together in one place."

"Have you never been to Belfast, then? Or London?"

She shook her head. "London once, but I was very young."

He smiled, taking pleasure in the questions she asked as they walked, and filling her in on what he knew of the city until they reached a small park. In the center, happy couples enjoyed a leisurely stroll beside a small pond. A fire had been built near the banks to warm chilled fingers when the temperatures became too stark. Rourke led her that way, mindful of the horse-drawn buggies that swished by.

Her face lit with pleasure. "You knew this was here?"

He nodded. "The ice be too thin now, but in the winter this is a favorite place for skaters. Do you skate?"

"No, but I'd love to learn."

"Next winter I'll teach you, though I need to warn you: I'm not the most skilled. We might both wind up polishing the ice with our backsides."

Cara laughed.

Next winter. Careful, he reminded himself, tearing his gaze from her face to focus on the pond. Being with her this way was pleasant, but he couldn't let himself forget how things really were between them.

She held her hands to the fire and took a deep breath. "It would be easy to forget where we are in this place."

He jerked his head toward her, his brows lifted in surprise. Had she heard his thoughts?

She smiled. "It's almost like we aren't in the city."

He relaxed and returned her smile. "Aye." A bench sat nearby. He motioned toward it. "Shall we rest a while?"

She nodded in eager agreement and waited while he swept away a thin layer of dirt and leaves. Once clear, she sat, and he sank down beside her. For several minutes they watched, unspeaking, the people and horses swirling past.

Cara dipped her head to tuck her face into the folds of her scarf.

"Are you cold?" Rourke asked.

"No."

But a shiver took her, and storm clouds filled her eyes before she looked away.

"What troubles you, lass?"

He asked it innocently, out of concern. Perhaps she sensed that. Tears sprang to her eyes. He caught them with his thumb before they fell.

For a long moment she studied him, measuring. Finally, she took a deep breath of air that grew colder the farther down the sun went. He felt the sharpness pierce his lungs, as though he, too, breathed deep. He waited, silent. He would not prompt her, would not compound his sin.

She hugged herself and stamped her feet. When she did speak, her lips moved slowly, as if they were frozen. "Rourke . . . I'm so afraid."

An ache flared in his chest. "Why? What frightens you?"

Like a child, she raised her hand and pushed the edge of her scarf between her teeth.

Not a child, he realized. Subconsciously she attempted to stem her words, to keep them from spilling out.

She cast her gaze from side to side like a panicked filly. "I don't . . . know what to do!"

The tortured cry seemed wrenched from her. She dropped her head into her hands and sat, shoulders heaving. He couldn't help himself. He pulled her into his arms. For a moment he couldn't breathe, could only revel in her nearness and the way her silken hair against his cheek made him feel. He closed his eyes and forced himself to consider his da.

"Sometimes . . ." His deceit sickened him, clogged his throat like a stone. Swallowing hard, he began again. "Sometimes sharing your burden with a friend helps lighten the load."

She lifted her chin, her face full of hope. "A friend?" The hope dissolved as quickly as a snowflake on a sunny day. "But . . . what if . . . I have been lying to that friend?"

The heat from his face raised beads of perspiration that trickled down his temples like rain. "We all lie, Cara."

Even that bit of truth failed to assuage his guilt. Still, he forbade himself from speaking more. She shuddered and pulled from his grasp.

Finally, as though she could bear the weight of her secret no more, she let go a sigh that rolled like mist on the air. "I overheard something today. Something troubling."

"At the boardinghouse?"

She shook her head. "In the alley where you found me."

"What did you hear?"

He asked too quickly, but she seemed not to notice. She straightened, and then her gaze fastened to him, open and trusting. "I'm going to tell you something, but you must swear never to repeat it. Someone's life . . . my life . . . depends on your silence."

Agony clawed at him, but unable to speak, he nodded.

She drew a quivering breath. "I . . . have a brother."

He licked his lips. "You told me. He died."

Slowly she shook her head. "I *thought* he died. The truth is . . . several months ago he wrote to me and told me he was alive."

Rourke's heart pounded harder, faster.

"At first, I hardly dared believe, but then it was like a miracle had raised my brother from the dead."

Her words came rapidly, as though now that the dam had been breached, nothing could hold them back. She clasped his hands so tightly, she shook.

"It took everything, every last pound I possessed, but I bought a ticket and boarded a ship to America. I had to find him!"

The chatter of people, a dog's happy bark— everything faded until he heard and saw only Cara. She stared at him, her eyes endless green pools that pleaded with him for understanding.

His mouth dry, he swallowed and tried to appear only mildly surprised. "Why have you said nothing before now?"

"He told me not to," Cara wailed, low and desperate. "His letter warned against telling anyone that he was alive, though he did not explain why. I assumed it had something to do with the reason he went into hiding in the first place. I've been hoping, clinging to the hope," she corrected, "that once he found me, he'd tell me the truth. But today—"

"He has not found you, then?"

She shook her head.

"And you have no idea where he is?"

Again, the gesture. Rourke took a deep breath.

Her grip on his hand tightened. "I cannot be certain, but I think, somehow, my brother's disappearance is tied to Deidre."

Her words startled his thinking. "What?"

She nodded. "I didn't understand her resentment before now, but today, in the alley, I heard two men talking."

"Go on," he said, his interest genuinely piqued.

"They were saying something about Deidre and a person named The Celt."

Rourke stiffened. So, the rumors regarding the Irishman were true. "Did you hear a name? Anything about who this Celt is?"

"No. Only that Deidre be kin to him."

He tucked the information away for his meeting with Malcolm and the others. "What else?"

Her gaze shifted up and left. "They mentioned

something about a traitor . . . someone who betrayed them and cost Deidre's husband his life. One of them said—" she swallowed and licked her lips—"he said she would do anything to find him."

If Cara was right, he wasn't the only person hunting for her brother. Deidre Sullivan had an issue to settle, as well. But did it matter? If a murderer died, would justice care whose blade ran red?

Aye. It mattered to him. He was the one who'd begged for mercy from a deliberately deaf God as his father lay dying. He was the one who'd vowed revenge.

Rourke cleared his throat and pushed the words past his stiff lips. "I can help you, Cara, but only if you trust me. Do you?"

Her breathing shortened and a wealth of agony swept over her face. Finally, she nodded. "Aye."

He leaned toward her, mingling the air from their lungs, reading the emotion and vulnerability in her eyes. He longed with every fiber and cell to kiss her and end the subterfuge, but his rational mind betrayed his wayward heart.

"Then I must know your brother's name," he said, lips tight. "Who is he, Cara? What is your brother's name?"

"His name . . ." Her chin trembled as her voice dropped to a whisper. "His name is Eoghan Hamilton."

26

The moment she spoke the words, peace filled Cara's heart. At last, an ally—someone to help locate her brother and protect her against Deidre's schemes.

And Rourke *would* protect her.

She'd glimpsed the concern in his eyes, felt the strength of his arms as he held her close. Yet he sat without speaking, his face as vacant and still as the nearby pond. She laid her hand on his cheek. "Rourke?"

He jerked to his feet. "I heard you. I'm . . . I just be thinking of a way to help. We do not dare move too quickly."

His words were stilted, forced. Doubt crept over Cara on spidery legs. She tucked her hands into her crossed arms. "Of course."

"It's getting late. I'd best get you home to the boardinghouse." At some point, his scarf had slipped from his neck onto the bench. He bent to retrieve it. "Be ya ready now?"

Ready or not, she sensed his impatience. Her knees trembled as she stood. "You do not want to know more? What he looks like? When I last saw him?"

Rourke gave a terse shake. "We'll discuss that

later, when we're not so exposed." His hand swept the park. "It would not be safe to say too much here."

A chill that had nothing to do with the weather reached through her coat and seized her bones.

He was lying.

The knowledge cut as sharp as any knife. Had she been wrong to trust him? Could he have somehow manufactured the concern she'd read in his gaze? If so, why? What had he to gain by urging her to open up to him?

Her thoughts swirled like the wind along the sidewalk as she took his offered arm and moved with him toward the boardinghouse. The distance seemed far greater than it had coming, perhaps because it was absent of lighthearted chatter. When they finally stepped into the brightly lit hallway, Cara's head pounded and her stomach felt ill.

Gratefully she slid out of her coat, wishing she could as easily shed the weight pressing on her heart. Rourke maintained his place at the door, as though he meant to go.

No voices drifted from the parlor, but Cara spoke in lowered tones anyway. "Are you not staying? It is late and Amelia will be locking the doors soon."

Disappointment bit her as he shook his head. She'd hoped to speak with him, rid herself of the doubts roiling inside.

"I still have a few errands I need to run before I turn in. Best take care of them now so I can get an early start on the repairs to the carriage in the morning."

"But Laverne will have supper ready soon. Can these errands wait?" She clamped her mouth shut, kicking herself for sounding so earnest.

Though he smiled, it was only a pale imitation of his usual cocky grin. "I'm sure I can render a crust of bread from somewhere. Good night, Cara. We'll talk in the morning."

He snatched open the door and ducked through before she said another word. For a long moment she could only stand numb and staring. Burning hot tears gathered behind her eyes. It had to be that he'd misunderstood her concern. Surely he would not have been so callous if he'd realized the danger. And of course he did not know Eoghan, so he couldn't know the seriousness of the situation if her twin had been forced into hiding.

The door swung open, releasing a blast of damp air. He was back! Relieved, she stepped forward.

Deidre's face registered her surprise as she swept into the boardinghouse and caught Cara staring. Her face puzzled, she unwound the scarf from around her neck and hung it on the wall hooks, followed by her coat. "You gave me a fright. What are you doing, standing there like a statue?"

Cara blinked rapidly to adjust her thinking. "I-I just got home myself."

Deidre's gaze dropped to the muddy puddles formed by Cara's boots. "Well, you'd best clean that up before Laverne catches sight of it." She grabbed a broom and thrust it toward Cara. "I took care of mine outside."

Indeed, her feet left no tracks as she sauntered through the hall toward the stairs.

"I'm going to change and then I'll be down for supper."

"I'll tell Amelia." The last word faded on Cara's tongue as Deidre disappeared around the corner.

Despair lent crushing weight to Cara's chest. Rourke. The water pooling on the floor. Deidre. Eoghan.

It was all too much.

The broom slipped from her fingers and clattered to the floor. She was alone and desperate, and God was silent, too far removed to know or care about her plight.

Whirling, she sped up the stairs to her room, slamming the door behind her. On the bedside table, feeble light flickered from an oil lamp. She reached to turn up the wick, then changed her mind and collapsed on the floor next to her bed.

Why? Why had God seen fit to take everyone she loved and leave her so completely alone and desperate for answers?

"Why?"

Guilt consumed her the moment she breathed the question. Who was she to question the Almighty? But did not the Scripture say to ask? To seek? To knock?

"Sure, and isn't that what I've been doing?" She cast her gaze heavenward, pleading for a sign that would calm her troubled heart. Instead, all she saw were the punched tin tiles that adorned the ceiling. She dropped her head onto her arms, defeated. "Why won't you tell me what I'm supposed to do? I'm so afraid. I don't know who I can trust. I just don't know . . ."

"God's help is nearer than the door."

Cara didn't bother stemming the tears that rose to her eyes. They burned fiery trails down her cheeks, falling faster and faster until sobs shook her body. Dimly she heard a soft knock on her door and Ana's voice calling her name. She ignored them both, and eventually Ana's light tread faded on the stairs.

Cara buried her face in the folds of her quilt. She couldn't see anyone tonight—not Ana, or Amelia and the others, and especially not Rourke.

Fully dressed, she climbed into bed and wriggled under the covers. Tomorrow she would think about the consequences of what she'd done by telling him the truth about Eoghan. Hopefully a solution for a way out of the mess she'd made would rise with the dawn. If not . . .

If not, she'd be forced to leave the boardinghouse and go into hiding for herself, until she found Eoghan or he found her.

Fending off another bout of disappointed tears, she yanked the covers over her head. She'd let her guard down because she'd wanted to believe Rourke a hero—some kind of knight upon whose broad shoulders she could lay her troubles. What a fool she'd been! He wasn't a knight. He was a man only, with feet of clay, and she'd been wrong to trust him.

Anger replaced the disappointment bruising her heart. She'd not make that mistake again.

Kicking her feet out from under the blanket, she tore at the buttons on her boots and tossed them onto the floor next to the bed. He'd used her, but for what purpose? She still didn't know.

Settling against the pillows to await the sunrise, she vowed to find out. Tomorrow she'd learn all there was to know about Rourke Walsh. If it was as she feared—if he had an underlying motive for asking about her brother—she'd disappear, and he'd never see her again. Or she him.

To her dismay, to her utter despair . . . the thought released an onslaught of fresh tears. She flopped onto her side. She might never see Rourke again, but she wanted to. Oh, how she wanted to.

A light tap on the door roused Cara from slumber. Groggily she lifted her head from the pillows.

"Who is it?"

"Breda." The door opened a crack, and the woman poked her head through. She looked like the groundhog searching for shadows Mr. O'Bannon had told her about. "Ana asked me to fetch you. Told me to tell you she'd not be going to the candle shop."

Though she'd slept little, and her shoulders ached from lying awkwardly, Breda's words drove the fog from Cara's mind. She sat up and swung her legs to the floor. "Why not?"

Confusion furrowed Breda's brow as she eyed Cara's rumpled dress. "She said she not be feeling up to it. Did ya sleep in your clothes, lass?"

Cara ran her hand over her rumpled skirt. "I . . . must have drifted off. What of Ana? Is she sick?"

Breda walked to the wardrobe, opened the door, and surveyed Cara's meager assortment of dresses. She pulled a gray wool skirt and matching top from the back of the wardrobe and carried them to the bed.

"Ana's running a slight fever. Laverne insists it be nothing to fret over, but Amelia doesn't want her taking any chances, what with the weather looking so rainy." She trailed her finger in the air. "Do you need help getting out of that dress?"

Cara fingered the buttons at her back self-consciously. "I can manage."

"All right then, but you'd best hurry or you'll miss breakfast." She patted the gray skirt. "Wear this. It's damp outside and the material will keep you warm."

"Thank you, Breda."

She bustled toward the door, her hand lingering on the knob as she looked back. " 'Tis nothing, lass. And, Cara?"

"Aye?"

She nodded toward the dresser and the washbasin sitting on top. Her face and her voice turned kindly. "There be fresh water in the pitcher. The cold will help draw the redness from your eyes."

A lump rose to Cara's throat as she watched Breda slip from sight. Though she'd only known them a short time, she'd made some fast friends here at the boardinghouse. Perhaps the accusations she'd made against God were not entirely true. By the light of day, she didn't feel nearly so alone.

Taken by a chill, she shivered and hurried to wash and dress. By the time she went downstairs, the others had left for the day—all except for Rourke. She heard him puttering about in the kitchen, his low tone mingling with Laverne's. Cara snatched a piece of toast from the sideboard and hurried to grab her coat. At least she'd missed him at breakfast. Though she was as determined as ever to find out what she could about him, it could wait until she got home from work.

But it didn't wait.

Again and again her thoughts drifted to him throughout the day, alternately going from regretting her honesty with him to hoping he'd somehow misunderstood her concern. She sighed with relief when at last the clock chimed five and she settled into her coat and gloves to leave.

"Good night, Mr. O'Bannon," she called, waving at the cheery chandler as she slipped out the door.

"You haven't left. Good. I was afraid I'd missed you."

Startled by Rourke's deep voice, she flinched and dropped one of her mittens in the muddy puddles lapping at both sides of the shop door.

"I've got it." He snatched the glove up and slapped it against his thigh, ridding it of dirt. "There now. Let me see your hand."

Cara stiffened and held out her hand, palm up, but instead of returning the mitten, Rourke drew close and slipped it onto her fingers.

His hand warm on her wrist, he looked into her eyes. "Better?"

Angered by his cavalier demeanor, she dropped her gaze. "You didn't have to meet me. I would have been fine on my own."

Thankfully he withdrew a step and dropped his hand. "I'm sure you would have, but I wanted to talk with you. To apologize."

Apologize? She narrowed her eyes in suspicion. "And what, pray, have you to be sorry for?"

For a lengthy moment it seemed, he said nothing. Finally he offered his arm. "Will you walk with me?"

What could she do? Her feet moved of their own accord, though she somehow managed to keep from taking his arm.

"I'm afraid I was caught off guard by your confession last night," Rourke began as he led the way onto the sidewalk.

Clad in dark trousers and a thick fuzzy sweater, Cara was hard-pressed not to look at him, though other women passing by were not so hindered.

He appeared not to notice their admiring glances and jammed his hands into his pockets. "I was surprised and, I admit, a bit disappointed."

"Disappointed?" She glanced at him askance.

"Aye. Forgive my churlish pride, Cara. I was disappointed that you'd not trusted me sooner."

They'd come to a broken spot on the sidewalk, where mud and slush combined to form a dingy puddle. Once again Rourke offered his arm. This time, Cara took it and allowed him to help her skirt the mess. Safely on the other side, however, she let go and resumed her pace.

"So, your mood, the sour attitude you displayed, it had nothing to do with the news of my brother?"

"How could it?" His long strides matched every two of hers. He shrugged and flashed a crooked grin. "I've never even met the lad."

She studied him critically. His cheeks were ruddy, but that could easily have been caused by the brisk walk. Indeed, he swung alongside her, blue eyes wide and pleading. Certainly he did not look to be lying. Traitorous tears burned the back of her eyelids, accusing her of longing to believe him. She walked faster, as though by doing so she might somehow escape the truth nipping at her heels.

"Cara, I was wrong to react as I did, but you must understand the ways of a man. When I found out that you'd been lying to me—"

"I did it only to protect my brother," she cut in sharply.

"Of that, I be certain."

So deep was the conviction in his tone, it slowed her steps. She stared at the sidewalk passing under her feet. "Then I don't understand . . ."

He reached out to grasp her elbow and drew her to a stop. Though his face twisted in a grimace, he still managed to look sheepish, a sight oddly humorous on a man of his stature. "We men are pitiful beasts. There is not one among us who does good. Not one. And yet . . ." His gaze softened as he looked at her, robbing her of breath. "We somehow expect our women to be better."

Sighing, he let his fingers slip to hold her hand. "I put you on a pedestal, Cara. 'Twas of my own making and unfair in its height. So, when you were honest with me, when you told me that you'd been lying to protect your brother, it was my own injured pride that made me act the fool."

Certain he could feel the ragged beating of her heart in her trembling hand, Cara tried to step away, but he refused to let her go.

"I was enamored with you, Cara—am still . . . enamored . . . with you." Rourke swallowed and licked his lips. "I have no right to say this to you, except that I hope it may convince you to let me help."

Not once had he looked away, or refused to meet her eyes. She felt her anger fade. Could it be?

"I want to help you find your brother, not because I want or need to prove to you that I speak the truth, but because I know it will make you happy."

He was saying the right words, yet something inside her hesitated. "My brother . . ." She paused and bit her lip. "He's all I have left in the world. You have to understand, I would do anything, say anything, to protect him."

Something flickered in his gaze and died. "I know."

"Do you? Are you certain?"

He dropped her hands. "Of course. Do you think you're the only one with ties to family?"

At the harshness of his tone, she flinched. He sighed and threw back his shoulders.

"I, too, know what it means to be obligated to

those I love, Cara. I do not fault you for feeling what I myself feel. I just wish . . ."

Here, a strange sadness overtook him, and Cara found herself tempted to lift her hand, as though she might with a wave sweep the sorrow from his handsome face.

Before she could utter a sound, Rourke spoke. "I want to help you, Cara. I swear to you, that much be true. And I'll do my best to spare you any more hurt, so much as it's within my power to do so." He stepped closer, near enough that his whisper roared in her ears. "Do you believe this?"

How could she not? His penetrating stare pierced her very soul. She nodded.

"And will you trust me to help you find your brother?"

The world swirled by in a wash of melting snow and bare-limbed trees. She wanted to look at the carriages clattering by, at the mothers scurrying home with their children in tow— anywhere but at Rourke. In the end, however, she could not avoid his endless blue gaze, as deep and turbulent as the sea.

She tipped her head back to stare at him. "I'll trust you, Rourke Walsh, but not because of the speech you made just now."

Confusion mingled with the storm brewing in his eyes. Drawing on her last ounce of courage, she closed the small gap that remained between them and laid her hand flat against his chest.

"I will trust you because I believe I have glimpsed the kind of man you are in here."

He drew a shuddering breath that might have made her knees go weak had she not already leaned against him. Instead of pulling her hand away, she pressed all the more firmly. "Still, I have a request of my own to make."

He tipped his head, lips tight, though he did not step from her touch. "Make it."

"I will trust you, Rourke Walsh, but in return . . ."

"Aye?"

"In return, I must ask that you also trust me."

27

For several heart-pounding seconds, Rourke could not move, hardly dared speak. Cara's demand served as a burning reminder of who she was . . . and why he pursued her. For years, he'd deemed the entire Hamilton clan as villains of the worst sort, incapable of honor and totally unworthy of trust. If possible, he'd have wiped every last one of them from the earth.

But that was before he'd met Cara, and it was most definitely not how his father would want to be avenged. How much further could he wander down vengeance's dark path and still hope to reclaim the man he'd been? The man that God, and his da, wanted him to be?

Determination rising, he laid his hand over Cara's. "Upon my oath, Cara, I will do my best."

Though the words rang hollow in his own ears, he could not bring himself to promise more. Hesitance dimmed the brilliance of her emerald eyes, washed the hope from them. To his relief, however, she nodded and slipped her hand from beneath his.

"Ah, but we're as slow as a late dinner. We should get on to the boardinghouse before Amelia begins to worry."

Indeed, the streetlamps had begun to glow, casting a cheery path before them. With the snow gone and the grass turning green, it almost felt inviting to be here, alone, with her. Rourke offered his arm, glad that this time Cara did not hesitate to take it. In fact, her full wool skirt brushed against the side of his leg in a most pleasing way as they walked.

"So?" She smiled up at him. "Are you and Giles settled at last?"

Not hardly. He hadn't felt settled since his da died in his arms. "Aye. After we spoke, I began the repairs to the carriage."

"Giles will be glad for your help. Amelia, too."

Rourke shrugged. "It's the least I can do."

"And tomorrow?"

He glanced sideways at her. "Tomorrow?"

"It's just . . . I wondered how you thought we might begin searching for Eoghan."

She peered up at him, her brows lifted high. The hope had returned full force. He squirmed under her stare. "I have some friends who work by the dock. Perhaps you should speak with them."

Friends? More like kinsmen. He shuddered to think of them questioning her, prompting her for details she might be reluctant to give.

Her grip on his arm tightened. "Of course. If you think it might help."

The muscles in his jaw clenched. Afraid she might sense his unease, he forced a smile. "Or I could seek them for you."

"Oh, well—"

Her foot slipped on a patch of mud, but with a quick hand to her back, Rourke kept her from falling.

"Thank you."

No doubt clouded her face as she looked at him, thanking him for such a minor task as saving her from a bit of soggy earth. "You're welcome."

"Would it be better, do you think, to let you speak with these men?" she continued.

Rourke shrugged, glad that for the moment he could at least be honest. "It may, for now, be best to keep you out of harm's way."

"Harm's way?"

"I mean only that they are unaccustomed to a lady in their midst. Their manners, and their speech, leave some to be desired."

"I see. Thank you, Rourke. I'm grateful for your help."

She nodded and then patted his arm in a sisterly way that made him even more uncomfortable. Nothing about the way he felt toward her could be described as familial. Turbulent, yes, perhaps even passionate. But not altruistic and most certainly not familial. Suddenly the need to prove that to her welled up in his gut, pressing on his insides like a most uncomfortable ailment.

The solid walls of the boardinghouse had risen into view. In a handful of strides they'd be at the door. Rourke stopped and pulled Cara to a halt in the shadows outside the circle of light cast by the streetlamps.

"Is something wrong?" She moved to stand in front of him, her touch lingering on his arm.

"No." How could anything be wrong when they were standing there together, alone and sheltered by the gloom of evening from everyone and everything? He stepped closer, took both of her hands in his. "Cara."

She shivered.

"Are you cold?" His voice was as harsh as a bitter wind.

" 'Tis not the night air that makes me tremble," she whispered.

In her gaze, he saw her defenses crumble, leaving a vulnerability she'd not shown before. She'd more than made good her word, standing before him so trusting. He drew her in until she pressed against him, encircled by his arms. Indeed, he meant to kiss her hard and fast, but the moment their lips touched, the anger inside him melted. Her hand rose to his cheek, and he wanted to tear the mitten from her fingers, to feel the warmth of her skin. Long and sweet they kissed, until finally Rourke forced himself to lift his head and step back.

Separated from him, her hand fell to her neck and was joined quickly by the other.

She was at a loss, embarrassed by her response if the color in her cheeks was any indication. He should say something to put her at ease. He took a deep breath. "There now. Our deal is sealed."

"Our . . . deal?"

He lifted one shoulder and folded his hands into his pockets. "To trust one another. We could have spat on it and shaken hands, but in this case a kiss was much more pleasant, don't you agree?"

He hated the words even as he spoke them. Certain she saw through the ruse, he turned from her toward the boardinghouse. "All right then, now that's settled we'd best be getting on."

This time he dared make no offer of his arm, not with his own senses still reeling. He lowered his head and strode the last few yards to the steps. Though she lagged behind, he threw open the door and waited at the threshold.

Her eyes did not meet his as she approached.

She walked with her shoulders thrown back and spine rigid, as though it were iron will that kept her upright and not muscle and sinew. He almost reached out to her as she passed. His fingers tingled for one last tempting touch and yet, somehow, he managed to keep his hand at his side.

Inside, Cara paused. Her lifted brow cut a fiery line against her pale flesh. "What is all that racket? It sounds as though the very hens have come in from the hen house."

Voices heavy with worry rang from inside the boardinghouse, growing louder as he shut the door.

"No, no, no, I tell ya. Sitting on their heels is what got 'em inta this mess in the first place. Squash the rebellion while they can, that be the answer, for sure and for certain."

"Giles, there's no need for stirring up everyone's emotions now." Amelia's voice, normally so gentle, carried a note of urgency.

Rourke slipped his cap from his head and deposited it and his coat on a hook near the door. Afterward he took Cara's coat and scarf and did the same before following her to the parlor, where the residents of the boardinghouse had assembled. With them stood Giles, one arm in a sling, the other high above his head, a letter clenched in his fist.

"Besides, who are you to say what's best for Ireland?" Fire sparked from Deidre's eyes, matching the riotous color of the curls she tossed over her shoulder. "Those 'rebels' you insist on squashing be someone's kin. Have you considered that?"

"Of course he has," Laverne protested. Her mobcap drooped over one eye as she waddled to stand next to Giles at the window. Grabbing the cap near the nape of her neck, she gave it a jerk and popped it back into place. "It's not that he wants bloodshed. They're going about it the wrong way is all."

"Says the Brit."

"Tillie!" Amelia's face was awash with horror. "Not you, too."

The unexpected remark surprised them all, especially coming from Tillie, who had proven to be of the gentler sort. Only Deidre had the gall to appear satisfied. She crossed her arms and clamped her lips, pleased for once to let someone else do the talking.

Tillie's face colored a deep red. "I'm sorry, Amelia. It's just . . . if you only knew how badly I want for all of this fighting to be over. It's gone on so long, and my Braedon . . . he would still be here . . ." She dropped her face into her hands, muffling her words. "Forgive me."

"There now, you see what you've done, Giles?" Breda bustled over and laid her arm about Tillie's shaking shoulders. "Waving that blasted letter about like it were a flag." She shot a disgusted frown at Giles, then gave Tillie a pat. "There, there now, me bairn. Do not fret. Giles be speaking out of turn, that's all."

Amelia posted herself at Tillie's other side and joined Breda in comforting the girl. "Indeed he has. He didn't mean to upset you—upset any of us, isn't that right, Giles?"

Two formidable flanks, the women directed a glare at Giles that would have melted iron. He nodded weakly and shoved the letter into the pocket of his breeches.

As always, Ana stood furthest from the fire near the door. Now that the attention had been diverted to Tillie, Cara crossed to her.

"What happened?" she whispered in a tone still loud enough to be heard in the quiet room.

"Giles got a letter from his kinsfolk back home. They tell of trouble brewing, of plans to form some sort of uprising against parliament."

"What kind of uprising?"

Ana shrugged. "They didn't say. Just that they be calling Giles home."

"What?"

"Something about Ireland needing all of her sons to help settle the dispute once and for all."

Cara's fingers pulled at her bottom lip. "Is he going?"

"He hasn't said."

"Why do you care?" Compared to Ana's and Cara's whispers, Deidre's voice was a clanging cymbal. It rang out in the quiet room, turning everyone's eyes to fix on the pair.

Cara quickly hid her startled expression and lifted her chin. "Your pardon, Deidre?"

Deidre's arms had gone from crossed to planted on her hips. Once again, Rourke found himself leaning protectively toward Cara.

"Why do you care if Giles sails back to Ireland to join in the fighting?"

Tillie's head lifted. "There be fighting?"

"Not yet, but I guarantee there will be." Deidre's gaze returned to Cara. "Well?"

"I asked not whether he'd be joining the uprising, but simply if he would be going," Cara insisted with a glance at Laverne.

"Besides, she isn't the only one with questions," Rourke added quickly.

At his response, Deidre lifted a brow and the corner of her mouth rose. What exactly did the woman know that made her eye him in such a way?

"Of that, I be quite certain, Mr. *Walsh*."

Ice settled in Rourke's veins. So, Deidre knew who he was, or at the very least suspected that he wasn't who he claimed. Perhaps it was time he could say the same. Just who was Deidre Sullivan, and what was her battle against him . . . and Cara?

Gritting his teeth, Rourke kept silent. Whether she was friend or foe had yet to be determined. He'd not risk exposing his true purpose in front of Cara and the others by saying too much.

Thankfully he didn't have to. Amelia led Tillie to the door, then turned to address the room. "In light of everything that's happened, I think it best if we take supper in our rooms. Breda, will you help Laverne prepare the trays?"

"Of course."

"I'll help, too," Ana offered, joining them at the door.

Amelia quickly shook her head. "That may not be wise, dear. You still look a bit piqued."

Remembering why she had not joined Cara at the candle shop, Rourke stepped forward. "I'll do it."

Cara stayed him with a touch to his arm. "No, let me. You see to Giles."

The women withdrew with a haste that said they were anxious to be rid of the unsavory conversation that had drawn them to the parlor. Even Deidre retired from the room like a shadow, gone to skulk in unknown parts of the house. For just a moment, Rourke indulged the wish that she be gone permanently, a thought that he firmly shook free.

"I guess we'd best be about our own chores, eh, Giles?" He patted the old man's bent shoulder and indicated the door.

Even so, the old caretaker appeared reluctant. His hand lingered on the pocket where he'd shoved the letter. "Blasted rebels. Not one of 'em with a lick of sense."

He continued mumbling as he shuffled from the room. Rourke followed close behind, but his thoughts were an ocean away. An uprising of any sort meant trouble for those members of parliament with whom his father had once served. He hated to think of the worry their families faced. Had he been wrong to leave? Perhaps if he'd stayed behind instead of pursuing his quest for vengeance . . .

It was an old argument, one he'd wrestled many times. Somehow he knew he'd fight the battle again, and it would be a very long, very sleepless night.

28

The path to the candle shop seemed unduly long the next morning, especially since Cara once again made the trek alone. As Amelia had predicted, Ana was not quite over her illness. It took hold with renewed vigor during the night and left her flushed and weak when she woke.

It appeared, Cara thought as she approached the door to Mr. O'Bannon's shop, that she wasn't the only one. A note fluttered from the jamb, and upon reading it she discovered that Mr. O'Bannon also was too ill to report to work. That meant she'd have to run the shop alone.

Sighing, Cara rounded the corner and went to

the woodbox at the rear of the store, where Mr. O'Bannon kept the spare key. By the time she unlocked the door and carried in enough wood to stoke the fire in the stove next to the desk, she was tired and sweaty, her hem soaked. She had just removed her coat and bonnet and thought to warm herself by the fire when the bell above the door jingled.

"I'll be right there," she called, not expecting a reply and therefore not surprised when she received none.

The apron Ana normally wore hung on a hook behind the door. Cara fetched it, dropped it over her head, and fastened the strings around her waist as she went to see to the customers.

Customer.

One man alone waited on the other side of the counter. His back was to her, but something about him seemed familiar. Cara slowed her steps. "Good morning."

The man turned. A ragged beard hid half his face, and he wore a cap pulled low over bushy brows. His eyes, behind a pair of thick spectacles, clapped onto her with an intensity she found unnerving.

She smoothed the apron with shaking fingers. "Can I be of help with something?"

Though he stepped closer, he could come no further than the counter allowed, a fact for which Cara found herself grateful.

"The owner of this shop." The man gestured at the candles lining the walls.

"Mr. O'Bannon?" Cara said, proud she did not stammer.

The man nodded.

What could he want with him? Cara swallowed and laced her fingers to still their trembling. "He is ill, I'm afraid. Won't be in until the morning, possibly longer."

The man's eyes gleamed. Fortunately the bell tinkled again, and she sidestepped to extend the same cheery greeting to a pair of women entering side by side, their loud chatter a welcome distraction.

It was a busy morning. Perhaps the foul weather created a need for people to replenish their stock of candles. Whatever the reason, Cara was glad that the shop seldom emptied. Though the man with the shaggy beard lingered a while, taking a somewhat unusual interest in their wares, he eventually wandered out. Cara breathed easier when he was gone, but the steady flow of customers kept her too busy to wonder what he'd wanted since he made no purchase and asked no more questions. By five o'clock she was exhausted and more than ready to make her way home.

With her scarf looped securely around her neck, Cara exited the shop, locked the door behind her, and then circled to the back to replace the key. She didn't linger long. The days were still short, and combined with a heavy gloom from an overcast sky, the space behind the shop was too dark to see well. In fact, it took her several attempts to find the hook in the woodbox where the key hung. Finally she took off her mitten and felt along the edge.

"Need some help?"

The voice behind her made her jump.

"Beggin' your pardon, miss. I dinna mean to frighten ya."

A hunched figure, broad in the shoulders, stood in the entrance to the narrow alley. Still clasping the key, Cara lowered both hands from her chest and did her best to sound calm. "You startled me, is all. No harm done."

The man stepped closer, but not until he left the shadow cast by the side of the building did Cara realize he was the same man who'd visited earlier. Her heart leapt to her throat, and of their own accord her fingers tightened around the key. Replacing it could wait. In the morning she'd explain to Mr. O'Bannon why she'd not returned the key to the box.

She swallowed and dipped her head. "Well, I'd best be on my way."

Only the man was blocking her path, and he stared at her in a way that was vaguely unnerving. Her bare hand rose to the scarf at her neck. "S-sir? If you don't mind letting me pass?"

A smile curled his lip. "Ah, but I do mind, lass. I mind very much."

Suddenly, Cara recognized the voice, if not the face. The wharf . . . the man who'd held her arm too long, only she'd been too concerned about finding Eoghan to be afraid . . . he was here. She stumbled until the back of her knees hit the woodbox.

"What do you want?"

"Ach." He rubbed his scruffy chin with one large hand. "So, you've seen through the beard. Well, it was a weak attempt anyway."

"Attempt at what? What have you to hide?"

"From you? Nothing, I suppose." He stepped closer. "From others?" His eyes narrowed until they glinted like razors. "Much."

Cara's heart beat erratically inside her chest. While he spoke, she edged sideways along the woodbox until she found the end, then moved the width of it to the wall of the shop. It increased the distance between them a total of four steps. "I don't understand. What has that to do with me?"

"You're a Hamilton," he growled. In a second he'd skirted the woodbox. Another second, he towered over her. "It has everything to do with you."

Cara couldn't move, could barely breathe. The man was huge, and she'd have had to be blind to mistake his black intent. "Who are you?" she whispered.

"Does it matter?"

"Aye, it matters."

His hands rose, drifted toward her throat. Cara fought to remain still. If she was to have a chance, any hope of escaping, he had to come closer.

"You've been asking questions, haven't ya, lass? Inquiring in places you dinna belong."

Cara scrambled for his meaning. "At the wharf?"

Or the church. She'd asked about the Fenians. But this was not the man she'd spoken to. Heart racing, she shook her head. "I meant no harm by my questions. It was simple curiosity what compelled me to ask about . . ." She trailed off, as if speaking the name would condemn her further. "What do you want?" she said, staring at the hand drifting closer, closer, until icy fingers grazed her neck. "Please, if you will just tell me—"

Before she could finish, strong hands closed around her throat. She reacted without thinking, bringing up the key and jabbing it into the man's neck. In the same instant, she let her knees go weak.

The man screamed, a cry of rage and pain so carnal it made Cara shudder. His hands left her throat to claw at his own neck, and Cara dashed around him, gasping as she felt nails grasp her arm and rasp across her flesh. With his other hand he snagged the flapping end of her scarf. It tightened briefly, threatening to cut off her air. She shrugged free of it and left it dangling from his fingers. Reaching the street, she ran, screaming.

"Help!"

Passersby gaped at her. Cara ran to the gentleman closest to the shop, a thin man in a black coat and matching top hat.

She clung to his arm, her face awash with tears that streamed unchecked from her eyes. "Please, sir! I need your help. I've b-been attacked."

The gentleman lifted full gray brows and peered back in the direction she'd come. "Attacked? By whom?"

"A man in the alley." Nausea swirled through Cara's stomach. "I think he was going to . . ." Bile climbed her throat. "He was going to . . ."

The man's grip on her arm tightened. "Yes? What is it, girl? You thought he was going to what?"

"I think he wanted to kill me," Cara spat.

A second later, she could no longer contain the roiling mess of fear and hysteria. Doubling over, she emptied the contents of her stomach onto the street.

29

An unfamiliar carriage trimmed in gilt and sporting a handsome team of sorrel horses rumbled to a stop in front of the boardinghouse. Rourke rested both arms atop the broom he'd been using to clear the stairs of rotted leaves and debris and watched as the door swung open and an older gentleman in a long black coat alighted the steps.

Visitors at this hour?

The man tipped his hat to Rourke, then turned back to the carriage and offered his hand to someone inside.

Returning the gesture, Rourke touched his fingers to the brim of his cap and then gave one last sweep of the broom to the mud and slush piling beside the stairs. From the corner of his eye he saw a wool skirt emerge, followed by a slender hand, and a sleeve encased in a coat that looked suspiciously like Cara's.

She stepped from the carriage. Her hair was in disarray and she wobbled when she set foot on the sidewalk, but the gentleman accompanying her was quick to take her arm and help her up the path.

Rourke's stomach plummeted to his boots. Casting aside the broom, he hurried to meet them. "Cara?"

The gentleman held up his palm as Rourke approached. "You know the young lady, sir?"

Reluctantly, Rourke drew to a halt. Cara was pale. Moisture pooled in her eyes and clung to her lashes. He would have preferred to wrap her in an embrace, to offer comfort and demand what cursed event had brought her to tears, but the old man's hand would not allow it. He drew a shuddering breath and nodded. "She is a resident in this boardinghouse. I am the caretaker, or rather I am filling in for the caretaker who is injured."

Giving a grunt, the gentleman lowered his hand and ushered Cara toward the steps. "Seems to be a bit of that going around."

"What happened? Is she hurt?" He assumed the place at Cara's other side, assisting as the gentleman walked her inside.

"Not that I can tell," the man said, "though I haven't been able to get much out of the young lady."

He had a kindly voice, and Rourke was glad he'd been the one to find Cara and bring her home. "In here," he said, motioning toward the parlor. "I'll get her something to drink and inform the others."

Cara caught his arm as he turned to go. Like a rabbit caught in a snare, she pleaded with him,

271

her eyes wide and chin quivering. "No, Rourke. Not the others. Just Amelia."

He glanced at the gentleman, then back at her. "Are you certain? Laverne, and Ana—"

She shook her head. "Just Amelia."

After a moment, he gave a nod and patted her arm. "Very well."

"I'll wait with her," the gentleman offered, looking to Cara, who agreed with a dip of her head.

Rourke squeezed her fingers and leaned close. "I won't be long."

He spun on his heel and exited the parlor, his long strides carrying him swiftly through the boardinghouse until he found Amelia in the library, a book in her hands and her glasses resting on the tip of her nose. She glanced up as he thrust the door open without knocking.

Catching sight of his face, she snapped the book closed and stood. "What is it?"

"Cara is in the parlor. She needs you. Something has happened."

Confusion mottled Amelia's features, although she did not ask questions. The book slid from her fingers and landed with a thump on the cushion where she'd been. Lips tight, she followed Rourke to the parlor where Cara sat, a glass of water clutched in her hands. The gentleman hovered at her side, his tall black hat gripped behind his back.

Hands outstretched, Amelia glided across the room. She gathered Cara close and sank beside her on the sofa. "Are you all right, dear?"

"I am, thanks to this man." She lifted her head and offered a grateful smile to the gentleman. "Amelia, this is Mr. Darby. He was on the sidewalk in front of the store when I was attacked."

"Attacked!" Amelia drew back to peer into Cara's face. "By whom?"

Slowly, Cara revealed the details of her ordeal. Each word fanned the rage building in Rourke's gut. Twice, he clenched the back of the sofa in order to keep from shaking his fists at the ceiling. At God. When at last she recounted her escape, weakness claimed his knees and he sank into a chair near her feet.

Amelia turned to the gentleman. Though pallor had crept over her cheeks as she listened to Cara's tale, there was no doubting the relief in her voice. "We are certainly glad you were near, Mr. Darby. I can never thank you enough for bringing Cara home."

"The man who attacked her," Rourke interrupted, "did either of you get a look at him?"

"Afraid not." Mr. Darby slapped his hat against his thigh with a glower. "By the time I got around to looking for him, the scoundrel had escaped over the fence." He lifted an eyebrow and squinted at Cara. "Miss Hamilton?"

She nodded and turned frightened eyes to

273

Rourke. "I think I've seen him before, on the wharf, the day you took me to look at the ships. I couldn't be certain, of course. It was getting dark, and I was frightened, but . . ." She paused, thinking, then gave a firm nod. "It was him."

Hugh? Afraid the wrong movement might betray his thoughts, Rourke focused his energy on holding every muscle tightly in check.

Twice, his kinsman had come near to claiming Cara's life. Twice, she'd escaped by the narrowest of margins. He shuddered to think what would have happened had she not been quick to act, or had not Mr. Darby appeared before Hugh could redouble his efforts.

Amelia fixed him with an incredulous stare. "Do you know this man, Rourke?"

"I remember the day Cara refers to," Rourke said slowly. "The man she saw takes odd jobs at the wharf. I pass him from time to time."

Even as he spoke, his conscience screamed him a liar. But he couldn't reveal the truth, at least not yet. Still, was his deception the cause of Cara's pain?

Agony over his divided loyalties tore at his soul.

Mr. Darby gave a loud *humph*. "No surprise, then. What disturbs me is that even good, hardworking folks can no longer feel safe on the streets." He directed a pointed stare at Rourke. "You think, perhaps, you might be able to provide the constable with a description of this chap?"

Rourke nodded, avoiding his gaze.

"Very well. I leave you ladies in this fellow's capable hands." Dipping low, he bowed first to Amelia and then to Cara. "Take care of yourself, young lady," he said, claiming her hand and giving it a pat. "And from now on, I don't recommend you walk home alone. Hate to see you fall into another spot of trouble and no one be there to help."

"Thank you, Mr. Darby," Cara said, her eyes filling with fresh tears.

Amelia, too, offered her thanks and said good-bye before Rourke showed the old gentleman out.

After he left, Rourke stood with his hand on the doorknob, noting the passing seconds by the ticking of the clock in the hall. If Hugh was determined to see Cara dead, Rourke couldn't let her out of his sight. But why? What drove Hugh's vendetta against this woman and no others before her?

His hand fell from the knob. Tonight, at least, the answer would have to wait. He couldn't risk raising the women's suspicions by leaving the boardinghouse to seek Hugh out. Circling back to the parlor, he found Amelia engrossed in tending to Cara's wounds.

His breath caught at the angry red slashes trailing her arm and neck. He'd not noticed them when she arrived. Swallowing hard, he drew a footstool close and sat. "How is she?"

A smile shoved its way onto Amelia's lips. She

followed it with a pat to Cara's shoulder. "She got quite a scare, but she'll be fine by morning, isn't that right, dear?"

A brief nod and then Cara turned her face away.

"Still, we'd best see about tidying up these scratches. Wouldn't want you catching some kind of infection." Suddenly businesslike, Amelia rose, her skirts swishing, and clasped Rourke by the arm. "Help her to her room, won't you, Rourke, while I go and fetch some water and clean bandages?"

Cara pushed upright, her palm smoothing her sleeve down to cover the scratches on her arm. "No, please. That won't be necessary."

"Fie," Rourke growled.

"Truly. I'm fine now—oh!"

Before she could protest further, Rourke stood and swept her into his arms. "We'll be upstairs, Amelia. While you're about the bandages, be sure to let Laverne know that Cara will be taking her supper in her room."

He didn't wait for Amelia's reply, but turned instead from her satisfied grin and strode toward the hall. What she thought of his actions was not important, at least not while Cara was tucked into his arms. Soon she'd be warm and safe in her bed.

That was the only thing that mattered.

Though her arms felt weak and her knees shook, Cara clung with all her might to Rourke's broad shoulders. He carried her with dizzying speed up the winding staircase, barely slowing his stride when he reached her door and forced it open with his foot.

"Rourke—" she began weakly.

"Quiet."

Though the word was terse, his tone was not. Neither was the glance he gave that settled over her like a blanket made of down. Reaching the bed, he let go with one arm and set her briefly on her feet while he drew back the covers, then swept her up again and laid her on the mattress as though she were no more than a bairn.

She spoke not a word as he moved to her shoes, his fingers managing the buttons without the aid of a hook. Scarcely did she breathe as his warm fingers cupped her calf while the other hand pulled her boot free and deposited it on the floor with a thud. This was soon followed by a second thud, and then he was tucking the blankets around her chin, his knuckles lingering lightly against the skin below her ear.

His gaze lifted to meet hers. "You could have been hurt—even killed—tonight."

So close was he, his hoarse whisper warmed her cheek. A thrill raced through Cara, vibrant and intoxicating. "I know."

"The other day, as well."

"The carriage."

"Aye." His gaze roamed over her face, lingering

on her lips until she blushed, then moving upward. "Cara . . ."

He would kiss her again, of that she was certain. She wanted him to, of that she was certain, too.

He leaned closer, his lashes sweeping down to cover the brilliance of his blue eyes, but instead of touching his lips to hers, his mouth grazed her ear and sent a shiver racing across her flesh.

"I could not bear to see you come to harm," he whispered. His hands stroked her shoulders, then moved lower until he gripped her arms. "I would rather die than see you hurt, and yet twice . . . twice I could not . . ."

He pulled away to look her fully in the face. Cara's heart thrashed against her ribs, longing for something she sensed only Rourke could give. She lifted her hand to stroke his cheek. As she did, her sleeve rolled back, exposing the fiery scratches.

Groaning, Rourke caught her fingers to his chest. "This is my fault. I should never have let you go to the shop alone."

"You didn't know Mr. O'Bannon would be ill."

Her breath caught as Rourke ignored her defense of him and pressed kiss after kiss to her palm, her wrist, and finally her injured arm.

Behind them a stair creaked, and Cara knew Amelia had arrived with the water and bandages. She touched Rourke's bowed head, letting her fingers curl in the dark locks at his temple a second before she tugged her hand free.

Amelia bustled through the door, a large basin in her hands. At the foot of the bed she paused and smiled. "You look better." Her gaze swiveled to Rourke. "Her color has returned, wouldn't you say? And the sparkle is back in those lovely green eyes. Can't tell you how relieved I am to see that."

"I as well," Rourke said, warming Cara through with the look he gave her before moving aside to make room for Amelia.

Once again she set her skirts to swaying as she crossed to the nightstand and set down the bowl. From her apron pocket she pulled a wide linen strip and laid it on the bed. "There now, we'll have you tidied up in no time. Let me see those scratches, dear."

Obediently, Cara lifted her sleeve and proffered her arm, aware as she did of Rourke's every move. Stooping low in front of the hearth, he scraped the thickest ashes into a bucket, reserving a few of the coals for the evening fire. Before long, he'd built a cheery blaze, Amelia had her arm cleansed and bandaged and the lamp beside her bed lit, and they were both moving to the door.

"Try and rest now, dear," Amelia said, her hands clasped at her waist. "I'll bring you up some supper as soon as it's finished. After that, I'll send Tillie to help you ready for bed."

It had been a long time since Cara had felt so

well tended. She smiled and offered her thanks before turning to Rourke. "My thanks to you, as well." She nodded toward the fire. "That should chase away what's left of the chill."

" 'Twas simple enough. I wish I could've done more."

Fearing they'd think her stalling their departure, Cara forced a smile and said nothing.

Pausing at the threshold, Amelia rested her hand on the jamb and cast one last glance at Cara. "Don't worry about tomorrow, dear. I've already sent word with Giles about your accident, and informed Mr. O'Bannon that you will not be in."

"Oh, but I'm sure by tomorrow—"

Both Amelia and Rourke fixed her with stern glowers, and Cara was forced to surrender with a giggle. "Very well, but when the rent is late . . ." She trailed off and wiggled her brows.

Amelia laughed. "You've already paid the rent. It's not due for another month."

Hitching her skirts, she spun and disappeared out the door. Rourke lingered a moment longer, then too soon the door closed him from sight.

Sighing, Cara dipped lower under the covers. Outside, the wind howled against the windows. Rain pattered lightly against the panes. The fire, cheery when combined with Rourke's presence, now cast shadows that jumped and leapt and made Cara strain to see into the furthest corners.

She shuddered as a pair of dark, forbidding eyes burned into her memory. Pain from her scratches flamed anew as she recalled the strong fingers scraping along her arm and tangling with the scarf at her neck.

She clutched the blanket to her chin. The man had intended to kill her. She'd read that with certainty in his powerful grasp. The question was, why? What had she done? Or perhaps not she, but Eoghan . . .

She shook the thought free. No one in America knew who she was, no one except Rourke. Why then? What other reason could there be for wanting her dead?

"You've been asking questions, haven't ya, lass? Inquiring in places you dinna belong."

Cara's heart rate quickened. She had asked questions—at the church when she inquired about the Fenians. Shortly after, Deidre had accused her of being a spy. With the memory came Giles's words about an uprising in Ireland. Could they all somehow be connected?

Cara shivered under the sheets, cold, despite what she'd said about the fire chasing away the chill. With night falling outside, she'd never felt so isolated or terrified, not even when she thought her brother dead.

"God, oh, God, where is Eoghan? Why hasn't he come for me?"

She pressed the blanket to her mouth to keep

from being heard, and still she could not silence the cry that raged in her heart.

She was alone.

And afraid.

And her enemy, at least one that she knew of, slept in the room down the hall. The other, more frightening, hid in every shadow.

30

Dawn crept over Cara's windowsill, the sun's watery rays tugging at her tired eyelids. She hadn't slept, hadn't eaten except for a bite of bread from the tray Amelia brought, but she couldn't help the thoughts that scuttled through her brain, keeping her alert to every sound.

Tossing aside the covers, she touched her toes to the cold floor and shivered. Another damp day. Maybe if she hurried, she'd be dressed and out the door before the others even slipped from their beds.

Her limbs shook as she washed her face and combed her hair, then scurried to the armoire to exchange her nightgown for a plain cotton skirt and blouse. Afterward, she found her boots where Rourke had dropped them on the floor and jammed her stockinged feet inside.

Downstairs, noise from the kitchen told her

Laverne already stirred despite the early hour. Cara skirted that room and made straight for her coat in the hall. Her scarf was lost for good, clutched in her attacker's grasp when she fled. She still had her mittens, but the sun rising in the east promised a warmth that said she wouldn't need them. Cara crammed them into her coat pockets anyway, quietly cracked open the door, and slipped outside.

The rain that had fallen during the night had hardened into spring frost. The rising sun sparkled off every tree and rooftop. Though she would have liked to pause to admire nature's beauty, she didn't dare tarry. One word, one question about her destination, and she'd be forced to lie.

Tugging her collar around her ears, Cara stepped onto the sidewalk and started the long walk to the wharf.

Ashberry Street was quiet this time of the morning. Cara made it easily past the rows of shops and vendors until she reached Broad Street and turned south. Here the swirling wind did battle with her hair. It tugged strands loose from her bun, whipping them into her eyes and filling them with tears. She lowered her head and pressed on. Still, the bitter norther dragged at her skirt, slowing her steps. She nearly sighed with relief when at last the columned entrance to the ferry landing appeared.

Travelers to Ellis Island were already milling at the gate. They were men mostly, but a few women as well, and Cara joined their ranks without causing so much as a raised brow. Across the way she spotted a red-haired priest whose blue eyes twinkled merrily despite the briskness of the day.

She wove through the sparse crowd to him and offered a shy smile. "Good morning."

He touched the brim of his cap and returned her smile. "Good morning."

"On your way to the island?"

"That I am. Make this trip often, sometimes two, three times a week."

So, despite her doubts, God knew her plans and had made provision. She thanked Him, a catch in her throat. "Then you know what time the first ferry leaves?"

"Aye. The boat'll be around in another half hour or so. I like to arrive early so as to purchase my ticket and be among those first to board."

Cara's brow wrinkled and dismay, heavier than any she'd felt last night, washed over her. A ticket? Why had she not thought to bring money for the fare?

The priest ducked his head and peered at her from beneath his cap. "Ya did think to purchase a ticket, didn't ya, lass?"

"I . . ." She cast about for the ticket window. "How much . . . ?"

Did it matter? She had no money. Her only option was to return to the boardinghouse, collect enough for the fare, and then hope to escape unseen . . . again.

Stepping back, she chided her foolishness, the sleepless night, everything that had led to her scrambling from the house without thinking through her plan first.

The priest put up his hand as she turned to go. "Wait, lass. Would this help?" Digging in his pockets, he retrieved a fistful of yellowed stubs, pulled one free, and held it to her.

Cara stared. "Is that—?"

"A pass to board the ferry?" He nodded. "I buy several for times such as this."

A blush warmed her cheeks. "You run into scatterbrained females often?"

His eyes twinkled and he held the ticket higher invitingly.

Still, she hesitated. "I cannot repay you."

The priest lowered his hand and motioned toward the side of a building where an over-hanging roof blocked the worst of the wind's bite. Glad for the shelter, Cara followed.

"My name's Edward Murphy," the priest said, "but ya can call me Father Ed." He smiled and tucked the tickets back into the pocket of his coat. "Most people do."

Cara extended her hand. "A pleasure to meet you, Father Ed. I'm Cara Hamilton."

Father Ed's handshake was solid, not too tight. A good handshake, like her daed's.

"Ya new to the city?" he asked when she let go.

Cara nodded quickly.

"Ya have family here?"

She mulled her reply. He was a priest, after all. It wouldn't be fit to be caught lying, especially to him. "So far, I'm alone," she said at last.

He bobbed his head sadly. "That be the way of it for many Irish girls. That's why I started a shelter in Battery Park." He lifted an eyebrow. "Our Lady of Deliverance. Ya know it?"

She thought, then shook her head.

Father Ed pointed across the harbor to the island in the distance. "Used to be, people coming off the boats simply had to be healthy. Now it's harder for single Irish women. They must have family or means of support. Most need some form of employment. Either that—" he paused to look at her—"or a husband to care for them."

Cara thought back to the day she'd arrived and grimaced. "Is that why you go so often to the island? To help young women traveling to America alone?"

He nodded, hitched his shoulders, then folded his hands into his pockets. "Two nuns help me run the shelter. We give the lasses a place to eat and sleep and help them find employment. Were it not for that, I fear many of these young women would be turned away before they ever set foot in America." His gaze turned somber. "Something drove them from their homes. I wager it was terrible to make them risk so much and travel so far?"

His voice lifted at the end to form a question. Affinity for the priest blossomed in Cara's heart. She smiled and pointed toward his breast pocket where he'd stuffed the tickets.

"Is that why you carry those with you?"

"The tickets?" He pulled one out. "Aye, that be why." He held it toward her a second time. "Often, doing the work of God is as simple as helping a seeking soul find what they're looking for, eh, Miss Hamilton?"

Cara secured the ticket in her palm. "Aye, Father Ed. And, thank you."

He shook his head. "No thanks necessary." His chin jutted toward the dock and a ramp that workers wrestled to bridge the gap between a rusting steamer and the shore. "There's the ferry." He offered his arm. "Shall we?"

She nodded and slipped her arm through his. The closer they came to the dock, the louder the noise of the wharf became. Gulls circled overhead, their cries lost in the hiss of the steamers and the shouts of the workers. Passengers lined up, their feet pounding the wooden pier until Cara knew she'd have to shout to be heard above the din. Father Ed, too, fell silent and simply pointed toward a spot along the rail once they were aboard.

The ship bobbed and rocked on the waves as passengers packed her deck. Finally the first mate gave the order to cast off and the ferry shoved from the dock. The wind rose as the ship picked up speed. Were it not for their position on the sheltered starboard side, Cara feared it might have picked her up and pitched her over.

"So, tell me, Miss Hamilton," Father Ed said, shouting to be heard above the rumble of the ship's engine, "what brings you to the island if not family? Be ya searching for someone?"

She nodded. "I am."

His brow furrowed. Eyes grave, he leaned toward her and cupped his hands to his mouth. "Ya know it be common for many folks to change their name or have it changed for 'em once they arrive at Ellis, don't ya, lass?"

Cara's brows rose. "What?"

"Some do it to fit in, make themselves less foreign. Others have it done for them by the inspectors. So unless they were blessed with a name simple to spell, they might be difficult to find." He shifted to stand closer. "Do ya know when this person arrived? That might narrow the search."

Cara thought back on her conversations with the members of the boardinghouse. Tillie said Deidre arrived some months before her, and she'd been at the boardinghouse almost a year. She glanced at Father Ed. "I think I can figure it pretty close."

"That's good."

Caught in the trough of a wave, the ship dipped forward. Father Ed grasped Cara's arm in one hand and steadied himself at the rail with the other. Once the ship righted, he grimaced. "Perhaps we'd best see about our sea legs and keep the conversation for later."

Grabbing the rail in both hands, Cara nodded. For several long, heart-pounding minutes, the ferry bucked the choppy waves. By the time the landing at Ellis Island came into view, her stomach was in knots and she had new sympathy for the man who'd made the trip to the lavatory on her first crossing.

The rolling ocean even made docking difficult. Cara's whole body trembled when at last she stepped from the boat onto shore. Staring up at the immigration building's imposing façade, she could only hope that locating the information she sought would prove an easier task than coming to the island had been.

Plucking another nail from the bunch clustered between his teeth, Rourke held it to the carriage frame and drove it home with two vicious swipes of his hammer. Ever since learning of Cara's disappearance at breakfast, he'd listened intently for her return. It was now nigh unto supper and still there was no sign of her. Had she received word from her brother? Was that where she'd gone . . . to meet him? If so, would she return? And what would Hugh say if he learned he'd been right all along but Rourke had somehow managed to let their one link to Hamilton slip through his fingers?

Picturing his kinsman's smirking face only made Rourke angrier. Though he'd waited outside Hugh's apartment long into the night, he'd seen no sign of the man—almost as though he'd known Rourke would come looking.

He placed another nail and gave the hammer a hefty swing, satisfied by the way the crash of metal on metal traveled up his arm.

At least repairing the carriage gave him something to do besides worry about Cara.

Shock slowed his swing, made his aim untrue. The hammer landed with a sickening thud against his thumb. Howling with rage and pain, he tossed the hammer to the stable floor and gripped his throbbing thumb in his other hand.

"*Tsk, tsk.* Done that a time or two me own self." Giles leaned against the stable wall, his bad arm nestled in a sling. He bent down, secured the handle on a water bucket, and carried it to Rourke. "Usually only happened when I was distracted, though. Got something on your mind, lad?"

Rourke yanked a handkerchief from his back pocket, shook it open, and dipped it into the bucket. Then, wrapping it tight, he used the cool pack to calm the fiery pain in his injured thumb.

"I 'spose I do." He grimaced and motioned toward the workbench, only too happy to sit and chat a while with Giles. Brows raised, he tipped his head toward Giles's arm. "We're a pair, eh? Only two good hands between us."

Giles gave a loud guffaw. "Only problem is, they be two right hands, not one of each."

Now that the pain had subsided, Rourke could chuckle.

"So?" Giles wagged his bushy eyebrows. "You gonna tell me what has you so befuddled you nigh took your thumb off?"

Rourke sighed. "It's Cara. When she's in the room, she's all I think about. When she's not . . ." He shrugged, angered by his inability to control his thoughts.

Giles nodded, his knuckles scraping at his cheek. "Ach . . . so that's it. You've taken a shine to Miss Hamilton." His lips split in a grin. "Kinna say as I blame you. I'd probably be heartsick meself if I were a few years younger."

Slowly his grin faded and his grizzled head wagged from side to side. " 'Tis a shame, though, to see such a pretty young lass carrying so much sorrow. Seems all of Miss Amelia's boarders are burdened with one sort of cross or another."

Of that he was certain. Rourke grunted his agreement.

"Take that young Tillie, for example. Have you ever seen a body so bowed with sorrow? And unforgivingness has about consumed Deidre. I wonder if she even realizes how bitter she's become."

Rourke stiffened, reluctantly compelled to see himself through Giles's eyes. Only his bitterness hadn't corrupted him as much as Deidre's, he assured himself . . . yet.

"And what about you?" Giles continued, nudging Rourke's arm with his elbow. "What's your secret?"

"Me?"

Giles lowered his chin and peered up at him. "Everyone's got secrets. What's yours?"

Rourke unwrapped the handkerchief. Though his thumb looked red and swollen, he'd not broken the skin. He grimaced. He'd probably lose his nail in a week or two, though. He let water dribble from his fingers into the hay strewn across the stable floor, then tucked the handkerchief back into his pocket.

Slowly he lifted his gaze to meet Giles's. "You're correct in what you say, but if I were to admit it to you, it would no longer be a secret, be that not so?"

A low chuckle rumbled from Giles's throat. Rising, he clapped his hand on Rourke's shoulder. "True enough, lad. True enough." He motioned over his shoulder with his thumb. "If you're finished out here, would you mind taking a look at the flue in the library fireplace? There's a good amount of smoke drafting back into the house. I'm thinking something be keeping it from opening properly."

Rourke nodded. Another chore meant his mind wouldn't wander to Cara and wondering if she was all right. It might even prove less dangerous than swinging a hammer. He left the stable and trudged up the back steps of the boardinghouse after Giles, pausing on the landing to stomp the mud and hay from his boots.

Inside, a fire in the kitchen's massive fireplace wrapped the room in warmth. Rourke crossed to it, took off his coat, and draped it over the back of a chair to dry. A moment later, Laverne appeared, the apron around her middle sagging beneath the weight of a goodly amount of potatoes.

"There you are. Finished with the repairs to the carriage?" She dumped the contents of her apron onto the table, scrambling to catch the ones that tried to roll away.

"Almost," Rourke said.

Giles ambled to Laverne's side and plunked his good arm about her shoulders. "Go easy on him, lass. He's injured."

Laverne snorted. "I'm a bit long in the tooth to be called a lass, and you know it." She quirked an eyebrow and peered at Rourke. "Where you be injured?"

He lifted his thumb. She strode to him, grabbed his hand, and jerked it down to look.

"Eh. You'll live." She released his hand and crossed her arms over her chest. "Well, maybe you can take a look at the fireplace in the library. Amelia says the smoke in there is thicker than an English fog."

"Now, Laverne, I've already told him," Giles said, sliding onto a stool and patting the one next to him. "You come over here and tend to these potatoes and leave the hard work to us blokes."

Her grunt rivaled that of any man, but she did as he bid and settled herself on the stool. Leaving them to their banter, Rourke exited the kitchen and wound his way to the library.

A damp chill gripped the room, as the fire had been allowed to go out. Rourke cleared the firebox of ashes, then laid his hand against the stones to test for heat. Warm, but not scalding.

Lying on his back, he inched up until he could see the flue. Indeed, it was positioned half open and no amount of finagling could get it to budge.

Wriggling out, he clapped the soot from his hands and stood. He'd need his tools. Hopefully it was nothing more than rust or debris that needed to be knocked free and not some bird or squirrel that had climbed into the chimney to escape the cold and wound up meeting with an unhappy fate.

In the hall, he was met by a whistling wind. Cara wrestled with the front door, her shoulder jammed against it and her feet braced as she shoved with all her might to get it closed. Rourke hurried to help, snapping out the blustery blast with a grunt before turning to glare at Cara.

"Where have you been?"

The wisps of hair that peeked from under her bonnet clung to her face, and her eyes were over-bright, her cheeks splotched with red.

"Never mind." Rourke stepped forward to undo the buttons of her coat and slip it from her shoulders. "Let's get you dry first. Then we'll talk."

He wrapped his arm about her, but instead of leading her to the library, he walked with her to the parlor. Though the fire had been banked for the night, there were enough embers to coax a blaze to life. He drew her close to the hearth, then bent to the task. Soon a fire crackled, but not quickly enough. Cara's teeth chattered as she rubbed her hands over her arms.

Moving to the chest at the back of the settee, he lifted the lid, drew out a lap quilt, and returned with it to Cara.

"Here. This should help you get warm."

She leaned forward so he could drape it around her and then sighed her thanks.

Rourke plunked down next to her. A thousand questions drummed his brain, but the one that most needed answering leapt to his lips.

"Did you find Eoghan?"

Cara stared at him askance. "What? No." She

glanced toward the door, her gaze suddenly hopeful. "Was he here?"

"No. I just thought . . . when you didn't come down to breakfast I thought . . ." A strange sense of relief warmed Rourke through. He motioned toward her. "You weren't in your room or at the candle shop, so I assumed he'd contacted you."

Cara's grip on the quilt loosened so that it drooped and fell to one side. Rourke scooped it up and patted it back into place. The fire had begun drying her hair, making it curl in damp tendrils at her neck. In total, she looked cold, wet, and completely helpless. In spite of his anger, he wanted to press her close and chase the chill from her bones.

Instead, he grasped her free hand and held it tightly. "Do you know how worried I've been?"

In the glow from the fire, her eyes were even more luminous, more alluring than by day. His breath caught. Though he hadn't wanted to admit it earlier, the thought that he might not see her again, that she would find her brother and leave without saying good-bye, had filled him with anguish. His grip on her hand tightened.

"I'm sorry, Rourke," Cara whispered. "It's just . . ."

"What?" he prompted. "Where did you go?"

She glanced at the door, then back. "To the island."

He lifted a brow. "Ellis? Why?"

She shifted so their knees touched. With one quick tug he could fold her into his arms. Rourke shook his head. "Well?"

"You remember last night, after I went to bed?"

He nodded.

"For a long time I couldn't sleep. I kept thinking back over the attack. The man said something . . ."

She shuddered, and Rourke truly had to fight the urge to pull her close. "What did he say?"

In the depths of her eyes, Rourke read confusion mingled with fear.

"He said I've been asking questions. Inquiring in places I didn't belong."

Reluctantly, Rourke let her go. "What do you think he meant by that?"

For a brief moment he dared to think she looked disappointed. She quickly took a breath and gave a little shake.

"The only thing I could think of, the only thing that made sense, was the day I went to the church. St. Paul's. You remember?"

"The day Deidre accused you of being a spy."

She nodded.

"You think the two are connected?"

"Possibly."

Rourke leaned closer. "Who did you talk to, Cara, and what did you say?" His fingers curled into fists. "Was it the same man who attacked you outside the shop?"

She looked puzzled for a moment, then shook her head. "No, that wasn't the man."

Rourke let himself relax. "But you did speak to someone."

Her gaze fell to her lap. "Aye."

"About?"

There was silence for a moment, broken only by the crackling of the fire.

"I asked about the Fenians," she said at last.

"What?" he hissed. Rourke could no longer bear to sit. He rose and paced the floor in front of the hearth. "Cara, have you any idea who the Fenians are? What kind of trouble you might have gotten into?"

She sat, still and small, her eyes bottomless pools. He had to turn his back just so he could think. Finally he sucked in a lungful of air, blew it out, and faced her. "You have to tell me everything, Cara. Do not hold anything back. You swear?"

Both of her hands clutched the blanket now. She nodded once, then twice. Rourke rejoined her on the settee.

For several minutes he simply listened as Cara explained how her brother had come to be involved with the group, how her daed had condemned him for it, and how Eoghan had refused to listen. Tears spilled from her eyes as she confessed how the newspaper article had prompted her to seek information at St. Paul's.

She finished by explaining how these things, combined with Deidre's accusation, had compelled her back to Ellis Island.

Rourke scratched his head. "So . . . you think Deidre may have some connection to the Fenians, who in turn may be linked to your brother?"

Cara bit her lip. "I think it's possible, don't you?"

"And you went to Ellis Island today . . . ?"

"To find out what I could about Deidre Sullivan."

"And?"

Cara hesitated, her eyes large in her pale face. When she grasped his hand, her fingers shook. "Rourke, there is no such person."

31

Cara's heart raced as she squeezed Rourke's arm, willing him to speak. Slowly he licked his lips, his raven brows drawn in a perplexed frown.

"What do you mean, she doesn't exist? Of course she does."

Cara forced her impatience aside to explain. "Father Ed, the priest who paid my fare to the island, told me that oftentimes people's names were changed when they came to America—either by choice, to make themselves sound less foreign, or by force, if the inspector failed to spell their name correctly."

"And Deidre's name?"

"Didn't appear in any of the registers."

"You were allowed to search?"

"Only the logs where the arriving passengers were listed."

Rourke's hand rose to his mouth, one long finger stroking his bottom lip thoughtfully. "Is it possible you simply overlooked her name?" His tone rang with doubt.

She gave a determined shake. "I was careful, Rourke. I knew she might be listed under a different last name, or maybe the same last name, but a different first name. In either case, I only found a few women with the name Deidre listed, and none whose last name was Sullivan. When I retraced the pages looking for Sullivan, I found no record of a female Deidre's age."

She waited, holding her breath. The discovery had somehow seemed important on the island, but now, with Rourke glowering so pensively, she wondered if he'd feel the same.

He lifted his chin and shrugged. "It could be something—"

"I knew it!"

He put his hand to her elbow. "Or it could be nothing. Until we know for sure who she is and what she's doing here, we cannot assume the worst, Cara."

Her excitement melted like snow on a hot day. He was right.

Rourke's hand fell to his side. "In the meantime, I do not think it would hurt to do a little investigating. Have you any way of inquiring about the boardinghouse? Maybe one of the residents knows something we do not."

Cara scratched her temple, then smiled and snapped her fingers. "Ana would know. She was the one who told me about . . ." She caught herself. Tillie's story was not hers to tell, and she already felt guilty enough for upsetting her the last time they talked. "Dinner won't be ready for a while. If Ana is upstairs, I can ask her now."

Rourke stood, drawing her with him. "Do that, but be careful. There's no sense riling Deidre further, especially if she has nothing to hide."

His touch on her arm lingered, lulling her senses until she almost forgot why she needed to find Ana. Finally he released her with a sad sort of smile that tugged at her heart.

"I understand why you left without telling anyone, Cara. Truly. But next time you get it into your head to go out looking for answers, do me heart a favor and take me with you."

His heart? Cara's pulse surged in response. Maybe by after dinner she'd have worked up the courage to ask what he meant. For now, it was enough to let her mind think what it would. Swallowing hard, she scooted toward the door.

One last glance and she was forced to press her hand to her chest to remind her lungs to breathe.

Rourke stood outlined in the glow of the fire, his broad shoulders and narrow hips casting a long shadow that stretched across the room and fell over the toes of her shoes. Indeed, it was almost as though a part of him still reached out to her. Were it not for the fact that he broke the spell by turning from her to the fire, she might not have been able to free herself from the spot on the carpeted floor. As it was, she managed to spin and dash from the parlor, through the hall, and up the stairs.

She slowed as she proceeded toward the bedrooms. Tillie's room was tightly sealed and no light seeped from under the door, but strangely a few feet farther down the darkened hall, a dim glow emanated from Cara's room.

Had she left a candle burning in her haste to reach the ferry? Surely not, for the dangers of such an act were widely feared. Yet there was no denying the flickering light spilling through the cracked-open door. Cara inched closer, some odd sixth sense warning her to proceed slowly.

Rustling sounded from inside, muffled, as though whoever was inside her room struggled to maintain silence. With just a touch, Cara pushed the door further ajar, enough to peek inside.

A woman bent at Cara's desk. Next to her, the drawer gaped open. Things precious to Cara lay strewn across the floor, including the leather pouch where she'd hidden Eoghan's letter. Her blood boiling, she thrust out her hand and gave the door a shove, then stepped fully into the room.

The woman whirled and Cara gasped.

"Deidre? What in blazes . . . what are ya doing in here?"

Now that she'd been caught, Deidre's alarm quickly fled. She crossed her arms and smiled. "You're back. We wondered where you'd gone."

"We?"

"Amelia and I."

Cara glanced about the room. "That does not explain your presence in my room." She crossed and snatched the pouch from the floor. "Or what you're doing looking through my things."

Quick examination brought a sigh of relief. The letter was still safely folded and tucked inside.

Deidre's eyes glittered in the dim glow of the candle. "What is that?"

Cara straightened, her voice low. "I don't think that is any of your business, Deidre."

Before she could respond, more light spilled in from the hall. Ana stood in the doorway, an oil lamp in her hand and a puzzled frown on her face. She looked from Cara to Deidre.

"Is everything all right in here?"

Her focus still locked on Deidre, Cara jammed her fists onto her hips. "I want to know what you are doing in my room."

Deidre squared to face her. "Perhaps I'm not inclined to tell ya."

"I don't care if you're inclined—"

"Cara? You're back?" Tillie crowded in next to Ana, her small face bronzed by the light of the lamp. Her tone quickly sobered. "What be the trouble here?"

Grabbing her skirts, Deidre whirled toward the door. "This is ridiculous. I'm going downstairs to help Laverne with supper."

Before she could ponder the wisdom of the action, Cara reached out and grasped Deidre's arm. Giving a jerk, she spun her round.

"Not yet, Deidre. You haven't answered my question."

The move startled Deidre. Something flew from her hand and landed at Cara's feet. She bent to retrieve it. Her bracelet! When she looked up, Deidre's eyes flashed fire, but Cara refused to be intimidated. Her own anger seething, she thrust out her chin. "How dare you!"

"What is that?" Ana drew closer.

Cara held the bracelet up between thumb and forefinger. "My da gave it to me. Deidre was going to steal it."

Ana turned to Deidre. "Is that true?"

"No."

"But you had it in your hand. We saw you," Tillie said.

Deidre's head snapped toward the girl. "Stay out of this."

Ana positioned herself protectively in front of Tillie. Lifting the lamp, she thrust it toward Deidre's face. "Why, Deidre? What have you to hide?"

When she failed to reply, Ana's jaw hardened and she turned to go. "Very well, then. It appears we will have to bring this to Amelia."

"Bring what, dears?"

All heads swiveled toward the door, where Amelia stood framed, her hands clasped at her waist and her eyes troubled. Towering behind her was Rourke. Cara met his gaze, but afraid the others would see, she quickly looked away.

"What is it? What has happened?" Amelia asked again.

Deidre stepped forward. "Cara's door was ajar. When I came upstairs to change for supper, I saw a rat scurry inside. I came in looking for it."

Tillie's eyes widened. "Why?"

"To kill it, of course," Deidre sneered. " 'Twould have been a most unpleasant surprise for dear Cara. I hoped to spare her."

Cara shook her head before she finished. "But my bracelet. You had it in your hand."

"What?" Furrows appeared on Amelia's brow. "Cara, is it valuable?"

"Only to me." Cara's gaze darted to Rourke and back.

Deidre's hand lifted, palm up. "There. You see? Why would I steal a worthless bracelet? I simply forgot I was holding it." Her chin held high, she dared them to challenge her words.

Cara squirmed at the uneasy stalemate. She sensed Deidre was lying, but how could she prove what was merely a feeling?

Rourke ended the standoff. "Deidre, how big was this rat?"

Amelia moved aside to allow him to enter.

Deidre's lip lifted as she turned her glare to Rourke. "What difference does it make?"

He held his hands several inches apart. "About this big?"

"Maybe." She jerked in a one-shouldered shrug. "I didn't get a clear look."

Her gaze, along with Cara's, circled the dubious faces. Finally, Deidre agreed with a toss of head.

"Aye, it was that big. Possibly larger."

"So you must have seen it climb into Cara's desk."

"What?"

Rourke gestured to the drawer that still hung open from the hinges and to the mess scattered on the floor. "Why else would you pull out her things?"

Deidre's eyes shone like daggers. "Aye. I saw it enter the drawer. Cara must have left it open," she added in obvious response to his next question.

"You were not afraid? Rats can be rabid, you know."

"So?"

Her voice had gone deadly low, matching Rourke's. Cara held her breath, looking back and forth between the two, but afraid to interfere, she remained silent.

"Did you intend to kill it with your bare hands."

It wasn't a question. They all sensed it, for like Cara, the others had searched the room for a weapon and found none.

Deidre had gone as rigid as a statue, her voice the only sign of life. "Are you calling me a liar, Rourke Walsh?"

Though he said nothing, his eyes spoke volumes and Cara shuddered.

Deidre's head swiveled slowly toward Amelia. "What, not a word in my defense? Are you going to allow him to speak so to me, Amelia?"

Instead of the expected uncertainty, Amelia met her glare with nary a flinch. She shook her head, her voice sad and mouth drawn with disapproval. "We will speak of this in private, Deidre."

"Nay," Deidre spat. With each rapid breath her chest rose and fell. She lifted a finger and jammed it at Rourke. "You take the word of a Hamilton and . . . a stranger? Who is this man? Do you even know him, Amelia?"

Ana spoke softly from the corner. "We all saw

you, Deidre. It didn't look to me as though you were chasing a rat. But if you were, why did you not say so immediately?"

"Of course you side with her," Deidre snarled, turning on Ana. "You never liked me, even from the beginning. From the first day I set foot in this house, you've been waiting for the chance to have me thrown out."

"Deidre, that is enough," Amelia said, gently but firmly.

Deidre's head swung from side to side and her finger shook as she pointed at Ana. "It's true. She knows how you feel about stealing. We all do. That's why she's so anxious to prove me a thief."

To her credit, Ana did not counter the accusation. She exchanged a quick glance with Amelia and kept her silence.

Amelia motioned to the door. "I'll not tolerate more of this, Deidre. Either we go downstairs—"

"Or what? I'll not allow her"—she thrust her chin toward Cara—"the satisfaction of seeing me tossed into the street."

"No one is leaving this house tonight," Amelia said, punctuating her words with a lifted finger. "'Tis true, I have said I will not harbor a thief, but I'm certain this is simply a misunderstanding—"

Deidre's face flushed red and her voice went shrill. "So you do believe her!"

"I did not say that."

"Besides, Cara never called you a thief," Ana added.

Amelia shook her head. "Don't, Ana."

"Not now perhaps, but who knows what lies she has spoken against me in private!" Deidre stared at Cara. "This is your fault."

"My fault!" Cara pointed at herself, then Deidre. "You were the one rummaging in my room."

Deidre moved like a striking serpent to slap Cara's hand. "Don't you dare point your finger at me, you—"

"Deidre!"

Cara sucked in a breath, too shocked for a moment to even move. A second later Rourke stood between them, his upraised palm blocking Deidre from pressing closer. "Enough. You leave now or I will carry you out."

"Oh, I will go," she hissed, her head bobbing. "But first—"

Rourke seized her arm. "Not another word, Deidre."

Her eyes narrowed and then widened with incredulity. "You already knew, didn't you? You know who she is."

He turned her to the door. "She is Cara Hamilton."

"She is Eoghan Hamilton's flesh and blood!" She spun and with a vicious jerk, tore her arm free and whirled to stare at Cara. "That be what the bracelet means, doesn't it! Who is he? Your brother? Your lover?" A hysterical laugh ripped from her throat. "Eoghan Hamilton is a traitor and a coward. His treachery killed my Sean!"

"I do not ken your meaning, Deidre," Cara said, afraid in the face of her rage to speak too loudly.

"Liar! If he hadn't betrayed them, my husband would be alive. Sean wasn't going to kill that politician. He was only trying to scare him, force him into changing his stance."

Cara almost couldn't think for the pounding of her heart. "What stance? What are you talking about?"

"Against home rule," Deidre spat. "But then that stupid Hamilton stepped in, pulled his dagger—"

She broke off and stood swaying, her eyes glassy and brimming with tears. All watched in shocked silence as she bunched her fist and pounded her chest. "It was supposed to scare him. That's all. They were going to scare him and then return Turner to his home. It wasn't supposed to end in a fight. Daniel Turner wasn't supposed to die."

"If what you say is true . . ." Rourke began hoarsely, and stopped.

Cara glanced at him. Lines of strain marked his features and his throat worked to swallow.

He refused to meet her gaze and stared at Deidre instead. "If it's true, then your husband's death and . . . the politician's . . . were an accident."

"No!" She flung her arm out to point at Cara. "It's her fault! Hers and that Eoghan. Who is he? Tell me!"

She lunged at Cara, but Rourke's feet were quicker. He caught her by the shoulders and held her at arm's length. "Stop, Deidre. You're distraught, I see that, but I'll not allow you to hurt Cara, or anyone else in this house."

"You think you can stop me?" Deidre demanded, still struggling. "You think anyone can?"

In answer, Rourke gave her a shake, and kept shaking until she quieted. For several long seconds, only her ragged breathing filled the air. Then, slowly, her bent shoulders straightened, her chin lifted, and she sucked in a breath and blew it out.

"Let go of me," she said at last.

To Cara's surprise, he complied.

Deidre turned on her heel, her normal icy resolve firmly fixed in place. Lifting her hand, she patted her hair and then marched to the door. The others cleared the way for her. Even Amelia stumbled aside, her laced hands pressed to her midsection.

At the threshold, Deidre paused to look over her shoulder straight at Cara. "Eoghan Hamilton kinna hide forever. I will find him. It's only a matter of time." She touched her finger to her lips and smiled. "When you see him, tell him that for me."

And then she was gone.

Finally free to breathe, Cara opened her mouth and let the air puff from her lungs. She was shaking, she realized with a start, and dropped her chin to stare at her trembling limbs.

"Are you all right?"

Cara's head shot up. Rourke had moved in such a way that his body shielded her from the others. Steadied by his gaze, she nodded.

"But Eoghan?" she whispered, clasping his arm. "I have to find him before Deidre . . ." She trailed off, afraid to say more.

Rourke took her hand and squeezed. "I'll follow her, find out where she's going. You wait here. Do you promise, Cara? You will not leave this house?"

With terror still paralyzing her limbs, she could only nod. Rourke's hand lifted to cup her cheek, and then he, too, disappeared out the door, leaving Cara to face Tillie, Ana, and Amelia's astonished stares alone.

Tillie's tongue poked out to wet her lips. "Is it . . . is what Deidre said true, Cara?"

"Tillie," Amelia chided, though her eyes, and Ana's beside her, shone with curiosity and dread.

Suddenly, Cara's legs refused to support her. She stumbled backward until her knees hit the bed. Collapsing onto the mattress, she curled into a ball, covered her head with her arms, and let the bitter tears fall.

32

Could it be? Could his father's death have been nothing more than an unfortunate accident?

Rourke shook the dampness from his eyes and plodded forward. His numb fingers curled into fists inside his pockets.

No. He refused to believe that the explanation that had driven him from his homeland, given by an old woman who'd seen the men grab his father as he left a local pub, had been wrong. But why would Deidre lie?

Up ahead, her slender figure dipped in and out of his sight, sometimes hidden by swirling fog and darkness, other times so visible he knew if she looked back, she'd spot him easily.

But she didn't look back. She walked, unswerving, up Ashberry Street and crossed several blocks, finally pausing at a corner to speak to the driver of a carriage for hire. The driver bent low to reply, then took something from her hand. A moment later, she climbed into the carriage and, giving a whistle, the driver set the horse in motion down the street.

Where was she going? Rourke sped up his pace. Waving to another carriage for hire, he waited impatiently as the driver pulled alongside him.

"Where to, sir?"

Rourke handed him several coins, then pointed at the retreating carriage. "After them. There be an extra coin in it for you if you follow close, but not too close."

The man's eyes gleamed. Tucking the money into the pocket of his coat, he waited until Rourke was aboard before setting off with a chirp and a jerk.

The ride gave Rourke plenty of time to contemplate the night's events. His thoughts winged to Cara and the look of desperation he'd read in her eyes before he left. Of them all, she was the innocent, for he believed without a doubt that such a look could not be feigned. Her desire was for her brother alone—not revenge, not malice, not even truth. So long as she could reunite with her sibling, she was content.

But was her brother so lacking in guile?

Rourke allowed his thoughts to journey to the day his father had come home lying in the back of a farmer's wagon.

"Fetch your ma, lad. Your daed's been shot."

" 'Twas them rebels what did it," the farmer's wife added. "Saw 'em with me own eyes, I did."

Rourke hadn't heard any more. Instead, he'd climbed into the back of the wagon, relieved to see his father was still alive. But when he pulled him into his arms, his hands had come away red.

Not until later, in agony of spirit, had he sought the woman.

Rourke closed his eyes against a sudden swell of pain. His da was undecided about home rule, but Rourke had convinced him to take a stand, pushed him to hold a hard line.

"For the good of Ireland," Rourke mumbled, jerking his eyes open.

Slapping his palm against his thigh, he leaned out the window and shouted to the driver, "Do you see them?"

"Aye, sir. They're just ahead. Looks like we be coming on Battery Park."

The carriage slowed and gradually rocked to a halt. As Rourke disembarked, the driver pointed with the tip of his whip.

"Over there, sir. The lady went into that there house at the end of the street."

Rourke thanked him, then tossed the promised coin up to the driver, who tipped his hat and set off with a brisk chirp. Once the rumble of the carriage faded, Rourke approached the house, keeping to the shadows outside the circle of light cast by the streetlamps but trying his best not to skulk, for though the streets were not busy, a few passersby eyed him curiously.

Rourke scanned the wrought-iron gate as he passed the great brick house where Deidre had disappeared. No name, only a number: 4723.

Ahead, a stout fellow in a gray coat and black

derby bustled toward him, his shoulders hunched and his head lowered so that Rourke was forced to sidestep in order to avoid colliding with him. Their shoulders brushed as he ambled past.

The man jerked his head up and jammed his derby back with his thumb. "Sorry there, chap. I wasn't watching where I was going."

Rourke waved the apology aside.

"Sure is a foul night out," the fellow continued, indicating the piling fog with a grimace.

Eager to move on, Rourke nodded.

"Well then . . . good night." The man tipped his hat, then paused and asked, "Say, are you lost? It's not exactly a fit night for walking."

Rourke shrugged. "No, I . . ." He hesitated and glanced over his shoulder at the house. "By chance, do you know who lives in that place?"

The man jabbed his thumb at the gate. "That place?"

Rourke nodded.

"Why, that's Douglas Healy's house," the man said, rocking back on his heels. "You know him?"

"I don't think so," Rourke said, though indeed the name sounded familiar.

The man's chubby hands clutched the lapel of his coat and his chin lifted. "Owns a shipping company. Heard he's made quite a fortune. Seems like a nice chap, too. Met him once outside Tammany Hall."

Interesting information, but worthless unless

Rourke could figure out why Healy's name niggled at his memory.

The man poked his hand out. "I'm Jonesy, by the way." He waited until Rourke shook his hand and then plunged his fingers back into his pocket. "Actually, my name's Elmer, but my last name is Jones, so everybody just calls me Jonesy."

"Rourke Walsh."

"Pleased to meet you, Rourke Walsh."

The wind kicked up and Rourke hunched his shoulders, hoping his demeanor and the dismal weather would encourage the man to shove off, but now that he'd started talking he seemed in no hurry to leave.

"So, Walsh—is that an Irish name?"

"It is."

"I have friends who are Irish. I'm English, myself. Moved to New York about six . . . no, seven years ago." He jabbed his chin toward Rourke. "You?"

Unwilling to spill too much information to a stranger, Rourke merely shrugged. "I haven't been here long."

Jonesy chuckled. "I daresay none of us have, unless you're a native."

His laughter grew louder, though not enough to draw attention. Still, Rourke was more than ready to move on. He tipped his cap and eased forward.

"Well, my thanks to you, Jonesy, but I'd best be going now."

"Of course. You have a good night."

"You too." Rourke took several steps along the sidewalk.

"Say . . ."

He glanced back. Jonesy stood with his hand held high.

"Aye?"

"If you're going to one of those meeting things, you'll want to circle round to the rear of the place."

Rourke lifted a brow. "Meetings?"

"I guess that's what they are, though I suppose I can't rightly say, having never been to one myself." His head tilted and he winked. "Like I said, I'm English."

In two strides, Rourke closed the distance between them. "I'm not following your meaning."

Jonesy pointed at the house with his thumb. "Well, that there fellow is Irish. I've seen several chaps going inside a time or two, all of 'em dressed like you and talking with a brogue. I pass this way on my way home from work, you see."

He fumbled to a stop, then leaned toward Rourke. His eyebrows bunched and his chubby cheeks fairly quivered. "I've been reading in the papers about . . . you know . . . the Fenians."

Rourke shot a glance at the house, then back at

318

Jonesy. "And you think that's what's going on in there?"

Jonesy's voice lowered to a conspiratorial whisper. "Possibly. Like I said, he's Irish."

Rourke matched his tone. "Indeed. And so am I."

Jonesy stiffened and drew back. "Right. I didn't mean—"

Holding up his palm, Rourke shook his head. "I'm Irish, but I'm not one of them. I will say this, though. The Fenians aren't to be trifled with. If you're right, and this is where they've chosen to meet, it may not be wise to be pointing them out, eh?"

Jonesy's eyes darted to the house and then he grabbed the front of his coat and hunched his shoulders. "No, I suppose not."

"So now, I guess we'd best be about our business."

"Right." Jonesy's feet tapped the bricked walk. "Well, good night, Mr. Walsh."

"Good night," Rourke replied, watching as Jonesy scurried in and out of the glow of the streetlamps like a rotund mouse. He turned and eyed the house.

If Jonesy was correct, Douglas Healy was a Fenian, and Deidre had gone straight from the boardinghouse to meet with him.

If Jonesy was correct.

Asking questions on the street would only draw

attention and might even get him killed, but he needed the truth, and there was only one way to be certain.

Jamming his hands into his pockets, he swung around and headed for the abandoned shoe store. He needed to call a meeting of his kinsmen.

Deidre poured a drink from the decanter on the sideboard, swallowed it down, then poured another. Behind her, Douglas paced, his fingers ruffling his graying hair.

" 'Twas foolish of you to come here. How many times have I told you we must not be tied to one another?"

She turned and rested her hip against the sideboard, one hand supporting her elbow, the other gripping the glass. Bitter tears burned her eyes. "And where would you have had me go?"

"That is up to you. 'Tis your own fault that Amelia had to toss you out of the boardinghouse."

Deidre slammed the glass onto the sideboard, sloshing the drink over the side onto her fingers. "She did not toss. I left. I couldn't stand looking at that Hamilton woman one more minute. Not one! Do you understand?"

Pulling a handkerchief from his pocket, Douglas crossed to her and dried her fingers and wiped the alcohol from the sideboard. "Calm down. It won't do any good succumbing to hysterics. That be what drove you here in the first place."

Deidre narrowed her eyes. Her father-in-law was nothing like her Sean. He lacked the passion, the zest for life that she'd always found irresistible in her husband. In truth, the one thing they shared was their loyalty to the Fenians, only deep down . . . she'd always wondered if Douglas cared more for them than his own son, and she knew Sean had wondered the same.

Remembering her husband's pain, she drew a ragged breath. Regardless of her suspicions, Douglas and his money were the means to an end. "What now?"

"You found nothing in her belongings? Nothing that might point us to Eoghan Hamilton?"

Her thoughts flashed to the pouch Cara had been so quick to claim. It appeared harmless enough, but why had she not thought to look inside? She lifted her chin. "Nothing."

Douglas stroked his mustache and resumed pacing. "But the bracelet—you be certain you've seen the likes before?"

"Aye. An artisan from northern Ireland makes them."

"And you said it was two strands, twisted together."

"That's what I said."

Douglas crossed to a writing table, withdrew a small box from one of its drawers, and carried it to her. Removing the lid, he reached inside and pulled out a bracelet identical to the one Deidre had found in Cara's room. "Did it look anything like this?"

"Exactly. Where did you get it?"

He replaced the bracelet and refastened the lid. "Never mind. The important thing is that I have it, and my hunch about Cara Hamilton was correct."

"Aye, you were correct. She's tied to him somehow, but why has he made no attempt to reach her?" Deidre gritted her teeth. "It makes no sense, and I grow weary of trying to figure it out."

Rather than answer, Douglas took his time restoring the bracelet to its place in the writing table. When next he met her gaze, his face was suspiciously blank. She glided to him, the rage simmering in her belly making her hands shake. "You be keeping something from me."

He acknowledged this with a slight tip of his head.

It took every ounce of control to keep from springing on him and clawing at his eyes. "What?"

Douglas appeared to think a moment, and then he sauntered to the sideboard, topped Deidre's glass, and carried it to her. She took it without a word.

"You remember our old friend, the one who told us that Daniel Turner would be in the pub the night he and Sean were killed?"

She nodded. She'd never met the man, but she remembered his name. "Hugh O'Hurly."

"That's right." A twinkle lit his eyes and he smiled. "He's in New York."

Interesting news. Deidre quirked an eyebrow. "Why did you not tell me?"

Douglas took the glass from her fingers and tipped it up, emptying the contents down his throat. Finished, he swiped his sleeve across his lips. "Because, my dear daughter-in-law," he began, his alcohol-laden breath drifting over her face, "I know you. You want the satisfaction of ending Hamilton's life for yourself. That puts you and anyone else who might want Hamilton dead at cross-purposes. I on the other hand do not care who holds the blade, so long as he ends up fodder for my garden."

He was right, and she saw no harm in denying it. Deidre shrugged and lifted a corner of her mouth in a smile. "So?"

"So . . ." He set down the glass and offered his hand. "Perhaps it's time we joined forces. After all, Hugh has as much reason to want Hamilton dead as you or I. Be that not so?"

She stared at his proffered fingers. Something told her Douglas had been working with O'Hurly all along. Aye, and the bracelet could be proof, but was that such a terrible thing? Together, they might be able to track down Hamilton, especially now that she'd exposed her intent to Cara and therefore could no longer hope to use her to dig for information.

She slid her hand into Douglas's. When he tried to pull away, she held tight. "You're up to something, old man."

His face hardened and he said nothing.

She leaned toward him. "I'm not blind. I saw how things were between you and your son. You want Eoghan Hamilton dead, but it's not out of revenge. What is it?"

The Celt's larger hand squeezed hers, bruising the bones, making her wince. She tamped a sigh of relief when at last he let go.

"Keep to your own business, darling Deidre. It's safer."

Resisting the urge to rub her fingers, she nodded. "Fine." She spun for the door, then paused with her hand on the knob. "Sean loved you, you know. Would have done anything for you if he thought it would have made a difference in the way you felt about him."

Her words did nothing to stir the hard, unreadable emotions on Douglas's face. He didn't even bother to refute them.

Which confirmed what she'd believed all along—it was up to her to see her Sean avenged. In the end, she'd find a way. She would look into Hamilton's eyes and feast on his fear . . . right before she plunged a dagger into his traitorous black heart.

33

Outside the library window, no rain fell, but the wind continued to lash the panes. Cara hunkered in the dark, tired and anxious yet determined to question Rourke the moment he returned to the boardinghouse. Only . . . where was he?

She glanced at the clock above the mantel. Dimly she could make out the numbers. Half past two. Rourke had been gone for hours.

She pulled her shawl tighter around her shoulders, little good though it did to ward off a chill that emanated from inside. Deidre's tirade had struck at her core, mainly because Cara had no idea how much of it was true. She snuggled deeper into the chair she'd drawn to the window to wait.

Long after Rourke and Deidre had disappeared, she'd sobbed into her covers. One by one the women of the boardinghouse had left her to her grief, except for Breda, who said nothing but remained, patting Cara's shoulder, until she'd fallen into a fitful sleep.

A low howl startled Cara from her thoughts. She bolted upright and strained to see through the darkened glass. At first, nothing, and then . . .

A figure emerged from the shadows.

"Rourke."

Just speaking his name brought a wave of relief. She'd imagined all sorts of evil things when she awoke alone in her room. The last hour had been torture. She sprang from the chair and ran down the hall to the front door, throwing it open in almost the same instant as Rourke lifted his hand to knock.

"Are you all right?" The words tumbled from her lips and hung in the air between them. At his nod she stepped aside to allow him to enter, then closed the door tightly. While he shed his cap and coat, she wrung her hands. "Well?" she asked when he finished.

"You're trembling." Rourke took her hands and pressed them to his lips. When he looked up, his eyes smoldered like blue fire. "Your fingers are like ice. The kitchen will be warm. We can talk there."

"No." She shook her head. "Laverne might hear."

Breathless, she motioned to the library, then spun and led the way. Inside, she waited impatiently while he lit a lamp. He carried it to the table next to the chair she'd vacated. Her shawl still lay on the floor. He picked it up and held it open for her. Her feet heavy, Cara crossed to him, but instead of giving it to her, he lifted it over her head and wrapped her in it, then held the ends closed. She lowered her gaze, afraid of what she might read in his eyes.

"Rourke, please . . ."

He sighed and stepped back, leaving her bleaker than she'd been before he arrived.

"Sit down, Cara."

She did. While he drew another chair to the window, she searched his face. "Did you find Deidre? Do you know where she went?"

His shirt rustled softly as he sat. "Cara, how much of her story was familiar to you?"

"You mean about Eoghan and . . . her husband?"

He gave the slightest nod and waited, unblinking.

"None." She clutched the shawl to keep from worrying the fabric to shreds. "But it might explain . . . it could be why Eoghan disappeared without saying a word."

"Aye."

Rourke lowered his gaze. In the dim glow of the lamp he was even more devastatingly handsome than in the day. His dark lashes rested like down against his skin, and his hands . . .

She reached out to clasp them. They were stiff, unyielding, and the moment they touched, a muscle began ticking in his jaw, but she refused to let go.

"Do you believe my brother is a traitor?"

"I don't know."

"But if what Deidre said is true, he must be."

He gripped her fingers and lifted his eyes to hers. "She also said he did it to save another. Do you believe that?"

Agony swept through Cara's heart. She took her time answering. "Eoghan can be carried away by causes he fancies. It is his nature. But an innocent man? Aye, I think he would have tried to save him if he could."

"You think that is what happened?"

She shrugged. "I don't know. He disappeared before I could ask him." She paused and looked down at their clasped hands. More than anything, she wanted to trust this man. She drew a breath and lifted her chin. "I do know that Da feared his new friends. Said they'd lead him into trouble."

"Friends?"

She nodded.

"Did you ever meet any of these friends?"

"No. Da would not allow them to be brought into the house."

"And when your father died?"

"Eoghan disappeared."

"But I thought—"

She shook her head. "What I mean is, he left Derry. Went to Belfast and who knows where else. I barely heard from him until . . ."

She fell silent, remembering.

Rourke stroked the top of her hand. "Cara, what made you think your brother was dead?"

Tears burned her eyes and spilled down her cheeks. She pulled her hand free to wipe them away, but he was there before her, his thumb gently catching the tears, soothing her grief.

"A parcel came to the cottage," she whispered, pinning her gaze to his beloved face. "Inside was Eoghan's shirt. It was bloodied and torn to shreds. I never found out where it came from or who sent it."

"But you were led to believe that it was a message—meant to inform you that your brother had died."

Unable to speak, she nodded.

Rourke pulled her close, his hands warm on her back. "I'm so sorry, Cara. I wish you'd been spared all of this. If I could go back . . ."

He trailed into silence, but Cara didn't care. She turned her face into his neck and closed her eyes, willing the morning to come and the sun to rise and shed its light on all that had transpired. Outside this room, Deidre and her hatred waited. Outside was fear and doubt about the future and her brother's fate. But inside . . .

She breathed deep of Rourke's masculine scent. Here, she never need fear heartbreak or lies. His strong arms held her. Beneath her cheek, his heart beat steady and sure. She could rest. She found peace.

She was safe.

She was safe.

Rourke closed his eyes, shutting out the room, the bitterness and lies, everything but the woman in his arms. As long as he could keep her there, protected, nothing else mattered.

Her breath caressed his neck, and her arms, slow at first, encircled his waist. As long as he lived, he'd remember this moment. Just as quickly he knew this moment would never be enough. He wanted more. He wanted a lifetime with Cara, but to get that . . .

He eased her from his shoulder, but unwilling to release her completely, he slipped his hand under her hair to cup the back of her neck. "The man who sent you here, the one you met on board the ship . . ." She nodded, her wide eyes hiding nothing. "Do you remember his name?"

She blinked and drew away. "Of course. It was Douglas Healy."

Rourke's stomach plunged to his feet. Healy had sent Cara to the boardinghouse—to Deidre. Deidre had fled from the boardinghouse straight to Healy. Perhaps the Fenians were not their only connection. He grabbed her hand and squeezed. "What do you know of him? Anything?"

"Not but what he told me on board the ship."

"And you be certain the two of you have never met before?"

"Never." She tilted her face to his. "What is this? Why do you ask about him?"

Doubt and fear wrestled in Rourke's mind. He refused to add to the lies he'd already told her, but revealing the truth might only endanger her further. Rising, he strode to the lifeless fireplace and stood with his back turned, the conversation he'd had with his kinsmen—with the exception of Hugh, who had been conspicuously absent—playing in his mind.

"This woman, Deidre—how can we be certain she spoke the truth?" Though the news had shocked them all, Malcolm remained resolute, his presence calming them.

Angus pounded the table with his fist. "There is no way, 'cept we find the man and see if his story matches hers. Even then, it stands to reason that someone *told the rebels Daniel's whereabouts. How do we know it wasn't him? How do we know he didn't cower and turn on his comrades when his plan soured? I say he is still the man we seek!"*

Rourke shuddered, glad for the shadows hiding his face. The threat to Cara hadn't diminished with the revelation of Eoghan's part in his father's death; it had intensified now that the others knew she was his sister.

Both hands tore at his hair. He lifted his gaze to the ceiling. Would he never find a way to reveal the truth without bringing her to harm?

Cara rose to her feet, but unlike him, the glow from the lamp illuminated her fully. "You know something. There is more you have not told me."

How could he look into those eyes and lie? Though he ached to hold her, he remained where he stood. "I have suspicions, Cara. Nothing more." He clenched his fists at his sides. "I must ask something of you."

She paled, her long red hair framing her face, making her look like a tortured soul held too long to the earth. "Go on."

"I must ask that you trust me, Cara. The things I keep, I keep for your protection. Will you believe this without knowing why it must be so?"

Her lashes fell, hiding her eyes, and she pulled her arms around her middle. "But, if this has something to do with Eoghan . . ."

"I will still help you find Eoghan. I swear to you, Cara, I will protect him, too, if I can."

"If?" Her gaze flew to lock with his.

"Deidre wants him dead. Though I know this to be true, I cannot foresee what she intends in order to accomplish that end. Before all else, I must know who she really is."

Cara sucked in a breath. "Rourke . . . what has Deidre to do with Mr. Healy?"

Pain filled her voice. When he crossed to her, she refused to meet his eyes. Placing his fingers under her chin, he lifted her head to look at him.

"After Deidre left here, she went to see him. But"—he continued when she opened her mouth—"we have no way of knowing why. Healy showed you kindness once. Who is to say she didn't go to see him for the same reason?"

A shudder shook her, but she nodded. "Aye, it could be as you say."

"Besides, it's Deidre we need worry about, not Healy."

The lines of worry melted from her brow as she raised hopeful eyes to him.

"I still want you to be careful," he added, cupping her cheek. "Though I cannot be certain . . . Healy . . . he may have ties to the Fenians."

Her lips parted as she took in the information, but then she drew a quivering breath. "All right."

Relief swelled in his chest, except . . . he ducked to see her face clearly. "We are agreed, then? Because of the danger, you'll stay at the boardinghouse and leave the questioning to me?"

She rested her hand over his in reply.

With her touch, Rourke felt the dread trickle from him. He would keep his word and find her brother. In the meantime . . .

He slipped his arms around her and breathed deep of her hair. Sensing his intent, she lifted her face and closed her eyes. The invitation was too powerful to resist. Lowering his head, Rourke drew her close and covered her lips with a kiss.

34

Eoghan's strength returned in thimblefuls. He could rise, even manage a few paces on his own, but each time he thought to leave the small, dingy apartment, the weakness and nausea returned.

Clutching the edge of the bed, he cursed his trembling limbs. Not that he wasn't grateful for Maggie's care or Charlie's good humor; he just needed to find his sister. Soon.

Maggie materialized in the doorway, as though his thinking her name had made her appear. In her hands was another bowl of weak broth. Eoghan grimaced. Maybe if a bit of chicken bobbed in the stuff, he'd gain his strength faster.

She shuffled to him, her thin lips spread in a smile. "Look at you, sitting up all by your ownsie. You'll be getting round in no time, that's what, and then what will poor Maggie do?"

She set the bowl on a table next to the bed, then fluffed the pillows and gave the ticking a pat. "Come on then, let's get you fed." Leaning close, she brought her face to within inches of Eoghan's nose. "I put a bit of potato in the broth for ya when Charlie weren't lookin'."

Eoghan immediately regretted pining for chicken. As it was, the couple had little to spare.

His lengthy recovery was taking food from their mouths.

Every muscle protested as he settled against the pillows. Though the pain no longer robbed his breath, he still favored his injured left side. Maggie consequently circled to his right. She put the bowl in his hands, watched as he swallowed a couple of bites, then perched on a stool, her hands clasped in her lap.

Eoghan eyed her warily over the spoon. "You look worried, Maggie. Is something wrong?"

"Wrong?" A breathy cackle puffed from her lips.

He lowered the bowl. "Maggie?"

She flinched at the firmness of his tone. He drew a breath and forced calm into his voice. "Look now, whatever it is cannot be so bad. Unless . . . Is it Cara?"

Her fingers worried the hem of her apron. "Cara?"

He narrowed his eyes suspiciously. "My sister —the one I sent you to see."

"Oh, her."

"Aye, her. You said she was well, safe from danger."

"Yea, she looked well."

"And you gave her my message, told her I would come for her as soon as I was able."

Maggie's chin fell and her fingers worked the apron hem faster.

Eoghan's pulse climbed. "Maggie?"

"You see, the thing is . . ." Her gaze scaled the walls, darted to the ceiling, and settled finally on her lap. "I didn't actually have a chance to say all that."

Eoghan bit his tongue so hard he tasted blood. Ignoring the burning pain in his shoulder, he set the bowl aside and shoved higher in the bed. "But you said—"

Maggie lifted a knobby hand. "Right pretty gal, that's what I said. Said she looked well enough."

"So, you did see her?"

"That's right."

"Then I do not understand. What happened? Why didn't you give her my message?"

Word by agonizing word she recounted the details of the carriage accident and how she'd been forced aside by the growing crowd.

"And if the carriages crashing together weren't bad enough," she finished, her eyes pleading, "my Charlie swears he saw that fellow what shot you standing not more than twelve feet away, watching the goings-on with a keen eye and muttering to himself 'bout his rotten luck."

Bowing over the covers, she grabbed his hand and gave it a squeeze. "Ya see why we couldn't tell ya, don't ya, love? It was too dangerous, is all. That man tried twice to put an end to ya and your sister. We couldn't risk leading him back here. Not with Charlie so old and frail and feeling like he'd have to defend me." Tears filled her rheumy eyes. "Ya understand, don't ya, boy?"

In fact, though his stomach felt weighted with lead, he did understand. Eoghan laid his hand over Maggie's and gave it a pat. "You risked your lives bringing me here. I was wrong to ask more of you, Maggie. You and Charlie both."

She clucked through her yellowed teeth. "I'm sorry, lad. I should have told ya. It's just, Charlie was so afraid, and I . . . well, I was scared, too, after I saw what was done to them carriages. All I could do was pray that sister of yours stayed close to that man what came to help her—hope he'd be some kind of protection."

Eoghan stiffened. "A man?"

She grinned. "Yea. A real looker he is, too. Your sister seemed taken with him, from what little I saw anyway."

Eoghan gave her gnarled knuckles a squeeze. "Maggie, did this man have a name?"

Her head bobbed. "Yea. Heard your sister call out to him . . . what was it?" She scratched her head, then snapped her fingers. "Rourke. That's it. Said his name was Rourke." Her eyebrows lifted. "The name mean something to ya?"

Nausea rolled through Eoghan's gut. Aye, the name meant something. It was as emblazoned on his brain as the politician's whose life he'd tried in vain to save.

Throwing aside the covers, he slapped his feet to the floor and forced his shaking legs to stand.

He had to get to Cara. His only prayer was that he wasn't too late—that her identity was still a secret and that she was safe . . . from Daniel Turner's son.

Making the promise to remain holed up in the boardinghouse proved much easier than keeping it. Twice, Cara made the trip down the stairs to peek out the front door for a glimpse of Rourke, and twice she returned to her room more anxious than before.

She gave the pillow on her bed a hearty smack, wishing it was his head, or hers for having agreed to his conditions. Why hadn't she demanded to go along, or at the very least asked where he was going when he left the boardinghouse at the crack of dawn?

A soft knock cut short her thinking. She scrambled from the bed, giving little heed to her skirt, which she'd taken pains to launder and iron just a couple of days prior.

In the hall stood Amelia. Her eyes twinkled with merriment, and when she clasped Cara's arm, her fingers shook.

"Cara, dear, we've a bit of good news at last. There's an old friend downstairs, someone I think you'll be glad to see. I've asked him to stay for supper, and he's agreed."

Wariness slowed her words. "An old friend?"

Amelia put her finger to her lips and gave a

wink. "He told me not to tell you, dear. Wanted to surprise you himself. You will come down?"

"Of course." Cara smoothed her hands over her wrinkled skirt. "Just let me freshen a bit. It won't take long. Will you let him know?"

"Certainly, dear." She gave Cara's cheek a pat. "Ah, but what a timely visit this is. God must have known you needed a bit of encouragement, as do we all." Her hand dropped to the knob and she lifted an eyebrow. "We'll wait for you in the parlor?"

Cara nodded and then the door clicked shut. A visitor? Who? Not Eoghan, for Amelia had called him an old friend. Puzzlement still muddied her mind a few minutes later as she descended the stairs and turned for the parlor. Voices drifted through the open door, one ringing with Amelia's light laughter, the other more masculine, but definitely familiar.

Both Amelia and the gentleman stood with their backs to the door. He was large and broad-shouldered, elegantly dressed, with a coat that brushed the back of his knees and trousers the same shade of burnished brown.

Cara's tread on the threshold drew Amelia's attention first. Her eyes lit with pleasure as she turned and extended her hand. "There you are, dear. Come and see who has finally decided to pay a visit."

Cara frowned as the gentleman set a cup and

saucer on the table, then straightened to greet her.

"Well, hello, lass."

"Mr. Healy?" Cara's eyebrows shot to her hairline.

"Aye. It's me, at last. It's been some months, eh? Glad to see you settled in, safe and sound. Not that I doubted it for a second. Knew I could trust Mrs. Matheson here to look after you." He patted his broad midriff. "Told you I'd check on you. Just didn't think it would take me this long. Business, you know."

Rourke's warning about his possible affiliations clanged like a bell through Cara's brain. "Of course. It be . . . good to see you."

Forcing her feet into motion, she crossed to him and stretched out her hand, which he took and brought to his mouth. He pressed a kiss to the back, then locked her smaller hand between his larger ones.

"Ach, 'tis good to lay eyes on you, lass. Mrs. Matheson tells me you're working for James O'Bannon?"

Cara's gaze flitted to Amelia. What else had she told him? "A-aye."

Circling to her side, Amelia wrapped her in a one-armed hug. "I knew Mr. Healy's visit would be just what you needed to shake the melancholy loose. I'm so glad he agreed to dine with us." She turned a broad smile to Mr. Healy. "I'll tell Laverne to set another place for supper."

Cara caught her arm before she could go. "I can do that, if you like, maybe help Laverne get the meal around."

"Oh no, dear." Amelia laughed, patting her hand. "You stay and visit with Mr. Healy. I'm sure you have much to catch up on."

"But you and he have been friends much longer. I'd hate to trouble—"

Amelia waved dismissively. "No trouble. In fact, he and I have already spent some considerable time chatting, haven't we, Mr. Healy?"

With Mr. Healy's chuckle, Cara's heart sank. She released her arm and watched silently as Amelia glided from the room, pausing long enough to slide the parlor door closed before she disappeared.

Though Mr. Healy's smile remained in place, it seemed somehow distant, less welcoming than before.

And now they were completely, utterly, alone.

35

Rourke's steps slowed as he approached the boardinghouse. It was late, almost quarter of seven, and darkness already gripped most of the street. Next to the sidewalk a carriage waited with a matched team of coal-black horses he did not recognize. Of course, there were many animals in New York, and many carriages whose owners he would not recognize. Still, his pulse quickened as he circled the rig and darted up the boardinghouse steps.

Inside, merriment that seemed pointedly at odds with the scene he'd witnessed last night rang from the dining room. He removed his cap and coat and went to investigate. Where there should have been a vacant chair at Deidre's place, a large fellow with graying hair and a cheery smile sat, eyes twinkling as he chatted with Tillie and shot outrageous winks at Breda. Ana, Laverne, and Giles, too, chuckled at his antics. But what puzzled him most was the way Cara leaned across the table toward him, as though every word the man spoke demanded her full attention.

A queer sort of jealousy fluttered in Rourke's gut. He stepped from the hall into the dining room, cutting short the man's jest and abruptly drawing Cara's focus to himself.

She half rose from the table, her lips slightly parted as she breathed his name.

Amelia laid aside her napkin and beckoned him to his seat. "Why, there you are, Rourke. We were just finishing our dinner. Come in, come in. Meet our friend."

The man across from Cara also rose and laid aside his napkin. He rounded the table, his hand outstretched. Rourke gave it a firm shake as Cara slid to his side.

"Rourke, this is my friend," she began, almost cautiously, for she spoke every syllable with a keen stare that begged his patience. "He's the man I told you about, the one who showed me so much kindness on the crossing from Liverpool."

Scarcely could he keep from dropping his mouth open. The gentleman's beaming smile only widened with Cara's introduction.

"Fie! Anyone with eyes could see it wasn't safe for a pretty young lass traveling alone to remain in steerage. I simply did what I hope any man would do for me own daughter, were she still alive, God rest her soul." He tipped his head to Rourke. "Douglas Healy, at your service."

Rourke used the moment to compose his thoughts. When Healy's gaze lifted, Rourke had wiped all trace of surprise from his face. "Rourke Walsh. Pleasure to meet you, Mr. Healy."

Healy clapped him on the shoulder. "Pleasure's mine, lad." His hand swept the table. "Come and join us. These fine ladies, and gentleman," he corrected with a nod to Giles, "have been regaling me with tales of Laverne's cooking."

"Call it what you will," Laverne said, the sparkle in her eyes belying her scowl, "but these here scalawags will be making their own oatmeal in the morning."

This loosed a fresh bout of laughter. Rourke

claimed his seat at Cara's side, his gaze questioning. When he bent to her ear, she gave a slight shake of her head and mouthed, *later.*

Indeed, it was much later before the table was cleared and the others had progressed to the library to continue their conversation. Rourke was reminded of a piper as Healy led them down the hall and was only partly glad he'd bothered to fix the flue.

Before she could join them, Rourke grabbed Cara by the elbow and pulled her into a quiet corner. "Cara, what is the meaning of this? What is Douglas Healy doing here? And what happened to my cautioning you about speaking with him?"

Her gaze traveled to the library and returned to fix on his face. "Rourke, you do not understand. There is so much . . ." She shook her head. "No, there is no time to explain. We'll talk later, after everyone has gone to bed. In the meantime, just know that we were wrong, Rourke. Douglas told me everything."

"Everything—wait. Douglas?"

"Aye."

The relief on her face sparked warning bells in his head. He squeezed her elbow tighter. "Cara, what did he tell you?"

Her eyes fell to his white fingers. He immediately loosened his hold. "I'm sorry, Cara. I didn't mean to hurt you. It's just . . .

you must tell me what you and Healy talked about."

She trembled beneath his grip. "Rourke, I told you, Douglas and I talked it out. I told him about Eoghan and he—"

"You—!" The word exploded from his lips. He bit short the ones that would have followed. "Cara, we have to talk. Now."

She craned her neck toward the library. "Can it wait? The others will think—"

"No. It can't."

Grasping her hand, he whirled and led her through the kitchen—ignoring Laverne's raised brows—through the back door to the stable.

Cara swatted at the moths circling her head. "The bugs will eat us alive out here."

He threw open the stable door and led her inside. "Better?"

"Better." She gave a reluctant smile. "But now I'll smell like hay."

He grunted at her attempt at humor and fixed her with a stern look.

She squirmed, her foot tapping the stable floor faster and faster until at last she breathed an exasperated sigh. "Fine. We'll talk"—she held up her finger—"but then I have something I must ask of you."

He agreed with a curt nod.

She spun and crossed to a bench covered with the rags and tools Rourke had been using to repair the carriage. He quickly swept them aside for her, then lit a lantern before grabbing a bale of hay and seating himself.

"Now, what exactly happened while I was gone?" he demanded, lacing his fingers to keep them from drumming.

Cara briefly explained the day leading up to Healy's arrival, then paused when she reached the point where Amelia had left the two of them alone.

"Douglas told me about Deidre's visit," she said slowly. "He told me everything she'd said, all she'd accused my brother of. I wasn't quite sure what to make of it, so I said nothing, just listened."

Even Rourke was taken aback, too befuddled for a moment to form words. "He . . . told you?"

She nodded and clasped his hand. "That's when I knew I'd been right to trust him. You see, he *is* one of the Fenians, just as you suspected. Deidre is, too, which is why she went to him, but the longer she went on about Eoghan and her husband, the more he realized the level of her madness. He wasn't interested in her plotting, Rourke. He listened to her story only out of concern for me, because he thought that by doing so, he might warn me of her intentions."

Her voice dropped to a whisper. "Rourke, Deidre told him she would stop at nothing to get to Eoghan. Nothing. I was so distraught . . . I begged Douglas for his help, and that's when I told him the truth about Eoghan."

Rourke stiffened. "And?"

"He asked me if I knew where to find him."

"What did you tell him?"

"The truth." Her chin fell to her chest. "I told him I didn't know."

Too agitated to sit, Rourke pulled from her grasp and paced the stable floor. Healy's story made sense. Cara obviously trusted him. Why couldn't he?

He felt it when she rose. His steps dragged to a halt, and soon she came to stand behind him, her small hand warm on his back.

"Rourke?"

He turned to her. Catching sight of her uplifted face, it was all he could do not to sweep her into his arms and press kiss after kiss to her lips. He tore his gaze away, shuddering as her fingers lightly caressed his cheek.

"I went to the wharf today," he said, his voice roughened by the emotions he fought to control.

The movement of her fingers stumbled. He quickly caught her hand before she could pull away.

"Why?"

"A man I spoke to the night I followed Deidre to Healy's house told me Healy owned a shipping company. I thought by asking questions at the wharf, I might uncover something of use."

She drew back and peered at him through narrowed eyes. "And did you?"

To his surprise, he found himself reluctant to admit that he had not, especially since the unease he'd felt since meeting Healy remained undiminished. "Not yet," he said instead. "Tomorrow I'll return and see if anyone else knows something other than what I learned today."

She moved to him, her hair falling gently over his arms, both hands clutching his biceps. "No. Rourke, tomorrow we have to go to the island."

He frowned. "Why? You've found out all you could about Deidre the last time you visited Ellis."

"Not Deidre. Eoghan. Douglas is convinced the island is the key to finding him. He told me he has friends, inspectors, who might be willing to help us track him down."

Tears filled her eyes, and he could no more resist pulling her to his chest than he could stop his lungs from filling with air. Where his shirt parted, her warm breath blazed a trail across his skin. He crushed her tighter.

"We have to find him, Rourke. We have to. If we don't warn him, Deidre . . ." Robbed of words, she shuddered.

Of their own volition his fingers rose to stroke her hair. "Shh now," he whispered. "We'll find him in time."

Her arms tightened about his waist. "You promise?"

"Aye, love," he said, dipping to press a gentle kiss to the top of her head. "I promise you, we'll leave no stone on the island unturned."

Gradually the tension trickled from her shoulders. When she pulled away, he felt bereft and would have drawn her back were it not for the anxiety etched deeply on her face.

He wrapped his arm about her shoulders. "I've kept you here too long. Let's get you inside so you can get some rest."

He reached for the knob, but she covered his hand before he could give it a turn. He lowered his gaze to soak in another glimpse of her face.

"Thank you," she whispered.

His heart jolted inside his chest. "For what?"

Her shoulder lifted in the barest of shrugs. "Everything."

He couldn't help it then—he dipped his head and stole a kiss before shoving the door open and ushering her inside.

Hugh rose from his crouched position in the stable and spit a blade of hay from his clenched teeth. It had taken every ounce of self-control not to spring on his cousin and the wretch of a woman with him. From his vantage point, it would have been a simple thing to disarm Rourke, even with his larger size and skill, and then kill the woman. In fact, were it not for the old man inside . . .

He caught himself. Healy's instructions were explicit: no one was to touch the woman until she'd brought them the information they needed about her brother. And though Hugh had dealt with him but a handful of times, even he knew better than to disobey The Celt's orders.

A smirk curled Hugh's lips. Healy thought he was so clever keeping his identity masked behind the shipping magnate façade, but Hugh knew who he was, thanks in part to his bumbling father, Angus. He probably wouldn't have recognized the truth if it bit him on the nose.

Hugh, however, was more observant, and in time he'd find a way of making the information profitable. For now, the man and his connections fulfilled a purpose—one that before long would no longer exist. Until then, there was no harm in indulging an ally.

Exhilaration spread like fire through Hugh's belly. Healy had promised an end to the threat to his secret, and if nothing else, The Celt was a man of his word. Tomorrow, he and Healy and Healy's wild-eyed witch of a daughter-in-law would set their plan into motion.

Settling into the shadows, Hugh resigned himself to watch . . . and wait.

36

Though she'd slept nary a wink, excitement prickled Cara's skin as she and Rourke stepped from the boardinghouse onto Ashberry Street just after noon the next day. She could hardly wait to get to the island, especially now that she had the name of Douglas's friend tucked safely into her pocket and they were finally on their way.

A storm had started before dawn and raged throughout the morning. Despite her ranting, praying, and eventually begging, the rain took its time fading into the gray overcast sky that frowned overhead. She darted an eager glance at Rourke. "Ready?"

"Almost." Drawing near, he grasped the flapping strings of her bonnet and snugged them into a bow beneath her chin.

Her breath caught. Even after he pulled away, the ribbon lightly tickling her cheek was as gentle as though his own hand stroked her skin.

"Th-thank you," she stammered.

His slow smile heated her through as no sun overhead could have done. She increased the distance between them and would have turned had not Rourke caught her elbow.

A cloud passed over his blue eyes. "Wait. I know another way."

Sensing his unease, Cara glanced down the street and back. "Why? Is something wrong?"

He shook his head. "Just a feeling. It might take a little longer to reach the wharf, but I think 'twould be wise to walk a different path than normal."

A shiver traveled her spine on icy fingers, and once again she was grateful for his presence. "All right."

Instead of turning south, Rourke headed north past the row of vendors until they reached a narrow side street. Tall buildings loomed on either side, protecting them from sight as they scurried along. Several twists and turns had Cara disoriented in short order. Even in broad daylight she doubted she could have found her way back to the boardinghouse alone. Finally they emerged onto a larger street and she thought she recognized a building Rourke had pointed out the first time they went to the wharf.

Rourke took her hand as her feet slowed. The lines of tension on his brow and around his mouth had deepened, sparking a flutter of nerves in Cara's stomach. She leaned into him until their shoulders touched, and she suddenly wished there were more people out and about.

She squinted up at him. "What is it?"

His stance reminded her of a tiger. He kept his

gaze fixed ahead, shoulders squared, head low and jutted slightly. With just a brief tug he brought her to stand behind him.

"Wait," he said.

The air dragged through Cara's lungs like razors. Though a drizzle had once again shaken free of the clouds, making discerning shapes difficult, she forced herself to stare in the direction he looked. She felt the rumble in her feet before she actually heard or saw the wheels of an approaching carriage. Black and foreboding, pulled by a matched team of horses colored the same as the carriage, it loomed from the shadows like a specter. She barely had time to gasp before Rourke spun and dragged her back into the alley.

"This way."

"Why? Who was that?"

He lowered his head and kept walking, faster and faster until she nearly had to run to keep up.

"Where are we going? The wharf—"

"We not be going to the wharf."

"But you said—"

"I know what I said, Cara." Without warning he jerked her against the building and pressed a finger to her lips. "Wait here," he whispered.

Never had she seen eyes so intense. She melted against the brick wall, barely able to nod, and was shocked when he whirled and disappeared.

The rain deepened and fell harder, pelting the earth and Cara's shivering form. She counted the seconds with each frosty breath that escaped from her lungs and circled on the air. Her ears strained for the slightest sound until finally she could bear the suspense no longer and poked her head around the corner to look.

Nothing.

The walls stretched out bleak and uninviting. The driving rain created a soot-filled river that carried mud and debris in its wake. But where was Rourke?

She clutched the strings of her bonnet, longing to call out to him, but afraid that doing so might bring him harm. Her heart leapt as a sudden breeze carried the sound of muffled voices to her ears.

Which way? She craned her neck from side to side. With the echo of the buildings, it was hard to tell.

But she couldn't remain where she stood.

She stepped away from the building, down another winding alley, then doubled back when the voices grew quieter. Another wrong turn and she faced a squat passage that ended at a brick wall. Frustrated and afraid, she spun and jerked her face to the sky. Never had it seemed so far away.

"God, help me!"

Her voice cracked and rippled along the damp bricks, finally returning to mock her ears.

Only it wasn't her voice.

Some distance away, a lone figure leaned, his form obscured by the falling rain. "Help me," he said again, following it with a bark of laughter that jolted Cara's feet to action.

She ran to the crux of the T formed by the merging alleys and swung left, no longer listening for Rourke's voice but moving without direction. She stumbled, caught herself against a wall, then kept going.

Her breathing grew ragged. Even so, she knew when she heard Rourke's deep tenor and turned instinctively toward it, bursting from an alley into a small square—straight into Rourke's arms.

"Cara! I told you to wait."

She fell against his chest, panting with relief and fear. "Rourke, s-someone—"

"Ah, Cara, there you are."

At the sound of Deidre's voice, Cara's head jerked up. In her hand, Deidre cradled a slim silver blade. A man whose face remained hidden beneath a wool cap hovered at her side.

Deidre held the dagger high, her eyes bright and blazing. "Do you recognize it? You should."

She glided closer, her smile widening with every step. Cara shrank against Rourke's side, felt him tense.

"Never fear, lass," Deidre purred. "I will be returning this knife to its rightful owner very soon."

"Leave her be," Rourke growled, springing to stand between her and Deidre.

Deidre paused midstride and quirked an eyebrow. Crossing her arms, she *tsk*ed in a way that made Cara shiver and then wagged the tip of the blade in the air. "Why, Mr. Walsh, don't you have your own reasons for wanting the Hamiltons dead?"

"No," he snapped, clipping the word with a quick glance at Cara. "Thanks to you, I realize now I do not."

She pressed the blade tip lightly to her chest. "Thanks to me? What have I done?"

"You revealed the truth about what really happened the night your husband was killed."

Her smiled faded, turned bitter, leaving her lifeless and pale. She lowered her chin and gave a slow shake of her head. "Come now, lad. Lest we forget, your father died the very same night."

Rourke threw his shoulders back. "As though I could forget."

Her hard stare softened. "Of course you couldn't, Mr. Walsh. Or should I call you—" she stole a glance at Cara, chilling her to the very marrow—"Mr. Turner?"

"T-Turner?" The name settled over Cara like a burial shroud. She tore her eyes from Deidre and stared at Rourke. "Your father . . . was Daniel Turner?"

He lifted a hand. "Cara, wait—"

"Aye, lass, that he was," Deidre interrupted. "You didn't know?"

Cara shook her head, backing away from Deidre, from Rourke, from the stranger whose eyes glowed from beneath his cap with deadly intent. Rourke took a step toward her, but she threw both hands in the air to stop him.

"You knew who I was?"

"Not at first," Rourke said, looking only at her, his eyes pleading.

"I told you about Eoghan." She pressed her hand to her temple, trying desperately to clear her thoughts. "You said Deidre revealed what really happened, but before that . . . you thought my brother . . . you were using me to get to my brother!"

"Cara, I can explain, but first we have to get you somewhere safe."

Each step brought Rourke closer to the alley from which Cara had emerged, though the tears building in her eyes and rain pouring down her face made it difficult to see. "Safe? How can I be safe with you? You lied to me. Even after you found out the truth—"

"I lied to protect you."

"Protect—" She got no further.

"Now!"

Deidre's scream cut off her words, made her knees go weak. Fire blazed from her eyes, wicked satisfaction curved her lips.

Cara barely had time to turn her head, to see the blur that sprang from the alley and consumed

Rourke in one fell swoop. They struggled for a moment, until the stranger with Deidre lunged in from behind and pinned Rourke's arms to his sides. Cara heard a sickening thud, saw Rourke crumple, his face a mask of shock and pain before his eyelids drifted closed, blocking the brilliance of his eyes.

His knees gave way and he slid, face forward, onto the ground. The men loomed over him, one with his feet straddling Rourke's prone body, a bloodied club gripped in both hands.

Fear clawed at Cara's throat as she recognized her attacker from the wharf, and again from the candle shop.

"You," she choked. In the scuffle, the other man's cap had been knocked free, and Cara recognized him as the man she'd spoken to at the church. "And you!"

The man did not look at her. She turned to see where he was staring. Blood was pouring from a gash on Rourke's head. He was lying so still, for a moment she doubted he was breathing. Before she could bend to check, she felt her arms secured, and then she was dragged around to stand face-to-face with Deidre.

Waking proved to be slow and painful. Rourke rolled onto his side, unable for a moment to make his eyes focus. Gradually the bricked walls of the buildings around him sharpened. The damp, muddy ground under his arm numbed his flesh.

Where was he?

A few feet away, something long and gray snaked through the trampled grass.

A bonnet, only Cara had been wearing it . . .

"Cara!"

Rourke pushed to his knees, then groaned and clutched his head when the movement made his temples throb. Crawling on all fours, he used the rough bricks of the nearest wall to pull himself to his feet.

The ground around him was trampled and muddy—except for a patch of red, which judging from the pain and the dampness running down his neck, had come from his own head. There was no sign of Cara. Where had they taken her?

Not *they* . . .

Rourke grimaced at a wave of fresh pounding. Deidre.

And Hugh.

He'd only caught a glimpse as his cousin barreled from the alley, but they'd wrestled enough for Rourke to recognize his muscular torso.

Hugh had hit him. But why would he be working with Deidre?

The shadows cast from the rooftops were long now. They poured like hot tar from the opposite side of the square. How long had he been unconscious? Three hours? Four? It had to be close to evening. Urgency took hold as he shoved from the wall.

The pain no longer mattered. His father, their quest for revenge—none of it mattered. Only one thing drove him, one thing kept him plodding forward as the world spun, threatened to tip, then righted itself as he stumbled into the alley.

He had to find Cara.

37

By the time Rourke reached Douglas Healy's home, the blinding hot pain in his head had lessened to a dull ache. The tension in his gut, however, had trickled into his limbs and set every nerve on fire. Only once did he allow himself to wonder what Cara might be facing— what his unforgivingness and misguided quest had caused. The panic that followed had nearly brought him to his knees.

Rounding Healy's estate, Rourke scaled the wrought-iron fence at the rear of the house and landed with a thud on the other side, near the carriage house. A surprised stableboy stared at him over the back of a sorrel mare, the curry-comb in his hand frozen midstroke.

Rourke strode to him. "You work for Douglas Healy?"

"I . . . that is . . ."

Rourke ignored him and walked from stall to stall inside the carriage house, searching.

The stableboy circled the mare. "Who are you? What do you want?" When Rourke did not answer, he grabbed the top of the stall wall and cocked his head. "Look now, I kinna let you in here. This be a private estate."

At the last stall, Rourke whirled. The stableboy stared at him, mouth agape.

Rourke jabbed his finger into the boy's chest. "How long has your employer been gone?"

The stableboy stared at the wound on Rourke's head. The currycomb shook as he lifted it to point. "Say, you should have that looked at—"

Before he could finish, Rourke grabbed him by the collar and jammed him against the wall. "Listen to me. I have very little time and no patience left. Either you tell me how long Healy has been gone or I break your scrawny neck."

The stableboy paled and licked his lips. "I dinna understand, sir. Mr. Healy isn't gone."

Rourke gave him a shake. "Then where is the carriage, the black one with the matched team?"

"Miss Deidre ordered it brought round this morning."

Rourke hesitated. "Did she say where she was going?"

"No, sir. They never tells me that."

Lights blazed from the main house, and

smoke rose from several of the chimneys. Rourke turned again to the boy. "Is Healy in the house?" When he failed to answer, Rourke shook him. "Tell me!"

"Aye! He be inside," the boy said, trembling. His Adam's apple bobbed in his skinny neck. "Sir, please . . . Mr. Healy . . . he's a good man."

"Then he has nothing to worry about," Rourke said, tossing him aside like an old sweater.

He marched across the yard until he reached the kitchen, the stableboy on his heels. One kick busted the door open, surprising the servants bustling around the table. Chaos erupted as he strode past them into the hall, past a formal dining room, where the housekeeper stared open-mouthed, and through a set of carved oak doors.

Rourke stalked to the first door and threw it open to reveal a den. Empty. He spun around and continued down the hall. By now, all of the household servants had gathered, along with a handful of men who looked more like they belonged in a barroom than a parlor.

The largest of them, a bullish brute with meaty hands and a dark scowl, cut into Rourke's path. "Hold it there. Just who are you, and what do you want?"

Rourke quickly sized the hallway. On a table to his left sat two large brass candlesticks. He grabbed one. Instantly the men behind the brute tensed. Several reached for the waistband of their trousers. Rourke directed his attention to the brute. "Where's Healy?"

The man eyed the candlestick in Rourke's hands, then crossed his arms over his chest. "That depends. Who wants to know, and why?"

Rourke's grip tightened. "Where?"

"You plan on stopping all of us with just that there stick?"

Rourke shook his head. "Just you."

For a second, doubt flickered in the man's face, and then he smiled. "We'll see about that."

With two fingers he motioned the men closer. Rourke relaxed his knees, prepared to strike.

"Enough!"

All heads turned to the top of the stairs. Healy stared down at them, a glass in his hand. "Mr. Walsh, what an unexpected pleasure." He turned to the stableboy. "Saddle the bay mare. Bring her round to the front."

The boy quickly fled to do his bidding. One snap of Healy's fingers and the men in the hall also retreated, like dogs given the command to heel. Another snap and the servants melted into the rooms, leaving Rourke and Healy facing each other alone.

Healy descended the stairs like a regent. Barely sparing a glance at Rourke, he passed him and continued down the hall. Rourke followed at a cautious distance, though if Healy had wanted him dead, he no doubt could have accomplished the task with just another snap.

The room they entered had doors that split off the dining room. It was good sized, with dark paneling, and smelled faintly of smoke and whiskey. Mirrors and paintings lined the walls; heavy drapes covered the windows.

Healy made his way to an ornate bar topped with several crystal decanters. He removed the stopper from one, replenished his glass, then held the decanter toward Rourke, who shook his head.

Healy replaced the bottle, took a swig from his glass, then grabbed a towel from the bar and tossed it at Rourke. Motioning toward the decanters, he said, "One of those is water. Clean yourself up."

"Where is she?" Rourke countered.

His face devoid of expression, Healy merely leaned against the bar and took another swallow from his glass.

Frustration roiled in Rourke's belly. He threw the towel aside and gripped the candlestick in both hands. "Where, Healy? Tell me."

"Or what?"

Rourke clenched his jaw. "I'll kill you."

Healy's gaze measured him from head to foot. "Aye, I believe you would." Slowly he set aside the glass and straightened. "Unfortunately I cannot help you."

Black rage fuzzed Rourke's vision. Healy was unarmed. Killing him would be murder. But if it meant saving Cara's life . . .

His thoughts winged heavenward as he silently begged God's forgiveness and took a step forward. "You lie. I saw the carriage. You were there outside the alley."

"I knew your father," Healy said, halting Rourke in his tracks. "Did you know that?" His head bobbed and he went on without waiting for Rourke's reply. "I made his acquaintance in Ireland, long before he went to parliament, and I, the Fenians. Always thought it was too bad we ended up on opposite sides. We might have made formidable allies."

Rourke froze. "How . . . ? Hugh."

A red flush colored Healy's cheeks. "It doesn't matter how I know who you are. Enough that I do," he barked, and then sighed. "Daniel Turner was a good man. I truly regret his death. I hope you will believe that."

"The Fenians kidnapped him. Tried to force him to end his resistance and bow to their agenda. How did you think that would end?"

Healy shook his head. "You're wrong, lad. We did not kidnap your father. My son acted without my authority."

"Your son?"

A flicker of sorrow flashed in his eyes and disappeared. "Sean Healy. Deidre's husband."

Rourke lowered the candlestick an inch. "He was killed in the skirmish, as well."

Lips white, Healy grabbed another towel from the bar, soaked it with water from one of the decanters, and held it toward Rourke. This time, he took it.

Healy's gaze clouded as Rourke wiped the blood from his face and neck. "I did not send Cara to the boardinghouse to be killed, you know. Like your father, she is innocent of wrong-doing."

"Then why?" Rourke demanded. Finished with the towel, he dropped it onto the bar.

Steps heavy, Healy lumbered to the fireplace and lowered his head to stare into the flames. "I did it for Deidre. She's been nigh mad with grief since Sean died. I thought if I helped her find his killer, if I helped her exact her revenge, she might finally find peace. It was a gamble, wagered solely on Cara's last name. I thought Deidre would use her to locate Eoghan. I never thought . . ." He turned to rest his arm on the mantel. "I see now I was wrong. Her lust for blood extends far beyond Eoghan. She wants all the Hamiltons dead."

"Including Cara."

Healy lowered his gaze. "Aye."

"Where did Deidre take her?"

He looked up, unblinking. "I kinna be sure . . ."

Rourke snarled and whirled to go. He'd wasted too much time already.

"But there is a place," Healy said, stopping him at the door.

Rourke glared over his shoulder at him.

"The wharf. My shipping company owns a warehouse there—Emerald Isle Freight."

Rourke's breath came hard and fast. "Where?"

"Liberty Pier." Healy held up his hand. "And, Turner?"

Once again, Rourke looked at him.

"Take the bay mare. You'll get there quicker, and my daughter-in-law?"

Rourke nodded.

"If you can spare her life . . ."

He spun and strode for the door. She had Cara. He wasn't making any promises.

Cara opened her mouth, forcing herself to take slow, measured breaths. The black sack over her head made breathing difficult, but struggling or giving in to panic was worse. Her jaw ached where someone had hit her. Her arms and shoulders screamed from being tied behind her. She wiggled her fingers, trying to force life back into limbs too long deprived of blood. The rope binding her wrists to the chair only cut deeper.

Behind her, heavy footsteps scraped the floor. "Why are we still here? Why don't we kill the wench and have done?"

Recognizing the voice of her attacker from the candle shop, Cara froze.

"Perhaps if you hadn't hit her so hard," Deidre snapped.

"What was I supposed to do? She fought like a wildcat when Rourke fell."

Nausea rolled up from Cara's stomach. She swallowed it back down.

He's not dead. Father in heaven, please do not let him be dead.

"You should have killed him, Hugh," another male voice said. "He'll be a liability to ya now."

"Aye, Kilarny, and he wasn't before?"

"So why didn't ya finish him?"

Deidre cut in. "Enough bickering!" They fell silent and her purr returned. "Once she wakes up, you'll both have what you need. Hugh, your kinsmen will never find out we paid you for the information on Daniel Turner's whereabouts. You'll go back to your kinsmen and tell them you only pretended to be my ally so you could track down Hamilton. And Kil . . ."

A shadow passed before Cara's eyes.

"You have my word that The Celt will never know you acted with Sean to kidnap Daniel Turner."

Her skirt brushed Cara's arm as she passed. In spite of herself, Cara shivered. A second later, she gasped as the sack was snatched from her head.

The sack hung limply from Deidre's fingers. In the other hand she held a lantern high. "You're awake. I wondered how long it would take."

Panic built in Cara's chest as she blinked repeatedly in a vain attempt to see her surroundings. In the light cast by the lantern she saw crates as tall as men. Row after row of them. Beyond that was nothing but gloom. She worked to steady her breathing as Deidre's face came into focus.

"Where am I?"

Deidre set the lantern on one of the crates, then wrapped her arm around her middle. The other hand fluttered upward and she rested her chin against her knuckles. "Why don't we let me ask the questions, eh?"

Cara glanced at the two men, both of whom glared at her with murder in their eyes. Where was Rourke? Or Eoghan?

She lifted her chin.

Deidre smiled. "There's a lass." Taking the sack, she draped it over Cara's shoulder and ran it across her throat. "Let's see . . . what is that old saying? 'Tis hard to fight with the wide ocean?" She leaned into Cara's face. "Aye, that be it. What say you, Cara Hamilton? No more pretense?"

Cara turned her face away. "What do you want, Deidre?"

Deidre clasped her chin and forced Cara to look at her. "Who is Eoghan Hamilton to you?"

Though the move made her wince, Cara tried to appear calm. "He is my brother."

She stared into Cara's eyes a moment, then

released her and straightened. "Hmm . . . 'twould have been better if he'd been your lover." She gave the sack a flick with her wrist. "No matter. You'll both be dead soon enough."

Cara's racing heart jerked against her chest. She knew where to find Eoghan? She closed her eyes and breathed a prayer for his safety. Deidre's laughter jolted them open again.

"It's far too late for that, lass. God can't help you here."

"God's help is nearer than the door," Cara whispered, more to herself than to Deidre. "There is nowhere He cannot go, His eyes cannot see."

She believed it. Peace flooded Cara's heart at the realization that despite her circumstances, or the doubts that had been her companion these many months since receiving Eoghan's letter, she still truly believed in the faithfulness of God.

Deidre's eyes glittered like jewels. "We shall see about that."

"Get on it with it," Hugh snarled, pacing the floor like a hungry animal.

To Cara's shock, Deidre strode across the room and struck him, hard, across the face. "I have waited a long time for this moment. You will not deprive me of the pleasure I take in it."

The ringing of the slap still hung in the air as Hugh's hand rose to rub his cheek. Black as coal, his eyes burned into Deidre's. "I'll kill you for that."

She simply smiled. "But not yet."

Kilarny shrunk further into the shadows cast by a row of crates. "You're mad—both of ya." He turned his gaze to Deidre. "I did my part, Dee, like ya asked. Helped ya get the girl. Now I'm finished here."

Deidre hesitated a moment, and then nodded. "Fine. Go."

Relief flooded Kilarny's face, though he paused at the large metal door to glance over his shoulder. "You'll keep your part of the bargain, woman. Friend or no, I'll show no mercy to Sean Healy's widow if you don't."

"I'll keep my word," she spat. "Do not worry about that."

He returned a snort before ducking through the door.

Cara's mind spun.

Sean. My Sean. Deidre's husband. Healy. Douglas?

She stared as Deidre approached. This time, she didn't bend to look into Cara's face. She circled the chair, round and round, plucking at Cara's hair or lightly caressing her cheek.

"Where is he, Cara?"

"Who?"

"Your brother. I know you know where he's hiding."

"I do not."

Her hot breath stroked Cara's ear. "I do not believe you."

A shudder rippled from her head to her toes. "Deidre, please—"

"You beg?" Deidre sidled around till she stood face-to-face with Cara. "Like my Sean begged your brother not to betray him? Did he listen?" She withdrew a dagger from the waistband of her skirt and held it to Cara's nose. "You know what this is?"

Afraid to speak, she nodded.

"Tell me."

"Eo-Eoghan's knife."

Deidre pulled it away and ran the blade lightly over her palm. "That's right. Eoghan's knife. And do you know where I got it?"

Cara stared, frozen as Deidre tightened her grip on the handle.

"I pulled it from my husband's chest, right after *your* brother put it there."

Sickened by what she heard, Cara closed her eyes. Still, she felt and heard when Deidre moved to stand at her back, one hand heavy on her shoulder.

"You will tell me what I want to know, Cara. You'll tell me or I'll sheath your brother's blade in your heart."

38

The bay mare raced through the city streets, the shoes on her hooves clanging dully against the cobbles. Rourke leaned low over her neck, urging her faster with his heels. If he was too late, if he failed to reach the wharf in time . . .

"C'mon!" he shouted into the horse's twitching ears.

Her mane whipped him in the eyes as she lowered her head and lengthened her stride. Trees and houses flew by, a shadowy blur in the moonlight streaming from breaks in the clouds. Still, it seemed an eternity before the buildings that crowded the streets thinned and he began seeing the outline of smokestacks from steamers stabbing the sky. Farther down, the boats were smaller, sailing vessels mostly, bobbing on the glistening waves.

Liberty Pier.

Rourke straightened and pressed down with his heels, strong in the stirrups, slowing the mare, then nudging her with his knees toward the dock where Healy said Deidre had most likely gone. The horse snorted, her sides heaving, the pounding of her hooves changing to a hollow thud as they left the street and entered the shipyard.

Lanterns cut the gloom on the ships they passed. Figures worked by their light, scrambling over cargo, barking orders to unseen deckhands. Bells clanged. Water lapped at hulls. Rourke's gaze shot across the muddy street. Forced to slow, he drew back on the reins and squinted to see the names painted on the sides of the buildings hunkered along the shore.

His impatience grew. Building after building passed, none of them bearing the name Emerald Isle Freight. Had Healy lied to him? Sent him on a vain mission in order to give Deidre the time she needed to exact her revenge?

He rounded a bend and saw it. The black carriage. Steam rose from the backs of the horses hitched to it, ghostly white in the light of the moon.

A hundred yards shy of the warehouse, Rourke dismounted just as a metal door squealed and a man stepped out. His bowlegged gait instantly identified him. He'd been with Deidre right before Hugh jumped him.

Rourke ducked behind the bow of an elegant sloop and waited until the man disappeared before poking his head out for a look. Except for the occasional head toss from one of the blacks, the street had returned to its former stillness.

He skirted the water's edge and covered the twenty-odd strides that remained to Healy's warehouse. The metal door was tightly shut, but voices drifted from inside, one of them Deidre's.

". . . do you know where I got it?"

Though he strained, Rourke heard no reply. He tugged on the door handle. It was locked. Panic swelled in his chest. Deidre was talking to Cara. She had to be, but if he couldn't reach her . . .

He threw his head back and stared at the building looming over him. Three small windows ran the length of the warehouse, but they were too high to reach. On the other side, more windows—still too high, but below them was a wooden door. The knob was old and rusted, and broke free as he yanked the door open.

Rourke dropped to his haunches and listened.

Nothing.

Either he'd given himself away and Deidre and Hugh lay in wait to ambush him, or they were too far from the door to hear him enter. He prayed it was the latter and pressed forward.

The gloom thickened the farther inside the warehouse he went. He discovered the room he'd broken into had once housed an office, which explained why it was walled off from the rest of the place. He breathed a prayer of thanksgiving for his good fortune and wound through the dust-covered furniture toward the exit.

In the main room of the warehouse, angry voices echoed from the walls and ceiling.

"She comes with us! I want him to see her die, the same way I watched my Sean."

"Fool! Have you considered what your cursed thirst for vengeance could cost? She doesn't know where her brother is. Kill her now and be done."

At Hugh's response, Rourke grit his teeth and hurried his pace—difficult in the dark, especially since he worked to keep his steps silent. Between him and Cara were bins of assorted sizes, crates, and machinery. On the floor, coils of rope threatened to snag his feet and send him sprawling. He picked his way until he could crouch just yards shy of where Cara sat bound to a chair. His heart constricted at the look of terror on her face.

Deidre gestured with a knife, coming sickeningly close to Cara's throat. "Nay! If she lives, Hamilton will come looking for her. We'll use her as bait to draw him."

Hugh took her by the arms. "Will you listen to me? I have as much reason as you for wanting him dead, but we can find Hamilton without her. We don't need her, I tell ya." He gave her a hard shake that rolled her head. "Deidre!"

Rourke tensed, braced his fingertips on the floor. Deidre had gone silent. Calm.

"No." He said it under his breath.

She glanced at the knife in her hand, then at Cara. Hugh released her arms.

Rourke rose to his feet. "No." Slightly louder.

Cara's lips parted. "Deidre . . ."

She eased to the front of the chair and lifted the knife above her head.

"Kill her now," Hugh said. "Do it."

"No!" The word ripped from Rourke's throat.

He leapt without thinking, watching in horror as the knife glimmered in the light of the lantern and arced downward, straight for Cara's heart.

Cara closed her eyes, bracing for a blow that never came. Instead, Rourke tackled Deidre and sent her sprawling. She let go a scream that ended in an *oomph* as her back hit the floor. The knife clattered from her hand and skittered to a stop inches from Cara's feet.

Rolling like a cat, Rourke pounced to his feet and came up swinging, catching Hugh on the chin and dropping him to his knees.

Tears sprang instantly to Cara's eyes. She strained against the ropes. He was alive. Alive! He was all right, and he'd come to rescue her . . . or had he? She bit her lip, sagging into the chair. Was it her or Eoghan he'd come to seek?

Behind him, Deidre sat up, gasping. Her head twisted to and fro as she scanned the floor for the knife. Finding it, she scrambled onto her knees and started after it. Her fingers closed around the handle and her head came up. Rourke didn't see. He was wrestling Hugh with his back to Deidre.

"Rourke, look out!" Cara screamed.

In the same instant she lifted her feet and kicked

Deidre with all her might. The force of the blow toppled the chair. Unable to catch herself, Cara gasped as pain shot from her shoulder to her elbow. Deidre, too, groaned as her head connected with the floor.

"Cara!"

She blinked and craned her neck to see. Hugh was slumped against the wall, his eyes closed and his jaw slack.

Her heart rate sped. She twisted the other way. "Rourke?"

"I'm here."

He was there, against the wall, fresh blood pouring from the wound on his head, but there all the same. She glanced again at Hugh. "Is he . . . dead?"

Rourke pushed from the wall. "Don't look at him, lass."

A second later, she felt the bonds on her wrists loosen, and then he lifted her to her feet and pulled her to his chest. His hands flicked from her head to her cheeks, her shoulders. "Are you all right? Cara, talk to me. I thought I'd lost you. I thought . . ."

He broke off and held her tight. "I will explain everything, I swear it. For now, we have to get you to safety. Can you walk?"

It was happening too fast. She felt light-headed. "I . . . oh, Rourke. You're all right."

His gaze softened. "Aye, love."

"And Deidre?"

The woman lay semiconscious on her side.

"She won't be out long. We have to go," Rourke urged.

Her knees felt weak, so Cara leaned on his arm and let him lead her through the large metal door. Outside, she froze, staring in horror across the harbor.

"Rourke."

She lifted her finger and pointed. A bright orange glow lit the night. Flames licked at the darkened sky. It couldn't be . . . and yet she knew immediately that it was . . .

Ellis Island was on fire.

39

"Oh, Rourke!" Cara clung to his arm, swaying, unable to tear her gaze from the awful sight. Flames engulfed the sides and roof of the immigration station. Sparks, millions in all, leapt into the air.

Beside her, Rourke stood as tall and straight as the copper statue lit across the water by the fire's glow. "Is that . . . ?"

"The immigration station, the records . . . they're on fire." Tears filled her eyes and flowed down her cheeks. She swung her head to stare up at Rourke. "What will I do? I'll never find Eoghan now."

His face was full of compassion. He said nothing as he squeezed her to his side. Cara watched helpless as a fireboat struggled to cross the choppy waves.

"It's too late," she whispered. "They're too late."

Letting go of Rourke's arm, her hand fluttered to her mouth as she stumbled to the water's edge. Never had the distance across the waves seemed so vast, the time it took to reach the island so great.

Rourke followed, stopping behind her to wrap her in an embrace. "Cara, we have to go."

She shook her head. She couldn't leave. Not yet. The flames were higher now. She heard the hiss of steam as water hit them, could almost feel the heat emanating from the island.

He squeezed her shoulder and whispered into her ear, "Cara, please. We'll find another way. I promise you."

Though she desperately wanted to believe him, her brother's name welled from her heart, the pain of losing him bruising, crushing, seeking release. She sagged under the weight of it, Rourke's arms all that kept her from falling on her face to the ground.

Gasping for air, she opened her mouth and let the cry spill out. "Eoghan!"

In her grief, she could almost hear him calling back to her, his voice as pain-filled as her own. She closed her eyes.

"Why? Why would God bring me this far, let me get this close, and then snatch him away? Why? I don't understand."

"I'm sorry, Cara. It's my fault. I'm so sorry."

Again, she imagined Eoghan calling her name, closer this time. She whirled and pressed her face to Rourke's chest.

"It's not fair. He is all I have. I have no one else."

"You have me, Cara. I swear, I'll never leave you." Rourke's fingers cupped her chin and then she was staring into his brilliant blue eyes. "I love you."

Her breath caught. "Rourke . . ."

"Cara!"

She swung to scan the wharf. It . . . couldn't be. It was Eoghan's voice, and he sounded close enough to touch. She jerked her head the other way. Her brother . . . her *brother* closed the last few feet between them. Her brow furrowed with confusion. In his outstretched hand, he held a gun.

"Eoghan?"

She could scarcely force enough air past her lips to whisper. He was thin, ghostly pale, but he was alive, and somehow he'd found her. She barely sensed when Rourke's arms fell away.

"Eoghan!" She took one step toward her

brother, then another, until she was running, wild laughter bubbling in her throat. But instead of taking her outstretched hand, Eoghan strode past her, his face black with rage.

Cara whirled. So close was the report of the pistol, she instinctively slapped her hands over her ears. In the same instant, the gun flashed orange and the acrid scent of smoke and sulfur filled the air.

Eoghan's shoulders hunched as he jerked a bag from the pocket of his coat and began reloading the pistol. Sweat dripped from his brow as he fired her a glance. "Run, Cara! I'll catch up."

Trembling seized her limbs. She stumbled to him. "What?"

"He's not dead! I have to finish him." He grabbed her arm and squeezed. Intensity blazed from his hazel eyes, so familiar yet so foreign with bloodlust shining from them. "Go!"

"F-finish—?"

Peering past him, she saw Rourke lying half prone on the ground. With one hand he struggled to drag himself to his feet. The other he clutched to his chest, his face contorted with pain.

Cara widened her eyes, horror rising like bile in her throat. "Oh, Eoghan, what have you done?"

"He's a Turner, Cara. He wants to kill us!"

In desperation she gripped his arm. "Eoghan, wait! You have to let me explain."

He shrugged her hand away. "There's no time,

Cara." Cocking the hammer, he lifted the pistol and aimed it at Rourke's back.

"No!" She acted without thinking. Driving her fist to his wrist, she knocked the pistol from his grasp, then dove to stand between him and Rourke, her arms outstretched.

Eoghan howled in shock and pain, then gripping his wrist he stared at her, his mouth agape. "What are you doing?"

She shot one hand toward him, palm out. "Eoghan, please, you cannot kill him. If you just give me time to explain—"

He straightened and cut his arm wildly through the air. "I told you, there is no time. His clan will be here any minute. They're trying to kill me, Cara! That's why I couldn't come to you sooner."

"No!"

His fist pounded his chest. "Are you listening to me, lass? They want us dead, both of us. They're still trying!"

"Hamilton!"

The scream rent the night air like a sheet. Deidre flew toward them. In her hand, Eoghan's dagger flashed orange and silver. Eoghan shoved Cara so hard, she fell to the ground. A split second later, he spun and threw his hands up to catch Deidre by the wrists.

"I'll kill you! I'll kill you the way you killed my Sean!"

Deidre's screams sent shivers coursing over

Cara's flesh. She watched, horrified, as she and Eoghan struggled with the dagger at the water's edge, both of them locked in a desperate life-and-death fight.

"Cara," Rourke groaned.

Her head snapped toward him, and then she crawled to him on her hands and knees. Sweat dampened his hair and dotted his brow. Cradling his blood-soaked body against her torso, she wrapped her arms around him and held tight. "Rourke, I'm so sorry. He didn't know—"

"You have to go, Cara. It's . . . it's not safe."

She shook her head violently. "I'm not leaving you."

"Eoghan was right." Rourke gasped and struggled to rise, blood oozing between his fingers. "My kinsmen . . . they're coming. They'll be here soon."

She stroked his pale cheek. "I don't care."

"But . . . I may not be able . . . to stop them . . ."

Terror squeezed her heart as he went limp, his eyes rolling back in his head. "Rourke! Please, darling, don't leave me." Sobbing, she pressed him to her chest. "Rourke, I love you!"

She had no time to think, no time to move, for suddenly Deidre screamed and dropped to her knees. Eoghan panted over her, his fingers curled and bloodied. Both stared at the knife that protruded from her midsection.

Slowly, Deidre's head lifted and a final sigh escaped her lips. Still, her clawed hands reached for Eoghan, grasping at air. He stepped away and she toppled from the edge of the pier. A second later, she disappeared beneath the icy waves.

Far away, men shouted and scrambled to douse the fire at the immigration station, though it was obvious now that it would not be saved. The flames danced in the sky above Eoghan's head, giving him a wildly eerie look that raised the hair on Cara's arms.

She stretched her hand to him, pleading. "Eoghan? Please . . . he needs your help."

He refused to take it. He stared at her, his face a mask of hurt and disappointment. "You love him? A Turner?"

"You don't understand—"

He shook his head. "No! I do not. I . . . do not." At last, silent, he spun on his heel and strode away.

Shock flashed through Cara's body like a lightning bolt. She was alone. Rourke was wounded, dying. She had to find help. But Eoghan . . .

She almost couldn't make out his retreating back for the teary haze that blurred her vision. In desperation she hugged Rourke tighter and looked about for help.

Three hulking figures separated from the shadows and made their way toward her. Three —all men. And one of them . . .

She gasped and bent protectively over Rourke. One of them looked exactly like Hugh.

40

The tallest of the men, the one in the middle, dropped to his haunches across from Cara, Rourke's unconscious form between them. He took in the wound to Rourke's head, the blood that stained his shirt. When he reached to investigate, Cara grabbed his fingers and shook her head.

For a split second, their eyes met. Like Rourke's, his were shockingly blue.

" 'Tis all right, lass," the man said gently. "We saw what you did. We're here to help."

He snapped his fingers then and pointed to the warehouse. The youngest of the group took off at a sprint. The third man, the one who favored Hugh, squatted next to Cara. She struggled to suppress a shiver.

"How bad is the wound, Malcolm?"

He grunted. "I've seen worse, but he's still bleeding. We'll need to get him bandaged up soon."

The tall man, Malcolm, looked at Cara. "What about you, lass? Are you injured?"

She shook her head.

"Are ya all right to walk, then?"

She managed a shaky "Aye," then reached out her hand when Malcolm moved to stand. "Wait."

He glared down at her, both snowy brows drawn in a glower.

Cara licked her lips. "Who . . . who are you?"

The frown cleared from his face and he returned to his haunches. "My name is Malcolm Turner. Rourke is my nephew." He gestured to the man next to Cara. "That is Angus O'Hurly, also an uncle, but on the lad's mother's side."

Hugh's father? Cara's gaze shot to him. No wonder they favored each other. Rourke stirred, and Malcolm laid his palm to his chest. "Easy, lad. It's all right now. You're safe."

"Cara?"

Malcolm lifted one brow and shot her a quick glance. "She's safe, as well—we'll see to that. Rest now." He motioned to Angus. "You get the horses. I'll do what I can to stop the bleeding."

"Aye."

Both men stood, pausing when the warehouse door opened and the youngest came jogging out. Angus strode to meet him, his gait stiff, shoulders squared. "Hugh?"

Cara's heart raced. She knew what his answer would be. He shook his head.

Malcolm crossed to them and clapped his hand on Angus's back. "I am sorry, Angus. We'll send the others to fetch him—"

"Nay," Angus barked, shrugging from Malcolm's grip. "He died a traitor's death. He'll remain where he lies."

He spun and marched away, his face hard. Malcolm, however, looked sad when he returned, the young man at his side. Once again, he squatted across from Cara, his elbows braced on his knees. "Cara, this is my son Clive." He looked at Rourke. "We're going to have to move him, lass. Will you let us have him?"

Rourke once again lay against her, unconscious, but until Malcolm mentioned it, she hadn't realized how tightly she was holding him. She gave a slow nod and relaxed her grip as Clive stepped in to take her place.

Within minutes he and Malcolm had packed the wound on Rourke's shoulder and somehow managed to move him onto the back of a gray gelding. Clive rode behind him, Angus beside on a black mare. Cara rode in front of Malcolm, shivering as they galloped down one unfamiliar street after another. Occasionally the glow from a streetlamp lit Malcolm's face. Though somber, she marveled at the similarity to Rourke's.

The horse's gait wavered, and Cara jerked her attention forward, to the road stretching out before them like a black ribbon. Just when she thought them hopelessly lost, Malcolm wheeled their mount onto a familiar cobbled street.

Ashberry? She peered over her shoulder at him.

He spared her a brief smile. "Aye, lass, we be returning ya to the boardinghouse."

Cara's lips parted. "But Rourke . . ."

She said nothing further until the steps came into view, but when Malcolm reined the horse to a halt and lowered her to the ground, she reached up to claim his hand. "Where are you taking him?"

"He'll be safe, lass. Do not worry."

Clive rode to a stop next to them. "Da."

He turned in the saddle to look at them. Rourke sagged against Clive, his face ashen. In the moonlight, the stain on his shirt looked even wider, darker than before.

"He cannot go much farther," Clive said. "I tried to go easy, but . . ."

Angus, too, rode up beside them. "He'll bleed to death before we reach shelter, Malcolm."

Suddenly light spilled down the stairs. Amelia stood framed in the open door, Breda, Tillie, Ana, and Giles all gathered at her back.

"Cara?" She hurried down the steps and wrapped her in a hug, the others close on her heels. "Praise God. We've been so worried."

"Where've ya been, lass?" Giles said.

Tillie clasped her hand. "Have you heard? The immigration station burned to the ground."

Amelia's gaze drifted to Rourke. She smothered her gasp with a hand to her mouth. Cara moved to her elbow.

"Amelia, Rourke needs our help. These men . . . they're his family."

Snapped from her paralysis, Amelia gestured to Giles. "Go, fetch the doctor. Tillie, Ana, draw the covers on his bed. Breda, wake Laverne. The doctor is going to need water and clean bandages."

Relief flooded Cara's heart. She whirled and clasped Malcolm's knee. "Bring him inside. There is help for him here." She motioned to the others. "And warm beds for your men as well if they are in need of rest."

Malcolm threw one more glance at his nephew before signaling the others to dismount. With Rourke in their arms, he nodded to Cara. "Show the way, lass."

She hurried up the steps, but only later—when the doctor had wrestled the lead from Rourke's shoulder and assured them all that he thought the bleeding had stopped—did she breathe a sigh of relief.

Malcolm clapped him on the back. "Ya done good, Doc. No doubt my nephew owes you his life, and the rest of us, our thanks."

Closing his bag with a snap, the doctor hefted it and shuffled to the door. "No thanks necessary." He gestured over his shoulder with his chin. "Just be sure to keep that wound clean, and send someone to fetch me if he begins to show signs of infection."

"Will do." Malcolm motioned to Angus and Clive. "Come, lads. Let's show the doctor out and leave the ladies to tend Rourke. We've much to discuss."

Amelia rose and joined them at the door. "I'll show you where the library is. It'll be quiet there, and you won't be interrupted."

Malcolm gave a nod and a slight bow, then followed her and the doctor out.

Left with Laverne on one side of the bed, she on the other, and Rourke in between, Cara finally allowed some of the grief and fear to seep from her eyelids.

Laverne rounded the bed and patted her back gently. "Are you all right, Cara?"

She swiped the dampness from her cheeks with the back of her hand. "I think so, or at least I will be in time."

Thankfully she did not push for an explanation, not that Cara could have offered one given the jumbled state of her thoughts. Laverne wrapped her in a hug before gliding to the door. "I'm glad you're all right. The lad, too." The knob twisted with a click in her hand. "I'll send someone up in a bit to check on you. Try and get some rest if you can."

As the door shut behind her, Cara sank into a chair and slumped forward to rest her arms on the edge of Rourke's bed. Despite Laverne's admonition, she would spend the night, what was left of it, close enough to hear should Rourke awaken and call out.

Her fingers sought his strong ones. Strange to think how close death had come to claiming him.

She shuddered and tried to close her mind to the memory of his groans. He was safe and resting. The doctor said he would recover. That was all that mattered.

Nearly half an hour later, a soft knock sounded. Breda entered and pressed a cup into her hands. "Drink this. It'll help calm your nerves."

She didn't ask what the cup contained, just downed the liquid in three large gulps.

Breda took the cup from her limp fingers and set it on the table next to the lamp. "Laverne says the lad is going to be all right?"

She hadn't the strength for more than a nod.

Breda patted her shoulder and then bent over the bed. Hands fluttering, she adjusted the blankets over Rourke and lowered the wick on the lamp until the barest glow spilled out. The oily light cast deep shadows over Breda's face. Cara shivered despite the fire someone had seen fit to kindle.

"Are you cold, lass? I can get you a shawl," Breda offered.

Cara shook her head. Now that things had slowed enough for her to think, to realize that while she had Rourke, Eoghan could well be lost forever, she felt tears threatening. "I'm fine. It's just . . ."

Emotion closed her throat.

Breda reached across the gap to clasp her hand. "What happened, dear? They're all a-whispering down there." She jerked her thumb toward the door. "Said Deidre is . . . that she tried . . ."

Cara swallowed before speaking the awful words. "She's dead, Breda. She tried to kill me. My brother, too."

"Your brother!"

Cara squeezed her fingers. "I'm sorry I couldn't tell you. He warned me not to."

Though confused lines still furrowed her brow, Breda clucked and patted Cara's hand. "Time enough for explanations in the morning, I suppose." She paused, and sorrow dimmed her gaze. "Poor Deidre. Never seen a soul more tortured by unforgivingness. I'm just glad . . . well, I'm glad she didn't hurt ya."

"Thanks to Rourke." Cara drew a shuddering breath and then both she and Breda fixed their gazes to his face.

Heavy footsteps sounded on the stairs. Cara went to the door, half expecting Malcolm, and surprised when it was Angus who gestured to her. "Mind if I come in?"

Breda crossed with him at the door. "I should be going. You'll call for me if you need anything?"

"I will," Cara said, squeezing Breda's hand as a way of saying thanks and then moving aside to allow Angus to enter.

Angus wound toward the bed, his steps surprisingly light for such a big man. Instead of touching Rourke, he clasped his gnarled hands behind his back. "How is he?"

"Resting."

"That's good."

He rocked back on his heels, and Cara thought she saw the slightest glimmer in his eyes from the light cast by the lamp.

Pity for him filled her. Whatever she thought of Hugh, Angus had lost a son. She motioned toward the window seat, far enough away that they would not disturb Rourke if they talked.

Once they were seated, the old man cleared his throat and nodded toward the cuts and bruises on her wrists. "You should have those tended."

She'd been so concerned with Rourke's welfare, she'd forgotten all about her own injuries. She tugged her sleeves down to cover the marks. "They're just scrapes. I'll be fine."

His bushy eyebrows gathered into a scowl. "No thanks to my son, eh?"

What could she say? She bit her tongue.

Seeming to appreciate her tact, Angus gave a curt nod and folded his arms over his chest. "Miss Hamilton—"

"Please, call me Cara."

Another nod. "Cara, then. My son . . . Hugh . . ." He struggled, as though speaking the name pained him, and ran his large palm over his grizzled face. "I would like to believe it was justice he was after, that he sought you and your brother out of loyalty to Daniel, but I'm no fool. I've suspected it was something deeper for a long time."

Deidre's promise rang in Cara's brain. *". . . your kinsmen will never find out we paid you for the information on Daniel Turner's whereabouts."*

Angus studied her, his gray eyes narrowed. "You know what that something is, don't you, lass? You overheard him tell it."

Surprisingly she felt no fear meeting Angus's gaze, only peace and an urging in her spirit prompting her to tell the truth. "He helped the Fenians find Daniel. I heard Deidre say they paid him for information on his whereabouts."

Anger twisted Angus's features. "So it was his own shame he was trying to cover by killing the two of you."

She nodded.

"And your brother?" Angus lifted a brow. "He really was trying to save Daniel's life?"

She clamped her hands tightly in her lap. "I believe so."

He grunted and lifted one of his arthritic knuckles to rub his temple. " 'Twould have saved us all a spot of trouble if he'd just confessed his part instead of going into hiding. He had to realize that running away only made him look more guilty."

Heat suffused Cara's cheeks, carried on a wave of ire. Her chin jutted out. "Would you have

395

believed him? You and your kinsmen thought him a murderer. Would you have even listened to his side of the story?"

After a moment, the scowl lifted from Angus's brow. "Ach. I suppose you're right. The Turners have a tendency to fight first, talk later. Guess that's what made Daniel Turner such a match for my sister." His eyes took on a devilish sparkle. "And I suspect it's what makes you such a match for my nephew."

Heat of a different kind swept over her then. Her gaze drifted to Rourke, from the dark thatch of hair that fell over his temple to the hard line of his jaw and wide set of his shoulders. She loved him, but was she his match?

Angus slapped both hands on his knees and pushed to his feet. He towered over her, half of his shaggy face hidden by shadows, the other a mix of ragged emotions that set her insides to quivering.

"My son betrayed our family and brought more shame to the O'Hurly name than I'd ever thought to bear. I regret the harm he's brought to both our families. I hope you can believe that."

Cara rose to look him in the eyes. "I do. Thank you."

Angus gave a curt dip of his head before shoving both hands into the pockets of his trousers and turning to go. At the door, he paused and looked back at her, one snowy brow raised to form a peak. "Our quarrel with your brother is ended. If . . . when . . . you see him next, be sure to tell him so. He'll have naught to fear from any of us."

A knot formed in Cara's throat. Having seen the anger that shone from Eoghan's eyes, she could only hope she'd have the opportunity to tell him of Angus's promise.

"I'll tell him," she whispered, though too late for Angus to hear. He had slipped into the hall and shut the door softly behind him.

Left alone with Rourke once again, Cara returned to her place beside the bed. There was nothing left for her to do but sit and wait for the dawn.

41

The sun's morning rays spilled from the window onto Rourke's bed, warming Cara's shoulders and coaxing her from sleep. The door behind her creaked, and she lifted her head from the bed-covers to see who'd entered.

Malcolm waited until she waved him in before moving to the chair next to her. "How is he?" he asked, his voice low.

Her eyes caressed the planes of Rourke's face, from the faint stubble that shadowed his jaw to the dark lashes brushing his cheeks.

"Resting." She slipped her hand from Rourke's

and tried in vain to massage the stiffness from her shoulders.

Malcolm watched her, one shaggy brow lifted. "You sat with him all night?"

Her hands stilled. Lowering her eyes shyly, she brought them to her lap. "Mr. Turner—"

"Malcolm."

She looked up and saw kindness twinkling from his bonnie eyes. Cara relaxed and nodded her thanks. "Malcolm, last night . . ."

"Aye, lass?"

She leaned forward. "How did you know where to find us?"

His chair protested as he shifted to face her. "Is that really what you be wanting to ask?"

Squirming under the directness of his stare, Cara felt a blush heat her cheeks. She shook her head.

Malcolm sighed and sat back in his chair. "You want to know about his father."

She said nothing, waiting.

"Rourke was close to him," Malcolm began, the hard lines on his face softening with remembrance. "They were both stubborn as mules, and they butted heads a time or two, mind, but there was always great respect between them. That's why, when Rourke asked his da to oppose the idea of home rule, Daniel was inclined to listen." Malcolm's voice roughened. "He never dreamed, none of us did, that it would lead to his death."

Understanding made Cara's heart heavy. "Rourke blamed himself."

"Aye," Malcolm said, his face somber. "And the bitterness of his guilt drove him to seek out the one who killed him."

Cara's head snapped up. "It wasn't Eoghan. My brother tried to save him."

Malcolm's large hand claimed hers. "I know, lass. Angus told me everything that you and he spoke about. 'Twas Hugh's treachery what led to Daniel's death."

Cara bit her lip. "I am sorry."

Malcolm nodded. "No more than I." He lifted his fingers to his mouth and cleared his throat. "Perhaps I am more so since it appears I owe your brother and you, and my nephew, an apology."

She and Eoghan, Cara understood, but Rourke?

Malcolm shook his head. "After Rourke told us what happened between you and Deidre, I got a little suspicious of his motives—sensed maybe his affection for ya had compromised his loyalties."

Blindly, Cara sought Rourke's hand and gave it a squeeze. "And?"

"I had him followed." He paused, then added, "He led us to a man named Douglas Healy. You know him?"

"Yes. Deidre was married to his son, though I didn't know that when I met him."

"Nor did we. Unfortunately, that is all we've

been able to discover about the man. He's disappeared. Word is he's headed back to Ireland."

Cara lifted a brow and Malcolm shrugged. "Someone paid Hugh for the information on my brother, Cara. Now three of the people who knew the identity of that person—Hugh, Deidre, and Daniel—are dead. Healy may be our only link."

A shudder passed through her. So, the Turner's quest for revenge wasn't over, only diverted.

"Last night," Malcolm continued, "after Rourke learned your whereabouts from Healy, Eoghan followed him to the wharf. He was on foot."

"And Rourke had Douglas's horse."

"That's right."

"But . . . if you saw him . . ."

"Rourke had already told us about Eoghan's innocence, remember. We had no reason to kill him, unless—"

"Unless Rourke was wrong."

Malcolm nodded.

Cara widened her eyes. "You wanted proof of Eoghan's innocence, so you did nothing? You stood by and let him shoot Rourke?"

"We're not as callous as that, lass. We arrived a second too late to stop Eoghan from shooting Rourke, but in time to see you keep your brother from killing him."

"And Deidre?" The dreadful image of the woman's lifeless body flashed through her mind.

Malcolm dropped his gaze. "That fight was

between her and your brother. We had no right to interfere."

She marveled at the insane logic. Rising from her chair, Cara went to the window and stood there, staring out at the sky. "You said Rourke learned of my whereabouts from Healy." She looked over her shoulder in time to see Malcolm nod his agreement. "I don't understand. Healy had as much reason as Deidre for wanting my brother dead. Why would he help Rourke stop her?"

Malcolm stroked his chin. "Why indeed?"

Cara shuddered as the implication of his simple words sank in. She left the window to join Malcolm beside Rourke's bed. "You're still hoping to find out who was behind your brother's death, aren't you?"

"Aye. As soon as Rourke is able, we'll be leaving. Going back to Ireland to see what we can uncover on Healy." He sighed and reached out to squeeze Cara's shoulder. "I truly am sorry you got caught up in all of this. I hope you and your brother . . . I hope you find him, work out the trouble between you two."

He turned to go, pausing before he slipped through the door to shoot her one last glance. "You look tired. Try and get some sleep."

The door clicked shut behind him. Rourke moaned, and Cara turned her attention to him. He was going to be all right. The doctor had assured them that with a few days' rest, he'd be back on his feet—a month and he'd be as good as new. But she?

She had saved Rourke, but lost her brother.

Again.

And according to Malcolm, as soon as Rourke was healed, she'd lose him, too. Sinking into the chair, she wondered if she would ever be well again.

42

The sunlight filtering through the bedroom window stabbed Rourke's eyelids, coaxed him toward wakefulness. Gradually he gave in to the sun's prodding, tried to roll onto his side, then groaned as a flash of white-hot pain reminded him of his condition. He grimaced and reached for his bandaged shoulder.

"Uh-uh. Don't touch that." Laverne bustled to him and slapped playfully at his hand. "Cara will have my head if I let you mess up her good work." She grinned and propped her hands on her hips. " 'Bout time you woke up."

Rourke dropped back onto the pillows. "How long have I been asleep?"

"This time? Two days."

Two days. So, it had been three since the night Eoghan appeared and Cara had almost been killed. A shudder took him at the thought. "Where is she?"

"Cara? Down in the garden with Ana and Tillie."

Rourke slid his legs over the side of the bed.

"Hold up there. Where do you think you're going?"

"Laverne, I have to see Cara—to talk to her."

"No you don't. I have strict orders to keep you in this here bed until the doctor says it's all right for you to be up and about."

"Orders? From who?"

"Who do you think?" Laverne pulled back the covers and directed a firm glare at his legs. He had no choice but to draw them back up, though he did so with a groan.

"Was that a cry of pain I heard, or something else?"

Rourke's heart beat faster as Cara's voice drifted through the door. A second later she appeared, holding a vase filled with flowers of every color. She set them on the table next to his bed, then grabbed the blanket from Laverne.

"Thank you, Laverne. I'll take over now."

"Good," she snorted, dusting her hands in the air and directing a glare at Rourke. "Seems the only time he behaves is when you're in the room."

She gave Cara a hug as she passed, then bustled out and drew the door closed.

Gently, Cara arranged the blanket over Rourke, her hands making his flesh tingle wherever her fingers touched his skin. Though he longed to simply soak in the sight of her, they had yet to speak of all that had transpired.

He caught her hand as she leaned over him. "Cara."

She froze, refusing to look at him.

"I am sorry about Eoghan."

"Oh, Rourke."

Tears gathered in her eyes, but she turned her face to the wall before he could wipe them away.

"I love you, Cara. I nearly went mad searching for you. When I saw Deidre with that knife to your throat, I wanted to tear her in two."

Her breath caught, but then her beautiful eyes sought his, and for the first time since she'd learned the truth about his father, he saw hope and wonder in their depths.

His mouth went dry. Exposing his heart, revealing the depth of his feelings, both were foreign and struck a fear deeper than any he'd known. Added to that, he felt at a decided disadvantage with her looking so lovely and strong and him as weak as a kitten. Already he felt a bead of sweat forming on his brow.

But he wouldn't risk losing her by remaining silent. He eased higher in the bed and pulled her to sit next to him. "I despised lying to you. From the moment I saw you at Ellis Island, I prayed you were not the one we sought, that Eoghan was not your brother, and that I . . ."

She grimaced and looked down at her hands, and he faltered.

"Rourke—"

"That I would not have to choose between you and my father's memory," he said, forcing the words through gritted teeth. "Until Deidre kidnapped you, I was never certain of the answer."

Her face softened, but was it with affection or pity? He steeled his heart and jerked his gaze away.

"But the moment I came to on the street and realized you were gone, that she had you and that I might not reach you in time to stop her from . . . killing you . . ."

Pain at the remembered fear made him wince. He drew a shuddering breath and closed his eyes as her fingers lightly caressed his cheek.

"Rourke, look at me."

He could not. He tilted his face away.

"We both kept secrets. If I had only told you the truth from the beginning . . ."

He dragged his head around. "How could you? I wanted Eoghan dead."

"But when you learned the truth—"

"When I learned the truth . . . Cara, I should have been honest with you. If I had, Eoghan might not have shot me trying to protect you, and you . . ." His heart ached at the loss he read in her eyes. "You might not have lost him again."

"Rourke . . ."

He grasped her hand. "Cara, I'll find him and explain. No matter how long it takes, or what I have to do, I'll make him understand."

"But—" she paused and licked her lips— "Malcolm said he was taking you back to Ireland."

"I'll find Eoghan first, make sure you're safe, and settled, and then I'll go. Forever. You'll never endure another moment's fear because of me or my family, I swear it."

For several seconds, she said nothing, and Rourke knew a moment of unreasoning terror— that she hated him, despised him, that she'd never again look at him with that same trusting smile.

"Cara—"

She laid her fingers over his mouth. "Rourke, I stopped Eoghan from killing you because I couldn't stand the thought of losing you."

"What?"

Tears soaked her eyes. "I knew Eoghan wouldn't understand. I knew, but I stepped between you and him anyway, because even if it cost me my brother, I knew I could bear that." Her hand slid to his cheek. "What I couldn't bear would be living without you."

His heart was so full he couldn't speak. When at last he was able to choke out words, his voice was rough, foreign to his own ears. "But . . .

you've searched so long, tried so hard to find him."

To his utter delight, she leaned forward and placed a kiss on the end of his nose.

"I love you, Rourke Turner." She sighed, and her hair, so sweet and silky soft, fell to drape his arm. "I love my brother, too. Finding him meant everything to me, until that moment when it came to choosing between him and sparing your life."

Her smile shook him to his core.

"I had to save you," she continued. "Nothing else mattered."

Forgetting the pain in his shoulder, forgetting the bitterness and lies that had held him captive for so long, Rourke leaned forward and swept her into his arms.

She loved him. She forgave him. As soon as he was strong enough, as soon as he could get back on his feet, he'd spend every waking moment making her happy, even if it took the rest of his life.

Epilogue

Cara leaned against the pier railing, her hand above her head, a salty sea breeze kissing her cheeks and teasing her hair. At her side, Rourke also waved farewell. From the steamer, his kinsmen returned the gesture with smiles on their faces, though Cara sensed they'd already turned their hearts across the ocean toward Ireland.

She slipped her arm around her husband's waist. He instantly tipped his head to smile at her.

"Do you wish you were going with them?" she asked, for a split second afraid of his answer.

He drew her against him, thrilling her with the look that gleamed from his eyes. "My father would never have wanted me to spend my life trying to avenge his death, I realize that now. It was my own bitterness and guilt that drove me to think so. My place is with you."

His head dipped and she instinctively lifted her mouth to receive his kiss, then laid her head against his shoulder, sighing with peace and contentment.

Rourke had kept his word. The moment his strength returned, he'd begun the search for her brother anew. Until now, there had been no word, but somehow, Cara sensed when the time was right, God would lead her to him, just as He'd led her to Rourke, and led Rourke to forgiveness and peace.

Her husband took her hand and pressed her fingers to his lips. "Are you ready?"

She flashed an impish smile. "For what?"

His eyes gleamed wickedly. "While I have enjoyed watching you get to know my kinsmen better, I am more than ready to have you to myself."

Cara feigned a frown. "I thought we might visit Amelia and the others today. It's been almost two weeks since the wedding. I've missed them."

Rourke growled low in his throat, sending a shiver of excitement racing through her. "We'll visit the boardinghouse later. Right now . . ." He pulled her to his chest and pressed a kiss to her neck.

Cara almost couldn't stand for the weakness in her knees. Sliding her arms around his waist, she closed her eyes and abandoned the farce. "Take me home, husband. Take me home."

Acknowledgments

I would like to thank my family for their steadfast support, their constant encouragement, and their faithful prayers. Mom and Dad, I love you guys. Thank you for being the best cheerleaders a daughter could have. To my sisters, Anne Byl, Maggie Granlee, Lori Schummer, and Cindy Delgado, I am beyond blessed to have four such amazing, talented women in my life. Thank you for always rejoicing with me when the newest cover comes out.

To my awesome critique partners, Jessica Dotta, Michelle Griep, Marcia Gruver, Ane Mulligan, and Janelle Mowery, thank you! Your critiques challenge me, make me better than I am. I love you all so much.

And to my agent, Chip MacGregor, there aren't enough words. Thank you for loving books, for caring about the authors you represent, and for seeking to please the God we both serve. You're awesome, and I am so grateful to be working with you.

Lastly, to my beloved husband, Lee, thank you for your patience and support. You are a miracle in my life and I fall in love with you every day. I couldn't do this without you. Without you, I wouldn't try.

About the Author

Elizabeth Ludwig is an award-winning author whose work has been featured on Novel Journey, the Christian Authors Network, and The Christian Pulse. Elizabeth's debut novel, *Where the Truth Lies* (coauthored with Janelle Mowery), earned her the 2008 IWA Writer of the Year Award. Her first historical novel, *Love Finds You in Calico, California*, was given four stars from *Romantic Times*. And her popular literary blog, The Borrowed Book, enjoys a wide readership, its first year seeing more than 17,000 visitors.

Elizabeth is an accomplished speaker and teacher, and often attends conferences and seminars where she lectures on editing for fiction writers, crafting effective novel proposals, and conducting successful editor/agent interviews. Along with her husband and two children, Elizabeth makes her home in the great state of Texas. To learn more about her work, visit ElizabethLudwig.com.